LATIN AMERICAN FOLKTALES

Stories from Hispanic and Indian Traditions

EDITED AND WITH AN INTRODUCTION BY

JOHN BIERHORST

PANTHEON FAIRY TALE AND FOLKLORE LIBRARY

PANTHEON BOOKS ❖ NEW YORK

All rights reserved under International and Pan-American Copyright
Conventions. Published in the United States by Pantheon Books, a division
of Random House, Inc., New York, and simultaneously in Canada
by Random House of Canada Limited, Toronto. Originally published in hardcover
by Pantheon Books, a division of Random House, Inc., New York, in 2002.

Pantheon Books and colophon are registered trademarks of Random House, Inc.

Permissions acknowledgments appear on pages 385–86.

Library of Congress Cataloging-in-Publication Data

Latin American folktales : stories from Hispanic and Indian traditions /
edited and with an introduction by John Bierhorst.
p. cm.—(Pantheon fairy tale and folklore library)
Includes bibliographical references.
ISBN 0-375-42066-5 (hardcover)
ISBN 0-375-71439-1 (paperback)
1. Hispanic Americans—Folklore.   2. Latin Americans—Folklore.
3. Indians—Folklore.   4. Tales—America.   5. Legends—America.
I. Bierhorst, John.   II. Pantheon fairy tale & folklore library.

GR111.H57 L37 2002
398.2′089′68—dc21   2001034056

www.pantheonbooks.com

Book design by Fearn Cutler de Vicq

Printed in the United States of America
First Paperback Edition
16 14 12 15 13 11

CONTENTS

Epilogue: Twentieth-Century Myths 307

PREFACE

The stories in this book represent the folktale tradition of Spanish-speaking America set within a frame of American Indian lore. As the scheme suggests, Latino folklore is two things at once. For the most part it is distinctly Old World, preserving medieval and even ancient story types. And yet in part it is new. That is, it has been embraced by Indo-America, which retains its own distinctive traditions while contributing a new, mixed lore of European and native elements.

The one hundred folktales at the core of this collection have been chosen to include the various European genres, ranging from the comic and the anecdotal to the heroic, the moralizing, and the religious. Familiar characters like the trickster Pedro de Urdemalas, the antagonistic two compadres, and the witch wife have been accommodated, as well as such quintessential tale types as The Bear's Son, Blancaflor, The Three Counsels, and The Clump of Basil. To suggest the atmosphere of live performance, the stories have been sequenced in the form of an idealized *velorio,* or wake, the most frequent occasion for public storytelling in Latin America. Riddles, games (here exhibited by a genre that will be called "chain riddles"), and of course folk prayers also help pass the time at a wake. Small selections of these are added to the tales.

Consequently, care has been taken to present material that is oral. In the preface to a book of folktales this should not have to be said. Yet in the region under consideration novelists are also folklorists and the distinction between literature and folklore has often been blurred. It is easy to set aside Valentín García Sáiz's *Leyendas y supersticiones del Uruguay* as an artist's creation rather than the transmission of a teller's performance, less easy to exclude the Colombian novelist Tomás Carrasquilla's *Cuentos de Tejas Arriba.* In the case of the Costa Rican short-story writer, novelist, and political activist Carmen Lyra, the nearly two dozen folktales she recorded have been accepted by folktale scholars, and one of them is included here.

The greatest debt, however, is to the company of dedicated folk-lorists and anthropologists that emerged at the beginning of the twentieth century and set about the task of recording Latino folklore nation by nation. Manuel J. Andrade, for the Dominican Republic; Delina Anibarro de Halushka, for Bolivia; Paulo Carvalho-Neto, for Ecuador; Susana Chertudi, for Argentina; and Ramón Laval, for Chile, are among the names that should be mentioned. Their publications will be found listed in the bibliography; their endeavors were a kind of systematics, akin to natural history, carefully preserving, labeling, and categorizing specimens of oral literature. Without their painstaking labor a compilation of this kind, which attempts to be panoramic, would not have been possible.

African-American folklore might well have been taken into account, especially for the Caribbean area—except that it has already been included in another volume in this series, Roger D. Abrahams's admirable *African American Folktales: Stories from Black Traditions in the New World.* Finally, there are no translations here from the Portuguese-speaking region, though there could have been in view of the overall unity of Ibero-American lore. It can be claimed, though, that the vast territory of Brazil is beyond the scope of the present offering. The folkloric riches of Indo-, Afro-, and Luso-Brazil deserve a volume of their own.

Timothy Knab, Richard Balkin, and Altie Karper jointly decided that I should undertake this essentially Hispanic volume. I thank them for giving me the opportunity. Barbara Bader provided information at a crucial moment; and I am grateful to Susan DiLorenzo, Jean Su, Rosalie Burgher, Ruth Anne Muller, Mary Hesley, and Jeanne Elliott for aid in locating texts.

J. B.
West Shokan, New York
July 2001

INTRODUCTION

L atin American folklore, or more precisely the recording of oral tradition in Latin America, has a five-hundred-year history marked by assiduous and highly skilled endeavor. Its span, however, is not continuous. There are two periods, the early Colonial era, lasting through the sixteenth century and into the first few decades of the seventeenth, and the twentieth century. In between lie nearly three hundred years of inactivity on the part of scribes and archivists, whose missed opportunities, to paraphrase the storyteller's closing formula, were carried off by the wind.

Understandably the two periods are not comparable. The first belongs to the era of early colonialism and religious conversion; while the second follows in the trail of two relatively recent phenomena—the rise of social science and the stirrings of romantic nationalism. The different agendas, set by the missionary on one hand and the folklorist on the other, produced results that were dissimilar in subject matter and even in style. This book is concerned mainly with the latter period. Nevertheless, it is in the earlier era, with its lore of the Conquest and of the advent of Christianity, that characteristic themes are first sounded.

Indian Background

One might have assumed that the initial voyages of Columbus had more pressing business than the collecting of stories. But in 1496, faced with the challenge of repeated insurrections among the Taino of Hispaniola, the Admiral himself ordered his chaplain, the Jeronymite friar Ramón Pané, to make a careful study of native custom. Pané lived with the Taino for nearly two years, made careful notes, and in his report included fragments of oral lore reduced to alphabetic script. Among the small but choice harvest of motifs were such typical Latin American Indian items as the ocean trapped in a gourd, the origin of women from trees, and the emergence of ancestors from inside the earth.

Less than two decades after Pané's discoveries, the royal chronicler Peter Martyr d'Anghiera was at work on a compendium of New World exploration that included a pioneering sample of the lore of the northwest corner of South America. From Peter Martyr comes the first notice of the typical Colombian Indian motif of the female supreme deity.

Collecting in depth, however, did not occur until after the conquest of the Aztec capital, Mexico, in 1521. Franciscan friars, who began arriving in Mexico City three years later, took charge of the intellectual culture of the new colony and made it their business to learn Nahuatl, the language of the Aztecs. The friars prepared Nahuatl-Spanish grammars and dictionaries that are still useful today, along with voluminous compilations of Nahuatl texts. Foremost in this work was the missionary-ethnographer Bernardino de Sahagún (1499–1590), whose twelve-book encyclopedia of Nahua lore, called *General History of the Things of New Spain,* included myths, legends, oratory, songs, sayings, and figures of speech. Repeatedly comparing himself to a medical doctor, Sahagún explained that he was recording these texts to supply preachers with the necessary information to "cure" the native people of their "blindness," because "the physician cannot properly treat the patient without knowing in which of the [four] humors, and from which cause, the infirmity arises." It is clear, nevertheless, that Sahagún was a man not only of the faith but of the Renaissance, whose researches served the interests of science, perhaps intentionally. In retrospect, Sahagún has been viewed as an experimenter in the techniques that would one day reemerge as anthropology.

Similar efforts, though not with the same thoroughness or subtlety, were initiated in the central Andes about 1550, gathering momentum in the 1570s during the term of the fourth viceroy of Peru, Francisco de Toledo. In order to support a program of reform and to substantiate his claim that Inca rule had been abusive, Toledo ordered an investigation of Inca history and custom, much as Columbus had done in Hispaniola three generations earlier. One result was Pedro Sarmiento de Gamboa's colorful *Historia de los incas,* drawn from the traditional histories chanted by Quechua bards.

The native chronicles to a large extent are the stories of kings, presented in chronological order, preceded by legends of tribal origin and myths of world creation. This is true of the sixteenth-century lore from Peru, Mexico, and elsewhere, including Colombia and Guatemala. Even in the fragmentary accounts obtained in Hispaniola, the names of a few Taino chieftains are preserved. Of particular interest, especially in the Peruvian and Mexican cycles, are stories of the final kings, the ones who were obliged to deal with the Conquest. In the view of native storytellers these rulers are tragic figures, and we hear that the Conquest was fated to occur. Such stories, from Mexico and Peru, are included as nos. 1/I–V and 2/III–V in this anthology.

It could be imagined that when the collectors of oral lore reawakened in the twentieth century and began finding the standard repertory of European folktales with their poor-boy-wins-princess plots and ubiquitous kings, the versions recorded in Indian communities would incorporate kings in Indian dress. But what we learn, in many localities, is that the Indian king has gone underground. In native folk belief, as if harking back to the Conquest lore of the old chronicles, the "king" is a remote personage who has been captured, killed, or hidden inside the earth, eventually to be reborn or to emerge as a deliverer. In the Andes this important figure is called Inkarrí, combining *Inca* and the Spanish word *rey,* or king. In the region from New Mexico to Panama he is sometimes called "Montezuma," evidently in allusion to the Montezuma of Aztec history. Among the Boruca of Costa Rica he is supposed to be living inside a mountain, guarding a treasure hoard. The widespread attitude is summed up by the anthropologist Robert Laughlin, writing of his experience with an accomplished tale-teller, Romin Teratol, of the Tzotzil Maya community of Zinacantán: "That Zinacantecs do not see kings in the same light as we do was driven home to me when showing pictures of contemporary European kings and queens to Romin. He asked if they were immortal. Not satisfied with my negative reply, he persisted, 'But they come from caves, don't they?'"

Meanwhile the familiar king of Old World folktales, in many of the versions composed by Indian storytellers, has been changed into the hacienda owner, or patrón, a character decidedly less persuadable than the prototype. Immediately the tales take on the coloration of modern short stories with sociological overtones. In short, reality breaks through. "The Pongo's Dream" (no. 36), from Peru, and "The Bad Compadre" (no. 96), from Guatemala, are two of several examples in the collection at hand.

At what date Hispanic folktales—the Cinderellas and the Dragon Slayers—arrived on American shores would be hard to calculate. Although modern folklorists have assumed these stories came with the conquerors, direct evidence is scanty. We do know that a group of forty-seven Aesop's fables was translated into Nahuatl in the sixteenth century, and such fables recur in modern Latin American collections. One of them, though it is not represented in the Nahuatl group, is given here as no. 53, "Good Is Repaid with Evil." A better example, representing a different kind of folktale, is no. 15, "What the Owls Said," a story from twentieth-century Mexico with a Peruvian variant recorded in 1608.

More important, it is clear that the earliest missionaries brought Bible stories, at least in the orthodox versions found in the various forms of the catechism known as *doctrina cristiana,* as well as in sermons and in other writings, all of which were translated into native languages. Often the stories are given in a connected series beginning with the creation of the world, followed by the appearance of Adam and Eve, the expulsion from paradise, God's visit to Noah, the world flood, the birth of Christ, the crucifixion, and the resurrection. By no means a Bible miscellany, the sequence economically illustrates the Catholic doctrine of original sin and redemption. That is, God created humans to enjoy eternal life in exchange for obedience; Adam and Eve, through their disobedience, broke the contract and bequeathed their sin to all subsequent generations. The flood was an attempt to wash away the accumulated sin, though only to temporary effect; it was Christ, finally, through his life, death, and resurrection, who restored the promise that had been withdrawn at the Expulsion. The earliest known native version, dating from 1565, is given here as no. 3, "Bringing Out the Holy Word." When the cycle reappears in the twentieth century it is found to contain numerous nonscriptural details, evidently borrowed from medieval traditions of considerable rarity in world folklore today. Indeed, the cycle has dropped out of the Hispanic repertory, surviving only in Indian retellings; it is one of the characteristic jewels of Latin American folklore, presented here in its twentieth-century form as nos. 55–73. Not surprisingly, it has been reinterpreted by native tellers. The doctrinal cues are now largely missing, and—again with sociological overtones—the emphasis is on escape from persecution.

🕸 Twentieth Century

Modern folklore research came late to Latin America. In Europe, by the mid-1800s, it was already clear that folktales were national treasures that might energize such groups as Germans, Finns, or Italians. In the Americas the overlay of new cultures made the opportunity less easy to recognize. Evidently it was the Indian tale that had grown from the soil, and it was decided that Indian folklore, for geographical if no better reasons, could serve Euro-American cultural interests. In North America the first resounding answer to the Grimms' two-volume *Kinder- und Hausmärchen* was Henry Rowe Schoolcraft's *Algic Researches* (1839), a two-volume collection of Algonquian tales, which the poet Longfellow turned into the enormously popular *Song of Hiawatha.* In Latin territory the situation was even less clear, for here there was more mixing of Indian and European culture than in the English-speaking region to the north. The first tentative steps were taken in Brazil, where oral tales from Amazonian Indian sources—still regarded as Brazilian classics—were published in the 1870s by Charles Frederick Hartt and José Vieira Couto de Magalhães. When the idea of folklore as a useful pursuit finally arrived in Spanish-speaking America, at the very end of the nineteenth century, it came first to the outermost parts of the region, Chile and New Mexico.

Rodolfo Lenz initiated the project in Chile with collections of Araucanian Indian tales published in the 1890s. Lenz, who has been called the Nestor of Chilean folklore studies, gathered around him a band of coworkers, including Sperata R. de Saunière, Julio Vicuña Cifuentes, and Ramón Laval, whose focus promptly shifted from Chilean Indian to Chilean Hispanic lore. Saunière, for her part, stated that she took her Hispanic narratives only from "persons of humble estate, house servants and country people who were not schooled and did not know how to read," scrupulously preserving "the idiomatic expressions and turns of speech." Among her informants was the eighty-year-old Juana González, of Chillán, a town in Indian country 250 miles south of Santiago, who provided the story "Antuco's Luck." If any Latino folktale could be made to stand for the whole it might well be this one. It has everything: the baroque opening and closing formulas, Hispanic narrative content, a hint of Moorish influence, profound Catholic symbolism, a hero with an Indian name, European kings, and a defiant touch of New World nationalism as the once-poor herdsman, now in Paris, takes the French princess as his wife, signing his marriage contract *Antuco de Chile.* The story is given here as no. 5. As for the "idiomatic expressions and turns of speech," these point to a dawning rationale for the collecting of Hispanic folktales not only in Chile but in Spanish America generally. Lenz himself was a pioneer in Hispanic linguistics, and he and his Chilean followers were soon in touch with another, younger researcher, Aurelio Espinosa of New Mexico, who would carry the work into new fields.

Of New Mexican Spanish ancestry dating from the sixteenth century, Espinosa was born in southern Colorado in 1880. He began his academic career at the University of New Mexico in 1902 and later joined the faculty of Stanford University, where he taught until his retirement in 1947. During his long career he brought the Hispanic folklore of the Southwest to an international audience and produced groundbreaking studies in the dialectology of New World Spanish. For Espinosa the folktale was a sampler of localized Spanish, rich in expressive and phonetic detail, waiting to be compared with specimens from other parts of Latin America and from Spain itself. Not satisfied with available Iberian texts, he traveled to Spain in the 1920s and recorded the tales for his massive *Cuentos populares españoles,* still the premier compilation of peninsular Spanish folk narratives. In addition, under his direction the first major folktale collections from Puerto Rico, Cuba, and Mexico were made.

It was becoming apparent that the Americas had preserved a Hispanic folk culture of great purity, perhaps especially in New Mexico. Here, a thousand miles from Mexico City, in a landlocked province the Colonial *gobernador* Diego de Vargas had called "remote beyond compare," were the oral literatures of Castille and Andalusia with their Arabic, Jewish, and South Asian roots still visible. Among the hundreds of New Mexican tales collected by Espinosa and his students were such durable standards as "The Three Counsels" and "The Twelve Truths of the World" in versions as complete as any that have been recorded in Latin America. Dressed up in the mock-serious numerology of far-distant lands, each of these tales preaches the straight and narrow, while promising reversals of fortune that break the rules. The poor man who sticks to the main road, keeps his mouth shut, and checks his impulses ("Three Counsels") or who insists on following the dictates of *compadrazgo,* even if it means taking the Devil as his compadre ("Twelve Truths"), in each case ends up living in a palace. It may also be noted that the hero who returns home to find his wife in the arms of a priest ("Three Counsels") or who escapes the Devil by having an angel invoke the eleven thousand virgins ("Twelve Truths") stands as the beneficiary of an unquestioning faith constantly inviting skepticism. One is reminded that in an irreverent Cuban tale the eleven thousand virgins are let out of heaven by St. Peter for a night on the town in Havana. As for one's wife in the arms of a priest, what else does one expect in folktales? Both conservative and revolutionary, authoritarian and subversive, pietistic and anti-clerical, this of course is the contradictory world of the folktale, whether Slavic, Spanish, Scandinavian, or Indic. But it belongs especially to versions recorded in Spanish America, where the contrasts are etched in sharp relief. "The Three Counsels" appears here as no. 45, "The Twelve Truths" as no. 23.

By mid-century "The Three Counsels" had been put on record not only from New Mexico but also from Chile, Mexico, Cuba, Puerto Rico, and the Dominican Republic. Other tales by this time were found to be equally far-flung, and the basic principle of Latino folklore—its unity—could be agreed upon. Another principle, seemingly confirmed again and again, is that folkloric influences do not normally travel from Indian languages into Spanish, though they move freely in the opposite direction. Consequently an overall distinction can be made between collections from Cuba, Puerto Rico, and the Dominican Republic, on one hand, and the mainland on the other. In the Antilles, where there are few if any Indian communities left to receive and rework Hispanic traditions, the familiar idols-behind-altars approach to Latino folklore has very little resonance.

The Antillean collections excel in tales that moralize, in sardonic inversions of such tales, and, as would be expected, in folkloric romances that end with the happily married living somewhere in the ever after. In "Don Dinero and Doña Fortuna," no. 6, from the Dominican Republic, the gentleman stands stubbornly on his money, while Fortuna proves her own version of nature's truth: Luck wins out over Money. "The Charcoal Peddler's Chicken," no. 44, from Puerto Rico, supplies the inversion: a poor man chooses to share his humble meal with Death rather than Luck, since Death, not Luck, treats everyone equally. In the romantic "Clump of Basil," no. 43, also from Puerto Rico, a clever young woman courts the king with impertinent riddles and outwits him, winning his mind, his heart, and of course his money. Stories like this are found on the mainland, too. But seldom in Indian communities.

Indian versions of Hispanic tales avoid outward moralizing. As a finishing touch, should one be needed, the storyteller prefers the etiological motif. Typically, "The Miser's Jar," no. 38, from the Kekchi Maya of Belize, ends not with a maxim about greed but with an epigrammatic theory on the origin of a certain bird: "As he sat down and began to weep, he was changed into the where-where bird. And to this day the bird may be seen near pools and in wet places, crying, 'Where, where? Where, where?'" Science, then, is the objective rather than philosophy, and we are led out of the folktale and into myth.

The happily-married ending, as in "The Clump of Basil," is the stock-in-trade of European folklore. It does find its way into Indian versions, as can be seen in at least two tales, "Riches Without Working" (no. 88) and "Rosalie" (no. 100). More usual in the folk fiction of native America, however, is the marriage that is left behind or the marriage opportunity that is rejected. In this regard the Puerto Rican stories, with their bride-and-groom finales, may be compared with the darker-hued tales from Colombia.

All five Colombian stories in this anthology were recorded by Gerardo and Alicia Reichel-Dolmatoff in the 1950s in the little village of Atánquez, 400 miles north of Bogotá. Located in the Sierra Nevada de Santa Marta, Atánquez is Spanish-speaking, its folklore essentially Hispanic with the full complement of moral and romantic tales. But there is also an undercurrent of Indian themes, as well as occasional terms recalled from Kankuama, the Chibchan language that had formerly been spoken in Atánquez. Nearby, in the heart of the Sierra Nevada, lies the tribal territory of the Chibchan Kogi, who managed to preserve their language and their traditional religious lore through the twentieth century. In folktales from Atánquez it can be noticed that marriage is turned aside and that the happy union, if there is one, is between parent and child. In "The Fisherman's Daughter," for example, the young heroine acquires a lover but goes on by herself to seek work, eventually returning not to a lover or a husband but to her father and mother. With the money she has earned she and her parents set themselves up as storekeepers and have whatever they want "from that time on." The daughter's work, we learn, had been aided by the proverbial old woman of Hispanic folklore, nearly always identified by Latin American storytellers as the Virgin Mother, especially when accompanied by her "little boy." But the work itself, in this case, is the retrieving of a magical hair from the "mother of all the animals." And here, so to speak, is the idol behind the altar, the old female divinity of the Sierra Nevada now in league with the Virgin of Catholic doctrine.

Through the 1960s, 1970s, and 1980s significant new collections of Hispanic folktales continued to appear, adding Argentina, Bolivia, and Ecuador to the roster of nations that can now be regarded as folkloristically well covered. Included in this group, notably, was Guatemala, where an ambitious program at the University of San Carlos was being carried out under the direction of Roberto Díaz Castillo, Celso Lara Figueroa, and Ofelia Déleon Meléndez. With its sponsorship of fieldwork, its bulletins, journals, and monographs, and its educational outreach, the Centro de Estudios Folklóricos has set as its goal nothing less than the integration of Guatemalan folklore and Guatemalan national culture. Among its most popular publications has been Lara Figueroa's edition of the tales of the quintessential Latino trickster, Pedro de Ur-

demalas. This folkloric figure is known throughout Latin America from
New Mexico to Chile, also in Spain and in Portugal (where he is called
Pedro de Malas-Artes). Lara Figueroa can write that he is "forcefully
alive in the hearts of the Guatemalan people, who have incorporated
him in their collective personality. Thus in reading the tales people re-
live his adventures, automatically identifying with this standard bearer
of our culture. For Guatemala he is the hero who challenges the ruling
classes; he is the originator of true popular values." A sequence of Pedro
de Urdemalas tales appears here as no. 18, including a version of the
widespread "King's Pigs" from the Guatemalan collection.

As the century progressed, folklorists became more and more aware
of the need to collect not only stories but information about the narrators. In this way they could preserve what Lara Figueroa has called "the
life of the story"; that is, its social context. Most of the twentieth-
century collections, especially the earlier ones, do not include that extra
benefit. In some cases, at least, we have the names of the storytellers,
enabling us to imagine that José so-and-so is giving us a man's point of
view or that a narrator named Bárbara offers a woman's version. Often
even this much has been withheld, necessarily, to protect the narrator
from repercussions in the home community. Nevertheless, collectors
have been able to sketch portraits of certain storytellers, sometimes in
Chaucerian detail.

Lara Figueroa presents his informant Antonio Ramírez:

He was born in Villa Nueva near Guatemala City. When he was
two years old he moved with his parents to the plantation country of Escuintla, where he still lives. In Escuintla they know him
as Uncle Chío, and the children call him Don Conejo [Mister
Rabbit]. Don Antonio is *analfabeto* [does not read or write]. He is
about seventy-five years old, now employed as a clerk in a brick-
yard in the barrio of San Pedro. He says he learned his stories
"here and there" and from a certain Colonel Julián Ponciano, who
was once his patrón and "who used to tell stories to the workers
while they scraped the seeds out of the pumpkins." Don Chío
tells stories mainly at wakes. He has a preference for tales of
Pedro de Urdemalas, "because that's what people like to hear at

wakes. Maybe it's because Pedro is such a devil and one-ups everybody. He isn't bad, though. He just goes after priests, con artists, and rich people, not really bad, just a one-upper." [no. 79]

The Costa Rican collector Carmen Lyra presents her beloved tía Panchita, whose name may be rendered in English as Aunt Franny:

She was a short, slight woman, who wore her gray hair in two braids [. . .]. She was always dressed for a funeral. And to protect her black skirt she wore a white apron around the house. [. . .] She and my Aunt Jesús, whose hands were crippled by arthritis, lived together in the vicinity of Morazán in a little house that was kept spotlessly clean. People called them The Girls, and even their own brothers, Pablo and Joaquín, when they sent me off to visit them, would say, "Now, you go see The Girls." She supported herself by making a thousand varieties of cakes and candies that flowed out of the house like water. Everybody wanted them. They were displayed in a massive old armoire with a glass front that stood in the tiny hallway next to the front door. [. . .] She would sit in her low-slung chair and tell me stories while her fingers, wasting no time, rolled cigarettes. I sat at her feet on a little leather stool that Uncle Joaquín had made for me. I could smell the tobacco, that had been cured with fig leaves, cane liquor, and honey. [. . .] How interminable were the moments when she broke off the story to take a puff from her cigarette or to light it with a coal at the edge of the hearth!" [no. 21]

From her Bolivian collection Delina Anibarro de Halushka presents the storyteller José Rivera Bravo:

Sixty-nine years old, married, no children. From an old and large family in Sucre. A cultivated man, a student of the humanities. Owing to the dedication of his parents and his brothers and sisters and his own determination and indomitable spirit he has amassed a store of knowledge in spite of his blindness. For many

years he lived on plantations owned by his parents along the Zudañes River in the department of Chuquisaca, where he learned
a great number of legends from Indians and from the townspeople of Zudañes. So keen is his interest in oral narratives that he
has published two little booklets of them, entitled *Tradiciones
chuquisaqueñas* (Sucre 1958). He uses the term *tradiciones* to mean
legends, or accounts regarded as true. He tells them with an air
of theatricality, as though inviting his listeners to believe. By
contrast he considers wonder tales to be "nursery stories" and
thus not to be taken seriously. [no. 19]

Knowing all this, whether we should or should not, we turn to the
stories with a subtext already in mind. For a tale like the Venezuelan
version of "The Horse of Seven Colors" (no. 12), we have only the
teller's name, Carmen Dolores Maestri. But even this is suggestive. The
hero of the story is a male Cinderella, who stays in the kitchen, washing
dishes, while his two contemptuous brothers go off to the tournament
to compete for the hand of the princess. Their swaggering dialogue,
with its rough camaraderie and bullying tone, amounts to a tacit com-
mentary on *machismo,* and we look to see whether the storyteller might
not be a woman.

Cultural matters, however, have usually been the province of the
anthropologist, while the folklorist has concentrated on plot and incident—technically, the tale type and the motif—with the idea of comparing these elements over time and distance to establish patterns of
diffusion. Shortly after the beginning of the century, when the boundary between professions had begun to harden, the peculiar nature of
each of these two disciplines dictated that Indian materials would be
collected by anthropologists, Hispanic materials by folklorists. This
has been the rule. But in the 1990s two deeply researched works by the
anthropologist James Taggart broke down what remained of the bar-
rier, bringing forward a double collection of Hispanic and Hispano-
Indian folktales. In *Enchanted Maidens* (1990) and *The Bear and His Sons*
(1997) Taggart presented fresh versions of old tale types gathered on
both sides of the Atlantic, along with abundant data on the men and
women who are the tellers, actually the re-creators. Their personal histories, together with Taggart's cross-Atlantic comparisons, make for an

original contribution to "the life of the story," suggesting a direction for future work.

🌀 *Performance and Translation*

Most tales in this as in nearly all collections were dictated or taped in one-on-one sessions with a folklorist or anthropologist, though sometimes with a few other listeners present. To do otherwise—to record performances in their natural settings—is inconvenient and would have been virtually impossible before the availability of magnetic recording devices. Although not taped, the Mazatec folk-Bible tales (nos. 55, 62, 71, 72, and 73) are among the few stories in this book that an anthropologist was able to witness *in situ*. The occasion was a wake in a tiny village in Veracruz State, Mexico, and among those present was Robert Laughlin, who writes:

> Inside, a table is set, adorned with arches of marigold and limonaria, two candles, religious pictures, and of course [the deceased's] favorite foods. The women enter to help grind the corn and prepare the coffee. When the prayer-man arrives the women kneel on straw mats before the altar. In candle-light he chants the "Three Mysteries." In response the women's sad nasal voices rise. Outside the men sleep or talk quietly together. Melchor García stands up. He is the religious leader of the village, also a prayer-man, wise in the knowledge of Spanish and the Bible. He offers to tell a religious tale. The others, sitting atop mounds of firewood, snicker and rock with laughter as he tells the tale that he, too, had heard at a wake and had learned by heart.

Fortunately, over the years, enough women have entered the field for there to have accumulated nearly as many versions from women narrators as from men. Male fieldworkers have often found it difficult to obtain stories from women, especially in conservative Indian communities. A notable exception was Father Martin Gusinde, who worked among the Yamana of southern Chile in the early years of the twentieth century. Gusinde went so far as to observe, "It is my impression that since they are less anxious than the men to display themselves by recounting their deeds and startling accomplishments, women find it easier to unravel the basic theme of a myth with fewer distractions and greater logical consequence."

Women, not surprisingly, have had much less difficulty in obtaining stories from men. The folklorist Elaine Miller tells of ringing doorbells in the Los Angeles area, asking for stories in Spanish. Some of her best informants were men, one of whom gallantly prefaced his recital, as the tape recorder rolled, "I dedicate a story to Señorita Miller, for her to include in her books." The story he then began to tell is no. 10, "Buried Alive."

Stories transcribed from tape are more likely to preserve the naturalness of live storytelling, the hesitations, the self-corrections, and the little asides. These features, not as numerous as might be wished, have been kept in the English translations given here.

Most of the translations have been newly made, largely because so few Hispanic folktales have been published in English. The reason, evidently, is that Spanish is one of the two principal languages of the Western Hemisphere, and serious authors can assume that the serious reader, even in North America, does not want translation. Glancing at the bibliography, one notices such English-language titles as Wheeler's *Tales from Jalisco Mexico* or Andrade's *Folk-Lore from the Dominican Republic,* implying that the contents are in English. Instead they are in Spanish, and in many cases a highly authentic Spanish, transcribed from the living speech with all the changed vowels and consonants and dropped syllables that give the live performance its flavor. For readers accustomed to standard Spanish a translation is not without value. Needless to say, the charm of localized Spanish washes off in translation. The temptation to compensate by peppering the English version with Spanish terms has been resisted, though certain words have been retained, especially if they have already been imported into English or, in a few cases, if there is no satisfactory English equivalent.

If Hispanic folklore in English has been relatively rare, the opposite is true of Latin American Indian lore, which has almost always been published in translation and very plentifully in English. The present collection includes English versions by the anthropologist Ruth Benedict, from the Zuni (no. 113); and by the poet Langston Hughes, from the Zapotec (III, following no. 84).

Idiomatic features of Indian speech can sometimes survive translation. Among these is the coupling found especially in Nahua and Maya storytelling. A clear example is the Nahua, or Aztec, account of the eight omens, no. 1/III. Another is in no. 96, "The Bad Compadre," where the beginning of the second paragraph has coupled phrases that stand out if printed as poetry:

> *His compadre, Juan, heard about it.*
> *Then Juan said to his wife,*
> *"Do me a favor,*
> *do me an errand.*
> *Go see our compadre,*
> *maybe talk to his wife."*
> *The woman went,*
> *she talked to the man.*

In addition to the wake, or all-night vigil, stories during the twentieth century have been told in a variety of settings. After-dinner storytelling at home, storytelling at the grocery store on Sunday mornings (while other people are at church), and storytelling during work breaks at large plantations are often mentioned. But the wake has been the principal occasion, at least for *public* storytelling, whether in Cuba, Panama, Mexico, Chile, or elsewhere. This is not to say that the custom has been universal. The Mexicanist Stanley Robe tells of extensive folktale collecting in the region east of Guadalajara, where no one ever mentioned storytelling at wakes. Robe was suspicious, however, and stated that he "would hesitate to declare that it does not occur." The point is that folklorists have found storytelling at wakes to be widespread, typical, and always to be looked for.

The selections that follow are identified by country, Indian culture (if applicable), and informant (if known). The name of the country stands alone or comes first if the text is of Hispanic origin. Thus "Mexico" indicates Hispanic, from Mexico; "Mexico (Nahua)" means basically Hispanic but from a Nahua source in Mexico; and "Nahua (Mexico)" means Nahua, or basically Nahua, from a Nahua source in Mexico.

PROLOGUE

EARLY COLONIAL LEGENDS

People say the dead are dead, but they are very much alive.

proverb / Cora (Mexico)

The story of the Conquest is the essential story of Latin America, centered on Mexico and Peru but shared across national boundaries as a common heritage. World history itself has no comparable story of the clash of cultures and its aftermath of irreparable loss. In the later years of the sixteenth century the conquistador Bernal Díaz del Castillo, who had participated in the events, could recall that when Cortés and his men had entered the Aztec capital with its towers and temples, "We said that it seemed like the things of enchantment that were told in the book of Amadis" and wondered if this were a "dream." Half a world away and after two more centuries had turned, the English poet Alexander Pope in one of his philosophical ruminations could ask, for the sake of world harmony, that

> *Peru once more a race of kings behold*
> *And other Mexicos be roofed with gold,*

confident that readers would grasp the significance. Told and retold by documentarians, the tale has an independent life in native legendary lore that is not nearly so well known as the more plausible, if none the less colorful, memoirs of European eyewitnesses. The folkloric accounts

19

are noteworthy for having taken shape so soon after the fact, even more so for the way in which they remove the Conquest from Western history, placing it within the realm of American Indian prophecy. The native raconteurs invite us to see that the entire disastrous episode was foreordained. Whether this is viewed as an act of resignation or defiance, it evidently puts the matter under native control.

For comparison, a few historical signposts from the European side of the divide may be offered here.

In 1502 a Maya trading canoe was contacted in the Bay of Honduras during the fourth voyage of Columbus, the same year Montezuma ascended the throne of Mexico. In 1518 the expedition of Juan de Grijalva touched the mainland at Cuetlaxtlan, an outpost of the Aztec empire, and reports of strangers on the coast were carried to the court of Montezuma. Hernán Cortés and his army put ashore in 1519 and began making their way inland, reaching the capital on the morning of November 8, when the famous meeting between Cortés and Montezuma finally took place. Several months later the Spaniards were driven out; they returned and laid siege to the city, conquering it in May of 1521. Afterward, Cortés was rewarded by the Spanish Crown and made Marquis of the Valley of Oaxaca. In native accounts Cortés is spoken of as the "marquis" or sometimes the "captain."

As background, it should be mentioned that the Aztecs—that is, the sixteenth-century Nahua—did not consider themselves an ancient people. According to their own traditions, they were latecomers to the Valley of Mexico, replacing the Toltecs, who had ruled from the old capital called Tula, fifty miles to the north. The last or near-to-last king of Tula, the hero-god Quetzalcoatl, was said to have gone away to the eastern coast, where he disappeared over the sea, promising one day to return. Possibly the Spaniards, now appearing on the eastern shore with firearms and various marvelous accoutrements, were returning Toltecs. Thus Montezuma, taking no chances, addressed Cortés as though he were Quetzalcoatl, coming back to reclaim his kingdom—an event made all the more probable in that Quetzalcoatl was supposed to return in a year 1 Reed according to the Aztec calendar, and 1519 was indeed 1 Reed.

In Peru the events unfolded on a slightly later schedule. In 1514 an epidemic of European origin, possibly typhus, arrived in the Caribbean and began making its way from Panama down the coast toward Inca territory. Huayna Capac, the eleventh Inca (king), died in 1526, and his son Huascar was installed as twelfth Inca in the capital city, Cuzco, in the southern highlands. Atahualpa, another of Huayna Capac's sons, was deputy ruler in the important regional capital of Quito, a thousand miles to the north. By the time the conqueror Francisco Pizarro and his men reached the highlands, Atahualpa had seized control of the empire and had arranged the murder of Huascar. In 1533 Atahualpa himself was executed by Pizarro's army at Cajamarca, approximately halfway between Quito and Cuzco, near the old religious center of Huamachuco. With no Inca at the helm the empire fell swiftly under Spanish control.

Like the Aztecs of Mexico, the Incas were upstarts in the long history of civilization in Peru. They are first noticed in native annals as a small tribe of the early 1200s in the vicinity of Lake Titicaca, where they claimed to have emerged from the underworld through cave openings. From there they made their way to the site of their future capital, Cuzco. Over the generations they added territory until by the 1500s they controlled a vast empire, which they called Tahuantinsuyu, "land of the four quarters," stretching from Ecuador through Peru and deep into Chile. The names and deeds of their kings were carefully kept by native chroniclers, and even as late as the twentieth century it was the duty of every schoolchild in Peru to memorize at least the bare list. The superior achievement was to rattle it off in a single breath:

1. Manco Capac (probably legendary)
2. Sinchi Roca (ruled about A.D. 1250)
3. Lloque Yupanqui
4. Mayta Capac
5. Capac Yupanqui
6. Inca Roca
7. Yahuar Huacac
8. Viracocha Inca
9. Pachacuti (ruled 1438–71)
10. Topa Inca Yupanqui

11. Huayna Capac (died 1526)
12. Huascar (died 1532)
13. Atahualpa (died 1533)

The eighth king, Viracocha Inca, is not to be confused with the god Viracocha, also called Coniraya or Coniraya Viracocha, often mentioned in Peruvian narratives. The Incas' own special deity, however, was *Inti*, the Sun. Over the years the Incas adopted the gods of tribes they conquered, including the god Viracocha, eventually developing a sizable pantheon, as can be seen in the story "The Storm."

It is probable that the great deity referred to in both the Aztec and Inca legends as "the Creator," "the Lord of Creation," or even "our lord who created the sky and the earth," is not a native deity but a latter-day reflection of Christianity. In the account entitled "Bringing Out the Holy Word" this figure is called God or Only Spirit, and the entire content is inarguably Christian. Nevertheless, the diction and the style of delivery are native. First performed in 1565, this "bringing out" song was chanted to the accompaniment of a two-toned log drum played with rubber-tipped mallets. Similarly, the Peruvian narratives, especially those recorded in the 1500s, are said to have been chanted by professional recordkeepers.

⇒ 1. Montezuma ⇐

I. THE TALKING STONE

Montezuma loved nothing more than to order great monuments that would make him famous. Beautiful things, it was true, had been commissioned by the kings who had gone before, but to Montezuma those works were insignificant. "Not splendid enough for Mexico," he would say, and as the years went by he grew to have doubts about even the huge round-stone where prisoners were sacrificed to Huitzilopochtli. "I want a new one," he said at last, "and I want it a forearm wider and two forearms taller."

So the order went out to the stonecutters to search the countryside for a boulder that could be carved into a round-stone a forearm wider and two forearms taller. When the proper stone had been sighted, at a place called Acolco, haulers and lifters were summoned from six cities and told to bring ropes and levers. Using their levers, they pried the stone from the hillside and dragged it to a level spot to be carved. As soon as it was in position, thirty stonecutters began to chisel it with their flint chisels, making it not only bigger than any round-stone that had been seen before, but more unusual and more beautiful. During the time that they worked, they ate only the rarest delicacies, sent by Montezuma and served by the people of Acolco.

When the stone was ready to be taken to Mexico, the carvers sent word to the king, who ordered the temple priests to go bring incense and a supply of quails. Arriving at the stone, the priests decorated it with paper streamers, perfumed it with the incense, and spattered molten rubber. Then they twisted the necks of the quails and spattered quail blood. There were musicians, too, with conch horns and skin drums. And comedians also came, so that the stone could be entertained as it traveled along.

But when they tried to pull it, it would not be moved. It seemed to have grown roots, and all the ropes snapped as if they had been cotton threads. Two more cities were ordered to send haulers, and as they set to work, shouting back and forth, trussing it with fresh ropes, the stone spoke up and said, "Try what you will."

The shouting stopped. "Why do you pull me?" said the stone. "I am not about to turn over and go, I am not to be pulled where you want me to go."

Quietly the men kept working. "Then pull me," it said. "I'll talk to you later." And with that the stone slid forward, traveling easily as far as Tlapitzahuayan. There the haulers decided to rest for the day, while two stonecutters went ahead to warn Montezuma that the great stone had begun to talk.

"Are you drunk?" said the king when they gave him the news. "Why come here telling me lies?" Then he called for his storekeeper and had the two messengers locked up. But he sent six lords to find out the truth, and when they had heard the stone say, "Try what you will, I am not to be pulled," they went back to Mexico and reported it to Montezuma, and the two prisoners were set free.

In the morning the stone spoke again. "Will you never understand? Why do you pull me? I am not to be taken to Mexico. Tell Montezuma it is no use. The time is bad, and his end is near. He has tried to make himself greater than our lord who created the sky and the earth. But pull me if you must, you poor ones. Let's go." And with that the stone slid along until it reached Itztapalapan.

Again it halted, and again they sent messengers to tell Montezuma what it had said. Just as before, he flew into a rage, but this time he was secretly frightened, and although he refused to give the messengers credit for bringing him the truth, he stopped short of jailing them and told them to go back and carry out his orders.

The next morning, as the haulers picked up their ropes, they found that the stone once again moved easily, sliding as far as the causeway that led to Mexico. Advised that the stone had reached the other side of the water, Montezuma sent priests to greet it with flowers and incense, also to appease it with blood sacrifices in case it might be angry. Again it started to move. But when it was halfway across the lake, it stopped and said, "Here and no farther," and although the causeway was made of cedar beams seven hands thick, the stone broke through them, crashing into the water with a noise like thunder. All the men who were tied to the ropes were dragged down and killed, and many others were wounded.

Told what had happened, Montezuma himself came onto the causeway to see where the stone had disappeared. Still thinking he would carry out his plan, he ordered divers to search the bottom of the lake to see if the stone had settled in a place where it might be hauled back to dry land. But they could find neither the stone itself nor any sign of the men who had been killed. The divers were sent down a second time, and when they came back up they said, "Lord, we see a narrow trace in the water leading toward Acolco."

"Very well," said Montezuma, and with no further questioning he sent his stonecutters back to Acolco to see what they might discover, and when they returned, they reported no more than what the king already knew. Still tied with its ropes and spattered with incense and blood offerings, the stone had gone back to the hillside where it had originally been found.

Then Montezuma turned to his lords and said, "Brothers, I know now that our pains and troubles will be many and our days will be few. As for me, just as with the kings that have gone before, I must let my-self die. May the Lord of Creation do what he pleases."

II. MONTEZUMA'S WOUND

Near the town of Coatepec in the province of Texcoco, a poor man was digging in his garden one day when an eagle swooped out of the air, seized him by the scalp, and carried him up toward the clouds, higher and higher, until the two of them were only a speck in the sky that quickly disappeared. Reaching a mountain peak, the man was taken into a dark cavern, where he heard the eagle say, "Lord of all power, I have carried out your command and here is the poor farmer you told me to bring."

Without seeing who spoke, the man heard a voice say, "It is good. Bring him here," and without knowing who took his hand, he found himself being led into a dazzling chamber, where he saw King Montezuma lying unconscious, as if asleep. The man was told to sit next to the king, flowers were put in his hand, and he was given a smoking tube filled with tobacco.

"Here, take these and relax," he was told, "and look carefully at this miserable one who feels nothing. He is so drunk with pride that he closes his eyes to the whole world, and if you want to know how far it has carried him, hold your lighted smoking tube against his thigh and you will see that he doesn't feel it."

Afraid to touch the king, the poor farmer hesitated. "Do it!" he was commanded. Then he held the hot tip of the tobacco against the king's thigh and saw that he felt nothing. He did not even stir.

The voice continued. "You see how drunk he is with his own power It is for this reason that I had you brought here. Now go back where you came from and tell Montezuma what you have seen and what I or-dered you to do. So that he will believe you, have him show you his thigh. Then point to the spot where you touched him and he will find a burn. Tell him the Lord of Creation is angry and that because of his arrogance his rule is about to end. The time is short. Say to him, 'Enjoy what is left!'"

With those words the eagle reappeared, took hold of the man's scalp, and carried him back to his garden. As it turned to leave, it said, "Listen to me, poor farmer. Don't be afraid. Strengthen your heart and do what the Lord commands, not forgetting a single word that he told you to say." Then the bird rose into the air and vanished.

The poor farmer stood amazed, but with his digging stick still in his hand he went straight to Mexico and asked to speak to Montezuma. Given permission to enter, he bowed low and said, "Lord, I come from Coatepec, and while I was working in my garden an eagle came and took me to a place where there was a lord of great power. He made me sit down where it was bright and shining, and you were there beside me. Then he gave me flowers and a lighted smoking tube, and when it got hot he commanded me to hold it against your thigh. I burned you with it, but you felt nothing and didn't move. He told me you didn't know what was happening because of your pride, and very soon your rule would come to an end and you would be in trouble, because your deeds are not good. Then he told me to come back and tell you what I saw. The time will be short. Enjoy what is left."

Remembering a dream he had had the night before, in which a poor man had wounded him with a smoking tube, Montezuma looked down at his thigh and saw that he had been burned. Suddenly the wound was so painful that he could not touch it. Without a word to the poor farmer, he called for his storekeeper and ordered him to lock the man up and give him no food until he died of starvation. As the prisoner was being led away, the pain increased and Montezuma himself had to be taken to his bed. For four days he lay suffering, and only with great difficulty were his doctors able to make him well.

III. EIGHT OMENS

Ten years before the Spaniards arrived, the sky omen appeared for the first time. It was like a fire tassel, a fire plume, a shower of dawn light that pierced the sky, narrow at the tip, wide at the base. Rising in the east, it reached all the way to the sky's center, the heart of the sky, right to the sky's heart, and so bright when it came up that it seemed like daybreak in the middle of the night. Then at sunrise it would disappear. It began in 12 House and kept coming up for a whole year. As soon as it appeared, men cried out, slapping their mouths with the palms of their hands. Everybody was afraid, everybody wailed.

There was a second omen here in Mexico. A fire broke out in the house of the devil Huitzilopochtli, the house known as His Kind of Mountain at the place called Commander's. Nobody set it. It flared on its own. When it was first noticed, the wooden pillars were already burning, and the fire tassels, the fire tongues, the fire plumes were shooting out, licking the whole temple. People were screaming. They said, "Mexicans, your water jars! Run! Put it out!" But when they poured water, it just fanned the flames, and then there was a real fire.

A third omen. The thatch-roofed temple of the fire god, the temple called Tzommolco, was hit by lightning. It was considered an omen because there was no heavy rain, just a sprinkle. It was a heat flash for no reason. There was no thunder.

A fourth omen. While it was still daylight, a comet that looked like three comets came out of the west and fell in the east, like a long-tailed shower of sparks, with its tail stretched out far. As soon as it was seen, there was a great roar, as though people were screaming everywhere.

A fifth omen. The lake boiled without any wind to make it boil. It sort of welled up, welled up swirling. And when it rose, it went very far, all the way to the bottoms of the houses, flooding them. Houses were crumbling. This was the big lake next to us here in Mexico.

A sixth omen. Often a woman was heard. She went weeping and crying. At night she cried out loud and said, "My children, already we're passing away." Sometimes she said, "My children, where can I take you?"

A seventh omen. One day when the water people were hunting, using their snares, they caught an ash-colored bird like a crane, and they brought it to the Black Chambers to show it to Montezuma. The sun had peaked, but it was still daylight. On the bird's head was a kind of mirror, a kind of reflecting surface, round and circular, and in it you could observe the sky and the constellation Fire Drill. When Montezuma saw this, he took it as a great omen. And when he looked again, he saw what seemed to be people coming into view, coming as conquerors with weapons, riding on animals. Then he called his astrologers and wise men and said, "Do you see what I see? It looks like people coming into view." But as they were about to answer him, the image disappeared and they could tell him nothing.

An eighth omen. Monstrous people kept showing up with two heads on one body. They were taken to the Black Chambers for Montezuma to see, but as soon as he looked at them, they disappeared.

IV. THE RETURN OF QUETZALCOATL

One day a poor man who had no ears, no thumbs, and no big toes came before Montezuma and explained that he had something to tell. Wondering what kind of creature this could be, Montezuma asked where he had come from. "From Deadland Woods," was the reply. And who had sent him? He had come on his own to serve the king and to tell what he had seen. He had been walking along the ocean, he said, when he noticed what seemed to be a large hill moving from one place to another on the water, and no such thing had ever been seen before.

"Very well," said Montezuma. "Rest yourself, catch your breath." Then he called for his storekeeper and told him to lock the man up and watch him carefully.

As the prisoner was being taken away, the king ordered his chief server, Tlillancalqui, to leave immediately for the seacoast to find out if the man with no thumbs had been telling the truth. "Take along your slave Girded Loins. Go to the ruler who serves me in Cuetlaxtlan and speak harshly to him. Say, 'Who stands guard here? Is there something on the ocean? Why hasn't the king been told, and what is it?'"

When they got to Cuetlaxtlan, they asked for the ruler and gave him the king's message word for word. "Sit down and rest," said the ruler. Then he sent a runner along the shore to find out the truth, and when the man returned, he was running fast. "I see something like two pyramids or a pair of hills," he said, "and it moves on top of the water."

The chief server and Girded Loins went to look for themselves. They saw the thing moving not far from the beach, and there were seven or eight men who came out in a little boat, fishing with fishhooks. To get a better view, they climbed a whitewood tree, a very bushy one, and watched until the fishermen returned to the twin pyramids with their catch. Then the chief server said, "Girded Loins, let's go," and they climbed out of the tree, went back to Cuetlaxtlan to pay their respects to the ruler, and rushed home to Mexico Tenochtitlan.

When they reached the city, they went directly to the palace to tell Montezuma what had been seen. "Lord and king, it is true. An unknown kind of people has come to the edge of the ocean, and we saw them fishing from a boat, some with poles, some with nets. When they had made their catch, they went back to the two pyramids that float on the water and were carried up into them. There may be fifteen in all, dressed in different colors, blue, brown, green, dirty gray, and red. They have headdresses like cooking pots that must be for protection against the sun. Their skin is very light, lighter than ours; most have long beards, and their hair hangs only to their ears."

At this news Montezuma bowed his head and without saying a word put his hand on his mouth and sat motionless for a long time, as though he were dead or dumb, powerless to speak. At last he said, "Who can I trust if not you, a lord in my palace? You bring me the truth every day." Then he told his storekeeper to go get the man with no thumbs and set him free. But when they went to the locker and opened the door, the man wasn't there. He had disappeared.

The storekeeper was amazed and ran to tell Montezuma, who was also amazed, but after a moment's thought said, "No, I am not surprised, because almost all those people from the coast are wizards." And then he said, "Now I will give you an order that you must keep secret on pain of death. If you reveal it to anyone, I will have to bury you beneath my chair, and all your wives and children will be put to death and everything you have will be taken away and all your houses torn down and their foundations dug up until the water spurts from the ground. Secretly, then, I want you to bring me the two best gold casters, the two best jade carvers, and the two best feather workers," and without delay the storekeeper went and found them. "Lord, they are here," he called.

"Show them in," answered the king, and when he saw them he said,

"My fathers, you have been brought for a particular purpose. Reveal it to any man and you will suffer death and all penalties, houses uprooted, loss of possessions, and death to your wives, children, and relatives. Now, each of you must make two works. There must be a gold neck chain, each link four fingers wide, with pendants and medals; and gold wristbands, ear jewels, fans, one with a gold half-moon in the center and the other with a polished gold sun that can be seen from far away. You must do it as quickly as possible."

In only a few days and nights the work was finished, and in the morning, when Montezuma was awake, they sent one of his dwarfs to tell him to come to the Hall of the Birds to see what had been made. "My lord, examine it," they said when they saw him coming, and when he examined it, he found it good. He called for his storekeeper and said, "Take these grandfathers of mine and give them each a load of coarse mantles of four, eight, and ten forearms mixed, also fine mantles, blouses, and skirts for my grandmothers, and corn, chilies, squash seeds, cotton, and beans," and with these things the workers went home contented.

Montezuma then showed the jewels and the featherwork to his chief server and said, "Here, the gifts are finished. You must take them to the one who has arrived, the one we have been expecting. I am convinced it is the spirit Quetzalcoatl. When he went away, he promised to come back and rule in Tula and in all the world. The old people of Tula are certain of this. And before he left, he buried his treasure in mountain ravines and in canyons, and these are the gold and precious stones we find today. Since it is known that he would return from the place in the sky beyond the ocean, the place called House of Dawn, where he went to meet with another spirit, and since it is certain that all kinds of jewels in this world were once part of his treasure, it can only be that he now returns to enjoy what is his. Even this throne is his, and I am only borrowing it.

"Return immediately to Cuetlaxtlan and have the ruler make up all kind of dishes, tamales, rolled tamales, tortillas with and without beans, all kinds of grilled birds, quail, grilled deer, rabbit, chili powder, stewed greens, and every kind of fruit.

"If you see that he eats these things, you will know he is Quetzalcoatl. If he does not eat them, you will know it is not he. If he likes only human flesh and if he eats you, all will be well because I myself will protect and maintain your houses, your women, and your children forever. Have no fear of it. Take Girded Loins with you, and if you see by these signs that their lord is Quetzalcoatl, adorn him with the jewels and give him the two large fans. Humbly beg him to let me die, and when I am dead he may come enjoy his mat and throne, which I have been guarding for him."

The next morning the chief server and Girded Loins set out with the gifts, traveling day and night. The moment they reached Cuetlaxtlan they told the ruler to prepare the food, using the finest ollas and baskets, and at midnight they carried it all to the edge of the ocean, so that at daybreak there they were, waving their arms and signaling across the water.

The small boat was lowered. Four men came rowing to shore to greet them and to ask who they were and where they were from. But the Mexicans answered them only in signs, saying they wished to be taken to their lord to give him the things they had brought. Then they loaded the food and the sacks with the gifts and rowed back across.

When they reached the ship, the captain appeared with the Indian woman, Malintzin, who translated his words. "Come here," she said. "Where are you from?"

"We are from the great city of Mexico Tenochtitlan."

"Why do you come here?"

"O lady, our daughter, we have come to see your lord."

Then Malintzin withdrew to an inner room and spoke to the captain. When she reappeared, she asked, "Who is your king?"

"Lady, his name is Montezuma."

"Why did he send you? What did he say?"

"He wants to know where this lord intends to go."

"This lord is your god, and he says he will go see King Montezuma."

"That would please him very much. But he begs this lord to let him finish his reign, waiting until after his death before ruling the country he left when he went away."

Then the Mexicans opened their sacks and presented the jeweled gifts and the two great fans, and when these had been received by the captain, they were passed from hand to hand, and the Spaniards admired them with much joy and great satisfaction. "O lady and daughter," said the Mexicans, "we have also brought food for the lord and chocolate for him to drink."

"The spirit will eat this food," said Malintzin, "but first he must see you eat from it yourselves." When the Mexicans had done as they were asked, the Spaniards all ate, offering the chief server and Girded Loins some sea biscuits, which were a little stale, and wine that made them drunk. They said that they wished to return with an answer to their lord Montezuma. "What is your name?" asked Malintzin. "My name is Tlillancalqui," said the chief server. Then she gave him this answer: "Tell Montezuma we kiss his hands and will be back in eight days and come see him."

Carrying these words, the Mexicans returned to their king and reported everything that had happened, describing the weapons they had seen and the horses, and showing him one of the biscuits.

"What flavor does it have?" asked the king, and touching it, he declared that it felt like tufa stone. He called for a piece of tufa, compared it, and found that the biscuit was heavier. Then he called for his dwarfs and ordered them to try it, and though they said it was good-tasting, Montezuma was afraid to eat it himself, saying that this was the food of gods. Instead, he ordered his priests to bring it to Tula and bury it in the temple of Quetzalcoatl. They took the biscuit, placed it in a fine jar all worked with gold, and covered the jar with a cloth. As they traveled north from Mexico, carrying incense burners, they sang songs of Quetzalcoatl, and when they reached Tula, they buried the spirit's food to the sound of shell trumpets, the roaring of conch horns.

V. IS IT YOU?

When the Spaniards arrived at the edge of the city, things came to a head, and it reached the point where Montezuma fixed himself and got dressed up to meet them, along with the other high lords and princes who were his chiefs and nobles. And so they all went out to make the greeting.

Fine flowers were placed on a gourd tray, with popcorn-, yellow to-bacco-, and cacao flowers surrounded by shield- and heartflowers in wreaths and garlands, and they brought gold necklaces, collars, and neck bands, so that when Montezuma met them there at Humming-bird Point he had gifts for the captains and warlords. Then he gave them the flowers, necklaced them with necklaces, with flower neck-laces, adorned them with flowers, and wreathed their heads. Then he showed the Marquis all the necklaces made of gold, and as he necklaced him with a few of them, the greeting came to a close.

Then the Marquis said to Montezuma, "Is it you? Are you he? Are you Montezuma?"

"Yes, I am he," said Montezuma, and he arose and went over to him and made a low bow. Then he pulled himself up to his full height, stood straight, and addressed him, saying, "My lord, you must be tired, you must be weary. You have arrived in this city of Mexico. You have reached this mat and throne of yours that I have held for you briefly. I have been taking care of things for you.

"Gone are those rulers of yours, Itzcoatl, Montezuma the elder, Ax-ayacatl, Tizoc, and Ahuitzotl, who briefly stood guard for you, govern-ing this city of Mexico. I, your servant, came after them. I wonder, can they look back and see over their shoulders? If only just one of them could see what I see, could marvel at what is happening to me now! For this is no dream. I am not sleepwalking, not seeing things in my sleep. I am not dreaming that I see you and look into your face. Indeed, I have been troubled for as many days as there are fingers on my two hands. I have gazed into the Unknown and have seen you coming out of the clouds, out of the mists.

"Those kings used to say that you would come back to your city and proceed to your mat and throne, that you would return. And this has come true. You are here, and you must be tired, you must be weary. Welcome to this land. Rest yourself. Go to your palace and rest your body. Our lords are welcome here."

Nahua (Mexico)

⮞ 2. Legends of the Inca Kings ⮜

I. MAYTA CAPAC

The Inca Lloque Yupanqui had grown old without an heir. And now it was widely believed that he was too old, too weak, to father a child.

Yet one day as he sat grieving, deep in sorrow, the Sun appeared to him in human form and consoled him, saying, "Do not grieve, Lloque Yupanqui, for your descendants shall be great lords. You shall father a child."

Upon hearing this, the Inca reported it to his kinsmen, who in turn made it known to the people. Then they set about to find him a wife. It was his own brother, being the one who knew best the Inca's nature, who selected the bride. He found her in the town of Oma, asked permission of her relatives, obtained her, and brought her to Cuzco. This woman was called Mama Caua, and by her the Inca was to have a son, whose name would be Mayta Capac.

Mama Caua had been pregnant only three months when her son was born. He was born with teeth. He was lively. And so quickly did he grow that at the end of one year he was as large and as strong as an eight-year-old. By the time he was two he was fighting with young men and could beat them and injure them severely.

They say that he joined in games with certain youths of the Alca-huiza, the Culunchima tribe, who lived in the vicinity of Cuzco; and he hurt a great many of them, and some were even killed. One day, in a dispute over who might drink water from a particular fountain, he broke the leg of the son of the Alcahuizas' chief lord, and he chased the other boys into their houses, where the Alcahuizas had been living in peace without troubling the Incas.

At last the Alcahuizas could no longer endure the attacks of Mayta Capac. And though they knew he was the Inca's favorite and well guarded by his kinsmen, they were nonetheless prepared to kill him. They were ready to risk their lives. They selected ten among themselves, and these were sent to the House of the Sun, where Lloque Yupanqui and Mayta Capac lived.

As they entered, intending to kill them both, it happened that

Mayta Capac was playing ball with some other boys in the palace court. When he saw his enemies arriving, bearing arms, he hurled a ball in their direction, and one of them was hit and killed. Then he attacked the others and made them flee; and although they escaped, they fled with many wounds. This then is how they returned to their chief lord.

When the Alcahuizas, the Culunchimas, were made aware of the injury that had been done to their people, they were filled with fear. Mayta Capac was only a child. What might he do when he became a man?

Now, truly, they were prepared to risk their lives. Gathering all their people together, they set out to make war against the Incas.

Then Lloque Yupanqui was troubled. He feared he would be destroyed, and he reprimanded his son, Mayta Capac, saying, "Child! Why have you injured these people? I am an old man. Would you have me die at the hands of our enemies?"

But the Inca's own subjects, who loved to pillage, who preferred war over peace and lived by thievery, spoke up in favor of Mayta Capac and told the Inca to keep still and not to speak against his son. Then indeed Lloque Yupanqui no longer reprimanded his son.

The Alcahuizas, the Culunchimas, prepared their troops. Mayta Capac likewise took command of his subjects. Both sides gave battle, and though at first the contest was even, with neither side prevailing, then at last when each party had fought long, each hoping to win the victory, the Alcahuizas, the Culunchimas, were defeated by the subjects of Mayta Capac.

But the Alcahuizas were not disheartened. They came again and with greater spirit. They attacked the House of the Sun and pounded it on three sides. At first Mayta Capac, having retired to his quarters, was unaware of what had happened. But then he emerged. He came out from behind the walls. He struggled fiercely with his enemies, and at last he routed them, he defeated them. Then he danced, adorned with fine regalia.

Still the Alcahuizas would not desist. Again they called Mayta Capac to battle, and again he accepted. But they say that now a hailstorm fell on the Alcahuizas, so that all of them were finally defeated. Then Mayta Capac took their chief lord and kept him in prison until he died.

Indeed this Mayta Capac was bold. He was the first since the days of Manco Capac to take up arms and win victories.

And they say that Mayta Capac inherited the Sun bird that Manco Capac had brought with him when he founded Cuzco. Always the bird had been locked within a hamper of woven reeds, handed down from Inca to Inca, and no one had ventured to open it, for all were timid.

But Mayta Capac was more daring than they. He wished to see what his forebears had kept so carefully hidden. He opened the hamper. He took out the Sun bird and spoke to it. Truly, they say, it answered him in oracles. And because of it he grew wise. He knew what would happen: he could foretell the future.

II. THE STORM

When Topa Inca Yupanqui was lord and had conquered many provinces, then for a long time he rested in great contentment.

But finally and in different places there came a rebellion of the Allancu, the Callancu, and the Chaqui. These tribes would not be subjects of the Inca.

And so the Inca fought with them for twelve years, enlisting many thousands of his people, all of whom, however, were destroyed. Then the Inca mourned. He was deeply troubled, thinking, "What will become of us?"

Then one day he thought to himself, "Why do I offer the gods my gold and silver, my woven robes, my food, and everything else that I have? Now, this moment, I will send for them, and they can help me against these rebels." Then he spoke aloud and summoned them with the words: "Wherever you are, come, you who receive gold and silver!"

Then the gods said yes and they came.

Pachacamac came in a litter, and so too, in litters, did the other gods from every part of Tahuantinsuyu, and they all came together in the great square at Cuzco.

Pariacaca, however, had not yet arrived. "Should I go? Or should I not go?" He was unable to make up his mind. Then at last he sent his son, Macahuisa, saying, "Go! And listen!"

When Macahuisa arrived, he sat down in the rear next to his litter.

Then the Inca began to speak: "O Fathers! Gods and Spirits! You know already how I have made you sacrificial offerings of gold and silver. My heart has been filled with devotion. And seeing that I have served you well, could you not come to my aid, now that I am losing so many thousands of my people? It is for this that I have called you."

But when he had spoken, not a one gave him answer. They merely sat there saying nothing. Then the Inca spoke again: "Speak! You made and created these people. Will you let them die in battle? Help me! Or I will have you all burned on the spot. Why should I serve and adorn you with gold and silver, with food by the basketful and drink, with llamas of mine, and everything else that I have? You hear my sorrow, and if you will not aid me, or even speak, you must burn on the spot." These were his words.

Then Pachacamac began to speak: "Inca, O Rising Sun, I who can violently shake all things, even you and the whole earth—I have not yet spoken, for were I to destroy these rebels, then you too and even the earth would likewise be destroyed. And so I sit here saying nothing."

Then at last, though the remaining spirits kept their silence, the one who was called Macahuisa began to speak: "Inca, O Rising Sun, I will go forth! You will remain behind and watch over your subjects and protect them with your thoughts. I will go at once. For your sake I will conquer!"

As he spoke, metal poured from his mouth like an out-flowing vapor; and there before him were golden panpipes. He blew on the panpipes and made music. Also he had a flute, and it too was of gold. Upon his head he wore a headdress. His staff was gold. His tunic was black.

Then, so that Macahuisa could go, the Inca gave him one of his own litters and selected strong litter bearers from among the Collahuaya, who in but few days could cover many days' distance.

And so they carried Macahuisa in a litter against the enemy.

When they had brought him to a little mountain, Macahuisa, being Pariacaca's son, began to make it rain, at first gently. And the people living in the villages below thought, "What is this?" and prepared themselves for the worst.

Then Macahuisa flashed lightning and made more and more rain until all the villages were carried away in a flood; and where the villages had been, he made gullies. With lightning he destroyed their overlord and all their nobles. Only a few of the people were saved, but had he willed it, he could have destroyed them all. Having conquered them totally, he led the survivors back to Cuzco.

From that time on, the Inca revered Pariacaca even more than he had before and furnished him with fifty attendants to make him sacrificial offerings.

Then to Pariacaca's son he said, "Father Macahuisa, what can I give you? Whatever you wish, demand it of me! Anything!" These were his words.

But the god answered, "I will have nothing at all, only that you worship me as our sons from Jauja do."

Then the Inca said, "Very well, Father." But he was filled with fear, thinking, "Perhaps he could destroy me too," and therefore he wished to make him an offering of anything whatsoever. And so he said, "Eat, Father!" and gave him food.

But Macahuisa replied, "I am not accustomed to eating food. Bring me coral!" Then he gave him coral, and he ate it at once with a crunching sound, *cop-cop*.

Though he asked for nothing else, the Inca presented him with sun maidens. But he did not take them.

And so Macahuisa set off for home to report to his father, Pariacaca. And after that, the Incas in later days would come to worship in Jauja and dance dances of veneration.

III. THE VANISHING BRIDE

Shortly before the arrival of the Spaniards, Coniraya Viracocha betook himself to Cuzco, where he met with the Inca Huayna Capac; and he said to him:

"My son, let us be off to Titicaca. There I will reveal to you who and what I am."

When they got there, he spoke again, "Inca, summon your people, that we may send forth to the underworld all the magicians and all those who are wise." He spoke, and at once the Inca gave out the command.

Then his people arrived, some saying, "I am created of the condor," others saying, "I am created of the hawk," still others, "I fly like the swallow."

Then Coniraya gave them this order: "Go to the underworld! Say to my father, 'Your son has sent me. Let me have one of his sisters.' This, then is what you must say," he commanded.

Then he who was created of the swallow, together with the other created beings, set out for the underworld, to return in five days.

Now it was he, the swallow man, who got there first; and when he had arrived and had delivered his message, he was given a small chest, together with the following command:

"Do not open this. The lord Huayna Capac himself must open it first," he was ordered.

But while this man was carrying the chest and when he had nearly reached Cuzco, he thought to himself, "I will see what it really is." Then he opened it, and there before him was a lady, very delicate and pretty. Her hair was wavy, it was like gold. She wore a splendid garment, and as she lay in the chest she was very small.

But the moment he saw her, she vanished. Then he arrived in Cuzco, very troubled; and Huayna Capac said to him, "Were you not created of the swallow, I would have you killed at once. Turn around, go back!"

Then he went back to the underworld and brought her forth again. Along the way, as he was bringing her, whenever he felt hungry and thirsty, he would merely speak the word and at once a table would be spread out before him and a place to sleep.

And so he delivered her in just five days. And when he arrived with her, Coniraya and the Inca received her with great joy.

But before the chest was opened, Coniraya spoke out, crying, "Inca! We will leave this world," and he pointed, saying, "I will go to this land," and he pointed again, saying, "You and my sister will go to that land. You and I will never see one another again."

Then they opened the chest. The moment they opened it the earth was aglow.

Then the Inca Huayna Capac uttered these words: "Never will I return from this place. Only here will I live with my sun maiden, my queen." Then to one of his vassals and kinsmen he gave this command: "You! Go in my place! And say, 'I am Huayna Capac'! Now return to Cuzco!"

And in that moment he and his bride disappeared, and so too did Coniraya.

Then some time later, when the supposed Huayna Capac was dead, his successors began quarreling among themselves. They fought over who would be ruler, each saying, "I am first," and it was then that the Spaniards arrived in Cajamarca.

IV. A MESSENGER IN BLACK

After a hard-fought campaign in the northern provinces, where certain rebel armies had at last been driven back, the Inca Huayna Capac withdrew to the town of Quito in order to rest and to issue new laws and new commands. At this time he received word of a pestilence raging in Cuzco. But again he pushed on, moving northward now against the tribesmen of Pasto and even beyond. As he continued his march, there were sudden bolts of lightning, striking close beside him, and convinced that these were an evil omen he turned back toward Quito.

Again he set out, marching westward toward the sea. But there, at the hour of midnight, he had a vision, in which he saw himself surrounded by millions upon millions of men. No one knows who they were. The Inca believed they were souls of the living, sent to warn him that a great many people would die of the pestilence. But the souls announced that they had come against the Inca himself and by this he understood that they were enemies and he saw that they were armed and hostile. He marched no more, but returned to Quito, and it was there that he celebrated the December feast called Capac Raymi.

Just at the dinner hour there came to him a messenger dressed in a black cloak. With great reverence he kissed the Inca and placed in his hands a small chest, its lid sealed. The Inca ordered him to open it, but the messenger excused himself, saying that it was the command of the Creator that the Inca himself must be the one to remove the cover. The

Inca believed him, and as he opened the chest, out came a scattering swarm of moths and butterflies, and this was the pestilence. Within two days the chief of all the Inca's armies and many of his captains were dead, their faces covered with scabs.

When the Inca saw what had happened, he ordered a sepulcher carved out of stone, and when it was finished he placed himself in it, and there he died. When eight days had passed, the Inca's body, partly rotted, was taken out and mummified and carried home to Cuzco in a litter as though it were alive. This Inca left behind him in Quito a son named Atahualpa.

V. THE ORACLE AT HUAMACHUCO

The Inca Atahualpa was inordinately cruel. He murdered left and right. He razed. He burned. Whatever stood in his way he destroyed. As he marched from Quito to Huamachuco he committed the worst cruelties, ravages, and tyrannical abuses that had ever been known in this land.

When he reached Huamachuco he sent two of his chief lords to make sacrifices to the idol that presided there and to question it as to his future success. The lords went and made their sacrifices, but when they consulted the oracle they were told that Atahualpa would come to an evil end as punishment for his cruelty and bloodshed.

Then the lords went and told the Inca what the idol had said and the Inca was enraged. Summoning his warriors, he started toward the temple where the idol was kept. As he drew near, he armed himself with a golden ax and advanced with the two lords who had made the sacrifice.

When he reached the entrance to the temple, out came an aged priest, more than a hundred years old, dressed in a long, shaggy robe tangled with seashells, which reached to his feet. This was the priest of the oracle, and it was he who had spoken the prophecy. So informed, Atahualpa raised the ax and with a single blow cut off the old man's head.

Then he entered the little temple, and the idol too he struck with the ax; he chopped off its head, although it was made of stone. Then he ordered the old priest's body set on fire and also the idol and its temple. When all had been burned, there was nothing but ashes, and these he allowed to fly off with the wind.

Quechua (Peru)

⤜ 3. Bringing Out the Holy Word ⤛

God says it, and he creates it: first was the light. And on the second day he made the sky.

The third day he makes the ocean and also the land. And the fourth day he establishes the sun. Oh, and the moon and all the stars.

On the fifth day the water creatures were made, then all the birds that fly along.

The sixth day our lord made the wild beasts and all the living things on earth, and at that time he created the first man. "Ah, let it be thus. Our very likeness, our very image shall be made. This is the one that will rule the earth.

"My creation, all that lies on earth, will be his property and his dominion."

When God had created the first people, then he blessed them. He says, "Increase, multiply! Dwell in all the earth!

"Behold, for I have given you every fruitful tree that exists in this world and every green herb that is here. Dwell in all the earth!"

For the briefest of moments did they assume the mat and throne of God the Only Spirit. And then the lord frowns and says, "Adam! O Adam, mark this well. You will get your food on earth with sweat."

And it is said that he expelled them. "When I say it and require it, then your life will finish here, for truly you are earth, and again you shall be earth."

As people on earth were scattered and sown, they multiplied. And
many were the sins. Because of these, indeed a second time God
grew angry. He flooded the world.

The mere eight people who were left, the children of Noah, were the
ones who reproduced. Truly they found favor. But does our lord
have a mind to frown? Indeed he is provoked!

But ah! Four thousand and three years went by, and God was compassionate: he sent his precious son, the savior.

Through Santa María he came to take his precious incarnation. Through
his precious death he came to save us, and he gave us everlasting
life.

Lords and princes, rejoice, be glad. Hear this: dawn appeared and the
true sun came out. It was Jesucristo, who came and laid his radi-
ance upon us. A blaze of light appeared from heaven.

At that time angels befriended us men on earth. And so it was not
without cause that María Magdalena was the first to see him at
the sepulcher.

How glad you were, Lady Magdalena, that our lord, the true God, the
true man, Jesucristo, spoke first to you where the sepulcher was!
Alleluia.

When the apostles San Pedro and San Juan heard that he was revived,
they were excited and came running to the sepulcher in the garden. Because of it their hearts were glad.

Forty days passed, and our lord gave orders to the apostles that in all the
world the gospel would resound. Then he ascended to the sky.

Mexico (Nahua) / Francisco Plácido

A TWENTiETH-CENTURY WAKE

The dead to the grave and the living to their business.

proverb / Texas

Stories are told at wakes in order to pass the time, or, more to the point, to prevent people from falling asleep. Although it is widely accepted that the soul of the deceased has set off for the afterworld by the time the wake begins, another, more sobering tradition has it that the soul is prepared to slip inside of anyone in the room who drowses off. For the mere sake of sociability, if not for the deeper reason, food, drink, games, and stories help to keep the wake in progress.

There are old reports of wakes being held in church in front of the main altar. The more usual setting is the home of the deceased, where the body is laid out in a room cleared of furniture or with the chairs placed along the walls. This would ordinarily be the room that contains a small altar, with the coffin placed on a bench or table with the head toward the altar. Prayers are recited in this room, while storytelling takes place in an adjoining room, perhaps the kitchen, or out in the yard around a fire.

The fast-paced twentieth century did not enrich the custom, and it has even fallen into disuse in areas like New Mexico that have entered the era of the funeral parlor. Times have changed in Oaxaca, where card-playing increasingly has replaced storytelling at wakes. And everywhere the old practices must confront modern sensibilities that frown on any form of diversion in time of crisis. Nevertheless, old-style wakes have been abundantly reported, at least for the early and middle years of the century. In areas where the custom survives people known to be good storytellers continue to be notified when the occasion arises, in order to ensure their attendance.

The usual pattern is for the wake to begin at the first nightfall after death has occurred, with burial the following morning. Then, frequently, the wake continues for another eight days and nights. Between the first and ninth nights of the nine-day cycle, or novena, participation is reduced, and fewer candles are kept burning. In parts of Guatemala storytelling is required especially during the wake, or *velorio,* proper—that is, the first night—and during the ninth night, or *acabo de novena,* the end of the novena. In Colombia, in the Sierra Nevada de Santa Marta, there may be visiting, with storytelling, on each of the nine nights, though guests do not stay past midnight except during the first and final nights.

Various foods are served at intermissions, as well as black coffee and, especially in southern South America, the herb tea *mate,* or, in Central America, cups of chocolate. Cigars and hard liquor may also be available.

Since the wake, either in its one-night or nine-night form, is the most typical occasion for formal storytelling, the selections that follow, instead of being grouped thematically, have been arranged as if told in this most natural of settings. That is, each tale suggests the next one, either picking up its theme or offering a contrast. The only group that has been tightly structured is Part Six, which has the folk-Bible cycle in the traditional order beginning with the Creation and ending with the Resurrection. Each of the other groups gravitates toward a particular theme but without observing a strict program. Part One centers on courtship and marriage, Part Two on the afterlife. A selection of folk prayers follows the last tale in Part Two, which itself is a prayer in the form of a narrative.

Part Three (romantic intrigue) and Part Four (wit) are followed by riddles. Riddles, too, are told at wakes, though they are reported in this context much less regularly than folktales. Manuel J. Andrade, describing his folklore-gathering tour of the Dominican countryside, writes,

"Twice I heard riddles in what seems to be their natural setting. One of the occasions was at a wake on a farm near Higüey, where no one expected a stranger, nor did any one know as yet that I was interested in riddles." Two of the riddles Andrade obtained, XVIII and XX, are reproduced here.

Tales of salvation and rescue, mostly without religious overtones, are in Part Five, leading into the Bible stories of Part Six. As noted in the introduction to this book, the Mazatec episodes given here were actually heard at a wake by the anthropologist Robert Laughlin.

For contrast, Part Seven turns to nonsense, with the final tale in this group exhibiting one of the most excessive of the storytellers' opening formulas:

> *If I tell it to know it you'll know*
> *how to tell it and put it in*
> *ships for John, Rock, and Rick*
> *with dust and sawdust, ginger*
> *paste, and marzipan, triki-triki*
> *triki-tran.*

At least some of these strange storytellers' formulas derive from patter-chants used in parlor games. The example shown above, from Chile, can be compared with an old Spanish rhyme chanted while dandling a child on one's knee:

> *Ah serene, ah Sir Ron,*
> *Ah the ships of St. John;*
> *And what's with John's? Eats a roll.*
> *And Peter's? Eats the cheese.*
> *And Rick's? It eats the ginger paste.*
> *Niki-niki {and so forth}*

Patter-chants often take the form of endless nonsense quizzes, or chain riddles as they might be called, that also escape into storytelling, either as closing formulas or as odd little tales complete in themselves. Several examples are given following Part Seven.

Part Eight then turns to the subject of greed, a necessary element everywhere in international folklore, with or without the moralizing that helps to wipe the curse away. Part Nine, finally, focuses on marriage and family, now in a darker key and with stories mostly from Indian narrators. These, strangely, suggest the ambiguity of the modernist short story rather than the transparent morality of the medieval folktale, even though the plots are basically Old World. Some are startlingly open-ended, transporting the reader or listener into another, untold story rather than winding up with a neat conclusion. The best examples are "The Bad Compadre," "Black Chickens," "Doublehead," and "A Day Laborer Goes to Work."

PART ONE

⇒ 4. In the City of Benjamin ⇐

The king of a certain city admired women for the stories they told. He ordered his vassals to collect all the loveliest women in the outlying districts and bring them in to be his wives. That way he would be able to hear good stories constantly.

None of the wives lasted more than three nights. They would run out of stories, and the king would toss them into a keep. Soon he had hundreds of women locked up like nuns in a cloister.

In the same city there were three sisters who had no marriage prospects. They were poor as could be. But they thought, "We'll go to the palace, and if we can just get an audience with the king, perhaps he'll marry us." The first of the three went off to try her luck and met with the same fate as the king's other women. It wasn't long until the second sister joined her.

Before the youngest set out she gave the matter some thought and decided to become the king's permanent wife by telling him a story that would have no end. The king married her without a moment's hesitation, and on their wedding night she began to recite. When morning came the story was not finished. Tired after hours of storytelling, she said to the king, "Allow me to rest, Sacred Crown. Tonight I'll continue." She had broken off at the most interesting part.

And that's how it went for an entire week, on and on with the story that never ended. After a while the king said, "This is my true wife. Such stories!" It was a marriage that lasted, the king always wanting to hear more. He never lost interest.

Tale followed tale but the story was never complete. Meanwhile the young wife was about to have a child, and one day she announced, finally, that the stories would come to an end.

For some time before this, since after all she was the queen, she had been performing her duties, keeping the palace in order, looking into every nook and cranny. Once, while making her rounds, she had come upon an enormous vault in the cellar beneath the palace. Inside it were thousands upon thousands of women. She was puzzled, because the word in town and throughout the country was that the king always beheaded his wives after the first three nights. She wondered what to make of her discovery but refrained from speaking openly.

Instead, as she went on with her nightly telling, she mentioned to the king that she didn't know, really, whether it would be right to finish. The story's end, she warned him, might be too shocking for him, because she knew what a tender-hearted man he was. She could tell, she said, that he wished no harm to anyone and that it was for this that the people of his country loved him. "Sacred Crown, I can't bring myself to let you hear how it all turns out. It would be too upsetting for you."

With his love for stories, the king's interest was now keener than ever. He ordered her to tell the ending. "I will," she said, "if you grant me one favor."

"What is that, my queen?"

"All those poor women you have in the vault, let them go."

The king was terrified. "What? If I turned those women loose, there would be an uprising. The people would drag me off the throne."

"Then the story is not going to end."

The king could barely contain his curiosity. "My dear, let me think about it." The days passed, and still no answer. At last the queen said, "I'd better tell you the ending, because I'll soon be going into labor. What if I should die in childbirth?"

"Oh no, my dear queen! Can't you put it off a few more days?"

In the meantime the queen was consulting with the women in the vault. After dark she was releasing them quietly, one by one, without causing a stir. The women were returning to their homes with made-up excuses. They'd been away traveling, they said.

When all were free, the queen declared she could no longer postpone the end of her story. She brought the tale quickly to a close, the child was born without mishap, and the king took notice that the women he had imprisoned were no longer in the keep. The dreaded revolution had not taken place, nor had the citizens pulled him from his throne. "Thank you, my queen."

With those words the king changed his ways, and the royal family lived happily from that time on. And that's the tale of the monarch named Benjamin, king of a far-distant city, and the city, too, was called Benjamin.

Ecuador / Rosa Salas

⪼ 5. Antuco's Luck ⪻

If you ask to hear it you'll listen and learn it, and any who can't will have to drink tea; for sleepy wits it's a mother's remedy.

There was an orphan boy, his name was Antuco, though country people called him the Little Blade, since he always liked to be sharply dressed. And this Antuco was a cowherd at a ranch in the mountains. His foreman was an old tippler they called Master Anselmo.

One day the overseer said to Anselmo, "Cut out the drinking or I'll replace you with somebody younger." Master Anselmo immediately thought, "Antuco!" who was a great favorite of the overseer, very reliable, and never touched a drop. So from then on the old foreman took a dislike to Antuco and tried to get him fired.

One night a cow was missing from the paddock, and the foreman told everybody Antuco was in partnership with the thief. Antuco denied it, but no matter; he was sent away from the ranch without his pay, and the overseer threatened to call the law against him if he didn't leave immediately.

So he bundled up what few clothes he had, and without a cent in his pocket he headed for Santiago to join the army, because without a recommendation how could he get a job at another ranch? Since he had never been to Santiago and wasn't sure which road to take, he lost time getting started. Before he knew it, it was dark.

He took shelter at an abandoned farm, picked up a few sticks to make a fire, and ate some bread. Then he wrapped himself in his blanket and fell asleep. He had a strange dream: an old woman was sitting there, warming herself by the fire. When he asked her who she was, she said, "I'm your luck."

"If you're my luck, how could you let me suffer for so long without helping me?"

"Because I've been lying asleep at this little farm where you were born, and to wake up I had to have the warmth of a fire only you could light. Now I won't sleep anymore, and I'll help you whenever you need me. You're going to be rich, and you'll make your mark on the world."

"How could I be rich when I don't have a pittance in my pocket?"

"You'll have the answer from the first Christian you meet on the road, if you don't fail to do him a favor." With these words the old woman vanished, and Antuco slept on.

At daybreak he set out again for Santiago. After walking awhile he came to a crossroads. Just then a man came by on horseback, and Antuco asked for directions. The man said, "It's the road on the right." Then he invited Antuco to ride behind him on his horse, since he was taking the same road himself.

As they went along, Antuco explained that he was going to Santiago to be a soldier, and the man said he had left home the day before and was just coming back from a distant ranch where he'd gone to get his brother-in-law. "And what bad luck! My wife's had a baby, and today there's a priest coming to our ranch to bless the new warehouse. So we thought we'd have the baptism at the same time. My brother-in-law and my wife's old aunt were supposed to be the godparents. But it turns out my brother-in-law is in bed with an injury. So what do we do now? It's a rough crowd at our place, and my wife wouldn't have any of them for a godfather. Are you in a hurry to get to Santiago? Would you mind being godfather to my little son? I'm sure my wife would be glad to have you as our compadre."

Antuco agreed to stay over until the next day, and when they got to the house he was introduced to the wife. Then the husband explained about the brother-in-law. Mena, for that was the woman's name, took a liking to Antuco and thanked him from the bottom of her heart.

"Don't mention it," said Antuco. "It's an honor to be godfather to your little son and compadre to such a fine woman as yourself."

The priest arrived and the baptism was performed. Then everybody sat down for chicken stew and some deep draughts of chicha, drinking to the health of the new baby.

During the meal Antuco told his dream of the night before and said with a laugh that it had come true, since already he had been asked to do a favor.

"Bah!" said Mena. "Such silliness! If dreams came true my husband would have found a pile of gold coins and precious stones by now."

"Is that so!" said Antuco.

"Oh yes," said the husband. "Just think! For three days I dreamed every night that a genie came to me and told me there was a spur on the side of the mountain where I'd find a dead hawthorn with three branches in the form of a cross, and buried at the foot of this tree would be a ball of red yarn. And if I'd tie the yarn to the tree and throw the ball over my shoulder it would lead me to an underground passage where I'd find a chest full of gold and jewels. Imagine, compadre! Where in the world would you find this famous hawthorn? Mena is right. It's silliness."

Antuco sat listening. He knew exactly the place in the mountains where there was a hawthorn shaped like a cross. And what had the old woman promised him? He made up his mind to leave as soon as possible. No need to explain to the compadres. They would only make fun of him. He simply told them he had decided not to join the military after all and would be looking for work at another ranch, and it would be better for him to start that afternoon instead of spending the night. He asked to borrow their horse. "I'll bring it back tomorrow."

Then he left the house and rode full speed toward the spot in the mountains where the hawthorn grew.

It was night when he got there. But the moon was shining and he had no trouble finding the tree. He hitched the horse to a boulder and unsheathed his knife, then he began to dig. He lifted out a piece of leather. Wrapped inside it was a ball of red yarn that looked as if it had been soaked in blood. He tied the yarn to the tree, just as his compadre had said, and gave the ball a toss. As it bounced and rolled, he ran after it until it stopped beside three stones.

He picked up the ball, which was still quite hefty, and stuffed it into his pocket. Then he began to pull at the stones. As he moved the first stone he heard rumbling inside the earth. He moved the second, and the ground shook. Then he moved the third, and a genie rose up surrounded by flames. The genie sprang toward him, nearly scaring him out of his wits, and to defend himself he threw the first thing that came to hand, which was nothing more than the ball of yarn.

The genie fell to the ground as if he had been hit with a hammer, and in that moment Antuco knew the yarn had power. As he was about to tie him up, the genie said, "Little master, don't tie me with that yarn. Let me be your servant. I am the guardian of the treasure, which I must hand over to the owner of the ball of yarn."

"Then get up," said Antuco, "and take me to the treasure."

The genie stood up. The two of them walked down a staircase into the earth, and there was a chest full of jewels and gold pieces. Antuco started to fill his pockets, but the genie said, "Little master, don't exert yourself. I'll carry the chest wherever you want it. As long as you hold the red yarn, I am your servant. Whatever you wish, command me."

"I command that we be transported to a palace in Santiago. And I command that this horse be returned to my compadres with a bag full of gold." In that instant Antuco and the genie were in a palace on the Alameda in Santiago. Such furnishings you've never seen, and in one of the bedrooms Antuco found a wardrobe fit for a lord. He shook a little bell and servants brought chocolate.

Meanwhile the genie put the treasure chest in a closet next to the bedroom and sat down on top of it to keep it safe.

Antuco, with his coaches and his horses, went out every day to take the air and began living the life of a prince. One day on the Alameda he passed his compadres. They too were dressed in style, and their baby was in the arms of a servant. Without making himself known, he followed them until they stopped and entered a fine house. That way he knew they'd received the bag of gold, and it made him glad.

Not long after that, he decided to travel. He wanted to see England and Paris France. He took out the ball of yarn and ordered a ship furnished with all the luxuries, so he could sail to Europe. And the next thing he knew, word came from Valparaiso that the ship was ready. Antuco went on board with the genie and the treasure chest, and after a few days they docked at Paris. Antuco had already sent a telegram to the authorities, letting them know a Chilean prince was about to arrive. So the king had his ministers waiting at the harbor with a gilded carriage.

When the ship dropped anchor, Antuco got off and started looking for a hotel. But the ministers said, "No, get in the carriage. If you don't stay at the palace the king will be offended." So Antuco had no choice but to say, "All right," provided the genie could come too. The ministers said, "Fine." But the genie said "No!" He would have to go on foot to carry the treasure. Everyone marveled at the way he handled the chest. Four men couldn't have lifted it.

That night at a banquet in his honor Antuco presented the queen with a crown of diamonds. He gave the king a sword all worked in gold, and the king's daughter got a pearl necklace with a brooch to match. Ask yourself whether such gifts were appreciated!

Now, the princess was engaged to the son of the king of England, but, to tell the truth, she didn't care for him. And once she'd seen Antuco, who cut such a bold figure, she started liking the English prince even less. So she whispered to her mother, who whispered to the king, and all three decided this prince from Chile would make the better husband.

When England heard about it, war was declared on France, and English ships set sail at once. Antuco was made admiral of the French fleet. With the genie at his side and the ball of yarn in his hand he gave the order for the red yarn to encircle the enemy. The genie drew the yarn tight, capturing the entire English navy. The prisoners were brought to Paris in chains, including the former fiancé of the princess, who had to pay a ransom before being allowed to return to England.

So Antuco married the princess, and on the day of the wedding he poured chicha for the people of France and drank to their health. When it was his turn to sign the marriage contract, he picked up the pen and wrote his name: Antuco of Chile, Prince of the Hawthorn.

The wind blows my tale out the door
And takes it to the farthest shore.
May it bring back a hundred more.

Chile / Juana González

⇒ 6. Don Dinero and Doña Fortuna ⇐

Don Dinero and Doña Fortuna were having an argument. Don Dinero pressed his claim, "My money's the answer. Without it there's nothing." Doña Fortuna shook her head. "Without good fortune your money brings nothing but trouble. It's my luck that's the answer. Watch, I'll prove it."

Just then a poor man appeared and stood before Doña Fortuna. She asked him, "And how is your life?" He said, "Life? What life? I'm tired of working, and all they give me is four reales."

She filled his knapsack with money and said, "Now, see if this helps. Come back in a while and tell me how things are going."

The man threw the knapsack on his back and went off. On the way home he passed through a forest. He started to have thoughts, "Who does Doña Fortuna think she is? Why should I go back to her? With a sack full of money I don't need anyone."

He walked on. Then wouldn't you know, the knapsack got tangled in a vine. The vine pulled down a wasps' nest, and the wasps stung him. He ran out of the woods as fast as he could, but when he reached the cleared fields, he discovered the knapsack had fallen off somewhere. He went back but couldn't find it. Something he didn't know: the wasps were thieves in disguise.

He returned sadly to the lady and told her what had happened. She said, "Don't worry about losing the money. Just go home."

The man had a neighbor who was better off than he was, thanks to

Doña Fortuna, who took good care of him. After the poor man had left, the lady sent this neighbor a basket of bananas. Hidden under the bananas was the poor man's knapsack with all the money. Not realizing the money was there, and knowing that his neighbor was in need, the good man told the messenger to take the bananas to his friend. "He is worse off than I am," he said.

The poor man was pleased with the gift. And when he took out the bananas, there was the knapsack. He was amazed. He hid the money and said nothing to his family. He ran to Doña Fortuna. "Now I know there's a God. And you! You knew the truth. Without luck, there can't be money."

The lady looked at him kindly. "Since you are repentant, I am going to tell you something. Find yourself a piece of land, whatever it costs, and offer to buy it. When you've made a deal, come to me for the purchase price."

The man went to see a landowner who owned a finca worth fifteen thousand pesos. The owner said to him, "If you bring me the money this afternoon, I'll give you my land for five thousand." He only said it to mock the poor man. But the poor man said, "It's a deal." And in no time at all the man who had been poor became rich.

Don Dinero turned to Doña Fortuna and said, "That man was so poor, now he's so rich!"

"Yes," said Doña Fortuna, "but it was only to prove that without my good fortune your money is nothing."

Dominican Republic / *José Guzmán Ribera*

⤷ 7. Mistress Lucía ⤶

Very well then. Here was a king who wished to marry the most beautiful woman in the world, and with that in mind he left his kingdom and took to the road. He looked everywhere and tried all the different countries. But although he was shown the prettiest young women, he was quick to see their faults and kept putting off a decision. At last, tired of the traveling and the disappointments, he decided to go home and forget the whole matter.

After he had been back awhile, it happened that a peddler arrived in the kingdom selling picture postcards and all kinds of portraits. Down the street he came, wheeling his cart with the little portraits arranged under an open umbrella. And who but the king should be on hand to hear his cry:

"Get your portraits! Portraits here! Pretty faces ready to go, some not so pretty, and some so-so. Portraits! Get your portraits!"

The king called the man over, took a look at the portraits, and saw one that pleased him. The longer he looked at it, the more he liked it. Unable to take his eyes off it, he asked who the young woman was and where she lived.

"Sacred and Royal Majesty," said the peddler, "she whom you admire is the mistress Lucía, who lives in the town of La Cañada. I must tell you, she's an orphan, whose brother Juan watches over her closely. In fact he lets her come out on her balcony only one day a year. I myself have never seen her, but those who have spend the entire year waiting for the day to come round again."

Hearing this, and already smitten by the portrait, the king suffered an attack of lovesickness and had to retire to his chambers, where he immediately dispatched messengers to find the young man named Juan and to ask him for the hand of his sister Lucía.

When Juan had been brought to the palace and had heard the king's proposal, he said he had never felt so honored. He would be pleased to allow the marriage. But first he would have to have a private audience with the king. The king drew him aside.

"Majesty," whispered the young man, "I must tell you this not because she's my sister, but because it's the honest truth. Beyond mere beauty she has three charms, and no one knows about them but me, and now you: when she brushes her hair, pearls fall to the ground; when she washes her hands, flowers drop from her fingers; and whenever she cries, it rains."

The king, who had never heard such marvels, was now more impatient than before, if that is possible. He ordered a coach to be outfitted and sent Juan with an escort to bring back Lucía at once, while he himself made arrangements for the wedding.

And now we will leave this king and turn to the mistress Lucía, shut up in her house and worrying her head over why in the world her brother had been summoned to the palace. She was torturing herself with first one idea and then another when Juan arrived and gave her the news that the king had decided to marry her.

Lucía, who was an obedient girl, made no objection to her brother's plans and even began packing her things. But she did have one requirement: she must be allowed to bring her pet parakeet and her pet mockingbird. And for the occasion she prettied up each of the two cages with a bonnet of ribbons. While she busied herself with this work, one of her servant girls said to her, "Mistress Lucía, you should bring me with you to clean the cages."

"Why not? Go ask your mother for permission."

The girl returned with her mother and said, "I can go if my mother comes too. And she'll do your laundry, just as always."

"Very well, I'll ask Juan, and if he says yes, you can both come."

Juan thought, "What could be better?" This way his sister would not be homesick. Besides, there was a brush fire just at that moment and the neighbors needed Juan to help put it out. So he had no choice but to entrust Lucía to the maidservant and her mother. No doubt she'd be perfectly safe. And of course he didn't want to keep the king waiting.

Up went the birdcages onto the luggage rack of the carriage. The two servants settled themselves comfortably. And Juan said good-bye to his sister, giving her many good counsels along with his blessing. Her carriage now ready, Lucía fluttered her handkerchief, saying:

> Good-bye, dear Juan, who mothered and fathered me.
> Good-bye, dear chapel, where I said my prayers.
> Good-bye, dear pebbles, that I used to play with.
> Good-bye, dear brook, where I used to bathe.

"Hush," said Juan. "You're making me weak." With that the carriage rolled off, Lucía started to cry, and the heavens, need it be said, opened up and poured.

Well, they hadn't gone far when they came to a deep woods where berries were growing. The old servant woman called out, "Look here! What should it be but strawberries! Mistress Lucía, why don't we stop and pick these for the king, so we don't come empty-handed."

"Very well," said Lucía. She ordered the coachman to stop, and as the three of them were jumping down, the parakeet caught Lucía's eye and said, "Mama Lucía, bring me too." And Lucía, who could never say no to anyone, took the cage off the roof and tied it behind her back.

They had just begun picking the strawberries when the old woman said, "Mistress Lucía, look! They're plumper over that way," and she ran farther into the forest. "Oh, darling! Look! They're fresher over that way, and more fragrant!" But in her heart she had a deeper plan. As soon as they were far enough from the carriage to be out of sight, the old servant woman took hold of Lucía, wrenched her arms, and slapped her all over. She pulled off Lucía's outfit and put it on her own daughter. Leaving Lucía with the parakeet and the daughter's clothes, the two servants ran back to the carriage and shouted to the coachman, "To the palace and hurry!"

When they arrived, the king was waiting with his entire court. At a glance he could tell that his bride-to-be was no rarity. She didn't even look like the portrait. He'd been tricked. But what are mere appearances? He consoled himself with the thought of the young woman's three charms. Anyway, since the king's word is for keeps, as people say, he had no choice but to go ahead with the wedding.

As the nuptials drew to a close, the king ordered his guards to throw open the doors to a balcony that overlooked the main square. All the king's subjects were to gather at once to witness a spectacle never before seen in the world. The queen would display her three charms.

The square filled up in no time. The king and his court arranged themselves on the balcony. But can you imagine? When the moment arrived for the maidservant to brush her hair, what fell out but lice? She washed her hands, and nothing came off but grime. And when she started to cry, the clouds flew away and hid behind the hills.

The king was humiliated. He lashed out at the queen. When she told him she had no idea what he was talking about, he began to suspect Don Juan of treachery. He summoned him to the palace for questioning.

At this the alert-minded queen pleaded a migraine and dotted her temples with paper discs soaked in oil of *alacrán.* No one was to disturb her, and all for the purpose of avoiding Juan, who would naturally recognize her.

On arriving at the palace, Juan had to be told that his sister could not see him, and when the king charged him with the crime of fraud he had no defense. After the king had pronounced him guilty, the ministers in council sentenced him to death.

The trial was held on the balcony, and the execution and burial took place in the commons just below. The mockingbird, whose cage happened to hang on the balcony, saw it all.

And now we must leave the palace and turn to Lucía. The poor dear, she'd been left alone in the woods without the slightest idea where to go. What's more, it was getting dark, and the farther she walked the deeper the forest. Worn out, she sank under a pine tree, ready to spend the night as best she could, when the parakeet said,

> *Dear mama Lucía*
> *Step it, stretch it!*

And this gave her a second wind. Suddenly there in front of her was the edge of the woods and in the distance a light.

> *Dear mama Lucía,*
> *Step it, stretch it!*

And before she knew it she'd arrived at the hut of a woodcutter and his family. Such beauty the poor little family had never seen. The terrified father cried out, "In God's name, speak! Are you of this life or the next?"

"Flesh and blood, but lost in the woods," came the simple reply, and moved by pity they took her in. The next morning she combed a few pearls from her hair and gave them to the woodcutter's wife to sell in town, wherever that might be. Believe it or not, the nearest town was the king's royal seat, and when the wife returned from her errand she brought the news that the king was in need of a seamstress.

Following the wife's directions and with the parakeet's cage strapped to her back, Lucía set off for town. No sooner had she arrived at the palace than a button popped off the king's shirt. He demanded a seamstress at once.

Lucía presented herself and was led to the king's balcony. Does it have to be said? The king was entranced. But the first one to speak was the mockingbird:

> *Mistress Lucía, O Mistress Lucía,*
> *Your brother Don Juan was done in,*
> *And his grave lies in the commons.*

Such news! Lucía burst into tears, and the sky answered with a sudden shower.

Yet another interruption. It was the chocolate hour. In came the king's page with chocolate and muffins on a sterling salver. The king invited Lucía to join him, and when she insisted on first washing her hands, he ordered a basin and a towel of genuine linen with a pictorial border. No sooner had she dipped her hands in the water than the basin was filled with flowers.

The king now knew: this was none other than Lucía. "Tell him," said the parakeet. "Tell what happened." And she told her story, strawberries and all, whereupon the king gave orders for the old servant woman and her daughter to be hanged by the neck from the uppermost branches of the tallest tree on the highest hill.

As for Mistress Lucía, she was wed to the king in a ceremony followed by feasting. As soon as it was over, the doors to the balcony were thrown open and word went out that the queen would exhibit her three charms. The people gathered, this time however with rocks in their hands to stone the queen in case they were cheated again. But it was not to be.

Lucía combed her hair with an ivory comb, and so many pearls tumbled forth that the people, forgetting the stones they had brought, scrambled to snap up the pearls.

A silver basin with a plunger and fountain came forth on a tray. When Lucía washed her hands so many flowers spilled over the rail of the balcony that women caught them with their aprons and men with their hats.

So nothing was left but to see it rain. In a time of such happiness who could cry? But all at once the mockingbird sang its song,

> *Mistress Lucía, O Mistress Lucía,*
> *Your brother Don Juan was done in,*
> *And his grave lies in the commons.*

At the first word Lucía began to weep. The heavens opened, and immediately the people ran for cover. They ran and couldn't stop.

And here we will leave them wearing out the soles of their shoes.

Mexico / Bárbara (surname not given)

⮞ 8. St. Peter's Wishes ⮜

St. Peter and a friend went out for a walk, and the exercise made them thirsty. St. Peter started asking for water. He got to a house, and when the woman came to the door and found out what he wanted, she took a glass, wiped it clean, and graciously gave him a drink.

St. Peter drank the water, and as he handed her the empty glass he said, "May God give you a bad husband."

The two friends continued down the road and came to another house. St. Peter asked for water, and the woman found a glass and scrubbed it until it was perfectly clean. Then she filled it with water and handed it to St. Peter with tender care.

He drained the glass and said, "May God give you a bad husband."

They came to another house, where an ill-tempered woman pushed a dirty glass of water in his face and said, "Drink it."

St. Peter drank it and said, "May God give you a good husband."

They walked on. The friend finally said, "How could you wish a good husband on that wretched woman after what you said to the women who were so good to you?"

"Because," said St. Peter, "a bad husband needs a good woman to straighten him out, and a bad woman needs a good husband for the same reason."

Cuba / Clemente Sarría

⇒ 9. The Coyote Teodora ⇐

Teodora, who knew the Devil's secrets, was married to a good, quiet man. He farmed his plot and lived in peace. The couple had barely enough to live on. And yet, their kitchen overflowed with delicacies. Teodora always had a juicy roast to serve her husband and her little boy.

The husband wondered. But when he asked his wife where she could be getting such food, she acted as though she didn't hear. Or she would say, "I bought it" or "A friend gave it to me."

The woman's husband was no simpleton, and he thought, "Are these the facts?" Day by day his suspicions grew. He took to watching his wife at night, but at first he could see nothing.

One night, however, as he lay awake, he felt the bed tremble and sensed that his wife was getting up. In the darkness of their little room he heard her recite a prayer of a kind he had not heard before. She turned around three times to the right, then three times to the left. He dared to look and saw that she had become a coyote.

Terror-stricken, he put his head under the covers and offered a prayer of his own, "St. Anthony and all the souls in purgatory, come save me!"

The next day, as usual, there were fryers and roasting hens on the kitchen shelf, and in the oven a suckling pig.

The husband was now on the alert. But the wife did not go out every night. A few days passed. Then one night, as before, she eased herself out of bed and recited her special words. This time her husband followed her tracks, and in the distance he could see a coyote running to the neighbors' barnyards and henhouses and into their kitchens, gathering provisions for the next several days.

Now fully aware that his wife was a witch, the man went to the priest and reported what he had seen. As Christ's minister the priest knew his duty and gave the husband a rope of St. Francis and a little holy water. "At precisely the moment she changes to her human form," the priest advised, "give her three lashes with the rope of St. Francis and sprinkle her with the holy water. She'll never be a coyote again."

The husband carried out the instructions. But as it happened, the next time the coyote returned from its midnight run and was just becoming a woman again, the husband delivered the lashes and sprinkled the water a moment too soon. The head and the upper body were restored to the form of a woman, as the husband already had seen, but the hindquarters were those of a coyote and could not be changed.

Unable to live as a human, the woman abandoned her husband and her little boy and fled to the woods, where she still roams, they say, as an example to witches everywhere.

Honduras / Pablo (surname not given)

⇒ 10. Buried Alive ⇐

Once . . . once there was a man, well, it was a couple who loved each other very much. And when they talked their little talks, it was always, "What if you died! What would I do?"

Then the other would say, "Ahhh, if you died, I'd die too." And they'd keep it up this way, night after night. The husband would say, "You love me how much?" "Ooooh, I adore you!" "Then what should we do?" "What do you mean?"

"If I die, you'll take your own life. And if you die, I will too, and I'll bury myself in the same grave." So they made a pact: whoever went first, the other would go too. That way they'd be buried together.

As luck would have it, the wife died. And the husband said, "Oh my heavens!" But there it was, the Mrs. was dead and they'd made that pact. "Here I go, off to be buried."

So he said to the gravedigger, "Make it a little extra wide, because I'm going to have to get in there with her. We had this pact: if she went first, I'd go too."

The gravedigger made it wider. And . . . they buried him.

But he wasn't dead. Somewhere, who knows where? he found a little pipe that he pushed up through the dirt so he could breathe and get some air. He had oxygen, then. It's how he stayed alive.

All of a sudden he saw a mouse coming out through a hole in the dirt, running this way, that way, this way, that way. He looked again and saw a she-mouse, the mouse's mate, lying there dead. And it came over and kissed her on her little snout. Then it ran off somewhere and came back with a tiny flower that it pushed into her mouth. With that the dead mouse stood up, and the two of them ran off into the hole, leaving the flower lying in the dirt.

When the husband saw how the little flower had raised the dead, he said, "For God's sake, this flower has . . . has power! I'm going to give it to my wife." He picked it up and pushed it into his wife's mouth, and would you believe it, she woke up.

Then he hears, "Where am I?"

"Don't you remember? You died. I'm here, too, because we had that pact."

"So what do we do now?"

"Oh," he says, "I'll call for help. I've got a pipe here that connects to the outside." So he calls, "Gravedigger! Gravedigger!" And the people who take care of the cemetery are hearing this, and they say, "Ghosts!"

"No, no," says the husband, "it's just us, the ones you buried yesterday."

"Still alive?"

"Still alive. Get us out of here."

So the gravediggers went and got their spades and dug them up. "How did it happen?" they wanted to know. And the man told them the whole story, about the mice.

Now, it turned out that this man, when his wife died, had some savings, some money they'd been able to put aside. He had taken it to the priest and said, "Father, here's a little something we had that I'm not going to need, now that my wife is gone because, well, I'm about to die, too." And he explained what the situation was.

And the priest had said, "That'll be fine. It'll pay for your Gregorian chants, sixty of them, for both of you. You'll get to heaven for sure. With sixty masses you'll go directly to heaven."

All right.

But now that they'd come back to life, they were poor. So the man goes to the priest to get the money back, and the priest says, "What money? Oh, I know! But only half of it's left. I already spent half for those chants."

The man says, "I'll take the other half, then."

The priest says, "All right, but you'll have to get out of town. You'll have to go some place where no one around here will ever see you, because if they found out you're still alive, I'd be ruined. They'd slit my throat. You've got to disappear."

So the man took the money and went to his wife, and he said, "You know what? We've got to disappear. Throw your clothes into a suitcase. Let's go."

And they did.

California / Candelario Gallardo

⇒ 11. The Three Gowns ⇐

A gentleman and his wife had a daughter named Rosa. The wife had a ring she always wore, and one day she said to her husband, "Take this ring, for I am dying, and whoever can fit it to her finger is the one you must marry."

The mother died, and within a few days word went out that the wearer of the dead woman's ring would have the rich widower for a husband. Eligible ladies from all over came to try on the ring. For some it was too big. For others, too small. And all this took many days.

With one thing and another the ring got lost, and it was missing for oh, about a year. In the meantime the gentleman's daughter had reached the age of marrying. And one day dear little Rosa was sweeping and found the ring. When she tried it on, it fit her exactly.

Her father, who was just returning from a sea voyage, noticed at once that his daughter was wearing the ring. He was enchanted. "You'll have to marry me," he said, "because your mother said so."

The daughter cried out, "Oh, Papa! How can I marry my own father?"

"Never mind. You'll do it and that's that."

"Very well, father. But before I marry you, you'll have to bring me a gown the color of all the stars in the sky."

"Why not!" And off he went to find such a gown.

After two or three days he came home carrying the outfit, and poor Rosa was more upset than ever.

"Very well, Papa, but I must have a gown the color of all the fish in the sea."

He rushed off at once. Three days later, when she saw him coming back with the gown, she started to cry. "Oh, Papa, I can't get married with only two gowns. I'd have to have three. Bring me one more, and it had better be the color of all the flowers on earth."

As she required, so he provided. The very next day, there it was, a gown the color of all the flowers on earth. And without pausing to rest he went into town to make arrangements for the wedding.

The moment he was out of sight she tied her clothes together, along with a magic wand she happened to have, and off she ran with the whole bundle, deep into the forest.

After living in the wild for a few days she came upon a young lioness and managed to kill it. She took its skin and put it on. Mind you, whatever she did she always asked the little wand for assistance.

Nearby in a certain kingdom, there was a prince who had gone into the forest to do some shooting. Spotting a dove, he took a pop at it and it started off. The dove flitted from snag to snag with the prince hurrying behind. He stumbled on. Suddenly he caught sight of a lion cub.

He said to himself, "I'll bring this back as a pet for my mother." He caught it easily and took it home. "Mama!" he cried. "Look what I've brought. A young lioness to keep you company."

The queen took the little lioness into her arms, then tied it to a leg of the stove. She put down a dish of food for it.

The following Saturday the young prince, Juanito, for that was his name, was hosting a ball, and when the hour arrived he tidied himself up. In no time he was on his way. When he'd gone and it began to get dark, the lioness, who spoke only to the queen, said, "I'd love to go to the ball."

"You must realize," said the queen, "that if Juanito found a lion in the ballroom he'd have it shot."

"Why worry? He wouldn't dream of shooting me."

"Then go."

On the way to the ball she asked the wand to give her a horse saddled in gold. She put on her gown the color of all the stars, mounted the horse, and rode off.

When she arrived at the ball, every guest came to the door to see this princess decked out in silver and gold. Juanito had come with his intended, but in his excitement he completely forgot she was there and began to dance with the princess. He was so infatuated that he made her a promise, which she did not reject, and when dawn came he gave her a gold band inscribed with his name. In exchange she gave him a gold band of her own. Then she jumped on her horse and sped away, slipping into the lion's skin as soon as she was out of view.

Later that morning Juanito came bursting into the palace, telling his mother all about a certain princess he had seen. He chattered on, with the lioness murmuring,

> *I might imply,*
> *I might deny,*
> *I might imply*
> *That it was I.*

The queen picked up the poker from in front of the stove and gave her a whack to shut her up. Juanito continued, "Mama, I must announce another ball for next Saturday."

He did just that, planning a ball even grander than the one he had held the week before. When the day came, and he'd sped away, the lioness said to the old mother, "How about it? Untie me!"

"God forbid that you shouldn't go!"

"I'm on my way."

As soon as she was out the door she instructed the wand, "As pretty as you made me last Saturday, make me prettier tonight. Make the horse nicer, too." Then she put on her gown the color of all the fish in the sea and rode off.

When she arrived at the dance, there were cries of excitement. And Juanito? He was enraptured. But at the crack of dawn she told him again, just as she'd told him the week before, "It's late. I must leave at once." Quick as a wink he gave her a little gold chain, and she gave him some token or other, mounted her horse, and vanished. They all ran to catch up with her but found no trace of her anywhere. And there was Juanito, panting with lovesickness.

Before she got back to the palace she changed into the lion's skin. When Juanito arrived, all he could say was, "Oh, Mama, I'm dying. That princess was more beautiful than ever," while the lioness, from her spot next to the stove, chimed in,

> *I might imply,*
> *I might deny,*
> *I might imply*
> *That it was I.*

The queen gave her a tap with the coal shovel, and Juanito went on, "But don't worry. There's going to be another dance next Saturday."

As delightful as the first two balls had been, the third, he hoped, would surpass them both. And when the day came he refused to eat. He went early to the ballroom to wait for the princess. When he had gone, just at the stroke of six, the little lioness asked her mistress for permission to follow him, and the dotty old queen threw up her hands and said, "Go ahead, get yourself killed!"

Once on the road, she changed into her gown the color of all the flowers on earth. Her horse was bridled in silver and gold, and as radiant as she had seemed the other two times, she was even more radiant now. Juanito rushed toward her and locked his arm in hers. He swept her into the ballroom. They began to dance. Just to be safe, he doubled the guard at the door so she couldn't escape. But nothing could stand in her way. When he'd given her a jeweled ring, and she'd handed him a gift in exchange, she suddenly disappeared.

The guards ran after her, but already she was far in the distance. Poor Juanito suffered a fainting spell.

Once more she pulled on the snug little lion's skin. Later, when Juanito returned to the palace, he went straight to bed, so badly smitten that even a swallow of water wouldn't go down his throat. His mother was beside herself; Juanito was her only child.

And this went on for a week, then another week. At last the little lioness asked her mistress if she thought the prince might like a few tarts. The prince was asked. He said no, he couldn't eat a thing. But shouldn't she make them anyway, just on a chance? No, no, said the queen. Goodness! If he knew that a lioness had made them, why would he touch them?

The lioness said, "Why would he know?"

So the little lioness made three tarts. In one she put the gold band, in another the gold chain, and in the third the jeweled ring. If the prince wouldn't eat them, at least he could cut them open.

The queen brought the tarts to his room, and when he opened the first, there was the gold band. In the second, the gold chain. And in the third, the jeweled ring. The breath of life returned to his body. "Mama, who made these tarts?"

Already the lioness had changed into her gown the color of all the stars in the sky, and when she came into the prince's room he said to his mama, "This is the princess I told you about."

He recovered immediately. There were royal feasts and dances. They called in a priest, who performed the wedding. Then Juanito became king. Rosa was queen. And they went right on living with Juanito's mama.

Puerto Rico

⇒ 12. The Horse of Seven Colors ⇐

A man with three sons had a wheat field that was being devoured night after night. He decided his sons should be his watchmen. He called his eldest and said, "Go out to the field and see what's eating up the wheat."

Just before dark the eldest son arrived at the wheat field, but instead of watching he dozed off. When morning came, whatever it was had been at it again and the wheat was torn up.

The father gave the boy a scolding and sent his second son. The boy went out to the field at nightfall, then lay down to sleep after finishing his supper bag. Again, in the morning, whatever creature it was had torn up the wheat.

The bewildered father surveyed his losses and began to grieve. The youngest son said, "Father, give me a chance."

"You're too young."

The boy insisted. He bought a guitar and a packet of straight pins and set off for the field. When he had hung his hammock, he stuck it full of pins except for a space in the middle where he lay down. Then he plucked the strings of the guitar and began to sing.

By midnight nothing had happened, and he dozed off. The moment he rolled over, the pins pricked him, forcing him to play another song. Through the night the pins and the guitar kept him awake, and just before daylight something came crashing into the wheat field. He threw his rope and caught a little parti-colored horse that looked at him mournfully and said, "Don't kill me. Let me go and I'll be your helper."

"I don't believe it!"

"You should, because I'm the Horse of Seven Colors. I'll help you whenever you need me, for the rest of your life."

"Do you swear you'll never eat Papa's wheat again?"

"I swear."

The boy untied the rope, and the grateful horse gave him a little wand. "Use this wand to call me. No matter where you are, I'll be there in a moment." The horse said no more and disappeared.

When the boy got home, he was praised by his father for saving the wheat. But he said nothing about the horse, and he kept the wand safely hidden inside his shirt.

As soon as the harvest was in, the father sent his eldest son to town with a burro and a double load of wheat to sell. Walking along behind the burro, the boy reached a ford in a river, where he met an old woman. She said, "My son, if only you'd be so good as to dip a little water into my jar!"

"What? Dip it yourself! I'm in a hurry."

"Where to, my child?"

"Mind your own business."

"What do you have in those sacks, my child?"

"Horse manure!" And he whipped the burro with a switch and kept going.

She cried after him, "Go, my son! May you sell horse manure!"

The boy got to town and made a deal for his two loads. The purchasers opened the grain sacks and what did they find? Horse manure. They gave him a thrashing, and instead of money he had to go home with a story about an old woman and a water jar. The father just rolled his eyes and imagined that his son had been cheated.

The next day the father sent the second eldest with another two loads of grain. The boy set off with the burro. When he reached the riverbank the old woman said to him, "Alas, my son, if only you'd take pity and dip me a little water!"

"What am I, your servant? I've got business elsewhere."

"And where is elsewhere, my son?"

"Elsewhere is where they'll sweep me off my feet!"

"And what do you have in those sacks?"

"Stones, busybody!"

"Go, my son! Good luck with the stones and may you be swept off your feet!"

In town the boy got an immediate offer for his two loads. But when the dealers opened the sacks, what did they find? Stones. They lifted him off his feet and strung him up, and only because they were trembling with rage was he able to wriggle loose and run away.

This time the father was in no mood to hear stories and gave both sons a scolding they wouldn't forget. "Rascals or dupes," he cried, "I can't tell which!"

On the third day the youngest son offered to go into town with the last two loads. The father shook his head, "You're too young to manage." But the boy wouldn't take no for an answer and set off by himself with the burro and the two loads. At the riverbank the little old woman appeared.

"Son, would you be so kind as to fetch me some water?"

"Why not, old woman?" He leaned over to dip it up. And when the old woman had slaked her thirst, she said, "Where are you off to, son?"

"I'm off to town, old woman."

"Son, what do you have in those sacks?"

"My father's wheat. I'm going to sell it."

"Go, my son! May you sell wheat!"

When he got to town the dealers, who were tired of tricks, refused to listen. But when he opened the sacks and showed them wheat of the highest quality, they paid well. Of course he took the money straight to his father.

In disgust the two older sons decided to leave home. Seeing them saddle their horses, the youngest boy pleaded, "Brothers, let me go with you!"

"Don't be stupid! Somebody has to stay with the old man, and it's not going to be us. Everything we try to do turns out wrong, so we're clearing out. Good-bye!" They dug in their spurs and sped off. When they were out of sight, the little brother packed a lunch and took off after them on foot.

All day and all night he walked without stopping, until at last in the distance he could make out two riders. They turned their heads and saw him coming. "Look who's here!"

"What do you suppose he wants?"

"Let's see what he's carrying!"

He was all caked with dust and sweat. "Brothers," he said, "let me ride on the rump of one of your horses."

"No, you belong at home with Papa. Go back!"

"Just let me ride on the rump!"

"Can we see what you're carrying?"

"You can!" He opened his lunch bag and showed them the food he had packed. "Can we take it from you?"

"You can!" He handed it to them gladly, and as he watched them stuff themselves, he pleaded again to ride on the rump. "Sure, climb up, if you'll let us pluck out your eyes."

"All right, I'll let you do it," he said. And what do you know? They did just that. And when they'd plucked out his eyes, they rode off, leaving him blind and stumbling in the middle of the road. With his hands in front of him he made his way to the trunk of a tree. There he settled himself to reflect on his brothers' cruelty and his miserable fate. Night came, and three witches flew into the top of the tree.

"*Kwok, kwok, kwok!*" laughed one of the witches. "Did you hear what happened?"

"No, my dear. What?"

"Well, I never thought we'd get this far. The whole world's coming to an end."

"Tell us more!"

"Well! It's gotten to where brothers are turning against brothers. Just today two of them plucked out the eyes of one of their own and left him blind. Imagine it! Their own flesh and blood!"

"Ah, yes, my dear, but you know, the cure for it is right at our fingertips."

"And what's the cure, woman?"

"All you'd have to do is pick three leaves from this very tree we're in, pass them in front of your eyes, and you'd see again."

"You're not serious!"

"But I am! *Kwok, kwok!*" And with that, the three rose out of the tree and flew off.

By now it was nearly dawn. The boy had heard the entire conversation. He broke off three of the leaves and passed them over his face. In that instant his eyes lit up and he could see again.

He continued down the road, walking day and night. Coming into a town after many days, he learned that his brothers had taken up residence there. He found their house, and when they saw him at their doorstep, they said, "It's our boy! What ever did you do to get back your eyesight?"

"It just happened," he said, then said no more. The two brothers wondered, "What should we do with him?" They decided to make him their cook and housekeeper. "And he can feed the horses, too!"

One day the brothers came home with news. The king in that town had issued a summons, calling all knights from near and far to ride past the palace gate. Whoever could toss an apple into the princess's balcony, hitting her on the bosom, would be given her hand in marriage. Each of the two brothers vowed to compete. The youngest, who by now had become a man, secretly decided to join them.

When the day of the competition arrived and his two brothers had ridden off, the youngest took out his wand and recited, "O little wand, by the power within you that God has allowed you, bring me the Horse of Seven Colors." As the words were spoken, the horse appeared. "What do you want with me?"

"Since I'm on my way to compete for the princess, don't you think I need something to wear?" In a wink he was dressed like a prince. Mounted on the Horse of Seven Colors he appeared at the tournament after all the other contestants had failed. At full gallop he hurled the apple up to the balcony, high as it was, and into the princess's open window. Then just as quickly as he had come, he disappeared. People were gasping. Such marksmanship!

When the two older brothers got back to the house, they found the youngest at work at the hearth, all covered with soot. They paid no attention to him and chatted away. "Say, buddy, that knight had some aim, didn't he?"

"Yeah, but he might not have hit the princess."

"You know something funny? The guy looked like our little brother here!"

The next day the two went back to the tournament, hoping for better luck. They took aim and let fly. But just like all the others they weren't able to get their apples even halfway to the royal window. Then here came the knight on the seven-colored horse in an outfit even more dazzling than the one he had worn the day before. His apple sailed up to the princess's window and grazed her cheek. There was a roar from the crowd. They were arguing. Some thought the apple had struck her bosom; others weren't sure. Meanwhile the dashing knight slipped away without a trace.

That evening when the two older brothers returned home, the youngest was in the kitchen quietly washing dishes. One of the two, who had just come in, said to the other, who had gotten there before him, "Today I saw that knight up close, buddy. He really looks like this one here!"

"Maybe you're on to something. He seems to be able to pull off anything he wants. Remember the wheat field?"

"And the two loads of grain?"

"And the eyes?"

They fell silent, then one of them burst out, "What's the matter with us? He's a country boy! Where would he get fancy suits like that? Or a horse with those wings and those changing colors?"

"You're right, buddy, we lost our heads for a minute."

"But whoever he is, he's going to be the winner."

"Seems that way. But we'll try again tomorrow, won't we, buddy? It's the last day."

"Who's a quitter? Not me!"

So they all went back for the final day, but none could hit even the bottom of the princess's window. Suddenly the knight on the little horse appeared, dressed with all the jewels and sparkle of a prince from a distant land. He paused for a moment so that his brothers could get an eyeful, then tossed the apple and hit the princess squarely on the bosom.

The crowd went wild. "A wedding! A wedding!" The king called the horseman to his side and presented the princess. She fell in love with him on the spot, and the marriage was celebrated without delay. There was a gala banquet.

Then the bridegroom summoned his two brothers. "So you see, you were right. And today I could punish you for everything you've done to me. But instead, you're pardoned. All I ask is that you go home and get Father. Bring him here so he can live with the princess and me."

The brothers were speechless, they wept. Then they hurried off to get the old father. The Horse of Seven Colors spoke up, "I've been with you until this day. Now you are content, and I have paid my debt." With that, the little horse vanished, leaving the happy prince standing next to his bride.

Venezuela / Carmen Dolores Maestri

⤜ 13. The Cow ⤛

A man and his wife had been married awhile and were expecting their first child. They were poor, but the wife had a nice little cow, and the husband, knowing they would need money, said, "What about it, my dear? Shall I sell the cow?" She said, "Very well." And he took the cow to market.

When he got to town, he passed a man with a lamb. The man said, "Where are you headed, my friend?"

"I'm about to sell this cow."

"Give me the cow, and you can have the lamb."

"Good enough, my friend." And he took the lamb and went on. At the next corner he met a man with a rooster. "Where are you going, my friend?"

"I'm on my way to sell a lamb."

"I'll give you my rooster."

"Good enough, friend." And he turned into the side street and came to a man with a goose. "Friend," he said, "will you take this goose for your rooster?"

"Good enough. I'll take it." He kept on going and passed another sharpster. This one had a sack of dried manure. "Friend, I've got a deal for you. Take this sack for the goose."

"Good enough, friend." And he headed for home. On the way he stopped at his compadre's house.

"How're things going?" asked the compadre.

"Not bad. I sold my wife's cow for a lamb."

"And where's the lamb?"

"I was able to sell it for a rooster."

"And where's the rooster?"

"Sold it for a goose, then sold the goose for this sack of manure."

"Are you crazy? Your wife will be furious."

"She won't."

"She will," said the compadre.

"You want to bet?" said the husband.

"What would you bet? You haven't a cent to your name."

"I'll bet you my life against everything you have, and you'll see. My wife won't be angry." Then the compadre's wife spoke up, "Don't do it, compadre. You'll lose, then your compadre will own you." But they brought in witnesses all the same, and they drew up a contract.

"Come hide outside the window, and bring those witnesses," said the husband, and he went off with the sack. When he got to his own little house, he said, "Here I am, dear!"

"And how did it go, dear?"

"Not bad at all, dear. I sold the cow for a lamb."

"Well, at least we can butcher it. We'll use the lambskin on the bed, and I'll dry the meat and save it for when I have my baby."

"What I was about to say, dear, is that I traded the lamb for a rooster."

"You make do with what you have," she said. "I'm an early riser. I'll have the rooster to get me up."

"Well," he said, "I was able to trade the rooster for a goose."

"So there!" she said. "Not everybody has a goose."

"And then I managed to trade the goose for this nice little bag of manure."

"Great!" said the wife. "Next time that awful neighbor insults me, I'll tell her to eat from the bag."

So what did the poor man get? All his compadre's riches. And the rich compadre? He was left with nothing.

New Mexico / Concepción Rodríguez

PART TWO

⤳ 14. Death and the Doctor ⤴

This was out in the country, and there was a man who kept thinking if only he could find the right work it would make him rich. Then one day Death stood in front of him and said, "I'm going to take care of you. I'm going to make you a doctor. You'll cure the sick just by laying your hands on them, and if you see me standing at the foot of the bed, you'll know there won't be any trouble. But if I'm standing at the head of the bed, don't bother. The cure won't work."

The man went to the city and began to practice his art. Time passed. He cured thousands, and word spread through the town that there was a physician working miracles. The news reached the king, whose daughter was gravely ill, and the king sent for the doctor.

When the man arrived, the king said, "My daughter is about to give up the ghost. Save her, you'll have half my kingdom and my daughter's hand in marriage. But if she dies, you'll be hanged at the gallows." The man started to cure the princess and saw that Death had stationed himself at the head of the bed. He thought, "Disaster! Instead of working a cure I'm going to be hanged." But an idea came to him. He turned the bed so that the princess's feet were where her head had been. And Death, seeing that he had been tricked, left the room. But not without planning revenge.

When the cure was finished, the king lived up to his promise and told the man to come back the next day for the wedding. But when the doctor walked out of the palace, Death caught him by the arm and said, "You're coming with me." He took him up to the sky and showed him acres and acres of little oil lamps. He said, "You see these lamps? These are the lives of all the people on earth, and this one that's sputtering and about to go out is yours."

The man said, "All right, but just give me fifteen minutes and I'll tell you a story you'll like." Death agreed, and while the man was telling the story, he looked around him, found where the oil was kept, and poured enough of it into his own little lamp to keep it burning. Today that man is still alive. I know him.

Dominican Republic / Feyito Molina

⤜ 15. What the Owls Said ⤛

It was in the old days. There was a hunter who told his wife to pack him a dinner bag so he could go out and bring back some game, and when it was ready he went.

The whole day he saw nothing. It started to get dark. He took cover in a woods where there were tall trees, rested his rifle against a tree trunk, and lay down next to it. Before long two owls flew into the tree and sat on a branch. The two began to talk, and this is what they said:

"You know, they're like that. We're the ones who can help, and what thanks do we get? They see us and chase us off."

"I know. They throw a hot coal to shoo you away."

"They throw stones. They try to hit you."

"They even pick up a rifle and try to kill you, when all you're doing is offering a little help. They don't seem to like it when somebody wants to do a favor."

"I know. They've got three doctors on the case already, and the patient isn't any better. They stick a needle in him, they give pills, and everything. But it doesn't work. Now, a good sorcerer would examine the patient and know there must be an animal under the bed and get rid of it and that would ease the sickness. All he'd have to do is throw a handful of kernels and one of them would roll to where the animal was."

"And after that he'd take an egg and roll it in paper."

"And then he'd put a little rum in a hollow reed and bury it in the earth and the sickness would go away. Any good sorcerer would do that."

Lying under the tree, the hunter could hear these instructions clearly. The next morning he went to the nearest ranch and asked what was happening. "Why are all these people standing around?"

"Ah!" they said. "The señor is gravely ill. Three doctors are in there right now, and still the patient is no better. The only thing that hasn't been tried is one of those witch doctors the Indians use. You wouldn't know anything about that, would you?"

"Me? Oh, no," protested the man. "But let me ask one thing. Would it have to be someone who *looks* like a healer?"

And already they knew they had their man. The patient's little boy ran into the house to ask his father if it would be all right to let the man come in, and he came back to say the permission had been given.

The man said, "Well, how am I going to go in there and stand next to those doctors who know so much? They know everything, and here I am in short pants. If I could be fixed up like a regular doctor, I might be able to visit the patient."

The boy went back inside. When he returned, he was carrying a pair of long pants and a clean shirt, because the señor, being rich, had everything.

"This is good," said the man. "But what about a hat? Doctors have nice hats. And shoes and everything."

The boy went back to his father and said, "He needs shoes and a hat. He says he can't come in and talk to you until he's dressed right."

Then the boy came back with the shoes and the hat, and the man said, "Doctors charge by the minute, and I don't even have a watch. You have to hold it in your hand to see how many minutes are passing. So what am I going to see if I'm not holding anything?" The boy went off to explain this to his father, and when he came back he put a watch in the man's hands.

The man said, "Now I'm just like the doctors. We work by the minute, you know." He followed the boy into the sickroom and asked for an ear of corn and a cloth to spread out on the floor. A nice twelve-row ear was brought. He twisted it back and forth to shell the kernels from the cob, all the while speaking under his breath the way sorcerers do, and when he had a handful he threw it across the cloth. One of the kernels bounced to the edge of the bed where the patient lay. He lifted the blanket that hung down from the bed, and there was a toad. He pulled it out and killed it.

Then he asked for an egg and a sheet of paper to wrap the egg in. After that, he put a few drops of rum into a reed, plugged it with a piece of cotton, and buried it outside in the yard, just as his friends the owls had said. Then the patient was cured.

The sorcerer did it all. The doctors did nothing. Who knows? That's what the story says. There, it's finished.

Mexico (Mazatec)

⋑ 16. Aunt Misery ⋐

Well, sir, there was an old woman up in her years whose only companion was a beautiful pear tree. It grew at the door to her cabin. But when the pears were ripe, the neighborhood boys came and taunted her and stole the fruit. They were driving her to the end of her wits.

One day a traveler stopped at the cabin and asked if he could spend the night. Aunt Misery, for that's what the boys and the whole neighborhood called her, said to the man, "Come in." The man went in and lay down to sleep. In the morning when he was ready to leave, he turned to the old woman and said, "Ask for whatever you want and your wish will be answered."

She said, "I wish for only one thing."

"Go ahead, ask for it."

"I wish whoever climbed in my tree would have to stay up there until I gave him permission to come back down."

"Your wish is granted."

So the next time the pears were ripe, the boys came to steal as usual, but when they climbed to the top of the tree they got stuck. They pleaded with Aunt Misery to let them go. She wouldn't. Then at last she freed them, but on one condition, that they never come bothering her again.

The days went by, and one evening another traveler stopped at the cabin. He seemed to be out of breath. When Aunt Misery saw him, she asked what he wanted. He said, "I'm Death, and I've come to get you."

She answered, "All right! But before you take me, let me have some pears to bring along. Would you pick me a few?"

Death climbed up the tree to get the pears, but he couldn't get back down. Aunt Misery wouldn't let him go.

Years passed, and there were no deaths. Doctors, druggists, priests, undertakers, they all started to complain. They were losing business. Besides, there were old people who were tired of life and ready to leave for the other world.

When Aunt Misery learned of this, she made a trade with Death. In exchange for her freedom she'd let him come down. And that's why, to this day, people are dying, and Aunt Misery is still alive.

Puerto Rico

➣ 17. Palm-tree Story ➢

A pregnant woman went to fetch water. She filled her jar, but when she tried to put it on her head she strained herself and couldn't lift it. All at once she was giving birth, just as three men passed by, out seeking their fortune; and now, suddenly, she had a little boy. The child said, "Mama, I'll lift the jar for you. There! Now give me your blessing to follow those men." And off he went.

Running after the three travelers, he called out, "Good friends, wait up!" One of them said to the others, "Now look at this! There's a little boy following us." They caught him and tied him to an anthill.

He freed himself and ran on. "Friends! Wait for me!" They caught him again and tied a stone to him; they dropped him into a deep pool.

Again he got free and kept on their trail. "Wait up!"

The three of them said to each other, "Let's fix him for good." But when they tried to catch him, he scurried up a tree. He called down to them, "In the distance I see a little house. There's smoke rising. People are living there." And this time it was the men who followed the boy. They walked on with the boy in the lead until they reached the house. An old woman came out. She said, "What wind tossed you here?"

"The wind that blows," answered the boy.

The old woman had some flesh sizzling in a pan. She gave it to them for their supper. Then, saying, "Night draws on," she put each of the men to bed with one of her three daughters. Since the boy refused to stay indoors, she sent him out to spend the night with the nanny goats.

As soon as she thought everybody was asleep, she got up and sharpened her knife, with her tongue fluttering,

> *Rrrr, rrrah, rrrrahh,*
> *Little knife, do your work, rrrrahh!*

But when she went after the boy, she heard him announcing in a loud voice, "These goats won't let me sleep!" She went back indoors.

While she lay in bed, waiting for the goats to stop bleating, the boy took logs from the woodpile and made three life-size dolls. Hearing nothing, finally, the old woman got up again, with her tongue fluttering,

> *Rrrr, rrrah, rrrrahh,*
> *Little knife, do your work, rrrrahh!*

But when she went for the boy, he had moved to the henhouse. "These chickens!" he was saying, "They won't let me sleep!" The old woman went back to bed. Just before dawn, at last, she was snoring. The boy brought the three dolls into the house and dressed them in the daughters' clothes. He whispered to the men, "Get up!" He put the men's jackets on the three sleeping daughters; and the three men and the boy slipped out of the house.

They were long gone when the old woman woke up again. She sharpened her knife and finished off the three sleepers in men's jackets, then realized she had butchered her own daughters. She put her strongbox under one arm, mounted a lean pig that she kept for riding, and gave a cry:

Piggy, get on!
Run with the dawn!

She had almost caught up with the boy when he saw her coming and ran up a palm tree. She opened her strongbox, pulled out a hatchet, and hurled it at the tree: "Slim down!" And the trunk of the tree became thinner.

The boy had filled his pockets with hens' eggs. He threw an egg: "Fatten up!" And the tree trunk became thick.

She threw the hatchet again: "Slim down!" He threw another egg: "Fatten up!"

"Slim down!"

"Fatten up!"

"Slim down!"

"Grandmother, throw it here!" She threw the hatchet again. He caught it and returned it, slicing off one of her arms. She flung it back with her good arm. He caught it and flung it again, and this time it did her in.

He climbed down the tree, and with the hatchet he took out her heart and sliced it into three little tidbits. He tucked the tidbits into the strongbox and ran back to the house. The three men had gotten there ahead of him and were tearing up the place, looking for the old woman's jewels.

The boy removed the tidbits from the strongbox and smeared the blood on the three daughters. They immediately came back to life. Then he presented the young women to his three companions, who had treated him so cruelly, and left them happily married with all the jewels in the old woman's strongbox. "Farewell," he said. And he was gone. They didn't see him again until they went to heaven. He was an angel.

Colombia

⟫ 18. Pedro de Urdemalas ⟪

I. THE LETTER CARRIER FROM THE OTHER WORLD

One morning Pedro de Urdemalas woke up without a cent in his pocket and started wondering, "How can I find some money?" He got on his burro and rode into town, facing backwards, crying, "Letter carrier from the Other World! Who has letters for Heaven? Bring them here!"

People looked out their doors, but no one brought any business until finally a woman came to the curb and said, "You're from Up Above?"

"Yes, madam, I'm the letter carrier for St. Peter. I'm on my way back right now."

"If only I'd known! I could have written a letter to my husband, who died last month!"

"Madam, I'm on a schedule and can't wait for you to write. But if you have anything to send your husband—money, clothes, food—I'll take it along. He's poor as a church mouse up there and getting thin."

"Oh, you're too kind! Wait a minute while I make up a box." And in no time she ran back to the curb with a bundle of men's clothing, a roast chicken, and two hundred pesos in fresh bills. "Give him this," she said, "and don't forget to tell him he's in my prayers every day."

Pedro bid her farewell and rode on down the street, still facing backwards, crying, "Letter carrier now leaving for the Other World! Last call for letters to Heaven!" As soon as he was out of sight, he turned himself around and rode out of town as fast as the burro would take him.

When he thought he'd gone far enough, he took off his old clothes and spruced himself up with one of the dead man's outfits and sat down to a peaceful meal of roast chicken. And with the two hundred pesos he kept on eating and drinking for several days.

Chile

II. THE KING'S PIGS

Pedro left home to try his luck. He came to a king's house, knocked on the door, and asked for work. The king said, "I have a job for you. Watch my pigs; keep them out of trouble. Mind you, keep an eye on them. Don't let them near the swamp."

"No problem," said Pedro. "Sounds easy."

The king went back inside, and while Pedro was tending the pigs, some passersby stopped and asked, "Are these pigs for sale?"

"Sure," said Pedro, "I'll sell them to you. Except for the tails. I'll keep those." When they'd paid him for the pigs, he stuck the tails in the swamp, one here, one there, and went and told the king, "Sir, the pigs are sinking in the swamp! I tried to pull one out and all I got was this, a tail!" He opened his hand and showed him the pig's tail.

"O my stars!" said the king. And he ran to take a look. He rolled up his sleeves and starting tugging at the tails, first one, then another. "Nothing but tails!" he cried. "The pigs are gone!"

Pedro started to back away. "I'll forgive you this time," called the king.

"Oh, thanks. I appreciate it."

The king came over to him, gave him his wages, and said, "Enough for today."

The next morning Pedro was back. But there was no more work at the king's house.

Guatemala / José Cleophas Arriaza

III. THE SACK

Pedro de Urdemalas put on a friar's robe and went out in the countryside begging for alms. At the end of the day he stumbled into a thieves' cave, and in the back of the cave there were bags of silver and gold, and jewels worth a king's ransom. A rocky nook had been set up as a kitchen. A lamb was slit open, hanging upside down ready for use, and there were two quarters of another, freshly butchered carcass.

Pedro was hungry from tramping through godforsaken fields and woods. He cut off a leg of lamb and started to grill it. Before it was done, the thieves came back. They grabbed Pedro and tied his hands and feet. "We'll throw him into the river," they said. "But first let's eat."

There were ten of them. When they'd finished the leg of lamb that Pedro had cooked, they put another on the fire. Meanwhile they stuffed Pedro into a sack and set him outside near the entrance to the cave.

Since Pedro was fortune's friend, who should come along at that moment but a cowherd with more cows and beautiful yearling calves than you could count, crying,

> *Hey, Bossy! Hey!*
> *Whoa, Bossy!*
> *Here, Daisy!*
> *Hey, Bossy! Whoa! Whoa!*

Pedro began chanting in a loud voice from inside the sack, "My Savior, protect me from drowning. For your sake, dear Lord, I resisted the temptation to take their money. Don't let them drown me, dear Lord."

The cowherd, who was a kind soul, overheard the prayer and opened the sack. Out popped the head of a friar, wrapped in a cowl.

"Father, what happened?"

"My dear little brother, such trouble! I was begging alms for my monastery when I ran into some gentlemen who tried to force me into taking whole bags of money. Our order forbids it! I can only accept small sums. We have a strict vow of poverty. I had to refuse, and it made them so mad they tied me up. As soon as they finish their dinner they're going to throw me in the river."

"Father, I can help you. Why don't we change places? When the gentlemen come back, I'll tell them I've thought it over and can take the money after all. Since it's getting dark, they won't know I'm not you. Let me put on your robe. You take my cows over to the next valley."

The two traded clothes, and Pedro took the cows and the yearling calves, leaving the cowherd in the sack with his hands tied. A moment later the thieves came tumbling out of the cave, their bellies full of roast lamb, tipsy from drinking the costly wines they'd stored inside. One of them threw the sack over his shoulder and trudged to the river, paying no attention to the cowherd's protests, "I'll take whatever money you've got, even if it's four bags. Even more!" They got to the riverbank, and two of the thieves swung the sack between them, letting it fly out over the water.

Pedro, who had climbed a tree to watch, stayed put until the gurgling sounds and the bubbles stopped rising from where the sack had hit. Then he climbed down and took charge of his herd. The next morning he drove the cows past the entrance to the cave, crying out with a full throat,

> *Hey, Bossy! Hey!*
> *Whoa, Bossy!*
> *Here, Daisy!*
> *Hey, Bossy! Whoa! Whoa!*

The thieves, who had just gotten up, recognized Pedro's voice and came out for a look.

"Father, what's the meaning of this?" said the thieves' captain. "Where's your robe? And who got you out of the river?"

"Providence, my brother, providence that takes care of the poor. A helping hand untied me. And the little people who live under the river, such good Christians! seeing that I was a poor friar in need, gave me these beautiful animals and led me safely to shore. All they asked in return was my friar's robe to keep as a relic. May God reward them!"

"Men!" cried the captain. "Where are those robes we took from the Dominicans the other day? Put them on, and let the padre tie us up and put us in sacks and drop us in the river. With the cattle we get from the little people we'll have enough to live easy for the rest of our days. I know the padre won't refuse us this favor."

"It would be a pleasure," said Pedro, "even if it makes me late getting back to the monastery. My reverend superiors will be anxious."

"Let's hurry," said the captain. And before another hour had passed they were all trussed up in their sacks at the bottom of the river. Pedro was now the owner of the cows and the calves and all the thieves' gold, silver, and jewels.

But Pedro's riches didn't stay with him. He went on a binge with his buddies and sweethearts. For as the proverb says, he who has figs has friends, and the money slipped through his fingers in less than a year.

Chile

IV. PEDRO GOES TO HEAVEN

Pedro was so poor he kept saying to himself, "Even the Devil won't come to see me." He said it over and over until who should appear but the Devil.

"So there you are," said Pedro. "I'll trade you my soul if you give me the money to set myself up as a blacksmith." The Devil did not have to be asked twice.

"But on one condition," said Pedro. "When you come for me, if I'm in the middle of a job, you'll have to wait."

"Why not?" said the Devil, and they drew up a contract and signed it.

One day not long after that, St. Peter lost his keys and went to God to ask what he should do. "You'll have to go to Pedro de Urdemalas," said God. "Ask him to make you a new set." So St. Peter gave Pedro the measurements, and Pedro made the new keys.

When Pedro was finished, God appeared and asked what the charge would be. "No charge," said Pedro.

"Well then," said God, "I'll grant you three wishes. Name them."

"Here's my first," said Pedro. "I wish the fig tree in my patio would bear fruit in all seasons." At that moment St. Peter, without being asked, chimed in, "And you'll be my guest in Heaven!"

Pedro continued, "My second wish is that if someone tries to pick my figs I can say 'Stick tight!' and he'll be stuck to the fig tree. Now here's my third: wherever I sit, no one will be able to make me get up."

"Your three wishes granted!" said God.

The day came when Pedro was ready to die, and one of the Devil's henchmen came after him. Pedro at the time was working on a set of tools. He said, "While you're waiting for me to finish, climb up in the tree and help yourself to some figs." The little devil climbed up, and

Pedro called, "Stick tight!" When he started to complain, Pedro took his hammer and tongs and beat the daylights out of him. "Now, unstick!" And the little fellow ran back to the Devil, who'd made the contract, and reported, "He won't come!" So the Devil said, "I'll get him myself."

The Devil came to Pedro and said, "Why wouldn't you come?"

"Because the little fellow wouldn't wait for me to finish my job. You've forgotten our contract? Be patient while I work on these tools. And have some figs!"

The Devil picked a few from the lowest branch.

"Those aren't the good ones. Climb up!"

The Devil climbed into the tree, and Pedro called, "Stick tight!" Then he picked up his hammer and tongs and started to give him a thrashing. "Stop!" cried the Devil. "You're killing me. I'll do anything, I'll tear up the contract."

"Then, unstick!"

They tore up the contract and the Devil went off empty-handed, with Pedro calling after him, "When they bury me, tell them to put my hammer in the coffin, and the tongs, too!"

Not long after that, Pedro died for sure. He went up to the gates of Heaven and knocked with the hammer. St. Peter answered, "Who's there?"

"It's me, Pedro de Urdemalas."

"Oh no you don't. Not here."

"You promised."

"But you didn't ask. Remember? Anyway, we can't let you in. You'll have to go down below."

Pedro went down below. But when the Devil's henchmen saw him coming, he made the sign of the cross with his hammer and tongs and they all fled. So he went back to the gates of Heaven and called out, "Old namesake, let me in! They don't want me down there. All they do is run away."

St. Peter consulted the Virgin.

The Virgin turned to Pedro and said, "Follow me. I'll take you myself." Pedro trailed after her, but when they got to the gates of Hell he made the sign of the cross behind her back and all the devils ran off again. The Virgin said, "You'll have to wait here until they come back for you."

"Oh, no," said Pedro. "I can't be by myself. You know that's against the rules." So they went back up, and the Virgin put a bench just outside the heavenly gates and told him to sit down. As she passed through the entrance, Pedro reached out to her, and she slammed the gate on his hand.

"Ouch! Open up!"

She opened the gate just an inch and Pedro stuck his head through. "Open wider, so I can get my head out!" She opened a little wider, and he sped through the gates and sat down on St. Peter's chair. St. Peter complained to God. God settled the matter once and for all: "Have you forgotten his third wish? Since Pedro was granted the wish to sit wherever he wants, he stays with us in the heavenly Kingdom."

Argentina / Noemí A. Pérez

➣ 19. A Voyage to Eternity ➣

It seems there were two men who'd been friends from school days. They went into different professions. Each made his own life, and they went their separate ways. But they kept in touch.

Time passed, and one day after four, maybe five years they got together again, and one of them said, "You know, brother, life is short. We aren't old, but we're not getting any younger either."

"You're right, brother, but we care about each other and we'll always have our friendship. That lasts. Or does it? You know, we ought to make a pact. Whoever goes to the grave first will communicate with the other one, send a letter to say whether eternity exists. If the survivor doesn't hear anything he'll know that life ends with the last breath and there's no other world."

"Yes, let's." And so they agreed.

After that they kept in touch. One, two, three, four years went by.

Then one day a messenger arrives at the house of one of the two friends. He's on a blooded steed, all rigged up, leading a second horse without a rider. He knocks. A servant opens the door.

"Is the gentleman in?"

"The gentleman is in."

"May I enter?

"Why not?" The messenger is well dressed, well built, what people would call a good-looking lad. Then the master of the house appears and says, "What can I do for you?"

"I have a letter from a gentleman."

"And who are you?"

"That isn't important. I'm under orders to take you back with me if you wish to go. Read the letter; it'll tell you . . . well, read it."

My dear friend: I send you this at long last, looking forward to seeing you soon. I don't ask that you reply but that you come in person, if only for a short while. The bearer of the letter will guide you. Trust him, there's no reason to be afraid. I want you to know that I am longing to see you. You must not forget, we promised to be friends in this life and in the next. I should have written you sooner, but I do it now with the tender regard we have always had for each other. I am confident you will not refuse this invitation, for if you do, our friendship will be ended forever.

The friend thought for a minute. Finally he said to the messenger, "I'll have to make arrangements. How much time can you give me?"

"Two or three days."

"Two or three days will be enough. While you wait, you must stay with me here."

"I'm sorry, I can't. I have other lodgings not far away."

"Then come for meals."

"Sorry, I'm committed elsewhere."

The friend thought, "How odd." He said, "At least you can leave your horses."

"Not even that. I must keep them with me."

The messenger rode off, leading the riderless horse. Then in three days the friend put all his affairs in order. He gave instructions to his servants. He went to the bank and the different government offices—I'm not sure, but I think this was in Spain—and he settled his accounts, paid the taxes on his house, no? That would have been it, because he didn't have a country estate. He was a rich gentleman, though, and got everything taken care of without delay, greased a few palms here and there to speed things up. Money talks, you know.

Then after the three days had gone by, the messenger reappeared. "Ready? Can we leave now?"

"Ready!" he said. "Let's leave!" He told his servants, "Take care of the house as if it were yours." He paid them their wages in advance and bid them good-bye.

They rode out of the city, which of course had new buildings under construction everywhere, the way it is with cities. So they didn't reach open country right away. But when they did, the man realized his horse wasn't touching the ground anymore, and the next thing he knew they were flying through the air. They kept on this way for three, four, maybe seven or eight hours. Well, when would this have been? It isn't told, but the speed was tremendous. Any neighbor's boy would have been amazed, because in those days they never even dreamed how fast an airplane could go.

Well, it seems they got to a great hall, where there was beautiful singing, and the man asked, "Where's my friend?"

Different people welcomed him, "Come in, come in," and they led him to an apartment, where his friend put his arms around him and said, "I'm so glad to see you! I was afraid you'd refuse my invitation."

"Brother, how could you think such a thing? Your letter gave me no choice. I put all my investments on hold, paid my taxes, and arranged my affairs so I could come see you. What else could I do? After all, we've been friends since we were children, and now we're at the mid-point of our lives. Or a little beyond."

Then his friend spoke, "I'm going to tell you something that might surprise you, though I hope it won't offend you."

"Tell me, friend. I can take it."

And they say that what he told him is this: "As you must remember, brother, I left the world four years ago. My promise was to let you know whether eternity exists. I've done that, and if you look around, you can judge for yourself. But for the first three years I went through torment because of my sins on earth. In my own opinion I was a righteous man, but once in the grave I came to realize that my good works had been few, not enough to bring me directly here. Now at last I'm on the road to Heaven, and you can imagine the beauty that lies ahead. My penance is over. I'm free now and on my way. I don't know when I'll arrive. Will you join me? Shall we travel together? Or would you rather go back to earth and wait for the Creator to call you? Answer me, so I can tell my messenger what to do."

According to the story, the friend hesitated. He wasn't sure what to answer. Finally he said, "I've got to go back home and get rid of all my worldly goods. When everything has been given away and the Everlasting can see that I have nothing left—when I'm naked—he'll gather me up, and you and I will meet again."

"I know what you mean," said the other friend. "Be sure to hold nothing back. Give away everything you have, because you never know when the Lord of the Universe will call you."

They talked for a little while longer, then the messenger took the friend back to earth. When he arrived in his city, he didn't recognize it. The buildings that had been under construction were now in ruins. There had been wars and other disasters.

The messenger left him at the door of his house and disappeared. But the house had been confiscated years before and sold for taxes. There were new owners. He showed them his deed of title, but they bounced him out on his ear. He had to seek shelter in a . . . well, in a monastery, I think it was a Franciscan monastery, and that's where he died. That's the story. There's no more.

Bolivia / José Rivera Bravo

🙾 20. Mother and Daughter 🙼

A mother's daughter who had led a good life died and, being a virgin, went directly to Heaven. The mother also passed away but found herself in Purgatory.

The mother fixed her gaze on Heaven and caught sight of her daughter. She called out,

> *Daughter María, spotless as snow,*
> *Let down your hair for your mother;*
> *Then fair as you were and now are,*
> *You'll be fairer than any other.*

The daughter bent her head down and let her hair fall into Purgatory. The mother climbed up and kept climbing until she reached Heaven. Of course, the mother had already been in Purgatory awhile and had purged her sins. Her daughter was simply waiting for her.

Colombia

🙾 21. The Bird Sweet Magic 🙼

A king lost his eyesight and could find no cure. Doctors came from everywhere and made promises to the king, to the king's three sons, and to the queen. But the king's eyes did not improve.

In the kingdom there was an old medicine woman who had made a reputation working cures where doctors had failed. Just in case, the king's family summoned her to the palace. Her instructions were these: "You'll have the cure if you can bring home the bird Sweet Magic. Rub its tail over the king's eyes. The bird is under the power of a king in a distant country. Remember this: the one who captures the bird is the one who must work the cure."

The king's three sons decided to give the medicine a try, and the king promised his throne to the one who could bring it back. The three set out that same day. The eldest left in the morning, the second-eldest at noon, and the youngest toward evening. Each took a good horse and a bag of money.

As the eldest son was riding out through the city gates, he saw a crowd in front of a church, and as the saying goes,

> *The crowd's noise*
> *Draws the boys.*

So he pulled up to see what was causing the commotion, and there was a dead man on the steps of the church. Someone had left the body without money for burial. The priest, even, was refusing to sing prayers for the dead because no one would come forward to pay for them.

The prince said, "There's nothing in this for me," and went on.

At noon the second son came by, and still the unfortunate man had not been buried. The second son shrugged and rode away.

Late in the afternoon, when the youngest pulled up, the corpse had begun to give off an odor. Dogs and buzzards were trying to get a piece of it, and the crowd was shooing them away.

Taking pity on the poor soul, the prince gave one of the bystanders enough money to go buy a coffin. He himself went to the priest and made a deal for the prayers. He helped open the grave and would not leave until the body had been laid to rest.

After he had traveled on for a while, night overtook him in a desolate place. Ahead in the distance was a little round light the size of an orange. It kept coming closer. The prince cried out, "In God's name, who are you?"

A voice answered, "I am the soul of the one you buried. Don't be afraid. Follow me. I will lead you to the bird Sweet Magic."

With the light directly in front of him the prince rode on through the dark. The next day he rested until it was dark again. Gradually he lost his fear. He and the light would talk to each other. During the day he would wait impatiently for night to come so that he could again be with his friend the little light.

After many weeks, traveling only at night, he came to the country of the king who was master of the bird. Following the light, he walked past the sleeping guards and into the palace, and there in a room paneled in gold and crystal was the bird Sweet Magic. It hung from the ceiling in a cage covered with rubies the size of coffee beans. The ceiling was paved with fresh roses. Their fragrance floated in the air, and when the bird sang, it was with the sound of flutes and violins.

The prince made a stairway of chairs and tables and was just touching the cage when the whole pile crashed to the floor. The king jumped out of bed, called his guards, and ordered the prince to jail with nothing but bread and water.

But then the king changed his orders. He thought, "This boy will risk anything to get the bird. Such a boy I can put to use." He freed the prince and promised to give him the bird if he would bring back a horse that the king favored over all his other horses and that had been stolen by a certain giant.

So said, so done. When night came, the little round light guided the prince to the pasture where the giant was guarding the horse. It was black as satin, with white shanks and a star on its forehead. On its shoulder was a knob, and the little light said to the prince, "When you turn the knob, you'll see what you'll see."

Well then, the prince climbed into the tree where the horse was tied. He reached down and began to loosen the rope. The horse, who could speak like a human, shouted, "Master, they're stealing me!" The giant, who had been napping, woke up but could see no one and went back to sleep. The tree where the prince was hiding was a mango tree and a very leafy one.

Again the prince reached for the rope, the horse cried out, and the giant looked around and saw only the tree. This time he spoke sharply to the horse and threatened to break its bones if it kept waking him. The horse knew better than to test the giant's patience. When the prince reached down once more and untied the rope, the horse kept still. The prince mounted the horse, turned the knob, and rode into the sky.

When they were over the king's palace, the prince twisted the knob in the opposite direction and they landed smoothly just at the palace door.

The king was beside himself with joy. But he was not yet ready to give up the bird. The prince would now have to rescue the king's daughter, who had been kidnapped by none other than the same giant who had stolen the horse.

Unsure, the prince conferred with the little round light. The light assured him that the task was possible. When night came the prince mounted the black horse once again and set off for the giant's palace, arriving at the supper hour.

The giant's dining room was on the second floor. The little light whispered to the prince that he would have to climb a vine to the second-story window. The vine held fast to the palace wall, as the light had promised, and when the prince looked in through the window he could see that the giant was just finishing his bottle of wine. The prince waited until the giant's head dropped to the table. Then he tossed a pebble at the princess. She looked up and saw her chance to escape, then ran to the window and climbed down the vine with the prince. As she could see, he was well put together and good-looking. His thoughts of her were the same. The fact is, they liked each other very much.

But when they got back to the king, they found he had changed his mind once again. The bird must not be taken away. The prince could choose anything else he wanted.

With the voice of the little light whispering in his ear, the prince asked permission to ride the black horse three times around the palace, with the princess mounted in front of him and the bird in its cage held in his hand. The favor was granted, and to make sure the prince would not escape, the suspicious king sent soldiers to guard every exit around the rim of the plaza.

The king had no inkling that the prince knew the secret of the little knob. After circling the palace for the third time, the prince suddenly turned the knob and rose into the sky.

So the prince flew home to his own country. When he got to the boundary of his father's realm, he twisted the knob again and came to earth. The first town he entered turned out to be where his brothers were staying. After weeks of partying, they had spent all their money and were only waiting until they could think of an explanation to take to their father. The sight of their brother, bringing home not only the bird Sweet Magic but a beautiful princess and a wonder horse, filled them with jealousy. But they took hold of their senses and pleasantly invited him to dine with them at the inn. In his innocence the young prince accepted their offer.

As they all sat at the table, the two older brothers slipped a narcotic into their younger brother's glass and the princess's glass, too, and when both had lost consciousness they dragged their younger brother to the top of a high cliff and dropped him over the edge. When the princess woke up, they told her the prince had gone off partying to another town and had abandoned her.

In triumph they came home to the king and the queen, who rejoiced to see them. No one seemed to know where the youngest son had gone, and the distraught princess was presented to their majesties as a madwoman.

The two brothers were ready to divide the kingdom between themselves. But when they rubbed the bird's tail over the king's eyes, it had no effect. The king was as blind as he'd been before.

Yet at that moment help was on its way. God's wish was for the young prince to live, and he gave to the little round light the power to save him. So, when the prince was dropped from the cliff, a branch caught him by the jacket. Not long after that, some mule drivers passed by, heard his cries, and lifted him to safety. When he told them who he was, they carried him directly to his father's palace.

No sooner had he arrived than the princess, who had been overcome by grief, regained her composure, and the bird Sweet Magic filled the air with its music of flutes and violins. The prince explained everything to his parents. The mule drivers verified his story. And, finally, he touched the bird's tail to the king's face, and the king's eyesight returned.

Now everyone knew that the two older brothers had lied. But the youngest brother, who was one of God's own children, would not permit his brothers to be punished. Instead, he embraced them and gave them their share of the kingdom. Then he married the princess, and she hung the bird's cage in her window, where she could hear its music every day.

When the little round light saw that his friend was safe, he came to say his last few words: "I am finished now. I have shown you my gratitude." The prince was unwilling to separate from his true friend. Then the voice came to him one more time: *Adiós y ahora hasta que nos volvamos a ver en la otra vida*—Farewell until we meet again in the next life.

And I? I went in one end and came out the other so you, my friends, could tell me another.

Costa Rica / tía Panchita (Aunt Franny)

➣ 22. Death Comes as a Rooster ⟨

A woman's husband was sick in bed. She did nothing but take care of the man, and every chance she got she prayed to the Lord, "Dear God, don't take him first. Let Death come first for me."

She repeated it constantly. Her compadre overheard her and said, "You'll know Death when you see him, comadre. He comes as a plucked rooster."

The woman kept on, begging Death, "Don't take my poor husband, take me instead."

Then the compadre caught a rooster, plucked its feathers, and put it out in the sun until it was crazed. When he turned it loose, it ran screeching into the sickroom. The wife took one look and said, "My God, it's Death!" She jumped behind the door and pointed her finger at her husband. "Over that way," she said. "The sick man is in the bed."

Cuba / Isabel Castellanos

⇒ 23. The Twelve Truths of the World ⇐

There was a poor man with so many children that he had run through all the available godparents in his village. Just when there was no one left to ask, his wife had another child. She said to her husband, "Who'll be godfather this time?" and the poor man stamped his foot and replied, "I'm going to invite the Devil!" With that he stormed out of the house.

After wandering awhile, he entered a forest, where a well-dressed stranger suddenly appeared from behind a cottonwood and asked the poor man, "Where are you going, my friend?"

"I'm trying to find a godparent for a child."

The stranger, who was none other than the Devil himself, said, "How about me?"

"I'm ashamed to accept," said the poor man. "You seem very rich, and I am very poor." To this the Devil replied, "Don't give it a thought. If you let me be the godfather of your child, you won't be poor anymore. There's a condition, however. You may keep my godson for twelve years less one day, and you must take away all the crosses and images of saints that you have in your house. Also you must not teach the child to pray. And after the twelve years less one day, I will come to claim him." The poor man agreed to everything. He told his wife, and she said nothing.

When the Devil arrived for the baptism, the poor man took him into the house and said to him, "I'm sorry to say that all I can give you to drink is coffee." The Devil told him not to worry. He ordered his servants to bring food and wine. They arrived with four wagons full. The Devil also had carpenters come, and in a just few hours they had built a palace for the poor family.

Soon after that, the Devil's wife appeared in a beautiful carriage, and the Devil and his wife took the child to have him baptized. When they came back, they said, "The boy's name will be Twelve and Less." The tables were set, and they had a feast. Then the godparents left, saying, "We'll see you again in twelve years less one day."

The years passed, and at precisely the time agreed upon, the Devil arrived for his godson. He had ordered that the child be placed in a room without crucifixes or images of saints. The mother of the child was the first to hear the compadre's footsteps, and she began to pray to God, asking him to free her child from the godfather's clutches. The Devil knocked at the door. No one opened. He cried out to his godson, "Open the door, Twelve and Less!"

There was no answer. He cried out again, "Open the door, Twelve and Less, for I am your godfather!" But the child was fast asleep.

The child's guardian angel then appeared and replied for the child, "I just can't open the door right now. I'm too sleepy."

"That's no excuse. Open the door!" said the Devil. And the child's guardian angel replied, "I'm telling you, I will not open the door! I'm too sleepy! Don't bother me!"

"If you don't open the door, I'll break it down!" said the Devil. "I'm in a hurry!" And indeed he was, for after twelve midnight his power over the child would be ended. For the third time the Devil said, "Open the door!"

"I will not!" said the guardian angel.

Finally the Devil got tired and said, "Tell me the Twelve Truths of the World, and I won't break down the door. Let's see if you can. I dare you to try!" The guardian angel replied, "But I can! I'll tell them!" Then the Devil said,

"Catholic and faithful Christian, tell me the Twelve Truths of the World. Tell me the One." And the angel replied,

"The One is God, Christ who came down to bless the holy house at Jerusalem, and there he dwells and will reign forever and ever, amen." The Devil gave a jump backwards and cried out,

"Catholic and faithful Christian, tell me the Twelve Truths of the World. Tell me the Two." And the angel replied,

"The Two, the two tablets of Moses, the One is God, Christ who came down to bless the holy house at Jerusalem, and there he dwells and will reign forever and ever, amen." The Devil gave another jump backwards and cried,

"Catholic and faithful Christian, tell me the Twelve Truths of the World. Tell me the Three." And the angel replied,

"The Three, the three persons of the Holy Trinity, the Two, the two tablets of Moses, the One is God, Christ who came down to bless the holy house at Jerusalem, and there he dwells and will reign forever and ever, amen." The Devil gave another jump and said,

"Catholic and faithful Christian, tell me the Twelve Truths of the World. Tell me the Four." And the angel replied,

"The Four, the four gospels, the Three, the three persons of the Holy Trinity . . ." Again the Devil gave a jump and said,

"Catholic and faithful Christian, tell me the Twelve Truths of the World. Tell me the Five." And the angel replied,

"The Five, the five wounds, the Four, the four gospels . . ." Again the Devil gave a jump and said,

"Catholic and faithful Christian, tell me the Twelve Truths of the World. Tell me the Six." And the angel replied,

"The Six, the six candlesticks, the Five, the five wounds . . ." Again the Devil gave a jump and said,

"Catholic and faithful Christian, tell me the Twelve Truths of the World. Tell me the Seven." And the angel replied,

"The Seven, the seven joys, the Six, the six candlesticks . . ." Again the Devil jumped and said,

"Catholic and faithful Christian, tell me the Twelve Truths of the World. Tell me the Eight." And the angel replied,

"The Eight, the eight choirs, the Seven, the seven joys . . ." And again the Devil jumped and said,

"Catholic and faithful Christian, tell me the Twelve Truths of the World. Tell me the Nine." And the angel replied,

"The Nine, the nine months, the Eight, the eight choirs . . ." And again the Devil gave a jump and said,

"Catholic and faithful Christian, tell me the Twelve Truths of the World. Tell me the Ten." And the angel replied,

"The Ten, the ten commandments, the Nine, the nine months . . ." And again the Devil jumped and said,

"Catholic and faithful Christian, tell me the Twelve Truths of the World. Tell me the Eleven." And the angel replied,

"The Eleven, the eleven thousand virgins, the Ten, the ten commandments . . ." And again the Devil jumped and said,

"Catholic and faithful Christian, tell me the Twelve Truths of the World. Tell me the Twelve." And the angel replied,

"The Twelve, the twelve apostles, the Eleven, the eleven thousand virgins, the Ten, the ten commandments, the Nine, the nine months, the Eight, the eight choirs, the Seven, the seven joys, the Six, the six candlesticks, the Five, the five wounds, the Four, the four gospels, the Three, the three persons of the Holy Trinity, the Two, the two tablets of Moses, the One is God, Christ who came down to bless the holy house at Jerusalem, and there he dwells and will reign forever and ever, amen."

The Devil disappeared with a roar of thunder, and the parents, no longer poor, kept their child and all the Devil's riches.

New Mexico / José Tranquilino Olguín

⇒ Folk Prayers ⇐

I. BEFORE RECITING THE ROSARY

Si en la hora 'e mi muerte	If in the hour of my death
el Demonio me tentare,	The Devil should touch me,
le diría: ¡No ha lugar!	I'll say to him, Stay back!
por qu'el dia'e la Cruz	For on the day of Santa Cruz
dije mil veces: Jesús.	I said a thousand times, Jesús!

II. FOR THE DECEASED

Bendita sea la hora	Blessed be the hour
cuando el Señor Consagrado,	When our hallowed Lord,
Nuestro Señor Jesucristo,	Our savior, Jesus Christ,
murió en la cruz enclavado.	Died nailed to the cross.
Así te pido, Señor,	I ask you, Lord, don't let
qu'es'alma no vay'en pecado.	This soul depart in sin.

III. AGAINST WITCHCRAFT

*Bendita sea la cera del Santísimo Sacramento del Altar, la Hostia Con-
sagrada y la Cruz en que murió Jesucristo. Mil veces me he de encontrar
el Domingo de Ramos frente al Crucifijo de Jesús. En la planta del pie
izquierdo traigo una cruz: ¡Malditos sean los mojanes! . . . Y para siempre, amén, Jesús.*

Blessings on the votive candle of the Most Holy Sacrament of the altar,
of the consecrated host, and of the cross where Jesus died. I will
do it: stand a hundred times before the crucifix of Jesus on Palm
Sunday and carry a cross on the sole of my left foot. A curse on
witches! Always! Amen, Jesus.

IV. TO REMOVE A CURSE

*Jesucristo, hijo de Dios vivo, por donde quiera que vaya y venga, las manos de
mi Señor Jesucristo adelante las tenga; las de mi señor San Blas, adelante
y atrás; las de mi señor San Andrés, antes y después. Mi Señora la Virgen vaya y venga en mi compañía; con mis enemigos tope; ojos traigan, y
no me vean; manos traigan y no me aten; armas traigan, y no me ofendan.
El velo que mi señor Jesucristo trae puesto, tenga yo puesto; el manto que
mi Señora la Virgen tiene puesto, tenga yo puesto; y que sea mi cuerpo cu-
bierto, que no sea preso ni herido, ni de malas lenguas perseguido. Tan
libre sea yo en este día como fué mi Señor Jesucristo en el vientre de la Virgen María. Paz, Cristo; Cristo, paz. Corpus, paz. Corpus, paz, Espíritu
Santo. Justo Juez Jesucristo, sálvame, sálvame. Padre Nuestro y Salve.*

Christ Jesus,
Son of the living God.
From where I've come
To where I go
I hold Lord Jesus' hands;
Before me and behind me
Hold my lord St. Blaise's hands;
Before and after

Hold my lord St. Andrew's hands.
My Lady the Virgin, be with me,
Intercept my enemies;
Let them seek
But not find me,
Stretch their hands
And not reach me,
Bear arms
And not touch me.
May I wear the cloak
Lord Jesus wears,
Wear the mantle
My Lady the Virgin wears;
Let my body be covered.
Let me not be seized or wounded
Or hounded by evil tongues.
May I be safe as my Lord Jesus
In the womb of the Virgin Mary.
Peace, in Christ's name.
In Christ's name, peace.
In Christ's body, peace.
Christ's body, peace.
Holy Ghost,
Christ Jesus,
Judge of the living
And the dead,
Save me,
Save me.
Our Father.
Hail Mary.

V. AGAINST ENEMIES

Padre Nuestro, Santo inmortal, fuiste clavado en la cruz con los tres clavos de acero. Así te pido, Señor, con la fuerza con que derribaste a los fariseos, me derribes a mis enemigos y a todos aquellos que quieran venir contra mí.

Tres tembló el infierno; tres tembló el infierno; tres veces fueron a tierra; tres veces los miraste y tres veces fueron desarmados. Así creo yo, Señor, cuerpo mío no sea preso ni mis brazos amarrados. Hicos traigan, se revienten; puertas de cárceles se abran de par en par y grillos se partan. Así creo yo, Señor, que puertas y candados sean falsos para mí.

Our Father, immortal *santo,* you were nailed to the cross with three nails of steel. By these I ask you, Lord, with your power that overthrew the Pharisees, throw down my enemies and all who come against me: Hell trembled three times, three times Hell trembled, three times they walked on earth, three times you gazed at them, three times they were powerless.

This I believe, Lord. Let my body not be taken or my arms be tied. Though ropes be brought, the ropes will break.

Let prison doors be opened wide and shackles break apart. This I believe, Lord. Let doors and locks be powerless against me.

VI. TO ST. ANTHONY

San Antonio bendito,	Blessed St. Anthony,
tres cosas pido:	Three things I ask:
Salvación y dinero	Salvation, money,
y un buen marido.	And a good husband.

PART THREE

⮞ 24. The Mouse and the Dung Beetle ⮜

A rich couple's son was soon to be married. Next door lived a girl as poor as could be, who loved the son desperately. Her mother, who worked for the boy's parents, would come home at night and tell her daughter what the talk was. The daughter kept hoping the boy would take an interest in her, but he never gave her a thought.

One evening the old woman came back and said, "They've set a date for the wedding."

"Who is he marrying?"

"A girl whose parents are as rich as cream. Who else would he be marrying?"

The daughter felt sick but said nothing.

The mother kept a statue of St. Anthony in the house. The next morning when she'd gone off to work, the daughter closed the doors and the windows. She stood before St. Anthony and asked him to give her the boy next door for her husband. When she prayed to the saint, he smiled. She prayed a little harder, but he was a sly one and made no answer.

The day before the wedding, as soon as her mother had left for work, the girl took St. Anthony out of his niche and stood him on the hearth. She kept talking to him while she heated a spindle over the fire.

"St. Anthony, listen to me, Blue Robe, I've asked you over and over again to give me that boy. They say you're powerful, but I'm beginning to wonder. You don't help me at all. And here he is, getting married to-morrow. I'm going to clean out your ears with this hot spindle, then maybe when I talk to you you'll hear me for a change."

St. Anthony just laughed. When she came toward him with the heated spindle, he ran from one corner of the room to the other.

Just as he ducked under the bed, the mother knocked at the door. Flustered, the girl opened up. The old woman asked, "What's going on?"

"Oh, nothing."

The mother noticed St. Anthony was not in his niche. She saw his feet sticking out from under the bed.

"I took him down to clean him," explained the daughter, "and I laid him there temporarily." The mother picked up the saint and put him back in his niche, all the while describing the banquet that had taken place next door. Hearing this talk, the girl felt sicker than ever.

The following day was the ceremony. Before the mother left for work she asked her daughter to come along and help her. The girl refused. "I can't," she said. "My heart's not in it." Later, when the wedding procession passed in front of her window, she couldn't even bear to look. She turned to St. Anthony and said, "I'll never pray to you again."

St. Anthony laughed and said, "Here's a mouse and a dung beetle. They're at your command. Give them orders and they'll obey."

When her mother returned, the girl asked which room had been prepared for the bridal chamber. The mother went to the door and pointed to a certain window in the bridegroom's house. That night the girl gave orders to the mouse, "Go look in the window and tell me if they're in bed yet."

"Not yet," reported the mouse.

She waited awhile, then sent him back. "They're getting into bed now," said the mouse.

"Gnaw a hole in the casement so the dung beetle can squeeze through." Then she instructed the dung beetle, "Crawl all over both of them and smear them with whatever you can find."

The dung beetle obeyed. First the bride and then the bridegroom leaped out of bed and ran to the bath. They threw open the doors to air out the room. The next night it was the same, and the night after that. After three nights, the bride and the bridegroom began blaming each other.

On the fourth morning the bridegroom was stopped by a little old man in front of his parents' house. "What's the matter?" said the little man. "You're in such a state! Weren't you married just three days ago? You're as haggard as a man who's been married a year or more."

"May I tell you something?" said the young man. And he spilled the whole story.

"You've married the wrong woman," said the little old man. "And this is the proof of it. You'll never be happy until you find the woman who's right for you. Better a poor woman whose heart is true. Believe in my advice and you'll know what to do."

The unhappy bridegroom turned away and for the first time took a look around the neighborhood. He went straight to the one who had prayed so hard to St. Anthony, who himself was none other than the little old man who had given the advice. St. Anthony blessed their union, and they lived happily from that time on. As the old people used to say: Eyes up before you sit down.

Colorado / Eva Martínez

⇒ 25. The Canon and the King's False Friend ⇐

A man and his wife who were childless vowed they would make a pilgrimage to Jerusalem if God would give them children. And at long last the wife delivered a son and a daughter. The children grew up, and when they were nearly of age the husband announced to his wife that it was time to be off for Jerusalem, as they had promised. Away they went, leaving the children with His Reverence, the canon.

When the parents arrived in Jerusalem, they wrote home to ask how the children were doing. His Reverence replied that the girl had not done well, while the boy had turned out to be a fine young man. The girl, he reported, had become a tramp.

The parents wrote back that since it had come to this the daughter was to be taken out and thrown to the animals after removing her eyes and one little finger, which must be shown to them as proof upon their return. Then the canon paid two ruffians to carry the girl off to the woods and bring back her eyes and her little finger.

But the girl moved those two men to pity, and they allowed her to go free after taking only the finger. They took the eyes from a wild boar, and when they'd gone off, the boar and a little coyote stayed with the girl and took care of her in their cave.

A king who lived nearby was out in the woods one day when he spotted the boar and the coyote. He chased them, driving them into their cave. Then, peering in, he saw the girl and ordered her to come forward. "I can't," she said. "I have nothing to put on." So the king took off his cape and threw it at her. She came out of the cave, the king fell in love with her, and what should happen but they rode off to his palace and got married.

Time passed and the king was called to war. Meanwhile the queen gave birth to a child. One day when the king had returned from the battlefield, the queen said to him, "Am I ever going to see my parents again?" So the king made arrangements for her to travel, selecting as her escort a friend in whom he had complete confidence. While on the road the friend became amorous, and when the queen rebuffed him he turned around and rode back. She, prepared for any emergency, had brought along one of the king's outfits. She slipped it on and continued her journey dressed as a man. When she reached her old home, her parents had no idea who she was.

As for the friend, when he got to the palace, he told the king that his wife had turned out to be a woman no better than she should be, who of all things had insisted on traveling by herself. Then the king, with his friend in tow, set out immediately to see what the truth might be. When they arrived at the parents' house, the wife was already there, but neither the king nor his friend recognized her in men's clothes. And who should be there as well but His Reverence, the canon, who himself had made false accusations years earlier when his advances had been rebuffed.

So there they were all together in the same room, and as they sat around swapping stories, each told his own tale. The queen in disguise, when it was her turn to speak, told the story of the canon and the king's false friend, not omitting a single detail. Before she had finished, the friend and the canon were shaking with fear. Then she turned around to the king and said, "Would you recognize your wife if you saw her?"

"Why, of course! I'd know her if she'd been changed into corn soup!" For the king had begun to realize who she was. In that instant she revealed herself and pointed to those who had tried to force her. The king begged her forgiveness, then asked, "What punishment for the canon and my old friend?"

"It's up to you, my dear." And the king ordered them tied to the tail of a horse and dragged until dead, then burned until there was nothing left but ashes. As soon as *that* matter had been taken care of, the king and his wife returned to their own country.

New Mexico | Juan Julián Archuleta

➢ 26. The Story That Became a Dream ➣

This was a young man out traveling, who came to a town he hadn't known before. Strolling along the streets he peered through an entranceway and saw a beautiful young woman sitting down to tea. She caught his fancy, and every day from then on he passed by her door just to catch a glimpse of her.

One day he came to a full stop and asked permission to light his cigar at her fireplace. With this little excuse he struck up a conversation and soon was asking, "Are you married or single?"

"Single," she said. But it wasn't true; the lady was married. Her husband, it seems, was an idler who had nothing better to do than crawl the streets up and down, coming home to his wife at night and sometimes not even then.

As it happened, the woman's admirer had the same occupation as the husband, and since the two of them frequented the same places, it wasn't long before they were friends.

All the while, the admirer was paying daily visits to the wife, and occasionally he would come to her when it was dark. After their first night together he pledged his love by giving her an expensive ring with his name engraved inside the band.

One night, just as the lovers were saying their good-byes, there came a knock at the door. The woman called, "Who is it?"

"Your husband!" came the answer.

The lover whispered, "What? You mean you're married?"

"We'll talk about that later. The important thing is to get you out of the way." She hid him under a pile a wool in one corner of the room.

Covered up and all muffled around the ears, the lover was unable to see the husband or recognize his voice. Finally, at three in the morning, he managed to slip away. The next day he recounted the adventure to his friend.

"Well! Aren't you the lucky one!" said the friend. "Good-looking girl, huh? And you're going to be there again tonight?"

"Why not? Fresh love, you know."

But if the husband thought it would be easy to catch his rival in the act, he was mistaken. The wife was too quick for him, always hiding the lover in a different spot. Worse, the husband had to listen to his friend's tales of adventure the following day. "Old buddy," he'd start out, "that husband doesn't have a chance. He's a louse, he's outrageous. She doesn't even want him around. And listen, he sticks his nose into every nook and cranny. But she knows where to hide me!"

"Oh, you don't say! She must be crazy about you. What luck!"

One night, at a loss for a new place to hide her lover, the wife put him in a little shed just off the kitchen where the cook threw dishwater and food scraps. It was a foul hiding place, but the man had no choice. The husband, after checking everywhere else, tossed a pebble into the waste shed, saying, "Take this, wherever you are, you piece of filth!" The stone splashed the lover with mud from head to foot. Yet he was able to keep still and not be seen.

The next day he reported it all to his friend, who pretended to be only mildly interested; and after giving his wife's lover a congratulatory pat on the back, he went off to see his father-in-law, who had a country place not far from town. He said, "You ought to know what kind of daughter you have!" and he explained what had been happening.

The father sent for the daughter at once and locked her in a room. Then he told his son-in-law to invite his friend to dinner. He would judge for himself whether his daughter was guilty. If he found that she was, he would kill the two of them on the spot.

The husband went back to town and soon returned with his friend. At noon the three men gathered at the table for a convivial meal, course after course washed down with draughts of wine. When dessert came, the host proposed that each relate his little adventures, beginning with himself, and he proceeded to tell an amorous tale he'd no doubt invented but that drew appreciative snorts all around.

"Now it's your turn," said the host, gesturing to the invited guest.

"Very well," said the guest, and without an inkling of what lay in store he began to relate his adventures with the host's own daughter, sparing not the smallest item. And the poor young woman heard everything through the door!

When he got to the part about the pebble and the waste shed, he started to feel his throat getting dry and he called for a cup of water. "Take wine!" they offered. But no, he needed water. And with that he was saved, because when the servant woman went out to the kitchen to get the water, the host's daughter called to her through an open window and, without attracting the servant's notice, she took off the ring her lover had given her and dropped it into the cup.

Seeing the ring, the guest drained the cup, slipped the ring into his vest pocket, and went on with the story: "So, after the husband looked all over the house and couldn't find me, he was so furious he picked up a stone and threw it into the waste shed and said, 'Take this, wherever you are, you piece of filth!' And it was a direct hit. I was splashed all over with mud—and just at that moment I woke up in a sweat, frightened to death!"

"What?" said the old man. "You mean it was only a dream?"

"Sir, what do you take me for?" said the guest. "Do you think I would have told such a story if it had been true?"

"Rogue!" cried the old gentleman, turning to his son-in-law. "Vile scandal monger! You've trifled with my honor. Now make your peace with God, because you've breathed your last." And with one thrust of his dagger he hushed him up forever.

They buried the dead man in the garden, and no one ever asked questions.

As for the dinner guest, he became a frequent visitor at the old man's country estate, and before the year was out he married the young widow who had figured so prominently in his story.

Chile | José Manuel Reyes

➤ 27. St. Theresa and the Lord ⬅

The Lord went walking with St. Theresa one day and they came to a house that had an open window. There in the window, for all to see, a husband and wife were kissing. The Lord noticed this and refused to give them his blessing.

They walked on, and they came to another pair of lovers, this time unmarried, and the lovers hid when they saw them coming. As the Lord passed, he gave them his blessing. St. Theresa was puzzled, but she didn't say a word.

They kept on, and they came to a humble little inn, a place so poor there was just one mug for the four people who were the customers, and two of them were fighting over it. The Lord went in and took away the mug, which made St. Theresa wonder. They went on and came to an expensive inn, and the Lord stopped and gave the mug to the innkeeper.

"Lord, tell me," said St. Theresa, "why did you bless those people who weren't married, and why did you take the mug from that poor little innkeeper?" The Lord said, "If you want to know, travel the main highway, and soon you'll find out."

St. Theresa went on by herself. She came to the highway and settled down at a mule drivers' stopping place. After a while a man on horse-back came along and pulled up to rest. He fell asleep, and when he awoke it was well after nightfall. In the dark he was frightened and confused. He jumped on his horse and rode off so fast he left his money on the ground where he had been sleeping.

Now, in that town there was an old man who had the habit of beg-ging food from a certain lady, who would always give him a few little *gordas* to keep him from starving. He came along, then, and sat down to build a fire to heat up his *gordas.* By the firelight he saw the purse that had been left by the horseman who had fallen asleep. In his excitement he forgot about the *gordas* and went off counting the money and prais-ing the Lord.

When he had gone, a mule driver pulled up. He was a poor man who had been traveling three days without food, and when he saw the *gordas* that had been left there for anyone to take he sat down and toasted them over the fire. He was a man who never remembered his Maker, yet on this occasion, when he was so badly in need, he praised the Lord over and over again. At just that moment the horseman who had left the money came back and heard the prayer of thanks. Enraged, he demanded his money.

"But, sir," said the mule driver, "I didn't see any money, only this fire and these little *gordas.* The other man said, "You're a liar. Hand over the money or I'll kill you." The poor mule driver kept protesting that he had seen no money until finally the exasperated horseman strangled him and rode away.

After witnessing all this, St. Theresa went back to the Lord and asked for an explanation.

The Lord said to her, "I blessed the lovers because they feared me. I did not bless the married couple because they were shameless.

"And the mug, I took it because the innkeeper allowed fighting and stealing, and I gave it to the other innkeeper because in him I found nothing to blame.

"And I took the money from the man on the horse to save him from damnation.

"And the old beggar who found the money, I allowed him to have it because I knew he would not forget me.

"And the mule driver who was killed, I permitted it to happen because he never remembered me until this day. I took his life to keep him from sinning again."

Mexico

⮞ 28. Rice from Ashes ⮜

People tell the story of a girl who lost her mother. They say her father turned around and married a woman who had two daughters of her own. The cruel stepmother made her husband's daughter the house servant, and right from the start the two stepsisters would have nothing to do with her. She had only a little lamb to keep her company, and one day her stepmother came into the kitchen and said, "Butcher the lamb!"

The girl started to cry. Then the stepmother held out a plate of rice and said, "If you don't kill the lamb, you'll have to separate this rice from ashes." She spilled all the rice onto the hearth and went off to take her midday nap.

The girl was wondering how she could ever separate the rice, when a dove appeared. "Why do you cry, child?" "Because my stepmother says I have to separate this rice before she gets up from her nap."

"Lie down and sleep," said the dove. I'll take care of it." As the girl lay down, a flock of doves arrived, and in no time the clean rice was heaped on the plate just as before. When the stepmother got up from her nap she hardly knew what to think. The next day she poured sand into a dish of lentils.

"If you don't kill the lamb," she said, "you'll have to separate these lentils. Do it before I wake up." The girl began to cry. But a flock of birds arrived and picked out the lentils while the stepmother napped.

The day after that, the stepmother threw sugar onto the hearth and ordered the girl to kill the lamb or pick the sugar clean. She went off to her nap. Hearing the girl's cries, a large ant appeared and told the poor child not to worry. This was the ant queen, who commanded many workers. Immediately the ants came crawling over the hearth, and when the stepmother got up from her nap the sugar was heaped in the dish.

Another day passed, and the stepmother came into the kitchen and said, "Kill the lamb, or you'll have to spin these two bags of wool into thread. Do it before I finish my nap." The girl began to weep. The lamb said to her, "Don't cry. I'll do it for you." As the girl watched, the lamb dragged the wool from the bags and stretched it out until it was all in a beautiful thread.

When the stepmother saw that the wool had been spun, she was furious. But when she examined the lamb, she found one wisp stuck to its little anus. Since every wisp had not been spun, she ordered her stepdaughter to kill the lamb and cook it for supper that very night.

The girl wept uncontrollably. But the lamb told her she should not be sad. "Calm down! Take me out and butcher me, and in my bowels you will find a little cup. This you must remove and keep always."

So she led the lamb to the riverbank, slit its throat, and quartered the carcass. When she found the cup, she set it aside.

Just then a little old man came by and asked for a drink. She dipped some water with the cup and gave it to him. Then she returned to the house and laid the cup in the bottom of the trunk where she kept her belongings.

The girl went often to the cemetery to visit her mother's grave. A little tree grew there, and in the tree there was a bird with a beautiful song. The girl would sit beneath the tree weeping, telling her troubles to her dead mother. As she told them, one by one, the bird's singing would take them away.

At home now, without the lamb, she had no one to be her friend. Out of meanness, just to remind her of her loss, her stepsisters had their mother buy them each a lamb of their own. The stepsisters' lambs grew quickly, and when not a leaf or a blade of grass was left in sight, the mother told her daughters that these lambs, too, would have to be butchered.

First the older daughter went out to kill her lamb. It made her cry to do so, but the lamb told her she must not be sad. She must look for a little cup inside the lamb's belly and take it for her own. She must also remember to be kindhearted and help those in need.

She butchered the lamb, and sure enough, there was the cup. At that moment a little old man came by and asked for water. The stepsister answered, "I don't give water to filthy old men."

This little man was God.

The following day the younger of the two stepsisters went out to kill her lamb, and the lamb gave her the same advice. She, too, found a cup in the lamb's bowels and met the same little old man asking for water. She answered him contemptuously, "If you want water, bend down and drink from the river." The old man got down on his hands and knees and drank.

Now, in the town there was a king whose queen had died and who had a son. On her deathbed the queen had told the prince he would someday marry a woman who would bring him a cup of gold, because this was the fate predicted by the prince's fairy godmother when he was born. The prince had now grown up, and the king proclaimed that any young woman with a cup of gold was to present herself at the palace.

When the stepmother heard this news, she drew up her skirts and ran as fast as she could to the center of town. She told the king that the girl with the golden cup was her own daughter. The next day the prince mounted a swift steed and set out to claim his bride. Arriving at the stepmother's house, he asked for the girl with the cup.

Both sisters stepped forward and began to shove each other. To settle the matter, the mother pointed to the older girl, "Go with the prince!"

The prince put her behind him on his horse and started off for the palace. But as they were passing the cemetery, the little bird that lived in the tree sang out,

> *Swift young lord,*
> *turn back, turn back.*
> *Your companion-to-be*
> *is awaiting you yet.*

The bird kept repeating its song until the prince turned around to the girl and asked her to show him the cup. She placed it in his hands and he saw that it was iron. Returning to the house, he said to the stepmother, "This is not my bride."

The younger of the two sisters now came to the door with her cup in her hand. It was all gold. The prince put her on the back of his horse and set off. But when they got to the cemetery, the bird sang out from the tree,

> *Swift young lord,*
> *turn back, turn back.*
> *Your companion-to-be*
> *is awaiting you yet.*

The prince asked for the cup, and when the girl handed it to him he saw once again that what had been gold was now iron. He rushed back to the house and asked the girl's mother if she had another daughter. The woman said no.

The prince insisted, "She has to be somewhere!" With the mother denying it, he ran into the house and started pulling everything apart. When he got to the kitchen, there was the orphan girl. He asked her, "Do you have the golden cup?" She had no idea why he asked but said simply, "Yes."

The prince told her to sit behind him on his horse, while the stepmother tried desperately to explain that this was only a kitchen girl. The prince replied, "It doesn't matter," for all he needed was to find the young woman who owned the cup.

As they passed the cemetery the little bird ruffled its feathers contentedly and sang,

> *You've found your companion,*
> *O swift young lord, keep on!*

To make sure there was no mistake, the prince looked over his shoulder and asked to see the cup once more. There it was, shining so brightly it blurred his vision.

When they reached the palace, the king was taken aback to see his son riding up with a barefoot girl in rags. But he saw the golden cup and knew she was the one who had been so long awaited.

The wedding took place at once, and when the kitchen girl changed into finery she was everything a princess should be. In time she had many children and became a great queen, known for her works of charity. She aided orphans especially.

Argentina / Aída Agüero de Agüero

⮞ 29. Juan María and Juana María ⮜

There were two women who lived together, and they were good friends. One of them had a son named Juan María. The other had a daughter named Juana María. The children grew up loving each other as brother and sister, but at a certain age they wanted to get married, and the two mothers put a stop to it.

So Juan María and Juana María ran away from home and took blood out of their own veins and wrote a contract with it. They swore in writing they would never marry anyone but each other. After a while they got to a strange city where there was no one to protect them, and they were arrested for vagrancy. Before they knew what was happening, they'd been thrown into prison in separate cells. Not even their prison guards were the same. Juana María had a woman as her guard. Juan María had a man.

Every day the prisoners were taken out into the street for exercise, and one time Juan María was noticed by the governor's daughter on her way to Mass. She fell in love with him at first sight and said to her father, "Let this man go free. I'm going to marry him." The governor granted his daughter's wish, and Juan María was taken to a hotel room, where they cleaned him up and put him into a fresh suit of clothes.

Juana María heard all about it. With the help of her prison guard she had a white shroud made for herself. Then she ordered a dagger, a lantern, and a long heavy chain. The night of the wedding a dance was held at the governor's palace. As soon as it was dark Juana María came out of the prison in her white shroud, wrapped in her chain, with the dagger tucked in her belt. When people saw her coming through the streets, carrying the lantern and rattling the chain, they fled in terror. They could hear her crying out:

> *This is the road of my desire.*
> *If any who stops me has two thousand lives,*
> *Two thousand times he'll expire.*

She was still wailing when she got to the governor's mansion. The dance was in full swing. Juan María came to open the door, and when he saw who it was, he took her into the bridal chamber without a word. She said, "You know why I've come. To honor our vow." Then he threw himself across the bed, and she drove the dagger into his heart.

Back out on the streets, she started wailing again:

> *This is the road of my desire.*
> *If any who stops me has two thousand lives,*
> *Two thousand times he'll expire.*

When she got to the prison, she allowed herself to be locked up again as peacefully as if nothing had happened.

Then somebody discovered the dead bridegroom, and the place was in an uproar. The dance turned into a wake. The next morning they put Juan María into a casket and carried him to church, to be buried the following day. That night Juana María came out of the prison again in her white shroud. The entire city was still in shock. She went through the streets, wailing and rattling her chain. When she got to the church, she opened Juan María's coffin and stabbed him once more for good measure.

Then just as she stepped out of the church a pack of devils snatched her and dragged her off. As they passed the prison gates, Juana María saw her guard waiting for her, and she called out, "Good-bye, Catalina. Take care. And thanks for your help."

The guard said, "Good-bye, my child. Be on your way! I won't forget you." But Juana María looked again and said, "My chain is long enough for both of us." And she threw the end of it around Catalina, and the two of them were carried off together.

Guatemala

➣ 30. The Witch Wife ➤

There was a bachelor who had no family. But he had many friends, and they advised him to marry. They introduced him to a certain Celina, a good woman, they said, and told him it was time to get serious.

He started making regular visits. When he was ready to declare himself, the woman said yes.

After they were married, whenever they sat down to eat, the wife would pick at her rice. She'd separate the grains and eat just one, maybe two. Her husband would say, "What's the matter? Don't you like what we're eating?" And the next day it would be the same. "Are you trying to save money?" No answer.

One night when they had gone to bed and the wife thought the man was asleep, though in fact he was awake, she got up quietly and put on her clothes. As she went out, the door made no sound.

The husband thought, "What could she be doing at this hour?" He got up and went after her. She crossed the street, crossed back again, went down another street, and stopped at the cemetery. He climbed a palm tree just outside the cemetery wall and watched as she went in. She walked directly to a fresh grave. Other women were there, too, chatting and laughing. Already they had dug into the grave and exposed the corpse. One of the women jumped in and tore off pieces of flesh with her fingernails. The man watched as she handed out the rotten morsels, one by one. "Here, sister," she said, and she tore off a large piece and gave it to the man's wife. The man nearly fell out of the tree when he saw what his wife was eating.

When the banquet was over, they closed the grave. The husband went home and lay down on the bed again. A few moments later the wife arrived, took off her clothes, and settled down next to him. Through the rest of the night, whenever she rolled over and brushed against him, he recoiled. He couldn't sleep, imagining how he would get rid of this woman. In the morning he was feverish from having slept not a wink.

At last it was time for breakfast. The wife pushed her rice around the way she usually did, eating only a grain or two. "You don't like it," he said, "because it isn't dead." She understood his meaning.

She got up from her chair and dusted some red powder into a cup of water. She spoke a few words that he didn't understand, then threw the water in his face and said, "Take your punishment!" At once he became a little red dog.

Not content with that, she picked up a whip and gave the dog a lashing. It jumped through an open window and rushed down the street yelping.

The dog ran into a baker's shop just as the baker was having a snack. "Here, little fellow!" said the baker, and he threw down a slice of bread. The baker had other dogs, and they pounced on the newcomer. But the baker was a dog lover and knew what to do. He gave the little red dog a corner of its own, and from then on it got all the affection it needed and all the bread it could eat.

The little dog helped its new owner. Whenever a customer tried to pass counterfeit money, the dog would bark and take the bad coin in its teeth. "My dog knows money!" the baker would say.

Before long the reputation of this clever dog spread through the town. When the king's daughter heard of it, she said to her mother, "I must see the baker's new dog. I wonder what it looks like." But princesses don't go out in the streets, so the mother had to go herself. When she returned, she said to her daughter, "It's true. The dog sinks its teeth in counterfeit money."

"What color is this dog?"

"It's red all over. And its eyes are human."

"Heavens! You must bring it to me."

The mother went back to the bakery and watched until the baker was busy. When he wasn't looking, she called to the dog three times, and it jumped into her arms.

She brought it straight to her daughter. The princess looked into the dog's eyes, and the dog looked into hers. She pulled a powder box out of her handbag and dusted some of the contents into a cup of water, pronouncing these words,

> *Whether man or dog,*
> *Be what you are!*

As she sprinkled the water on the little dog, it became a man again. He fell to his knees and said, "I'm yours, I'll be your servant." And he told her his story, not omitting a single detail.

"Goodness!" said the princess. "You married Celina? We went to the same school. I knew her perfectly well, and I stayed away from her. She used her science for the wrong purposes."

The man stayed on for a while and worked. When he left, the princess paid up his wages and gave him a flask filled with a solution she herself had prepared.

On the way home, the man kept thinking, "How shall I punish my wife? I can't! She's my wife. It wouldn't be right to harm her."

When the wife caught sight of her husband, she was frozen with fear. She started to run, but he opened the flask and sprinkled a few drops. Immediately she changed into a mare. His conscience was clear now. He gave the mare a good kick and sold her to a miller.

The miller had cane to be ground for sugar. But the mare wouldn't turn the millstone, no matter what the miller tried. Meanwhile the husband married another woman.

At last the miller, tired of the mare's tricks, beat the life out of her, and that was the end of Celina.

Colombia

⮞ 31. O Wicked World ⮜

Juan was a good man who poured his whole life into sheepherding. He loved his wife, and she, for her part, helped him keep their little house in good repair, sharing all the labor with him as an equal. Apparently she was happy in her poverty and in her work. But the truth is she did not particularly love her husband, and there were times when she was bored.

One day poor Juan had an attack of some illness or other and fell over dead. When this happened Juan and his wife were on a hillside herding their sheep toward the corral. The wife shouted toward the houses below, "Send three strong boys to help me bring down Juan!"

A voice called back, "What's the matter?" She answered, "I need three boys. Juan is dead. Ay, my poor Juan." She kept repeating, "Ay, my poor Juan."

They shouted up to her, "We're coming! Four of us!"

"No, no," she said. "Three is enough. I'll be the fourth." Taking her at her word, three boys climbed the hill and helped her carry her husband's body. As they made their way down the path, the wife cried aloud, "Ay, poor Juan. How he loved this beautiful countryside!"

When they had gotten the dead man into the house, the boys left, and the widow, as calmly as you can imagine, fried a batch of *buñuelos*. She had worked up an appetite.

News of Juan's death passed from mouth to mouth. In no time the townspeople arrived to express their condolences, crowding into her house, and the widow had to put away the frying pan full of *buñuelos* just as they were ready to be eaten.

One of the neighbors from close by had brought his busy little dog, who followed him everywhere, and because of it the dog was called World. This little World was well known to the widow, and when she saw him speeding like a bullet toward the pantry where she'd tucked the fritters, she started to scold him, "O wicked World! You keep on taking them, one by one! Oh, no! You've taken the best of them all!"

Juan was buried the next day. But the neighbors, who knew nothing of the *buñuelos,* could not forget the widow's grief. "The poor thing, how good she is!" they said. "How she cherished her late husband!"

Argentina / Clara Chamorro de Silva

32. The Three Sisters

There were three sisters, and they were quite charming. Although they lived in one of the poorest neighborhoods in the city, they managed to be glamorous.

Now, in those days there was a night patrol. Guards went around to keep watch on people and to listen for suspicious conversation. One evening the first watch passed the house of the three sisters, and the patrolmen heard talk.

"I'd marry the king's baker," one of the sisters was saying, "so I'd have sponge cake all the time."

"I'd marry the king's steward," said the second sister, "then I'd have everything in the pantry that's good to eat."

The third said, "Why take one of the servants? I'd marry the king himself."

"Aren't you the uppity one!" said the other two. "Imagine marrying the king!" And all three burst out laughing and continued chatting away.

But the guards heard everything and reported the conversation to the king. The sisters were called to the palace. When they arrived, the king greeted them in a pleasant way, sat down with them, and engaged them in conversation. Finally he said, "I hear one of you wants to marry my baker and one wants to marry the steward. And you're the youngest? You want to marry me!" The sisters, all flustered, said: "Who ever told you that?" "I never said such a thing." "It was only a joke."

"But do it you will," said the king. "You'll marry the baker. And you? The steward will be your husband. And you, my dear, will be married to me." So it was all arranged. They had three weddings and settled themselves in the palace.

After a while the one who had married the king became pregnant, and when it was time for her to give birth, she called her sisters to be her midwives. She delivered a boy. But the two jealous sisters had already gotten a little dog ready to take the baby's place. As soon as the child was born, they put the dog in bed with the queen, then put the baby in a chest, nailed the lid shut, and threw it into a river that flowed through the palace garden. They told the king to come see, and when he arrived they showed him the dog. The king said, "Why be amazed by the work of nature? If my wife gives birth to a dog, so be it."

Later, when the king's gardener went to the riverbank for water, he found the little chest. He brought it home to his wife and said, "Look what I found."

"Open it up!" she said. "There might be treasure." He pried the lid loose, and there was an infant.

"Why, look! It's a little boy," said the wife. "Since we have no children, he can be our son." They began to bring him up.

Another year went by and the queen was again taken to childbed. She called in her two sisters to help with the delivery; this time they brought a cat. They laid the child in a box, dumped it in the river, and put the cat in the bed. The king just shrugged, "What's meant to be was meant to be."

The gardener found the box, again with a little boy inside, and his wife cried, "It's God's work! Since we had no children of our own, he's sending them to us in this manner."

The following year the queen gave birth again. This time her sisters put a piece of kindling in the bed. When the king saw the stick of wood, he showed no surprise and just shrugged it off as before. But when the gardener found the box in the river and opened it up, there was a baby girl. So the gardener and his wife had three young ones to raise.

One day after many years, the queen was out walking in the garden and noticed the gardener and his children, now nearly grown. The queen starting thinking out loud, "What a beautiful place! Only three things are lacking. If only we could have them, it would be paradise."

"And what would the three things be?" asked the gardener.

The queen replied, "A bird that speaks, an orange tree that dances, and water that jumps and leaps." The gardener's son interrupted, "I'll find them for you."

Without delay the boy's mother, who was the gardener's wife, packed him a lunch, and he headed for the mountains. Along the way he met a hermit, who asked, "My boy, where are you going?"

"I'm off to find the bird that speaks, the orange tree that dances, and the water that jumps and leaps." The hermit then said, "Just keep to the path, and after you've climbed this mountain you'll come to a plain. You'll find everything there. The bird will be in a cage hanging from the orange tree, and the water will be close by. If the bird speaks, take it. If you see the tree dancing, break off a few branches. And if the water is jumping and leaping, fill your bottle. But if all's quiet, touch nothing. And one more thing: Before you get there, a voice will be shouting insults. Make no answer and don't look around."

The boy went on, and as soon as he reached the top of the mountain he heard the shouting, "Throwaway child! Shame!" But he didn't answer or turn around. The plain lay straight ahead. He saw the bird, but it wasn't speaking; the tree, but it wasn't dancing; and the waters, but they weren't leaping. He touched them all and was instantly frozen.

Meanwhile at home, his sister and his younger brother were watching a glass of water he had left on the windowsill. He had said to them, "When half is water and half is blood, you will know I am in danger and must come look for me." The two had been watching every day. When suddenly the glass was half blood, the younger brother said, "I must go and get him." And he set off for the mountains.

When the boy came to the hermit, he received the same advice that had been given before. And like his older brother, he paid no attention and fell under the same spell.

In that instant the glass on the windowsill was entirely filled with blood. Wasting no time, the sister put on a suit of men's clothes, packed scissors and a little comb, and set out on a mule to find her brothers.

When she came to the hermit, he asked, "Where are you going?" And instead of just answering, "I'm on my way to find my lost brothers," she got down from her mule and combed the hermit's beard and with her scissors trimmed his nails, which had gotten much too long. After that, all he said to her was, "Pass ahead! Keep to the road!"

At the top of the mountain she heard the voices, "Throwaway child! Shame!" And she answered,

> *Try as you might*
> *To blame me,*
> *Your names and threats*
> *Can't shame me.*

And there in the distance she saw the bird. It was speaking. The orange tree was dancing. And the waters were jumping and leaping. From its cage the bird shouted, "The heroine comes forth!" She took the bird-cage in her hand, cut some branches from the orange tree, filled up a bottle at the spring, then asked, "Divine bird, where are my brothers?"

The bird said, "Listen, stick your hand in the spring. Pull out two crystal balls, blow your warm breath on them, and they'll return to their human form." In this way she made them flesh and blood again, and I'll tell you their names. One of the brothers was Bamán; the other, Párvis. And all three rode home on the mule.

When they had planted the boughs in the garden and put the bird-cage there, they dug a little hole and poured in the water. The king and the queen were called, as well as the queen's two sisters. "What a beautiful garden!" said the king. "Just what we wanted!" said the queen. Then the bird turned to the two sisters, who were the baker's wife and the steward's wife, and said, "I hear you throw away other people's children," and before the bird could say more, the sisters backed off and kept going till they were out of the garden.

Meanwhile the king was saying, "Show me around this garden!" The gardener's wife thought, "Good heavens! Unexpected company! What can we possibly serve the king?" But the bird told her, "Look on the other side of the orchard. See what you find." Nestled among the roots of the last tree were two little squashes. "And whatever will I do with these?" asked the poor woman. "With these you'll please the king," said the bird.

When the gardener and the king had made the rounds, and the king had had his fill of admiring the talking bird, the dancing tree, and the leaping waters, they all sat down to the table, and the king cut into the squashes. Out came pearls, pouring all over the table. The king was amazed. "Squashes full of pearls! I've never seen anything like it!"

"Squashes with pearls surprise you," said the bird. "But you weren't surprised when your wife gave birth to a dog, a cat, and a stick of wood."

"What!" cried the king. "Tell more!"

The bird told all. Then finally it said, "Here are your three children, right before your eyes." The king embraced them and took all three into the palace, together with the gardener and the gardener's wife, and gave them much better jobs than the ones they'd had before. Then he issued an order for his two sisters-in-law to be rounded up and sent to the firing squad.

It's what they deserved, isn't it?

Colombia

➤ 33. The Count and the Queen ⇐

The count and his dear sister, the countess, lived together in town. One Sunday when the count went to Mass he fell head over heels for the wife of the king and wanted nothing but to be alone with her. Since it wasn't possible, he came home in a gloomy mood. His sister questioned him, "What's the matter?"

"Nothing you can help me with," he said. Then he called an old woman and gave her a letter to carry to the queen.

When the queen read the message and understood it, she smudged the old woman's face with charcoal and tied a flagstone to her back. The count saw the woman returning and said, "How did it go?"

"Oh, she was horrible to me! Just look at my face and this load on my back!"

At that moment the count's sister came into the room and said to her brother, "May I be your interpreter? The queen's answer is favorable. The black marks on the face mean she wants you to come at night, and the stone signifies that you are to come in through the window."

So! The king would be away. And the count was off to the playing field. His sister advised him to stay only until midnight, then return. He followed her instructions.

The next night he went back but overstayed. At six in the morning he was still asleep in the queen's bed. When the king came in and saw a man with his wife, he sent his servant after a priest to confess the two of them so he could have them put to death.

As the servant was hurrying along the street, who should be standing there but the sister of the count. She asked, "Where are you headed?" And from the servant she learned the truth, that the king had caught the queen with her dear brother. She said, "I'm going to give you this moneybag. You let me be the one to go for the priest."

So the count's sister went and told the priest the whole story. And the priest, not one to be judgmental, loaned her his cassock.

Dressed as the priest, she presented herself to the king and asked, "What's this I hear?" And when the king had filled in the details, the count's sister said to him, "Leave it to me. I'll confess them."

She went into the room, rousted her brother, and made him put on the priest's cassock. Through the closed door she called to the king, "You can come in now. There's been a mistake. Your wife wasn't with a man but a woman!" The king entered the room and took a look for himself. He wasn't completely satisfied. He said to the queen, "Tomorrow in church you must swear in the name of God, before a priest and before your husband, that no man has touched you but me."

The next day, early, they made their way to church for the queen to take her oath. Meanwhile the count found a poor shepherd and paid him well for the loan of his clothing. Then, dressed as a shepherd, the count stood alongside the roadway, and about thirty minutes later the royal carriage came by. The queen insisted on stopping a moment. She got out of the carriage easily, but when she tried to climb back up she couldn't quite manage. The shepherd came forward and said, "Young lady, I'll hold your foot so you can get back in." Then off they rode to the church.

When they got there, the king explained to the priest what was wanted, and the priest said to the queen, "Do you swear before God, the church, and the king, that no man has touched you but your husband?"

The queen replied, "Yes, I swear before God, before the church, before this priest, and before my king that no man has touched me but my husband and the poor shepherd who held my foot when I climbed into my carriage. No other men have I known, so help me God."

Colorado / Félix Serna

PART FOUR

‖‖‖‖‖‖‖‖‖‖‖‖‖‖‖‖

⋙ 34. Crystal the Wise ⋘

Listen and learn it, learn to tell it, and tell it to teach it; if any can't learn it they'll buy it if any can sell it. The shoe fits, yes? No? Ouch! It pinches my toe.

There was once a gentleman who had quite a daughter. Her godmother had been a fortune-teller and had given her a little slipper that knew all and told all whenever it was asked a question, though it spoke only to the goddaughter and wouldn't tell anybody else a thing.

The gentleman was rich beyond words. He hired private teachers so his daughter could learn foreign languages, history, and Castilian. But she knew more than they did just by talking to the slipper. They couldn't think what to teach her. She was quicker at history and all the rest than the people who had invented those subjects. And arithmetic? She knew more about it than her father's own cashier. In a trice she could add up the household accounts. The whole world marveled at what she knew.

People who couldn't learn anything from teachers came to her, she explained it, and they went away knowing it. Since she made no charge, naturally she had lots of students. They called her Crystal, and the name suited her well because her mind was like a crystal ball.

Word of this young wisewoman reached the ears of a king who had a son and daughter, and he summoned the young woman's father for a talk.

"Greetings to you, sir."

"Greetings, Sacred Crown. At your service."

"Good sir, could you lend me your daughter for a couple of months? They tell me she's a genius, and I have a son and a daughter in need of instruction. My son is a young man already and a good student, but the girl is lagging behind. If your daughter could go over her lessons with her, she might learn more than she's learning from her tutors."

"At your command, Sacred Crown. Ready to serve you." And when the gentleman returned to his daughter and explained what the king wanted, she said, "Very well."

Off she went to the palace, where the king, the queen, and the princess greeted her warmly. But the prince looked down his nose. He himself had offered to go over his little sister's lessons, and the king had said to him, "Someone else can do a better job than you."

So the instruction began, and the king and the queen were delighted with the results. The princess for a change seemed to understand her lessons.

One day while Crystal was with the princess, the prince came into the room and sat down. Immediately he objected to the manner of instruction and said so. They had a heated argument. And from then on, day after day, the prince interrupted the lesson and contradicted the teacher.

Once when Crystal and the princess were having tea in the princess's room, the prince came in and started his usual nagging. "That's no way to teach. That's not how I learned it." And on and on, until finally the teacher threw down her teacup and gave the prince a slap on the face. He got up and left the room without a word.

Time passed and the princess mastered her lessons. Her parents were well pleased and offered to pay for the instruction. But Crystal refused, saying it had been an honor for her to be the teacher of a princess.

Then a strange thing happened. The prince, who had never come again to taunt the teacher, told his father he wanted to marry Crystal in order, as he put it, to pay back a debt. The king, who knew nothing of the incident, imagined that the prince had attended the classes as a dutiful student and was simply filled with gratitude. Since the young teacher's father was a gentleman of high standing, the king gave his permission and the marriage was celebrated with all the festivities.

The prince had made arrangements for a cottage on the palace grounds to be fixed up as a retreat where he and his new wife could settle comfortably. And on their wedding night, when all the guests had gone to bed, he came into the room where his bride was getting into her nightclothes and said, "Crystal, do you remember the slap you gave me? Are you ready to apologize?"

"Apologize? I wouldn't dream of it. In fact I'll give you another if you keep on like this."

At that he flew into a rage and shoved her into a corner of the room where there was a trapdoor, which he pulled open, saying, "Since you won't repent, off to the underworld!" He pushed her down a staircase and locked her up in a cell he had prepared for just that purpose. She made no complaint and spent the night sitting upright in a little chair.

In the morning the prince came back and asked if she was ready to say she was sorry. Again she said no. To deceive the king and Crystal's father, the prince sent a carriage off at daybreak carrying a maidservant dressed in the bride's clothes, while he himself rode alongside on a horse as if accompanying her. He let it be known that they would be spending time at a friend's place in the country.

He was determined to keep his bride locked up until she relented. But as she would not, he became more and more enraged. Every night he would open the trapdoor and call downstairs, "Aren't you sorry?" And every night she would give the same answer. Her prison cell was wearisome, but nothing could move her to ask his forgiveness.

One day she noticed that a mouse had gnawed a hole in the floor boards. Bending over for a closer look, she heard rushing water. An underground stream flowed directly beneath the floor. With a table knife that had been left in the cell she enlarged the opening and saw that the stream was quite deep and that daylight appeared not far in the distance. Slipping into the water, she swam out into the open, then ran home to her father, who all this time had thought she was vacationing in the country.

When she had told him everything, he was as angry as you can imagine and was about to go storming off to the king. But she said, "Keep quiet. Just send me decent food, and I'll let you know if I need anything else."

"As you wish," he said, and under the king's very nose he had the underground stream diverted so he could go visit his daughter, who meanwhile had returned to her cell without being missed. The prince only opened the trapdoor at night and never went down the stairs; he just lowered her meals in a basket tied to a string. So he had no idea what she was up to.

One day, after shouting down the stairs, "Do you repent?" and receiving her usual answer, "Never!" the prince added, "I'll be in Paris for a while, enjoying myself, and while I'm gone a servant will lower your food." She replied, "That's perfect. Have a good time and don't get into trouble." Exasperated, he slammed the trapdoor with his foot and went on his way.

Meanwhile she crept out of her cell, ran home to her father, and told him she needed lots of money and a special sleeping coach to get her to Paris nonstop. By the time the prince arrived, after dallying along the route, she was already installed in a magnificent palace across the street from the very palace the king of Paris had rented to the prince himself.

Every day she swung out in a coach drawn by four horses. The prince, who also took rides, noticed her and was struck by how much she looked like his wife.

He started off by greeting her. Soon he was stopping to talk. In no time he was paying her visits, asking her if she was married. She said no. Smitten, he asked her to be his wife. She said yes, and they had a wedding.

Nine months later she gave birth to twins, a boy and a girl. She decided to name them Paris and Frances. And so that's what they were called.

After three years of marriage, the prince broke the news that he had gotten a telegram calling him home. His father, the king, had dropped dead. Crystal wanted to go, too. "Not yet," he said. "I need time to calm my mother's nerves." But she managed to have him sign two declarations, one for each child, stating that they were his own and would be his heirs.

Then off he went. But the truth is that the prince had written home to say that his wife had died in childbirth, and the king, who was alive and perfectly well, had written back saying, "Come at once. I've found the ideal bride for you. And no dallying. The bride's father, who is the king of Spain, insists that she be married immediately."

Need it be said, Crystal had her suspicions. She and her two children boarded the night train and got home ahead of the prince, who was delayed choosing gifts for his new bride. She went straight to her father's house, having sent him a telegram the day before, so that he would expect her.

When the prince arrived, he called the servant that had been paid to lower the food every day. In fact the servant had pocketed the money and never opened the trapdoor once. He said to the prince, "She died of a broken heart not long ago, and I nailed the door shut so no one will ever find her."

Completely satisfied with this report, the prince got ready for his wedding. As it happened, the king of Spain's daughter was no beauty, but she was young and as rich as you could ever wish. Besides, she struck the prince as timid, and he thought, "Now here's one that won't cross me."

When the prince and his bride entered the cathedral, which was all lit up for the wedding, he was taken aback at the sight of a lady dressed in white, heavily veiled, and at her side two little children, also veiled. Suddenly the lady came forward, and as she stood in front of the prince she dropped her veil, and there was Crystal dressed like a queen, wearing a diamond tiara. The children, likewise, dropped their veils, and there they were: Paris and Frances, waving papers that turned out to be the declarations the prince had signed.

The children rushed at him, shouting, "Papa!" And the prince, dazzled by his wife's beauty, fell on his knees and begged her forgiveness, confessing to all his crimes. Everybody clapped their hands and cried, "Cheers!" to the prince, his wife, and their two little heirs. And the poor Spanish princess, mad as could be, just stood there with no husband and no kingdom.

My tale is done, and the wind blows it off.

Chile / Carmen Rivera

⇒ 35. Love Like Salt ⇐

A king who had three daughters called them to his side and asked each one how much she loved him. The eldest replied that her love for her father was more than all the world's gold. The king then turned to his second daughter, who declared that her love was as precious to her as all the necklaces, rings, bracelets, and dresses in her wardrobe. Then he turned to the youngest, who said, "Father, I love you as dearly as I love salt."

Hearing this, the king was filled with rage and vowed to have his daughter put to death. She wept. She begged him to change his mind. But the king was convinced that he had been mortally insulted and paid no attention to her pleading. Instead, he ordered one of his servants to take her directly to the woods and bring back only her eyes and her little finger.

When the princess got to the woods with the servant, she pleaded for her life. She promised to live deep in the forest where no one would ever see her. The servant said, "How can I help you? I have to bring back proof that you've been killed."

She got down on her knees and spoke to him from her heart, and seeing how graceful and lovely she was he was moved to pity. He would spare her, he said, but they would have to cut the fifth finger from one of her hands. He forgot, in his moment of compassion, that the king had also asked for the two eyes.

The princess reminded him. Then they noticed a little dog that had followed them into the woods. They made up their minds to kill it and take out its eyes. When the deed was done, the princess gave up her little finger, and the servant, leaving her alone in the forest, went back to the palace. The king examined the proof and was satisfied that his daughter had been put to death.

Meanwhile the princess wandered into the deepest part of the woods. At last, too tired to walk farther, she stopped to sleep. When she woke up, it was morning. She was hungry and went off in no particular direction, hoping to find food. She walked all day, not knowing where she was headed. That evening she came to a cave where a hermit lived. "My dear child," said the hermit, "what are you doing in this wilderness?"

She answered, "I'm looking for a place to spend the night." Then she asked if she could stay and live with him in his cave, be a daughter to him, and help him. He was willing, and after the first night she stayed on.

It was a different life from anything she had known. The cave was no palace. For food she had to dig roots, and like any good shepherd she drank water straight from the brook. One day a young prince who had lost his way in the forest surprised her as she was gathering an armload of flowers. Overwhelmed by her beauty, he proposed marriage, and she accepted at once.

He lifted her onto his fine horse and galloped away to his palace. When they arrived, he told his parents, "I want your permission to marry this woman. No other can be my wife." Caught up in the spell of the princess's beauty, the parents gave their immediate consent. Wedding preparations were made, and invitations went out to all the neighboring kings and queens, including the princess's parents.

On the day of the wedding the princess saw that her father had arrived, and she pointed him out to the prince and said, "Tell them not to put any salt in the food where that king is going to sit." The prince and the princess then settled themselves at the very same table. When the king started to eat, he complained at once and spit out the food. He said, "Where's the salt? This has no flavor!"

At that the princess rose up and said, "Salt never meant anything to you before. Why would you want it now?"

"You can't eat without salt!" he cried.

Then she said to him, "Wasn't there someone who offended you once by saying they loved you as dearly as salt?" Suddenly the king remembered what had been done to his daughter, and he asked the princess how she knew. She said, "I am your daughter."

The king refused to believe her. Then she held out her hand with the missing finger. "My daughter, forgive me," he said. "I never realized how much you loved me. You will enter my palace under an arch of flowers, and I will honor you with eight days of feasting."

Well, they had that feast, and they killed peacocks and chickens and had all sorts of food. I was there, too. They made me eat pig's feet.

Mexico

⇒ 36. The Pongo's Dream ⇐

A little man came looking for work in the great house of a hacienda owner. The man was a menial, a pongo. He was miserably made and poor in spirit, and his clothes were worn out.

The master could not help laughing when the little man greeted him in the long gallery. In the presence of all the men and women who served him, he demanded, "Are you human or something else?"

The pongo bowed his head and made no answer. Terrified, he remained standing, his eyes frozen.

"I have my doubts," continued the patrón, "but at least we'll see if he scrubs pots or if he can hold a broom." He gave the order to the foreman, "Here, take this filth!"

Dropping to his knees, the pongo kissed the master's hands. Then, crouching, he followed the foreman to the kitchen.

Small as he was, his abilities were equal to those of an ordinary man. Whatever he was asked to do, he did well. Yet there remained a touch of fear in his face. Noticing this, some of the peons would laugh. Others were sympathetic. "Orphan of orphans, child of the wind," said the cook when she saw him. "Those freezing-cold eyes must have come from the moon."

The little man spoke to no one. He worked without making a sound and ate in silence. He obeyed every order. "Yes, dear papa," or "Yes, dear mama," was all he would say.

At nightfall when the peons assembled in the gallery of the great house to recite the Ave Maria, without fail the patrón would torment the pongo in front of all the others. He would pick him up and shake him like a hide. He would give him a push on the head and make him fall to his knees, and as he knelt he would slap him lightly across the face.

"I believe you're a dog. Bark!" he would say.

The little man was unable to bark. So the order would be changed. "Then get down on all fours!" And he would obey, scurrying back and forth.

"Run sideways!" the master would say. Then the pongo would run sideways, imitating the little dogs of the high plains. And the patrón would laugh. His whole body would shake with laughter.

"Turn around!" he would cry, when the little man had reached the far end of the gallery. And the pongo would turn around and run back, veering just a little to one side. When he had finished he would be tired out.

Without kicking him too hard, the patrón would strike the little man with his boot, sending him sprawling on the brick pavement of the gallery. Turning to the servants who were lined up waiting, the patrón would say, "Let us recite the Paternoster." And a moment later the pongo would rise to his feet. But he would not be able to recite because he would not be in his proper place.

In the growing darkness the peons would step down from the gallery and into the patio and begin making their way toward the little cluster of living quarters. Then the patrón would call to the pongo, "Out of here, you paunchy runt!"

And so it went, every day. The patrón would make his new pongo grovel before the entire household. He would command him to laugh, or make him pretend to cry.

But one evening at the vesper hour, when the gallery was overflowing with all the members of the household, and when the patrón had just begun to notice the pongo, the little man suddenly spoke up loud and clear, his face retaining just a trace of fear.

"Sire," he said, "may I have your permission? My dear father, I wish to speak."

The patrón could not believe his ears. "What? Was it you who spoke, or someone else?"

"Your permission, dear father, to speak. With you. I wish to speak with you," repeated the pongo.

"Speak—if you can," said the master.

"My father, my lord, my soul," began the little man, "last night I dreamed we were dead, you and I. We were together in death."

"With me? You? Let's hear the rest of it, Indian."

"We were dead, my lord. And it seemed we were naked, the two of us, together. Naked before our great father, St. Francis."

"And then what? Speak!" commanded the patrón, torn between anger and curiosity.

"There we were, dead and naked, standing side by side, and our great father, St. Francis, was searching us with those eyes of his that can see farther than anyone knows. He searched us both, you and me, and I believe he was weighing our souls, judging us for what we had been and what we were. And you, being rich and great, you looked straight into those eyes, my father."

"And you?"

"I know not what I am, sire. I have no way of judging my own worth."

"True. Go on."

"Then, after that, our father opened his mouth and spoke: 'Let the most beautiful of all the angels appear. And let this incomparable one be accompanied by another little angel, who likewise shall be the most beautiful of all. Let the little angel bring a gold goblet filled with the sweetest, clearest honey.'"

"And then?" asked the patrón.

All the servants were listening to the pongo with rapt, yet fearful attention.

"Master, scarcely had our great father, St. Francis, given the order when a brilliant angel appeared, way up high like the sun. He came nearer and nearer until he stood in front of our father. Behind the great angel came the little one, so beautiful. All soft and bright like a flower. In his hands he carried the gold goblet."

"And then?" asked the patrón.

"'Great angel, take the gold goblet and cover this gentleman with honey. Let your hands be like feathers as they pass over his body.' That was the order the great father gave. So the heavenly angel dipped his hands into the honey and made your whole body bright, from your head to your toenails. And then you rose up tall, just you. And even against the bright sky the light from your body shone out, as if you were made of clear gold."

"Yes, that would have to be," said the patrón. Then he asked, "And you?"

"While you were shining in the sky, our great father, St. Francis, gave another order: 'Let the angel of least worth, the commonest angel of all, come forth. Let him bring a gasoline can filled with human excrement.'"

"And then?"

"Then a worthless angel with scaly feet, not even strong enough to hold up his wings, came before our great father. He arrived all tired out, with his wings drooping, holding a big can. 'Here, old fellow,' said our great father to this poor angel, 'smear the little man's body with that excrement you have there. All of it. Any way you like. Cover him the best you can. Quickly!' Then with his gnarled hands the old angel took the excrement out of the can and slopped it all over me. It was just as if mud were being thrown against the wall of a plain old building. And there I was, up there in the bright sky, ashamed and stinking."

"That too would have to be," said the patrón. "Go on. Or is that all?"

"No, my dear father, my lord. For now, though things were different, we found ourselves once again standing before our great father, St. Francis, and now he was taking a long look at the two of us, you and me. His eyes were as big as the sky and he looked right into us, how far I don't know—as far as to where night becomes day, where forgetting becomes remembering. And then he said, 'The angels have done their work well. Now lick each other. Slowly. And keep on licking.' Just then the old angel became young. His wings regained their usual black color and their great strength. Then our father charged him to watch over us, so that his will would be done."

Peru (Quechua)

⮞ 37. The Fox and the Monkey ⮜

Both the fox and the monkey were thieves. One night they went out together and came to the little hut of a pongo. A pot of quinoa mush was on the fire. Scooping up the mush with his hands, the monkey ate until he was full. Then the fox put his head in the pot and said, "I'll finish this up." But before he knew it his head was stuck. He whispered to the monkey, "Get me a stone to break the pot!"

The monkey felt around in the dark and put his hand on the head of the sleeping pongo. The monkey called to the fox in a loud whisper, "Over here! There's a round stone you can hit the pot on."

"All right!" whispered the fox, and he knocked the pot against the pongo's head. The pongo woke up and grabbed the monkey, while the fox escaped. Next day when the pongo reported for work at the great mansion he brought the monkey and gave it to his patrón. "We'll throw boiling water on him," said the patrón, "and then we'll skin him."

The fox came around to see what had happened to the monkey. As soon as he saw the fox, the monkey cried out, "Oh, you can't imagine what trouble I've gotten myself into! They're forcing me to marry a woman!"

The fox, out of curiosity, came closer and asked, "How is that possible, brother?"

"The master of the house has a daughter, and he tells me I have to marry her."

"In that case," said the fox, "let me untie you. I'll take your place."

"Oh, thanks!" said the monkey, and the fox freed him. Then the monkey tied up the fox and ran away.

That afternoon the master and his pongo came back with a pot of scalding water. The fox cried, "Stop, stop! I'll marry your daughter!" But they paid no attention and doused him with the hot water. That night the fox bit the rope in two and escaped from the house of the patrón. Then he began to hunt for the monkey.

He found him on a mountainside. Seeing the fox coming, and with no way to escape, the monkey pretended to be holding up a ledge as if it were about to fall. "Hah!" said the fox, "I've got you now!"

In a quiet little voice the monkey said, "Brother, if you make me move, this stone will fall and crush us both. Worse, it'll kill all the people below and wreck their houses. You're stronger than I am. Hold it up for me while I go get help."

"Of course," said the fox. He raised his hands and held the ledge as the monkey went off pretending to look for help. After a while the fox grew tired and thought, "Well, in any case, I can escape myself." So he let go and jumped aside. He looked around trembling, but the ledge had not moved. "He's done it again," said the fox. "This time I'll find him and kill him."

That night he saw the monkey sitting near the riverbank with a piece of stolen cheese. "Brother," said the monkey, "are you wondering why I never came back? Those people! Not a one of them would help!" He offered the fox a taste of the cheese. The fox tried it and asked, "Where did you steal this?"

"Promise you won't lay a hand on me, and I'll show you."

"I promise," said the fox. The monkey led him to the water and pointed out the reflection of a half-moon. "There it is, brother. I took only a little piece for myself and left the rest for you." The fox, hardly waiting for the monkey to finish speaking, jumped into the river and drowned.

Bolivia (Aymara) / Moisés Alvarez

⇒ 38. The Miser's Jar ⇐

There was once an old miser who had a beautiful jar. It was so beautiful that anyone who saw it wanted to buy it. Yet no one could meet the old man's price.

One day when he came home from his work in the cornfield, his daughter, who was grinding cornmeal, said, "Father, three people came to see the jar this morning, a gentleman, another man, and a priest."

"And what did you tell them?" asked the old man.

"I told them to come back this afternoon."

"You are a wise girl, and you have made good use of your wisdom," said the father. "When these three return, as they surely will, you must say to each one that you have decided to sell the jar for five hundred pesos without my knowledge. Tell the gentleman to come for it at eight o'clock tonight, the other man to come at half past eight, and the priest to come at nine."

The girl did as she was told, and at eight o'clock the gentleman arrived. But just as the girl had finished counting the money he had brought, there was a noise at the door of the hut, and throwing the money into one corner, she cried, "Go up into the loft! If my father finds you here, he will kill you."

While the gentleman was hurrying up to the loft, the other man came in. But before he could leave with the jar there was again a noise at the door. "Go up to the loft," cried the girl, "or my father will kill you!"

The man climbed quickly into the loft, and the priest came in. He was in a great hurry and had the jar already in his hands when the voice of the old man was heard outside. The priest trembled with fear as the girl cried, "Put the jar down and go up to the loft!"

When the girl's father came in, he asked, "Where is the gentleman's money?"

"There in the corner."

"And the other man's money?"

"There in the corner."

"And the priest's money?"

"There in the corner."

After a pause the old man asked, "And the gentleman, where is he?"

"Up in the loft."

"And the other man?"

"Up in the loft."

"And the priest?"

"Up in the loft."

"You are a wise girl," said the old man. Then he took his large carrying sack off his shoulder, put it in the middle of the floor, and set fire to it. The three men in the loft were soon dead from breathing the smoke, for the sack was full of dried chilies.

"Well," said the old man, "we still have the jar and three times five hundred pesos as well."

"But we have three dead men in the loft," replied his daughter.

"The fool will get rid of them for us tomorrow," said the old man.

"In the morning I will go find him and tell him you have sent me to ask him to come have breakfast with us."

The girl knew that the fool was in love with her and would do whatever she asked. So the next morning, when the three of them had finished their breakfast, she told the fool that she and her father were troubled because a priest who had eaten with them the night before had choked to death, and, fearful that it would be found out, they had put him in the loft, not daring to take him out for burial.

"Don't worry about a dead priest," said the fool. "Promise to marry me, and I'll get rid of him without any trouble." The girl gave her promise, but no sooner had the fool set out with the dead priest on his back than she sewed a cassock and put it on the gentleman.

When the fool returned and began talking of marriage, the girl laughed and said, "Don't try to deceive me. I know very well that while I was at the stream getting water, you sneaked into the house and put the priest back in the loft."

Seeing the gentleman in the cassock, the fool said, "I buried you once and I'll bury you again." Then he set out with the gentleman on his back, and the girl sewed another cassock and put it on the last of the three dead men. And when the fool came back and said, "He'll lie where I put him this time, because I piled heavy stones on the grave," the girl frowned and said, "Why don't you tell me the truth? I know very well that while I was out getting firewood, you came in and put the priest back in the loft."

"Well, I'll bet he doesn't come back after I bury him the third time," said the fool when he saw the cassock. As soon as he had set out with the last of the dead men on his back, the girl called to her father, who was hiding nearby. He came in, filled the beautiful jar full of money, and strapped it on his back. The girl strapped the grindstone on her back, and after setting fire to the hut they began walking toward the east.

They had not gone far when the old man caught his foot on a root and, stumbling, fell into a deep pool that lay next to the road. The girl plunged in, trying to save him, but with the weight of the grindstone she sank, too, and that was the end of them both.

The fool, coming back and not finding the hut, followed the tracks of the old man and his daughter all the way to the edge of the pool. As he sat down and began to weep, he was changed into the where-where bird. And to this day the bird may be seen near pools and in wet places, crying, "Where, where? Where, where?"

Guatemala (Kekchi Maya)

⇒ 39. Tup and the Ants ⇐

There was once an old man who had three sons. When they had grown up, and he had said to them, "Now you must marry," the eldest wrapped some food, asked for his father's blessing, and set out to find a wife. Meeting a man who had three daughters, he promptly married the eldest.

After a while the second son came along and married the second daughter. Finally the youngest son asked for his father's good words of blessing. Then he, too, prepared food for the road and set out to search for a bride. Before long he had joined his older brothers and in no time had married the youngest daughter of the old man.

Now Tup, the youngest boy, was a do-nothing, as his father-in-law soon found out. He was constantly being scolded for his laziness, and his mother-in-law would say to her youngest daughter, "What use is an idle husband?"

When the time came to clear cornfields, the old man called his three sons-in-law together and told them they must start the next day. "Cut trees!" he commanded.

Next morning the brothers set out to work, carrying tortillas and corn soup to last for three days. But Tup carried only a little, because his wife's mother hated to waste corn on such a worthless son-in-law.

The two older brothers quickly found a spot that suited them and began working. But Tup went on through the forest, not stopping until he had left his brothers some distance behind. Sitting down to rest, he fell asleep. When he awoke, it was quite late in the afternoon, too late to do any work. So he gathered a few palm leaves and made himself a shelter. After he had eaten some of his tortillas and drunk some of the corn soup, he went back to sleep.

Next morning, when he awoke, all his tortillas and corn soup had disappeared. Looking around and seeing a leaf-cutter ant carrying off the last piece of tortilla, he realized that while he had slept, the ants had robbed him of his food. He picked up the ant and said, "I'll kill you unless you take me to your nest." The ant did not disobey. When they arrived, Tup knocked three times, and the lord of the nest came out. "What do you want?" he asked.

"Your people have stolen all my tortillas and corn soup," said Tup. "Either you must give me back my food or you must do my work."

The lord of the nest thought for a few moments, then said, "I will do the work." So Tup showed him where to make the cornfield and went back to his shelter to sleep while the forest was being cleared. All the ants turned out to work that night, and being so many, they had cut down all the trees and bushes by the end of three days.

On the way back to his father-in-law's, Tup passed his two brothers. Instead of clearing the forest, these two were busily making holes in the tree trunks. When the old man had said, "Cut trees," they had thought he meant cut into them instead of cut them down, and on and on they worked.

When Tup got home, the old man cried, "Here comes Idle-bones, the last to go and the first to return. Don't give him anything to eat." In spite of this, the mother-in-law managed to grind some cornmeal and make a few tortillas. Later, however, when the other two brothers arrived, the old man greeted them heartily and ordered chickens cooked.

After several days, when he judged that the fields would be dry, the old man sent his three sons-in-law to burn the brush. The older two were given large supplies of corn soup and honey, while little Tup, for being so lazy, got only a small portion of each.

The two older boys, when they got to their spot in the forest, gathered all the wood chips and twigs they could find and burned them, but the column of smoke that rose to the sky was miserably thin. Meanwhile Tup took his honey and corn soup to the ants' nest and gave it to the lord of the nest on the condition that they do the work of burning his field. Then Tup rested all day, while the ants hurried about their task, burning the entire field. The columns of smoke that rose were so thick even the sun was hidden.

But the old man thought the smoke from Tup's field came from where the other two brothers were working. So when Tup returned, he again scolded him.

When all was ready for sowing, the older brothers took three mules loaded with corn seed. Tup took only one sack. The older brothers planted a little of their corn beneath the trees, but most of it they left in a storage hut they had built in the forest, and the rest they hid in one of the hollowed-out tree trunks.

Tup, meanwhile, took his seed to the ants, but when they saw such a small sack they said it was not enough. The fire had spread far beyond the cleared area, they said, and the amount of land to be planted was now enormous. "You may find more seed in my brothers' storehouse," said Tup, and when they had started to work, he went to sleep. After the planting was done, the three returned home. Tup received his usual contemptuous welcome, while the older brothers were feasted.

When the corn was in ear, the old man sent the three sons-in-law back to their fields to make earth ovens and roast the young corn. The two older brothers, with little else they could do, dug a small hole in the ground, then put in the few stunted ears that had just managed to survive in the shade of the forest. As for Tup, he went straight to the lord of the ants, and all the ants came immediately to his aid. They brought fifteen loads of the yellow ears, made the earth oven, heated it, and packed it with the corn while Tup slept. Toward evening he awoke and returned home.

On the following day the old man and his wife, his three daughters, and their husbands set out with a team of mules to harvest the field and eat the roasted ears. Arriving at the cornfield of the two older brothers, the father-in-law found that there was no clearing to be seen and no corn except for the few miserable plants growing in the shade of the forest, and these were more like grass than corn. When the old man saw the heap of rotting corn in the hollowed-out tree, he cried, "Where is your earth oven?"

The tiny oven was uncovered, and when the father-in-law had been shown the handful of stunted ears, he flew into a rage. Refusing even to speak to the two older brothers, he turned to Tup and said, "Let us see if you have done any better."

They started off again, Tup leading them through the forest until they came to the path the ants had made from the ant nest to the field. The path gradually widened, becoming a highway. "Where does this fine road lead?" asked the old man, and Tup replied, "To my cornfield."

Eventually they reached a huge field, stretching farther than the eye could see. "This," said Tup, "is my field." But the old man, knowing his son-in-law, could not believe it. As they climbed a small hill at the edge of the clearing, the old man's wife asked Tup where the earth oven was, thinking he would not be able to answer her, for she, too, doubted that this could be his cornfield. "You are standing on it," replied Tup. "This hill is the earth oven." Then the old man said, "You have worked enough. Let your two brothers uncover the roasted ears."

While the brothers worked, the mother-in-law tried to walk the field to see how wide and how long it might be, but it was so immense she got lost, and Tup, once again, had to call his friends the ants. Told that the old woman had lost her way, the ants spread out over the cornfield, searching until they found her.

After they had all eaten their fill of the roasted young ears and the mules had been loaded, they started for home. That night chickens were killed in honor of Tup. As for the other two brothers, they were ordered out of the house and told never to return.

Mexico (Yucatec Maya)

⋙ 40. A Master and His Pupil ⋘

Don Gumersindo Drydregs had a son, and the boy was getting big. The time had long passed for him to start in a job. So one day Don Gumersindo called him and said, "My son, how tall you are already!

And still you don't know how to do anything. I've decided to apprentice you to a trade. Tell me which one you like."

The boy said, "Me? I don't even know the names of any of those what-do-you-call-them, trades. Start naming them, and I'll tell you what I think."

"All right, son. Let me see. How about carpenter?"

"No, I'd cut myself to pieces."

"Blacksmith?"

"Goodness! I'd burn myself."

"Bricklayer?"

"Heavens! I'd get lime in my eyes."

"Tailor?"

"I'd stick myself with a needle."

"Shoemaker?"

"Never. I'd hit my knees with the hammer."

"Potter?"

"What's that, with clay? I hate it."

No matter what Don Gumersindo suggested, the boy found something wrong. The old man was desperate. Finally he shouted in anger, "I've got the job for you! Idler!"

"If you say so," said the boy, "I'll try it."

The following day Don Gumersindo delivered his son into the hands of Juan Idler, a man without any known trade, who lived off tricks and thievery.

The first day of the apprenticeship, Juan said to the boy, "Let's go out to the street, my son. We'll see what's available." They walked up and down, begging alms, then watched for a while to see if there were any drunks they could roll. Nothing turned up.

Since they were really quite hungry, they stopped under a fig tree, and Juan said, "Here we are! This at least will keep us from starving. I'll climb up and drop a few figs, and when you've eaten all you want, save the rest for me." So he climbed up into the tree, and when he'd dropped a few of the figs he jumped back down. And there was his apprentice lying on the ground with his mouth wide open.

"What's this?" said Juan. "Did you eat enough already?"

"Well, no, master," said the boy. "Not a single one fell into my mouth."

Juan said, "Ah, what a finished product you are. Why does your father bring you to me? I should go to you. You could give me lessons."

Guatemala

⇒ 41. The Louse-Drum ⇐

In a country a long way from here a king had a pretty daughter who played a drum that could be heard all over the kingdom. Since kings in those days used to invite princes to their palaces so that their daughters could look them over, this king held a banquet, and princes came from near and far. The one who guessed what the princess's drum was made of would win her hand.

Not a single one guessed correctly.

Now, the princess was in love with a certain prince who lived in town but hadn't dared show up at the palace because he was an enemy of the king. So one day the princess was on her balcony when this prince was standing at his window, and she called out to him, "Come guess! Tell them the drum is made from the skin of a louse that my maid-servant found on my head." Unfortunately the prince was not close enough to catch this information.

But an old man sitting under the balcony heard every word. He got up and went straight to the palace guard and asked for an audience with the king. The king took one look at him and said, "It's guess or be hanged by the neck. Here, if you're such a wise man: What's my daughter's drum made of?"

The old man answered, "The drum you're talking about is made from the skin of a louse that a maidservant found on the princess's head, and you yourself gave the order for it to be fattened up until its skin was large enough to make a drum."

Since kings' promises are promises for keeps, the king had to call his daughter and tell her he was about to give her away to a graybeard, and a pauper at that. No matter that the girl protested, the king arranged for their marriage and immediately banished them both from the palace.

The princess had an idea. She suggested to her old husband that they go bathing together at the head of a roaring falls. Off they went, and when the old man had bathed awhile he lay down to rest beside the falls. As soon as he had dropped off to sleep, the princess pushed him over the bank. He disappeared in the spray, but at the same moment something jumped up on her back, and suddenly she had a lump on her shoulder. From then on, whenever she spoke, the lump answered her.

On and on she traveled, through forests, across rivers, and past villages, until at last she came to the city of a king with a son that interested her. Pretending she couldn't speak, so that no one would discover the talkative lump on her shoulder, she found employment in the king's kitchen. They called her The Mute.

She caught the prince's eye, and he wondered if the new kitchen maid might not be more than a humble servant girl, perhaps some kind of princess. But the prince had already been promised to a young woman of that city. When his engagement day arrived, the date was set for the wedding.

One day the queen asked the new kitchen girl to make her a corn-dough pudding. As the princess started to cook it up, she remembered the lump on her shoulder, which was quite fatty, and she said to it, "Hey, lump, want to come down on my arm?"

Needless to say, it answered her. "Sure, why not?" Then she said, "Hey, lump, come down to my hand."

"Sure, why not?"

"Hey, lump, come down to the tip of my finger."

"Sure, why not?" And when the lump was dangling from her fingertip, she quick took a knife and sliced it off. As it dropped into the pudding, it shouted, "*Ayayay, ayayay!* I'm melting!" But she was unmoved by its cries.

When she tried her voice and found that she was at last free, she was greatly relieved. For the time being, however, she remained silent.

The queen thought the pudding was delicious.

That evening The Mute put on a green dress and shoes to match, rouged her face the way princesses do, and when she finished she was quite presentable. She knew where the prince's bride-to-be lived, so she went there and walked in front of the house. The prince and his betrothed were standing on a balcony. The prince recognized The Mute and completely forgot himself. He blurted out, "You look like the princess my heart has dreamed of." She answered, "You've seen your princess in dreams. Now you see her in life."

The prince shook himself loose from his betrothed's arm and ran after The Mute. "How can it be?" he asked. "You are not mute at all." He took her hand in his and led her to his coach. By the time they reached the palace they were ready to announce their engagement. You can imagine how surprised the king and the queen were when the princess told them her story.

To celebrate the wedding they invited all the neighboring kings and queens, and the guests included the princess's father and mother, who found nothing to fault in their new son-in-law.

Panama

⤜ 42. The Three Dreams ⤛

Two students, once, were on their way to a town. The road was long and they had only ten centavos between them. In the distance they could see something moving. What was it? They stepped up their pace and, sure enough, it was human. An Indian, they realized. They got closer, hailed him, and called out, "Do you have any money on you?"

"Five centavos."

That's just what each of the two students had, five centavos. They'd been discussing it, how it wasn't enough to buy a meal, and so they'd kept on walking until they'd come to this something or other that might be human, and they'd stopped to ask about the money; and the man had said, "Five centavos."

So one of the students said to the other, "Since we've got ten already, and our friend here has five, that makes fifteen. We could do something."

They kept on down the road, and after a while it got dark. They decided to ask the Indian to make camp with them for the night. Then the three pooled their resources and bought a half-pound of rice and a pound of sugar to cook in a little pot that one of them had brought along. When it was time to go to bed—well, let's just say, lie down—one of the two intellectuals made a proposition, "This rice? In the morning we'll cook it up for breakfast to get some energy for the road, but the one who gets to eat it will be the one who tells the best dream."

So the pressure was on to start dreaming. The two students went right to sleep. In the morning all three were ready with dreams to tell. One of the two students was the first to wake up. He said to his friend, "Did you dream anything?"

"Yes I did."

"What was it?"

"In my dream there was a broad avenue stretching from here all the way to Heaven, and it was lined with flowers. I walked along until I came to the end. There was a church. It was so beautiful, I walked right in. When I got inside, I saw all the statues of the saints, and I myself became . . . a statue! And what about you? Did you dream?"

"Yes, I dreamed there was a broad avenue stretching all the way to Heaven. I walked along until I got to the church, and I saw that you were a statue, but then I raised my eyes and there was a cloud coming down. It got closer and I could make out three angels. They lifted me up. I became an angel, too, and the four of us floated into the sky."

"So we both had dreams! What about you, Indian? Did you dream?"

"Yes, patrón, a little bit like your dream. Imagine it, patrón, there was an avenue, and at the end of the avenue was a church. I went inside, and there was my patrón, changed into a statue, and I looked up and saw my other patrón carried away by the angels. So what else could I do, all by myself in the world? I ate the rice."

Guatemala / Luis Arturo Hernández Castañeda

➤ 43. The Clump of Basil ⬅

Well, sir, there was once a carpenter who had three pretty daughters, Carmen, María, and Pepita, and they lived in a little house not far from the king's palace. The house had a garden full of flowers and a handsome clump of basil.

The poor carpenter had to be out nearly every day working his trade, while his daughters labored at home by themselves.

Now, the king who lived in this city was a great lover of riddles and would propose them not only to his courtiers but to anyone he happened to meet. One morning, while out for a ride, he passed the carpenter's little house and saw Carmen, the eldest of the daughters, watering the basil. He called out to her,

> *Young lady, grant me your best appraisal:*
> *How many leaves on your clump of basil?*

The girl was embarrassed and went inside without answering.

The next day the king came by again. The second eldest, María, was watering the basil plant. The king repeated his question. But like her sister, the poor young woman went into the house, ashamed, without answering.

The following day Pepita, the youngest and prettiest, was out watering, and when the king caught sight of her he asked,

> *Young lady, grant me your best appraisal:*
> *How many leaves on your clump of basil?*

Without hesitation Pepita called back,

> *Caballero, give me your best reply:*
> *How many stars are in the sky?*

Having imagined that the girl would be caught off guard like her sisters, the king was embarrassed. He rode away without answering, but promised himself he would get even.

A few days later the king appeared again, this time disguised as a street vendor selling candies. Since the carpenter's daughters had a taste for sweets, they called to the vendor the moment they saw him. He came into the house and announced he would sell his candies only for kisses.

The two older daughters were indignant. They showed him the door. But the youngest struck him a bargain and gave him one kiss for each of the candies he had in his jar.

After returning to the palace, the king changed his clothes and waited until he knew it was time for the basil to receive its daily watering. Just at the right moment he rode by the house and called to Pepita,

> *Young lady, grant me your best appraisal:*
> *How many leaves on your clump of basil?*

She answered,

> *Caballero, give me your best reply:*
> *How many stars are in the sky?*

But the king called back,

> *You with your answers so smart and handy,*
> *How many kisses did you give for candy?*

And Pepita, ashamed, ran back into the house.

The days passed and the king did not come riding by the garden. Pepita heard from someone that the king was deathly ill. Without a moment's hesitation she knew what to do. She dressed up as Death and went to the palace leading a mule. Frightened, the palace guards stepped aside and allowed her to enter the king's bedroom. She said to the king, "I've come to take you. Your years and days are counted up."

The king begged, "Let me live. I'll do anything you ask. Just give me a few more years." So Pepita told him, "There's only one way." And what was it? To kiss the mule under its tail. And since the king wanted so badly to live, he raised up the tail and began kissing, and kept on until he had planted a great many in that very spot. Death promised him a year of life for each kiss.

Then Pepita, still dressed as Death, left with the mule. The king began to improve and was soon completely well.

Before long he appeared once again in the street, rode past the garden, and found Pepita watering the basil. He said,

> *Young lady, grant me your best appraisal:*
> *How many leaves on your clump of basil?*

She answered,

> *Caballero, give me your best reply:*
> *How many stars are in the sky?*

The king called back,

> *You with your answers so smart and handy,*
> *How many kisses did you give for candy?*

To which she replied,

> *Clever, my lord! But answer without fail:*
> *How many times did you lift the mule's tail?*

In spite of himself the king began thinking, "This wise young woman will be my wife." Still, he would have to find a way to get even with her. He had the old carpenter brought before him. "I'll take your daughter to be my queen," he declared, "but she must come to the palace neither naked nor dressed, neither riding on horseback nor sitting in a carriage nor simply walking. And if she doesn't do it, both you and she will be put to death instantly."

The poor carpenter returned to his house in despair. But when Pepita heard what the king had commanded, she sent for a fisherman's net and wrapped it around her body. Then she told her father to hitch her up behind the mule. Off she went to the palace, neither naked nor dressed, neither riding nor sitting nor simply walking. The king, seeing how clever she really was and knowing she would make an excellent queen, married her without further delay.

> *Their life thereafter was perfectly nice;*
> *They even gave me some chicken with rice.*

Puerto Rico

⇒ Riddles ⇐

I.

Fuí a un cuarto,
Encontré un muerto,
Hablé con él
Y le saqué el secreto.
libro

I entered a room
And found a dead man,
Spoke with him
And came away with his secrets.
book

II.

Monte blanco,
Flores negras,
Un arado
Y cinco yeguas.
la escritura

White mountain,
Black flowers;
One plow,
Five horses.
writing

III.

Uno larguito,	One tallest of all,
Dos más bajitos,	Two not so tall,
Uno chico y flaco	One skinny and small,
Y otro gordonazo.	And a butterball.
los dedos	five fingers

IV. PARAGUAY (GUARANÍ)

Maravilla, maravilla,	Wonder, wonder,
¿Mbaé motepá?	What can it be?
Ycure mante oguatava.	It walks with its tongue.
el arado	plow

V.

No tiene pies y corre,	It has no feet but runs,
No tiene alas y vuela,	It has no wings but flies,
No tiene cuerpo y vive,	It has no form but lives,
No tiene boca y habla,	It has no mouth but speaks,
Sin armas lucha y vence	It has no defenses, yet persists;
Y siendo nada, está.	And though it is nothing, it exists.
el viento	wind

VI.

Más bueno que Dios	Better than God,
Más malo que el diablo;	Worse than the Devil,
Lo comen los muertos	The dead eat it;
Y si lo comen los vivos, se mueren.	The living who eat it die.
nada	nothing

VII.

El que lo hace no lo goza,
El que lo goza no lo ve,
El que lo ve no lo desea
Por bonito que lo esté.

el ataúd

Its maker doesn't use it,
Its user doesn't see it;
Those who see it never want it,
As fine as it may be.

coffin

VIII.

Cantando olvido mis penas
Mientras voy hacia la mar;
Las penas van y vuelven
Más yo no vuelvo jamás.

el río

I sing away my troubles
As I travel to the sea;
Troubles go, troubles return,
But there's no return for me.

river

IX.

Blanca como la leche,
Negra como la hez,
Habla y no tiene boca,
Anda y no tiene pies.

carta

White as milk,
Black as soot,
Has no mouth but speaks,
Travels but has no feet.

a letter

X.

Cuesta arriba,
Cuesta abajo;
Y, sin embargo, no se mueve.

la carretera

Rises up,
Dips down,
Yet never moves.

highway

XI.

Verde en el monte,　　　In a forest it's green,
Negro en la plaza,　　　In a market it's black,
Colorado en la casa.　　In a cottage it's red.
　　　el carbón　　　　　　　　　charcoal

XII.

Pino, lino, flores,　　　Pinewood and linen and flowers,
Y alrededor amores.　　And all those around it are ours.
　　Mesa de comedor　　　　　　　　dinner table

XIII. MEXICO (NAHUA)

Se tosaasaanil, se tosaasaanil　　A riddle, a riddle.
Maaske mas tikwaalaantok　　You hate to do it,
Pero tikpiipiitsos.　　　But you give it a little kiss.
　　　tecomate　　　　　　　　　beer bottle

XIV.

Cuando joven, amarga,　　Sour when a young girl,
Cuando anciana, dulce.　　Sweet when an old woman.
　　la naranja　　　　　　　　　orange

XV.

Cuando chiquita, costillita,　　A sparerib when it's young,
Y cuando grandecita, tortillita.　　A tortilla when it's grown.
　　　la luna　　　　　　　　　moon

XVI.

Mi madre tenía una sábana
Que no la podía doblar;
Mi padre tenía tanto dinero
Que no lo podía contar.

cielo y estrellas

My mother had a sheet
That she could never fold;
My father had more silver coins
Than he could ever hold.

the sky and the stars

XVII. PERU (QUECHUA)

¿Imallanpas, haykallanpas?
Mama killa watan,
Tayta inti paskan.

escarcha

What is it, what is it?
Mother Moon ties it up,
Father Sun sets it free.

frost

XVIII.

El agua la da,
El sol la cría;
Y si el agua le da
Le quita la vida.

la sal

Water provides it,
The sun creates it,
But water that touches it
Always destroys it.

salt

XIX. ECUADOR (QUICHUA)

Imashi, imashi.
Shuj yacupipish yaicun
Mana shuturin,
Ninapipish yaicun
Mana ruparin,
Imashi?

chaimi can llandu

What can it be?
Lies on the water
Yet never gets wet,
Falls on the candle
Yet never burns.
Can you guess?

shadow

XX.

Cuando iba,
Iba con ella,
Y cuando volvía
Me encontré con ella.
            la huella

When she went away,
I went off with her,
Yet when she returned
I was there to meet her.
            footprint

XXI.

En el camino la encontré,
Me la busqué
Y no la hallé
Y siempre me la llevé.
            la espina

I found her on the road,
Then tried to find her,
Couldn't find her,
Took her with me everywhere.
            splinter

XXII.

En el cielo no lo hubo,
En el tierra se encontró,
Dio con ser Dios no lo tuvo
Y un hombre á Dios se lo dió.
            el bautismo

In heaven it doesn't exist
And yet on earth it can;
God himself, who lacked it,
Received it from a man.
            baptism

XXIII.

Uno que nunca pecó
Y nunca pudo pecar,
Murió diciendo Jesús
Y no se pudo salvar.
            el loro

One who never sinned
Even if ill-behaved,
Died speaking the name Jesus
Yet never could be saved.
            parrot

XXIV. ECUADOR (QUICHUA)

Tutamantaca chuscu	In the morning it
chaquihuan purin,	walks on four legs,
Chaupi punllaca ishqui	At noon on two legs,
chaquihuan purin,	
Tultu chishitaca qumsa	In the evening on three legs.
chaquihuan purin,	
Imashi?	What is it?
runa	human being

XXV.

No recuerdo si fuí niño,	I don't remember childhood,
Pues hombre fuí al nacer.	For I was born a man;
Aunque me quiten la vida	My life is taken every day
Mil vidas he de tener.	Yet has a longer span;
De los besos amorosos	The kisses that a lover gives
Yo siempre testigo fuí,	I never fail to see,
Que por hacerlo a su novio	And those who kiss their lovers
Muchas me han besado a mí.	End up kissing me.
la barba	beard

XXVI.

Chiquita como un ratón	No bigger than a mouse,
Y guarda la casa como un león.	Like a lion it guards the house.
la llave	key

XXVII.

Mientras que estoy preso, existo,   Hold me captive and let me be,
Si me ponen en libertad, muero.   Make me die if you set me free.

el secreto   secret

XXVIII.

El que me nombra, me rompe.   Whoever names me breaks me.

el silencio   silence

XXIX. PERU (CASHINAHUA)

Rawa ix′ta möxô mörã nimiç′   What is it that travels by
mãekãi?   night?

iôxĩnã   ghosts

XXX. MEXICO (YUCATEC MAYA)

Tanteni′ tantetci′.   I am doing it and you are
doing it.

tanktcaik′ik′   breathing

PART FIVE

➣ 44. The Charcoal Peddler's Chicken ⇐

There was a charcoal peddler always down-and-out. He would say to God, "Please someday let me have an extra fifty centavos, just an extra fifty, to get a chicken I could sit down and eat all by myself." And the day came when he had the fifty, and he bought the chicken.

When he'd put it on the fire, and it was still in the pot, a handsomely dressed man stopped by, claiming to be hungry. The peddler said, "Who are you?"

"I'm Luck, come to help you eat your chicken."

"Scram, you handsome dog. You don't help me. Luck helps only the rich."

The well-dressed man went on. A moment later another man, badly dressed, showed up. "And who are you?" said the peddler.

"I'm Death, come to help you eat your chicken."

"Come, sit down," said the charcoal man. "Let's eat. Take half and enjoy it, for Death treats everyone the same, rich or poor. Luck may be a dog, but he isn't faithful to his owner."

Puerto Rico

⇒ 45. The Three Counsels ⇐

A man in need of work set out from home, leaving his wife and his six-teen-year-old son. In a remote country he found a master who hired him and treated him well. Seven years passed and he went to the master for his pay. They had agreed he would be given seven bags of money for seven years' work.

The master knew what the man had come for and said, "Very well. You've earned your wages. But let me ask, would you rather have seven bags of money or three counsels?"

The man thought a moment. Which would be better? Then he said out loud, "I'll take the three counsels."

The good master answered, "You've chosen well. And here they are. The first is: Never leave the road for a bypath. The second: Never question what doesn't concern you. The third: Never act on the first piece of news."

The man took the counsels to heart, and when he had bid the good master farewell he started for home. After traveling a few leagues he came to a spot where a couple of paths branched off. Some men were standing there, and one of them said, "Come along with us and take this short cut. You'll get home faster." The man refused, remembering the first of his master's counsels: Never leave the road for a bypath.

He'd walked another league when he heard shouts. Somebody was running up behind him. It was one of the men who'd been at the fork in the road. The man was wounded. "We were attacked by highway-men, and they murdered my friends. I was the only one who got away." Then the traveler congratulated himself, realizing that his master's good counsels had saved him from death.

He walked on, traveling the main road. In a while he came to a house, large and grand, yet strangely quiet. He knocked at the door, and a tall, thin man received him courteously, inviting him to enter and make himself comfortable. He settled himself in a chair. The hours went by. He didn't dare move a muscle for fear of breaking the silence.

When it was time for dinner the thin man appeared in a doorway and motioned him to come forward. He led him into a magnificent dining hall, to a table laden with all the delicacies you could ever wish for. There were wines and liquors of all kinds, rare game meats, pastries, and fruits from different countries. The dishes were gold and silver, the knives and spoons were silver.

When the two men had seated themselves, the host's wife came into the room carrying a skull. She placed it on the table with loving care and began to eat the food it contained, dipping it up with her fingers. The guest could barely conceal his amazement and was at the point of asking what it all meant when he remembered the second of the three counsels: Never question what doesn't concern you.

Afterward the host directed him to a bedchamber and left him to spend the night, terrified by what he had seen at dinner.

The next morning he was called to breakfast, and he witnessed the same thing. The woman appeared with the skull and sat down to eat from it. The guest pretended not to notice, and when it was time for him to be on his way he said his good-byes. The host drew him aside. "I'm surprised you never asked about the skull. Why not?"

"Because I was given a piece of advice that I've vowed to follow: Never question what doesn't concern you."

"Since you didn't ask," said the host, "I'm going to tell you. My wife and I are not of this world. During our time on earth we were as rich as could be and as greedy. God punished us by putting us here, where my wife would take every meal from a human skull and every traveler would stop at our door. As each guest would ask, 'Why the skull?' he would go to his death. Come, I want you to see how many have perished for asking the question you never asked."

The lord of the manor took him into a cavernous cellar, piled with cadavers, skeletons, and loose skulls, some freshly dead, some old and dry. He continued, "We have remained prisoners in this terrible place, waiting for the traveler who would ask no questions. You are that traveler, and now we are free."

With those words he handed his guest the keys to the manor. "Great riches are hidden here. Now they are yours." As he was speaking he vanished together with his wife, and the traveler found himself alone with all that wealth. He was not sorry to have followed his master's counsels. Seeing how rich he now was, he set off contentedly for home, where he had left his wife and son.

As he approached his house it was getting dark. The lights were on, and he looked through a window and saw his wife reclining on the bed, caressing the hair of a young priest who was holding the woman's head in his arms. The poor traveler, finding his wife in the arms of a lover, was about to rush in and plant a knife in the man's throat. Then he remembered the last of his master's three counsels: Never act on the first piece of news. Restraining himself, he went to the door and knocked.

The woman and the priest came to greet him, and when he asked, "Who is this?" his wife replied, "This priest is your son, who was still a boy when you left home."

The traveler embraced his wife and his son joyfully and told them all that had happened in his travels, how he had received the three counsels, and how he had made his way home. Then together they went off to the manor house to enjoy their wealth.

The master, who had wished to reward the good worker by giving him three counsels, was Our Lord Jesus Christ.

New Mexico

⇒ 46. Seven Blind Queens ⇐

In a faraway country there was a cruel king who took pleasure in making his people suffer.

One day while out hunting in the woods, he saw a beautiful young woman standing at the door of a cottage. He brought her back to the palace and married her.

The new queen's happiness lasted no more than a month. At first, charmed by her loveliness, the king behaved himself. But as the novelty wore off he revealed his true nature and began tormenting everybody.

Since the queen was closest to him she paid the heaviest price. One morning he woke up in a fury, ordered the queen's eyes plucked out, then shouted to his guards, "Take her to the dungeon! And keep her on bread and water!"

Not long after that the king married a second young woman, and she, too, had her month of happiness, then her troubles began. Before another month had gone by the king had blinded her and thrown her into the dungeon with the first queen. The same fate befell five additional brides, one after another.

Each of the imprisoned queens gave birth. But only the first of the seven was able to protect her child. The others, driven by hunger, ate their newborn infants. The first queen carefully hid her little boy, and as though he knew what would happen if his mother's companions discovered him he never made the slightest cry.

He was a beautiful child and grew quickly. At night, while the other queens were asleep, his mother taught him to speak. Bit by bit she passed along to him what little knowledge she had. He absorbed it without having to be told twice, for he was blessed with a quick mind.

One day the boy found a key that had been dropped on the floor of the dungeon. Playing with it, he poked it into the damp wall, and the mortar crumbled away. There was a tiny shaft of light. He kept working at the stones until he made a hole large enough to crawl through. "Mother," he said, "I'm going out to see what I can find. Stand in front of the hole so the warden won't notice."

On the other side of the wall was a garden filled with flowers and fruit trees. The boy gathered as much fruit as he could carry and brought it to his mother. Only then did she tell her companions that she had a son, and she said to her boy, "Share the fruit with the other queens!"

From that moment on he was the darling of them all. He repaid their affection by bringing them fresh provisions from the garden each day.

Every time he went out his mother felt her heart pounding. She thought, "What if the gardeners find him and take him to the king?" Finally she said to him, "Son, if they catch you they'll ask you, 'Where are you from? What is your name? Who are your parents?' Tell them,

'My home is the world, my name is Wind, my father and mother are Thunder and Rain.'"

More than a year went by without anyone discovering him, because the boy made his excursions first thing in the morning, and the gardeners were not early risers. At last, however, one of the gardeners got up earlier than usual, caught the boy, and took him to the king. But the child found favor with the king, and when the king began questioning him, "Where are you from?" the boy answered, "My home is the world."

"And who is your father?"

"My father is Thunder."

"And who is your mother."

"My mother is Rain."

And so the king suspected nothing.

Now, shortly after gouging out the eyes of the seventh queen and locking her up in the dungeon, the king had married again. This time he had met his match. The new wife was a strong-minded woman with a heart of stone, who lorded it over her husband until he gave in to all her demands and became soft and weak.

I've already told you how the boy pleased the king at first sight, and even more so with his ready answers to the king's questions. The king had issued these orders: "Dress him well! Give him free run of the palace and the grounds!"

The boy lived with the palace staff, who adored him. They gave him his fill at every meal, and when he got up from the table he gathered the leftovers and brought them to the blind queens. He would stay and chat for a while with his mother and the other women, especially in the evenings before retiring to his room.

Eventually the boy's reputation reached the ears of the new queen, who demanded to see him. She, too, wanted to hear his smart answers, and when she had satisfied herself that he was as confident and strong-willed as everyone said, she made up her mind to have him killed.

Pretending to be ill, she called the king and said, "My dreams tell me that nothing will cure me except the milk of a lioness, which must be delivered by a lion—and in a lion's skin. And no one but the young man must go after it."

The king, who obeyed all the queen's orders, even if they were distasteful, sent the boy to get the cure. Alarmed, the boy went first to his mother to tell her what the queen had commanded, and his mother then advised him:

"The queen only wants to get rid of you, but you won't be harmed if you follow my instructions. Before you go, ask the cook for bread, milk, a saucepan, and salt for seasoning. Keep traveling until you reach an open country where you will see a cliff rising beside a stream shaded by trees. Make a milk sop with the bread and leave it next to the water. Then hide behind a tree. A lion will come along, sniff the sop, and gulp it down. He'll say, 'What a sop! Who brought this?' You'll come out of hiding and say, 'It was I, sir.' And the grateful lion will do your bidding."

So the boy did as his mother instructed, and when the lion had licked the last of the sop from his jowls he looked around and said, "What a sop! Who could have brought it?"

"Sir Lion, it was I!"

"What can I do to show my gratitude?" asked the lion.

"Here's what I need," said the boy, "the milk of a lioness in a lion's skin, brought to the palace by a lion, to cure the queen, who is deathly ill."

"Nothing could be easier," said the lion. "A little lion cub will go with you. Just take this wand, and when you get to the palace, tap the lion cub on the head three times and say, 'Go back where you came from!'" And before the lion had finished speaking, the lion cub appeared, carrying a lion's skin on its shoulders.

When they got to the palace, the queen was out on her balcony. She caught sight of the lion cub carrying the lion's skin and flew into a rage.

Just at the palace gate the boy lifted the skin onto his own shoulders and gave the cub three taps, saying, "Go back where you came from!" and the cub disappeared.

After this the queen hated the boy more than ever and swore to herself that she would see him killed. In no time she took sick again. She said to the king, "I've dreamed of a cure, and nothing else can save me. I must lay my eyes on the singing towers and the dancing battlements, and the young man must be the one to bring them to me."

The king gave the order to the boy, who went directly to the dungeon to ask his mother what to do.

She said, "My son, don't worry. The queen wants you to die. But follow my instructions and you'll be protected. Before you go, ask the gardener for a burro and tell the gardener's wife to give you a guitar. Saddle up the burro and keep traveling for seven hours. You'll reach the Enchanted City, where you'll see no one but the old sorceress who lives there. Strike up the guitar, and she'll come out. As long as you keep playing, she'll be under your spell, and from then on you'll know what to do."

When he reached the gates of the Enchanted City, he began to play. An old woman came out and asked if she could buy the guitar. "Later!" promised the boy. "First you must show me the sights of the city."

He continued playing without a moment's pause, as the old woman shuffled along beside him in her slippers. They came to a piglet in a beautiful little pigpen. "Grandmother, what's this?" he asked. "You mean the little pig? It's the life of your father's new queen. Now please, give me the guitar!"

"Later, grandmother!" He kept on strumming. They came to a fountain of gold-colored water surrounded by flowers. "What's that, grandmother?"

"It's the water that restores sight to the blind. Now give me the guitar."

"Later!" he said, and he kept plucking at the strings. They came to a platform made of a single diamond, and in the middle was a tiny castle of ivory, vibrating with the soft sounds of angels singing inside it. "Grandmother, what's that?"

"That? It's the singing towers and the dancing battlements. But let me have the guitar!"

"Not yet!" And he kept on playing. They came to a place where there were many lighted candles, some long, some of medium length, some short. "Grandmother, what are those?"

"Those are the lives of all the people who live in the kingdom."

"And the tallest one, whose is that? My father's?"

"No, it's mine, my child. Now let me have the guitar!"

But before she could finish, the boy put out the flame with one corner of his poncho, and the sorceress fell to the ground, dead forever.

He filled a flask with the golden water, slipped the ivory castle into the burro's saddlebag, and, leading the pig by a rope, rode back to his father's palace.

The queen was waiting on her balcony. When she saw the boy arrive, she tore her hair in frustration. He picked up the little pig and dashed it to the ground, killing it instantly. The queen drew one last breath and gave her soul to the Devil.

After that, the boy rushed to the dungeon of the seven blind queens. He restored their eyesight with the golden water, then went to the king and told all. Hearing that this boy who had become his favorite was none other than his own son and that the troublesome queen was no more, the king exclaimed, "I'm doubly blessed!"

The king remarried the boy's mother and made sure that all his subjects enjoyed themselves at the grand wedding banquet. The past served him as a lesson, and from that time on he governed wisely. As for the other queens, each married a grandee of the court and lived happily. Here ends my story, and the wind carries it out to sea.

Chile / Luis Smith

⤳ 47. The Mad King ⥵

An evil-minded king woke up one morning in a frenzy. As soon as he settled his wits he announced he would get rid of all the old people in his kingdom. He called his soldiers and gave the order, "Heads of gray, let them roll!"

The order was carried out. All the old people were beheaded with the exception of one man who took cover at his son's ranch far out in the bush. Rumors of an escape filtered back to court. The king sent soldiers deep into the countryside to find out if the stories were true and to take no mercy on the lone survivor.

The soldiers arrived at the ranch where the old father was hiding.

They turned the house upside down, but in vain. The son had hidden his father in a bunker outside.

The soldiers returned empty-handed. "It's no use, Your Majesty. The old man is lying low." Furious, the king ordered the son brought to the palace. When the son arrived, he denied everything. The king, who was no fool, asked, "You live in the bush?"

"Yes, sire."

"Then find me the herb-of-all-cures. Bring it here tomorrow or you'll be skinned alive."

The young man went back to the ranch and told his wife what the king had commanded. "You'd better ask your father," she said. And he ran to his father's hideout. "Father, I must find the herb-of-all-cures."

"That's easy," said the old man. He explained where it grew, and his son brought it to the palace next day, still fresh. The king's suspicions were strengthened. He thought, "Only a wise elder would know where to find the herb-of-all-cures." Then he proposed another test: "Bring me the king-of-all-birds, and do it by this time tomorrow or you'll be strung up!"

The son ran back to the bush. "Father," he said, "I must catch the king-of-all-birds or they'll string me up."

"But it's easy," said the old man. He explained where to find the bird, and his son brought it to the palace in the nick of time.

The king now knew the son had lied. Only an elder would have been able to find the king-of-all-birds. Not to be defied, the king set a trap to catch the young man once and for all. He demanded, "Come back tomorrow. And when I see you, you'll have to be inside and outside the palace. Otherwise, death!"

"Father, how can I be inside the palace and outside the palace?" asked the son when he got back to the father's hiding place. The father explained how it could be done, and when the son appeared in front of the king the next day, he had tied one end of a rope to the edge of the palace roof and the other end around his waist and was swinging into the palace doorway and back out again.

Still not satisfied, the king said, "Come back tomorrow with your wife and your dog." When they arrived the next day, the king handed the young man a whip and ordered him to beat the dog until it told where the old father was hiding. The master used the whip, but the faithful dog refused to speak. "Then flog your wife!" ordered the king. But the wife spoke up, "He's in the bunker!"

With all haste the guards brought the old man before the king, and the king put his hands on the old man's shoulders and said, "You raised a good son." Then he repented his sins, calmed down, and pardoned the old father. Together the father, the son, the son's wife, and the dog went back to the ranch, and there they lived out the rest of their days.

Florida

⤜ 48. A Mother's Curse ⤛

Well, sir, a woman was starching clothes, and when she turned her back for a moment her little boy put his dirty hands in the tub and spoiled the starch. When the mother saw what he had done, she flew into a rage and said, "Go to the Devil!"

Hardly had she spoken the words than a whirlwind came up and darkened the sky. She was frightened and began to tremble. The storm was over in a few minutes, but when she looked for her little boy he wasn't there.

She wept bitterly. She called his name. But it was no use. The Devil had taken her child.

One day as she passed by a woods, she noticed a little pile of bones. She brought them back to her house and buried them. After that, at night, a flapping of wings could he heard near the house and the croaking of a large bird, as if asking for something.

People say it's that woman's child, who comes especially on windy nights to ask his mother's forgiveness.

Puerto Rico

⇒ 49. The Hermit and the Drunkard ⇐

Two brothers were born in a country town. One of them became a hermit and went to live on a mountaintop where the angel of mercy dropped down at mealtimes to give him his daily bread. The other brother became a hopeless drunkard, and from that time on he had a special place in the underworld, where he slept on a bed made of iron, though he didn't realize it, having convinced himself he was still living in his own house. Every day he went out with enough money in his pockets to buy a bottle and cover his other expenses.

Along the route that he always took, day after day, there was a picture of the Virgin of Lourdes hanging from an urn in front of the house of a devout family. As he passed by, he never failed to tip his hat, saying, "Dear Virgin, don't forget me."

Sometimes he was so drunk he missed her completely. But if he did, he would ask a passerby for directions and retrace his steps in order to greet her, always with the same words, "Dear Virgin, don't forget me."

One day as he passed through a particular neighborhood, he heard the sound of weeping. He stopped to see what was the matter. A man had died, and there was a wake in progress. Entering the house he asked to speak to the widow. When she came forward, he reached into his pocket and gave her a handful of money. "Take this," he said, "and feed your children. Don't be afraid. I'm going to help you."

Then he saw that the widow was pregnant and in the last stages at that, and he added, "When your child is born, he'll be my son. I'll take care of him."

From then on, every time he passed that way, he left money for the widow. When she gave birth to a little boy, he paid all the expenses. As the child grew and began to speak, he was taught by his mother to say "Papa" whenever they saw the drunkard, until finally the mother said, "Here, he's yours." The drunkard picked up the boy and carried him off in his poncho.

As soon as they got to the drunkard's home in the underworld, the man passed out on his iron bed, while the boy ran round and round the bed, saying, "This is some place to sleep!" Then he touched it and burned his finger. Astounded, he looked under the bed and saw a fire burning.

He shook his adopted father to wake him up. "Papa, your bed is on fire!"

Suddenly the man saw what he had never seen before. In a panic he scooped up the boy and ran with him back to his mother's house. "You must take care of your son yourself," he said, "for I may never return."

In desperation he ran on until he came to a river. He threw himself into the water, picked up a heavy stone, and began pounding it against his chest. He begged the Virgin of Lourdes to forgive his sin. In answer, two angels descended and carried him into the sky.

About the same time, his brother the hermit started wasting away with hunger. The angel of mercy had stopped the daily deliveries. After a week God himself took stock of the situation and gave the angel an order. "Here, take some bread to the hermit. Tell him his brother was saved, and we were so busy celebrating we forgot all about him."

Hearing this from the angel, the jealous brother cried out, "Don't you know my brother's a mugger and a thief? If he can be saved, I should be saved twice over."

No sooner had the words left his mouth than the hermit was handed to the demons in the underworld, where from then on he slept in the same iron bed that had formerly been reserved for his brother the thief.

Ecuador / Isabel Rivadeneira

⮞ 50. The Noblewoman's Daughter and the Charcoal Woman's Son ⮜

In a faraway country—I can't remember which one—there was a rushing river with a castle beside it and beautiful gardens in every direction.

In the castle lived a noblewoman named María, who was expecting a child any day. This child, she thought, would be all her happiness, and she was predicting great things for its future. One afternoon, while walking in the gardens, she passed a woman of the village who had just delivered some charcoal. The charcoal woman was also expecting a child. When she saw the noblewoman, she stopped and said, "Milady, how good it would be if you had a daughter and I had a son! They would marry each other!"

The haughty noblewoman said nothing and turned her back. But she could not get the charcoal woman's words out of her head. A few days later she in fact gave birth to a daughter. Then she summoned a trusted servant and said, "Go immediately to the charcoal woman. If she has had a daughter, let her be. But if it's a son, you must put the child to death. As proof, bring me the tongue and the little finger."

The servant made his way to the charcoal woman's hut. And what should be there but a pretty little boy all ruddy and blue-eyed, just like an angel. In a moment the poor mother realized why the servant had come. She clung to the child with all her force, but the man snatched him and ran off.

The trusty servant raised his knife, but in that instant he was struck with shame. He could not kill the child. Yet he knew that her ladyship would put him to death if he failed her, so he cut off the baby's little finger. Then he killed a puppy that was passing by, and cut out its tongue. Gently he laid the child in a basket, padded it with straw, and placed it on the river so that the current would carry it off somewhere. When he returned, his mistress asked, "Did you do what I told you?"

"Milady, here's proof."

The noblewoman was well satisfied and had a sign put up at the castle gate: WHAT GOD MADE, I DESTROYED.

Now, the king and the queen of this country were wise rulers who lived well. Yet their happiness was not complete, for they had been unable to have a child. One day, as it happened, the king went walking by the river and found the basket with the charcoal woman's little boy. He brought the child to the queen and said, "Look what I found in the river. This will be our son."

The queen was overjoyed and ordered a little gold finger to be made for the child.

In time the boy grew into a manly young prince. When he reached the age of twenty, the king and queen took him aside for a talk. They told him how he had been found in the river and how they had come to love him as their own flesh and blood and had made him their heir.

The prince adored the king and the queen. But now he began wishing he could find his real parents. He wanted to help them, and the thought that they might be poor, suffering somewhere, made him sad.

"What's troubling you?" asked the king.

"Sire, you know how much I love you. But I must search the kingdom for my parents. I'm sure I can find them. When I do, I'll bring them home with me, and there'll be happiness all around."

The king consulted with the queen. They ended up giving permission for the search and sent the prince off with an escort of twenty knights and twenty squires.

The prince was received with open arms in all the towns he rode through. Yet he himself was sad. His parents were nowhere to be found. At last he reached the town where the noblewoman lived and took lodgings at an inn across the street from her castle. The first thing he noticed was the sign on the castle gate: WHAT GOD MADE, I DESTROYED. He asked at the inn what the sign might mean, but no one could tell him.

That afternoon, as he stood at his window staring at the inscription, a radiant young beauty appeared on one of the castle balconies. The prince was dazzled. "Who is she?" he asked. "Milady's daughter," he was told.

His heart leaped. Her ladyship had invited him to the castle that evening for a reception in his honor. Naturally he would be introduced to her daughter.

The hour arrived, and when the daughter met the prince she fell in love with him just as he had fallen in love with her, for as I have said, he was handsome and manly.

And with everything else this prince was naturally good. He mingled not only with the guests but with the servants. When he talked with the old retainer who had set him afloat on the river, he happened to ask, "Tell me, what is the meaning of that sign at the castle gate?" Having noticed the prince's gold finger, the servant knew without asking that he was speaking to the son of the charcoal woman.

"I'll explain," he said, "if you promise to keep this quiet." When the story had been told, the two made plans to meet the following morning. "Wait for me at the edge of the woods," said the prince, "then take me to the charcoal woman's hut. But don't tell a soul, do you hear?"

"I hear," said the old retainer.

The next morning, when the charcoal woman saw the two men approaching, she went up to them warily and asked, "What do you want?" The prince said, "Madam, remember the little son, who was taken from you at birth? I am that son." The poor woman couldn't speak. She threw her arms around the prince. "But don't tell a soul," he said. "Wait here until I send for you."

The prince returned to the castle to ask the noblewoman for her daughter's hand in marriage. The answer was an immediate yes. It had been her ladyship's dream for her daughter to marry the royal heir and become his princess.

On the day of the wedding a mysterious guest arrived, heavily veiled. When the ceremony was over, the prince said, "Madam, remove your veil." And there she stood, the charcoal woman, face to face with her son's new mother-in-law. "And this," said the charcoal woman, "is the son you tore from my arms. God saved him from death."

Her ladyship, hearing the truth, choked on her own rage and fell over dead. The princess at first was sad, for this was her mother. But she dried her tears, and she and the prince, together with the king and the queen—and the charcoal woman—lived happily from that day on.

Cuba

≥ 51. The Enchanted Cow ⪇

If you learn it you'll know it, so listen and learn how to tell it; now, don't pick the fig until it's big; if you want a pear you'll need a ladder; and if you'd like a melon, marry a man with a big nose.

There was a woman called Dolores who had two children, a boy, twelve, whose name was Joaquín, and a baby girl, Chabelita. Dolores had had a husband, but not now.

And such a good-looking, hardworking, honorable husband! But one day, not long before Chabelita was born, this husband went off to the fair in Chillán to sell a fatted cow and never came back. The cow showed up the following day with a rope caught in its horns and its hide all wet. The husband, they thought, must have drowned crossing the river, and the cow somehow got away. But when they looked for the body, they found nothing.

A few days later some workmen mentioned they'd seen the husband and a woman who lived near the river, riding off together on a horse. This woman was the one they called the Lost Soul, because she had commerce with the Devil, it was said, and at night you could hear singing and carrying on at her ranch.

In spite of it, Dolores could not believe that her Pancho, for that was his name, would leave his family and run off with another woman. But how could she argue? Her husband was gone without a trace. Originally she'd come from a small village near Constitución, so she decided to go back there with her son and her newborn baby. She sold off what little land she had, and the few animals, keeping only the cow that had come home that day from the river. She loved this cow. When it looked her in the eye, it seemed human. Besides, it gave plenty of rich milk, and she was using it to feed Chabelita.

With the money she'd gotten from the sale, she bought a little farm not far from her old home village, close to the sea. She could gather shellfish to make ends meet, and with the milk from the cow there would be cheese. Joaquín helped, too, watching after his little sister.

One day while his mother was in the village, Joaquín decided to take the baby for a bath in the ocean. He picked her up in his arms and waded in. In a flash a giant wave pulled him head over heels, and what happened to the baby he had no idea. When he could breathe again, he let out with a scream, then plunged into the water. But there was no sign of his baby sister. Wild with grief, he fell down on the beach and sobbed.

Suddenly he heard his name called. He raised his head, and there was the cow, speaking to him with a human voice. It said, "I knew this was going to happen. It was the same with your father. He tried to cross the river and that woman came after him. She's a witch, you know, and the water spirits are her in-laws. She used her wicked arts against him and doomed him. Now she's got the baby. You'll be next, unless you do what I'm about to tell you."

"And what would that be?"

"You must take your knife and kill me, then skin me immediately. Spread the hide on the water, and it will take you over the waves. Be sure to hang on to the tail. If you find yourself in danger, pluck one of my tail hairs and it will be your salvation. And don't forget: take out my eyes and put them in your pocket. They're powerful. They'll let you see through water and earth, even mountains and stone walls."

The boy followed these instructions, and before he knew it he was gliding over the waves. When he was far from shore, hundreds of fish started snapping at the hooves of the cowhide, threatening to drag it to the bottom of the sea. But he remembered what the cow had told him, plucked a hair from the tail, and when it turned into a hefty oar he clouted the fish until they were all floating bottom side up.

Night came fast, dark and gloomy. But he took one of the cow's eyes out of his pocket and gazed into the water. Far below he could see rocks, fish, monsters of the deep, and old shipwrecks. There was not a thing in his way, however, and with the eyeball close at hand he sailed on through the night.

When morning came, a flock of black birds larger than condors came swooping down to land on the cowhide. Before they could sink it, he pulled another hair from the tail, and when he looked at it a second time it was a loaded blunderbuss. He pulled the trigger, and some of the birds flew off screaming. Others dropped to the water, and their blood turned the ocean red.

Another couple of hours and icebergs came into view. In what seemed no more than a few moments they were on top of him. In his haste to pluck a hair he yanked nearly the whole tuft from the end of the tail. As he threw the tuft at the icebergs, the hairs burst into flames. The ice melted, and the cowhide sped on its way.

Finally, with one of the eyeballs as his telescope he spotted an island on the horizon. In the middle of the island was a castle surrounded by walls as high as mountains. He thought, "My little sister's there." And as the cowhide landed, he adjusted the eyeball and looked through the castle walls. There was an enormous room with a column of black marble in the center. Chained to the column was a man; and close by, a pan of live coals. Bending over the coals was that woman they said had stolen his father. She clutched a baby in one hand and a butcher knife in the other, ready to skin the baby. She seemed to be talking to the man, who turned his face away as if he didn't want to see what she would do.

Without wasting a second, Joaquín snatched the remaining hairs from the cow's tail and put them in his pocket. He laid one of them against the wall, and it became a ladder. Up he climbed, until he reached a window. With a single bound he jumped through the window, landing next to the woman. Then he tore the knife from her hand and gave her a whack that sent her rolling across the floor.

He picked up the baby and untied the prisoner, who was none other than his own father, so thin and pale he seemed more like a skeleton than a live man. Then with one of the cow's eyes Joaquín peered into the black marble column. He saw a staircase leading downward. He found the door, opened it, and descended into a treasure cave. He and his father filled their pockets with gold and precious stones, then followed the winding passageway out to the sea. They jumped onto the cowhide and were pushed home in no time by the hands of invisible beings.

Dolores was on the beach waiting for them. She'd picked up a scent in the wind. And when she saw her lost husband and her two children, she threw her arms around them and cried for joy. Her husband explained how the Lost Soul had carried him off by speaking a few magic words and how she had tied him up in her castle when he refused to marry her.

While his father was telling the story, Joaquín was running back and forth on the beach, gathering up the cowhide and the cow's bones. He bundled them all together and put the eyes back in the sockets. Then he reached into his pocket and pulled out one last hair from the cow's tail. He struck a match to burn the hair but burned his fingers instead and dropped the match. It fell on the hide, and the cow stood up. It was as plump and healthy as ever and started ambling home.

With a portion of the gold and jewels they'd stuffed in their pockets, Joaquín's father bought a ranch, lots of animals, and everything else you'd need to be rich. They all lived happily till the day they died—and here we are, still waiting for our luck to change.

My tale is done, and the wind blows it off. When the wind brings it back, I'll tell it again.

Chile / Magdalena Muñoz

➲ 52. Judas's Ear ⋐

There was a young wife who had a son. When her husband died she left the boy with his grandmother and went off to see the world. Arriving at the edge of a forest, she changed into men's clothing and fell in with a couple of hunters who had a camp. They invited her to join them. "Come work with us," they said. They had no idea she was a woman.

One day when it was the young widow's turn to stay back and prepare the meal, they warned her, "There's someone who keeps coming here spilling the food while we're off hunting. We don't know who it is."

"I'll keep an eye out," said the widow. When the men had gone, an old woman came into the camp and began knocking over bowls, spilling food left and right. The young widow picked up a club and chased her off. When the two hunters returned, the widow said, "It was an old woman. Just look at the mess she left! When I tried to catch her, she ran down a hole."

"We'll have to pull her out, but how?" said one of the men.

"We'll cut a hide into strips, make a towline," said the other, "and go down hand over hand."

But the one who tried it first got cold feet as soon as he reached the bottom of the hole, and he came shinnying back up the rope as fast as his hands and knees would take him. The same thing happened to the second man.

"What did you see down there?" asked the widow.

"A little white light," said the man. "It scared me out of my wits."

The widow picked up her club and shinnied down the rope. There was the light. She waited a moment. Nothing happened. She moved forward slowly. What should she find but three shining maidens! As she approached, the maidens drew back in fear. One of them cried out, "Stay where you are! Can't you see we're under a spell? We're prisoners of Judas himself, and his old wife looks after us and brings us food."

"Stop worrying," said the widow. "I'll get you out of here if it costs me my life."

"And how will you do it, sir? We were kidnapped by Judas, who is king of the underworld, and even though our father is king of the country above, he hasn't been able to set us free."

"Come with me," said the widow. She led the princesses to the towline, and all three of them shinnied to the top. When the two hunters saw the shining princesses, they were smitten. "Who gets which one?" "We'll decide that later!" And they yanked the rope out of the hole before the princesses' rescuer could even think of climbing back up.

Down below the widow turned around and saw the old woman coming after her. "Stop, thief! You've stolen our princesses!" In reply the widow lifted her club and with one blow reduced the old crone to a pool of blood.

Judas appeared in an instant, snorting and bellowing. "I smell blood! Hand me my meal, or I'll eat you alive!" The widow brought down her club a second time. Judas dodged, and the blow knocked off one ear. She pulled out her rosary and threw it around his neck. He fell backwards, and the rosary pinned him to the ground.

"Set me free immediately!"

"I'm not the one who's holding you down," she replied. "But I can help you if you'll get me out of here."

"It's a promise. King's honor."

She took back her rosary, stood on his shoulders, and was just tall enough to crawl out of the hole.

"Now give me back my ear!"

"Not a chance! I'll keep *that* for good luck." And she headed straight for the city, still in men's clothes. Her son, who was living in town with his grandmother, had no idea his mother had arrived. As for the two selfish hunters, they themselves were in the king's city, now married to the king's two older daughters and living like princes. And the youngest princess? She could do nothing but wait for her rescuer, hoping that he—as she thought—would arrive before long to ask for her hand.

When the widow got to the palace and asked to see the king, the guards paid no attention to her. The young princess, however, was at the window and saw the one she had been waiting for. She went to the king and announced grandly, "My husband is here. Let him in."

The king gave the order, and when the widow came before him, still in her manly outfit, the king said, "Is it you, who broke the spell and freed the three princesses?" The hunters, who were now the king's sons-in-law, were called forward as witnesses. They had no choice but to tell the truth. What else could they say when the widow produced the ear? Then she spoke up, "Your Majesty, I have a son who is flesh of my flesh. Let him be the one to marry the princess."

"What? A red-blooded man like yourself refusing to marry my daughter? You won her fair and square. She's yours."

"Your Majesty, I cannot marry a woman."

"Why not?"

"Because I am a woman."

"You, who swung the war club that defeated King Judas?"

"Never mind. I am a woman."

"Give me your word on pain of death."

"You have my word."

"Then bring me your son," said the king. "He'll marry the princess, and I'll make him my heir."

The widow's son was brought to the palace at once. The young princess liked him from the first moment, and they were married without delay. The king called the widow to one side, "Madam, shall I have those traitors put to death? The ones who left you in the cave and came rushing to marry my poor daughters?"

"Not at all," said the widow. "They were disloyal to me, as you say, but they are happily married now. For the princesses' sake let's just forget it. After all, the princesses are not to blame." The king agreed. Then he said to the widow, "Next time there's a war, I'll make you captain of all my armies!" And mind you,

*This tale will last if it's true;
If it's just a tale, it's through.*

New Mexico / Sixto Chávez

➣ 53. Good Is Repaid with Evil ⇐

While out walking with his son one day a man saw a snake trying to get into its burrow. A branch had pinned it to the ground and it couldn't move. The boy started to free it. But the father stopped him and said, "Don't! Snakes are bad neighbors. One little bite, if it gets the chance, and we'll be finished."

The boy paid no attention and gave the snake its freedom, and when the snake rushed at the boy to bite him, the father cried, "Snake, my friend! How can you bite him, when he's just saved you?"

"Don't you know?" replied the snake. "I'm repaying good with evil like everyone else. Isn't that the rule?"

The snake kept insisting. But the boy and his father stood back. A burro was passing by at that moment, and they asked for its judgment. The burro turned to the snake and said, "Bite! Good is repaid with evil. That's the rule. The same thing happened to me. After I'd worked all my life my master stopped feeding me and turned me out."

The snake was just ready to bite, when the boy's father saw a horse coming down the trail. He called to it and asked for its judgment. The horse rendered the same verdict as the burro. And so did a dog who came along later.

The snake was just at the point of biting when the father, who still hadn't given up, appealed to a fox who happened by. He explained the case in a whisper and said, "Friend fox, be the judge. If you save my son, I'll reward you with a pair of fat chickens I've got at my ranch."

"Don't worry," said the fox. "I'll be impartial." And with his well-known gifts of persuasion the fox convinced the snake to drop the matter completely. Inch by inch the snake backed away. "Wonderful," said the man. "Now let's be on our way and I'll pay you what I promised."

When the man got home, he said to his wife, "If it hadn't been for our friend the fox, we wouldn't be alive," and he told her all that had happened. "I promised our two fattest chickens."

There was the fox waiting on top of the woodpile. "What? Our two fattest chickens?" The wife reached for a sack, stuffed their meanest dog inside, and handed it over. The fox ran off as fast as it could. And as it took to the road, it kept turning over in its mind, "What they tell you is true. Good is repaid with evil."

Venezuela

➢ 54. The Fisherman's Daughter ◁

A man and a woman were married, and let me tell you they were poor. Every morning the man went fishing and would come back with no more than enough to get through one more day.

Then one time he pulled up his net and there was nothing at all, not a single fish. He heard a voice from the depths, "Promise to bring me the one who greets you lovingly when you arrive home, and I'll give you as many fish as you want."

The man thought, "Couldn't it mean my little dog, who always runs from the house and jumps up to greet me when I come with my catch?" Three times the voice called from below. Hearing it for the third time, the man said, "Very well, I'll bring you what you ask. Where shall I find you?"

"Right here!" said the voice. Then he cast his net again, and when he pulled it up it was filled with fish. He went home contented.

When he got within sight of his house, his little daughter ran out to greet him. "Papa, you're home!" And she gave him a hug.

"Ay!" he said. "If only you knew, you wouldn't hug me!" He entered the house, and his wife asked, "Why are you crying?"

"If you knew, you wouldn't ask." He kept quiet while his wife cooked the fish. When dinner was ready, he said, "I'm not hungry."

"Tell me why not?"

He repeated, "If you knew, you wouldn't ask."

"Tell me!" The husband was crying. Finally he said, "I couldn't catch a thing. My net was empty, but a voice promised me fish if I'd pay for it with the one who greets me lovingly. And when I got home, who should greet me with a hug but our own little daughter!"

The wife said, "You made a promise. Now you must do what the Lord requires."

The man had three days to comply. On the third day they dressed their daughter nicely and the father took her to the deep place in the river where he had heard the voice. He called out, "Here's the treasure you wanted."

"Bring her to my house in the middle of the river," came the answer, "and leave her there."

They went into the water and found a house with chairs and tables and everything else a home should have. The man said, "Daughter, I must leave you now." She was pleased with what she saw. "Very well," she said, and he shut the door and went away. Night came.

When it was time to light the lamps, the lamps were lit. At suppertime the supper appeared, at bedtime the hammock was slung. Not a soul could be seen. Then all on their own the lights went out.

When morning came, breakfast appeared, but there was not a living soul. Yet the table was set. That night, when the lights went out again, a man's voice called to her, "There's a louse on the top of my head. Come kill it." The girl got up, found the louse, and began rumpling the man's hair. "That's enough! Go back to bed now." After all, she was still just a child.

On a different night, the man said again, "There's a louse on my head, come look for it." She began rumpling his hair, then touched him farther down on his face and felt something strange and woolly. In the dark she could hardly tell what it was.

Another night he said, "In the morning you will find a horse all saddled, waiting for you. You must go to your parents. But don't let them touch you."

"As you wish."

"And here, take this money for your father."

The next day, when she arrived at her parents' house, her mother reached out to embrace her, but the girl shrank back. "Get down from your horse and come in," they said. She answered, "No, I must go back now." They were astounded to see that she had become a young woman. She handed them the money and rode away.

When she got back, she dismounted. She did not see who led the horse away or who unsaddled it. Night came.

When the lights went out, someone entered her room, just as before, and she began rumpling his hair. "Did you do as I told you?"

"I did. And no one touched me."

"Good," he said. "Now on Sunday you'll go again." And she did, and all went well. Then one night, when she had begun to rumple his hair, her hand grazed his body and she felt fish scales. "Oh my!" she thought. "He's a charmed creature!"

He read her thoughts and said, "In the morning you must go to your parents again. But don't bring anything back with you."

"As you wish."

The next day, when she arrived at her parents' house, she allowed them to embrace her. She went inside, and the three of them sat there eating, smoking, and drinking. As she was about to leave, she said, "Mama, let me have a box of matches and a candle." She tucked them into her bag and rode off.

That night she rumpled the creature's hair as usual, and he relaxed into sleep. She waited until his breathing became regular, then said to herself, "Now I will see what he looks like." She struck a match, and there before her was a man, but only from the waist up. His lower half was a fish. He awoke and gave her a fright, "I've caught you, you wretch! I told you not to bring anything from home, and here you are with matches. Your easy days in this house are finished. You'll soon know what hard labor is. No breakfast tomorrow. Instead there'll be trousers, a shirt, a hat, sandals, and a machete."

In the morning she found the clothes laid out on the table. She was given an order: "Put them on. For your disobedience you must go to the king's palace and ask for work. Take the road on your right." She did as she was ordered and left the house.

When she came before the king, she saw that he was not an old man but still young. She greeted him, and he answered her tenderly, "What can I do for you?"

"I'm looking for work."

"My pleasure," said the king. He could see that she was not a man but a woman in men's clothing. Everything about her was womanly. She was given a room.

In the morning she asked, "Now what must I do?"

"Pay close attention," said the king, "I'm going to give you a task. You will find it hard because of the traveling and the long distance. But here it is: I must have a strand of hair from the mother of all the animals."

She started out, with no idea which way to go. After many hours she met an old woman and a little boy. She herself was headed up the road, the old woman was coming down.

"Where are you headed, my dear?" asked the old woman.

"To get a strand of hair from the mother of all the animals."

"That isn't hard. I can help you," said the woman. "And since I see you are carrying food and water, could you let me have a little for myself and my child?"

"Yes, of course," she replied. And when they had taken the water and eaten the food, the old woman said, "You see this mountain? When you get to the top you will find the mother of all the animals. A meadow is there. If it's covered with grass, the mother is asleep. Step on her without fear, and pick one strand. But if the meadow is bare, keep away. It will mean she's awake."

When the young woman reached the meadow, it was covered with grass. She picked one strand, rolled it up, and came away.

The king was delighted when he saw what she had brought and began to unroll it. It unrolled and unrolled, making a heap that kept on growing. It had no end. The strand was infinitely long.

"What ever can I pay you?" cried the king.

"It's up to you."

He gave her thousands and thousands of pesos. A nice little sum! "Now you're free to work elsewhere," he said. And off she went, carrying the money.

On the road she met another old woman. Really the same old woman as before. And she said, "I'm lost! How do I get home to my mother and father?"

"Don't worry about a thing," said the little old woman. "Just take this wand and hold it in front of you as you walk along. Whenever you're lost, say, 'Little wand, little wand, by the power that's yours and that God allows you, show me the way to go home.' It will take you directly."

And so it did. She pointed it straight ahead until she reached her own house. And there was her mother, happy to see her, and her father, too. Although she was dressed as a man, they knew her face. Her mother complained, "What are these men's clothes?" She took them off, put on the clothes she had worn before, and was their daughter again. With the money she'd brought they were rich. They set themselves up as storekeepers and had whatever they wanted from that time on.

Colombia

PART SIX

⇒ 55. In the Beginning ⇐

Ah, think of it, friends!

Once there was nothing to be seen, once there was only water.

At last God spoke: "This water must be dried away. Let the world grow."

And so the world grew, but still there were no mountains.

Again God spoke: "Tomorrow is a day of work. Monday. Let us begin our work. We will build the mountains, so the plants can grow."

It was done.

The second day, Tuesday. More work! God made the channels where all the water would run; river and stream.

The third day, Wednesday. God shaped the clouds. "Let the rivers fill with water. Let the plants be born."

The fourth day, Thursday. Fishes it was that God made. Now the water has animals, now the water is clean.

Friday, the fifth day. God built the mountainsides.

Saturday, the sixth day. All the animals of the world He made, and man.

The seventh day, Sunday. Now God spoke: "Now our work is over. Let us hold a Mass. Let us go to the church to pray. So the work we have done will last through all the many thousands of years that are still to come on this earth. And just so shall our sons, who come the day of to-morrow, do as we are doing now."

Here ended the work of God.

Mexico (Mazatec) / Melchor García

⮞ 56. How the First People Were Made ⮜

The true God took up one ounce of earth and began to work it. "What are you doing?" asked God's sister.

God answered, "Something that you may not know more about than I know." He made an image in the shape of a man and set it to dry. He blessed it with the sign of the cross, and it changed into a man.

"What were you doing?" asked God.

The man answered, "I was sleeping."

God gave him a pick and a shovel and took him to a spring and told him to make a ditch. The man dug the ditch, and water flowed through the ditch into a garden that God had made. In a little time the garden began to give fruit.

Then God made an oven. He made images of oxen in clay and put them into the oven. When he took them out they had turned into live animals. God said to San Lucas, "You will be the patron saint of animals, so they will abound."

San Lucas said, "If you want them to abound, you will have to make a cow." God agreed to this and gave all the animals to San Lucas. And so San Lucas is the patron of the animals. And in time the animals abounded.

The man began to cultivate his field. San Javier would go to the field to take him a breakfast of tortillas, and one day the man did not want to eat. God asked San Lucas and San Javier why the man was not eating.

San Javier said the man would not eat because he wanted a wife. God said, "I will give him a wife, but today I will not send him any food."

San Miguel went to the man and said that God agreed to give him a wife but that today he would not send him any food. The man said that would be all right. The man went to sleep in his field and as he was sleeping God came and opened his left side and took out a rib and put it alongside the man, and when the man awoke his arm was around the woman.

Now when you die, there stands San Miguel with a balance. The dead who weigh one ounce go to heaven, and the dead who weigh more than one ounce go to hell.

Mexico (Zapotec) / Miguel Mendez

➣ 57. Adam's Rib ⪦

Said God, "You are the first man. Since I am very busy, you are going to take care of the garden that I have planted."

"Very well," said the man. But after a few days he said to God, "Well, I am not able to cook, because I spend all my time working in the garden. If you would listen to me, I would like a cook to prepare my food."

"It can be done," said God. "Next Friday at noon knock on your rib seven times and in this way a cook will appear."

The man returned and did as he was told, but no cook appeared. The man was very sad. Then God appeared and said, "Knock again." The man began to knock on his ribs. Said God, "Now you see a woman is coming out. She is going to be your wife."

"But I only wanted a cook," replied the man.

Mexico (Popoluca) / Leandro Pérez

➣58. Adam and Eve and Their Children⪦

God created the sun and the moon and the stars and the world. He created man and called him Adam. But Adam was not satisfied and God made Eve from one of his ribs. Then he put Adam and Eve in the Garden. He told them not to eat of the fruit of a certain tree. The serpent tempted Eve and they ate. God then told Adam that they had to work now and that they had to die. And he told Eve that she had to give birth to her children with pain.

And Eve had twenty-four children. When they grew up, God told Eve to bring out the children to be baptized. And Eve took only twelve children to be baptized. She was ashamed and hid the other twelve in a cave. So God baptized only twelve of the children.

From the twelve that were baptized came all the white people. And from the twelve that Eve hid in the cave and that were not baptized came the Indians. When God found out that Eve had hidden them in a cave he put them in Mount Blanca in Colorado. From there the Indians came out later and went to the different pueblos. Some went to Taos, some went to Isleta, some to Sandía, others to San Juan, and others to Santa Clara and Laguna and the other pueblos.

New Mexico (Isleta)

⇒ 59. God's Letter to Noéh ⇐

There was a man called Noéh who was much respected by the people. As Noéh was a Catholic he went to church. He did not forget God, nor was he forsaken by God.

God sent a letter to Noéh. The angel came down from the sky and gave it to him, at seven in the evening. The letter said that if the people did not go to church God was going to put an end to the world. The people were unmannerly and gross. Noéh was to hold a meeting so that all might hear that if they did not go to Mass, God would put an end to the world.

Sunday morning Noéh went with his letter to the town secretary, who was busily writing. All assembled to hear what Noéh had to say—to hear the letter. The secretary read from the letter Noéh had brought,

"God says you are to hold Mass and say the rosary. If not, Holy God will put an end to the world."

They laughed. "Noéh is crazy!" They did not believe God had sent the letter. "Noéh himself has sent the letter. He is crazy. Let us kill him."

Noéh said, "I am going now. I will explain to God that you do not believe what he says." At seven that night the angel came again. The angel was Gabriel. He asked, "What do the townspeople say?"

"They are going to kill me because I am crazy. They do not believe what the letter says."

"Very well, go and see them again, and if they still do not believe, God will put an end to the world, next week."

Mexico (Zapotec) / Agustín Santiago

⪼ 60. God Chooses Noah ⪻

Father God, when he was old, went from house to house, asking the farmers, "What work do you do? What do you plant, my children?"

There was one who answered contemptuously, "I'm planting stones." Father God went on his way. The next day, where there had been corn, there were stones all over the field. The repentant farmer said to himself, "It was the Holy One who came to my house."

The old Father journeyed on. He came to another of our ancestors, and he asked, "What do you plant, my child?"

The man answered rudely, "I plant phalluses." The next morning when the man awoke, his corn plants had been changed into phallic stones. He said to himself, "It was the Holy One who was here."

The Father went on. He asked a third man, "What work do you do?"

"I plant a little corn and a few beans. Would you like some meat broth to drink?"

"Yes, my son," said the Holy One. "I will take it." The farmer gave him a dish of broth. Then God said, "Do you have room for me to spend the night?"

"Yes, I would be glad."

"My child, I hope you will not be disgusted," said the Old One. "I am sick with a rash."

"Father, don't worry," said the farmer. "I will nurse you."

"Then stay here," said the Father. "Don't go out to your field."

When he had nursed him back to health, three days had passed, and Father God said, "Your field is already planted. The corn is in ear and the little beans are forming."

"I don't believe it," cried the man.

"Go see for yourself."

The farmer ran to the field and saw the new ears and the beans. When he returned to the house, Father God had already gone. The farmer said to his wife, "Where is he?"

"He just left."

"Then shake the bed!" They did, and out came a little package filled with money. They ran after the Father to tell him he had left his money.

"My son, my daughter," said the Old One. "I left it for you, so you could buy something."

"Thank the Lord!"

"Do me a favor," said the Old One. "The Devil is following me. When he comes, tell him it was three years ago that I passed this way."

Then Satan arrived. "Where is he?" he asked. "What road did he take?" The farmer pointed in the opposite direction. Satan went on. The farmer continued his work in the field. The days came, the days went.

Mexico (Mixe) / Atanasio de Dios

⮞ 61. The Flood ⮜

The Old One allowed one man to be in the world, and he said to him, "My son, this is not the time to work at chores. The whole world is going to be destroyed. The land will become water." He also said, "Plant the seed of the cedar tree, and in the morning look for a carpenter to make a big canoe with a lid. Get into it with all your family and seal yourself inside."

In one night, quickly, quickly, the cedar grew up. Wind blew, and the leaves of the tree rustled. From the tree the carpenter made a big canoe.

Rain came at midnight. In the night the rain filled the earth with water, and with the water the canoe rose to the sky. The earth and the world were destroyed. The land became water.

Then the water subsided, and the world became dry. There were new people. The Old One allowed others, new people, to exist.

The man came out of the canoe, caught fish, and ate them.

The Old One had said, "You must not make fire."

But up above, the Old One was smelling fire. He came down to see who had made the fire, asking, "Where is this fire smell?"

When the Old One arrived, he said, "Who gave you permission to catch fish?

"And you were not to make fire," said the Old One, "yet you are doing it. I told you not to make fire, you fool. Now you will have to serve as an example for the new people." And the Old One hit him over the head.

"Because you did not listen, I am going to change you into a howler monkey."

Mixe (Mexico) / Serapia Ricarda

⇒ 62. A Prophetic Dream ⇐

And there was a woman who had planted many flowers, of every kind. And many times people arrived who wanted to take her flowers to decorate their homes.

One day it was a little girl who came—she wanted a gardenia. Well, quickly the woman went to cut it. But on the bush was growing a flower in the shape of a finger. Out from under the fingernail came words.

"Do not touch me," said the flower.

How that woman ran!

Soon after arrived another person who also wanted a flower. Well, this time it was a face she found there. And that face, too, told her not to come near. Again the woman—don't think she hung around there! Well, she told everybody that *she* was not going to cut that flower, for it was a person who was sprouting there. And a third time she went, but now she could see even its chest.

This same day she had a dream. The dream told her that the person who is being born is called "God Almighty." So she said to her husband, "Listen to me, I slept and I dreamt, and my dream told me that God is coming to Earth."

He became very angry, her husband. "Ha! It's God who's coming, is it? You think that? What if you aren't fooling me? What if it isn't your lover who is coming?"

"And you, hear what I say. What if it be true? What if it be true that it is God, then only you will be speaking evil," said his wife.

Now a fourth person arrives to ask for a flower. She goes again, but the bush is bare, there is no one. Now God is among his people, the angels, telling what will come to pass in the world.

Mexico (Mazatec) / Melchor García

⇒ 63. The White Lily ⇐

My grandmother told me this story. How did it go? The dear virgin mother was one of three sisters. Of the other two, one was a recluse who devoted her life to prayer, and the other was a matchmaker.

When the virgin mother was ready for marriage, suitors came to look her over. But no one chose her. People kept saying, "Who's missing? Who's missing?" No one wanted to marry the virgin mother. Finally someone said, "Joseph is missing," and they went to look for him. Someone brought him around, and when he came forward, he threw a white lily against the virgin's breast. Then he turned and ran away.

After a while he came back, and the two were married. One day, when they had been living together for some time, Joseph gave Mary a hug. Just as he did that, he felt a baby stirring inside her body. He realized what it was and said, "This isn't my son, this isn't my daughter. Whose child is inside you? It can't be mine."

Knowing that he could not be the father, he packed his carpenter's tools on his burro and went away, leaving the virgin mother.

Ecuador (Quichua)

⇒ 64. The Night in the Stable ⇐

Jesus Christ was born in the night in Jerusalem, as we know. His parents were St. Joseph and the Virgin Mary. They were merchants, and they traveled together. They went from house to house asking rich people to give them lodgings, but the people refused because they thought Joseph and Mary were thieves.

Eventually they came to the house of a rich man who said they could not stay with him, but if they wanted they could spend the night in the stable where the sheep, cows, and other animals were kept with their herders. So that's where they went.

At about three o'clock in the morning, or a little later, when the morning star came out, Mary gave birth to a boy who had stars on his palms and forehead. He lighted up the world.

All the herders came to look at the child, and the owner of the house came, too.

That night it snowed very hard, and the child was so cold he stiffened as if dead. The herders ran to take care of their animals. But the sheep and the cows breathed on the child's body and warmed it, and the child revived. Then Jesus blessed these animals. But the horses and mules, when they had come close to the child to look at him, had not believed that this could be God. Instead of breathing on him to warm him up, they broke wind. God was angry with the horses and mules and said they would never be favored, would never be eaten by humans, and would have to serve as beasts of burden from that time on.

Guatemala (Quiché Maya) / Tomás Ventura Calel

⋙ 65. When Morning Came ⋘

I. WHY DID IT DAWN?

When Jesus was born, it was dark in the stable. Many came together and began looking for him.

It was dark, very dark. And why did it dawn? He was appearing. It was dawning. He was appearing beautifully; he was shining as he came. But he appeared down there, and they said, here is where he is. There he came, rising. They all saw him. Many had gathered, and they all saw him. Behold it was dawning, it was dawning, it was dawning until it dawned completely.

Mexico (Nahua)

II. THAT WAS THE PRINCIPAL DAY

Our Lord was born now.

So the next day, they saw the man who wouldn't lend his house, crying, "Oh, I thought it was a beggar who spent the night," he said the next morning.

They saw now that it was Our Lord. With priests and bishops they went to look, to watch them celebrate a wonderful fiesta on the principal day, Christmas. So it's called Christmas. You see, when morning came they had a fiesta. The Christ Child was born already by morning time. When morning came the baby was already born. But he wasn't a human being. He was Our Lord.

Then when they saw him, they held a wonderful fiesta, when morning came. There was music and everything. Yes, indeed! Now that was the principal day, Christmas. It's been just the same ever since, just like it is now.

Mexico (Tzotzil Maya) / Manvel K'obyox

⇒ 66. Three Kings ⇐

When Jesus was born three kings came to visit him and adore him. One was an American, the other was a Mexican, the last was an Indian.

When they arrived, all three knelt and worshipped the child Jesus. Then each gave Jesus a present. The American king gave money. The Mexican king gave Jesus some swaddling clothes. And the Indian king, who was very poor, had nothing to give, so he danced before Jesus.

Then Jesus told them he would grant each a gift and asked what they wanted. The American king said he wanted to be smart and have power. And Jesus granted his wish. For that reason Americans are powerful.

When he asked the Mexican king what he wanted, he said he wished to believe in the saints and pray. And for that reason Mexicans believe in the saints and pray.

Lastly Jesus asked the Indian king what he wanted, and the Indian king said he was very poor and humble and would take whatever Jesus would let him have. So Jesus gave him seeds of corn and wheat and melons and other fruits. And that's why Indians have to work always to live.

New Mexico (Isleta)

༂ 67. The Christ Child as Trickster ༃

Time passed and the child Jesus was growing. One day when he was about four years old he disappeared from the virgin mother's poor little hut. No one knew where he had gone. They hunted and couldn't find him. They looked everywhere. Suddenly he spoke up and said to the virgin mother, "Ha! Where do you think I've been? The whole time you were looking for me I was right at your side."

Not long after that, the little boy's father got a contract to build a house. It was work he needed, so the virgin mother could buy food for the family. While he was working on the house, he opened a sack of cement. He hadn't mixed it yet when the child poured out the water and let it run over the cement. "You little devil, look what you've done," said Joseph. "You've ruined the cement."

But when the father turned his back for a moment, the child fixed it, and the cement was dry again, exactly as it had been before.

Another time, when the house that Joseph was building was partly finished, they invited him to come in and eat. They called the little boy, too. "Come on, child. Come eat." Now, in the yard there were a dozen chicks, and the child decided to bring these with him. He killed them all and came into the house with the chicks wrapped in his poncho. When he dumped them out on the floor, the people cried, "Look what you've done, you little devil! You'll have to pay for these."

He just stood there laughing. Then he said, "All right, throw them out. I'll pay you for them."

He went back outside and gathered them into a heap. While the people on the inside were having their dinner, the chicks on the outside were coming back to life. The little boy put them into his poncho again and brought them back into the house. The chicks were peeping.

"Hail Mary! A miracle!" they said. But the child Jesus just laughed.

After the meal he went back out again. While his father was taking measurements for the upper stories of the house, he picked up a saw and cut all the beams into bits and pieces. "You little devil, what have you done? All those beams were cut to length and ready to be nailed. Now what will I do? I don't have the money to replace them. Here I am working to make myself poor!"

Then the child picked up the bits and pieces and made the beams whole again.

Ecuador (Quichua)

⮞ 68. Christ Saved by the Firefly ⮜

When Jesus Christ was a prisoner, they thought he was smoking in jail. They thought they saw the end of his lighted cigar. But it was not he, it was the firefly, and Jesus Christ had already fled.

Cakchiquel Maya (Guatemala) / Matias Sicajan

⇝ 69. Christ Betrayed by Snails ⇜

He came to a river and crossed over. But as he was crossing the river, he stepped on freshwater snails. When the ones who were chasing him reached the river's edge and could not see which way he had gone, they questioned the snails. The snails replied, "Don't you see that he has trampled on us and turned us over?"

Belize (Kekchi Maya)

⇝ 70. Christ Betrayed by the Magpie-jay ⇜

Jesus hid under some banana trees. "That's him, he's near now," said the ones who were chasing him. The magpie-jay was there. He was a human once. "Is it Our Lord you're looking for? He's here," said the magpie-jay. "Seize him! He's here now." Then they captured Our Lord. They made him carry a cross.

Mexico (Tzotzil Maya) / Romin Teratol

⇝ 71. The Blind Man at the Cross ⇜

The soldiers came to take Christ to Calvary. Ah, friends, these thoughts are bitter to the taste.

All the townspeople were gathered together. Said Pilate to the people: "Which of the two who are bound do you want set free? One is named Barabbas, the other is the Son of God, who is surnamed Christ."

"Free Barabbas!"

Barabbas was freed. Our Lord they took to Calvary, beating him as they went. Five thousand lashes they gave him. Three times he fell, bearing the cross on his back.

Magdalene, Mary Cleopha, and the Pure Virgin saw Jesus there. Deep went their hurt. They asked the soldiers if they could wash Christ for a moment.

He came now almost stinking. Covered with worms, lice, fleas, and every kind of sore. His whole body covered with spit.

"Let us cure his sickness while we bathe him."

Then they washed him. And after he was clean, they washed his clothes, too.

But when they wiped his face, there on the cloth appeared a picture of Jesus' face. Now the soldiers were angrier than ever.

"This man has much magic!" they said.

He came to that place where he was to die.

They stripped off his clothes. They divided them amongst the whole town.

They gave him a hammer blow on his chest—even his mother, at this time, far away, was nearly killed with grief. By the blow she knew they were putting her son to death.

They spread out Christ's arms; to put each one against each arm of the cross.

They nailed him. They stood him up so that he could be seen by all.

He does not die.

At last, they bring soldiers. To shoot him.

Everyone wanted to shoot him, but Christ defended himself. Not one bullet found him.

One man alone had not taken his turn—a blind boy.

"What use is this blind man, he's only listening to what's going on, he's doing nothing," the soldiers were saying.

The soldiers gave the blind boy a spear. They showed him.

"Here is where you can spear him, right here."

"*Now,* the spear."

Pu—sh!

Sun and moon blackened.

The earth shook mightily. Many soldiers, many, fell down, nearly dead.

A drop of Jesus' blood fell. Fell into the eye of the blind boy. And he saw!

He opened his eyes—Christ.

"Ah, Father of my heart, I did not know it was you, *hombre.* If I could have seen, I could not have done this."

The blind man was pardoned.

There died Jesus.

Mexico (Mazatec) / Melchor García

⤳ 72. The Cricket, the Mole, and the Mouse ⤶

Some friends of Jesus came now, Joseph and several others. They were talking about what to do with Jesus now that he was dead.

"He is dead, we had better bury him. We don't want him to remain here. First, let's go to the king to see if he can't be buried."

And they went to the king to ask if they could lower Christ, so he would not be hanging there, gaped at by all the people.

"Well, good." The king was even pleased to have him taken down.

"For my part," says Pilate, "it hurts me, too, but it was the people's fault. Only because they said so did I do it."

When the apostles came, the Virgin was at the foot of the cross, weeping and praying. They took a white cloth, a sort of hammock, so that the Virgin could hold him to her, while they were building the coffin. They brought the coffin.

Well, now everything is ready. There is nothing more to do, but take him to the sepulcher. They sealed the coffin.

When they had finished burying him, they placed a great stone there so that he could not leave. And a soldier stood watch so that no one could come to dig him up. Everyone else left. Now all was silence.

Quiet, friends, listen carefully.

A cricket came, singing. *A pro nobi*—pray for us, the poor thing was saying, three times, four times. And this means surely now he is dead, now he cannot be wakened.

But within the sepulcher, where the corpse was, Jesus heard. He answered that he was still not dead.

"I am, I am alive, but I do not know how I am going to get out, because of that rock that is on top."

The little animal, hearing Christ's words, fled, calling out: "Don't worry, I'll be right back."

And on the way he met a mole.

"See here, where are you going, mole?"

"Why, I'm just walking along here."

"Look, friend, I went to where the body of Our Lord is. Christ has *not* died. Already he has spoken, but he doesn't know how to get out, because that stone is very large, and he isn't able to get out. Couldn't you dig just where the coffin is? I, as I haven't enough strength, can't dig."

"Sure, why not. Yes, I'm coming."

He digs, digs, digs above Christ's coffin.

Now you can almost go on the mole's road to see the coffin.

Then some other little animals came to see Christ's burial place.

A mouse came.

The mouse ran down the mole's road. With his teeth he gnawed open the coffin.

Jesus awoke and departed.

Again the earth shook with terrible force.

That soldier who was on top of the rock almost died. He was scared enough! He ran away. He said nothing.

Now, on the morning of the fourth day three women also came to Jesus' sepulcher. One, the mother of Jesus; the two others, family relations.

When Mary saw her son's tomb, the stone that had been placed there now was floating in the air, and on it was sitting an angel, like a dove.

Mary seeing this: "Why is the stone in the air? Who is on the stone? Why doesn't it fall?"

After a moment the angel spoke to Mary. "What do you come to see here?"

"Why, I come to see my son's grave. I come to leave some flowers on the fourth day." Even as our women do now.

"Well, look, Jesus is still not dead. Already he has left. Jesus can be found now at a certain place. It is best that you go to your house to give the news to the others."

Mexico (Mazatec) / Melchor García

⇒ 73. As If with Wings ⇐

Jesus departed through the air, as if with wings. He rose to Heaven. The apostles stood watching him as he rose.

On the forty-seventh day, when Jesus reached Heaven, the twelve apostles rose to Heaven, to govern until this day.

The tale is ended.

Mexico (Mazatec) / Melchor García

PART SEVEN

|||||||||||||||||||||||||

≥ 74. Slowpoke Slaughtered Four ≤

Once and twice makes thrice upon a time there was a king, and the king had a daughter who solved every riddle that was put to her. No riddle was too difficult.

The time came for the daughter to marry. The king sent out criers to spread the word that whoever brought a riddle the princess couldn't solve would become her husband and inherit the kingdom; but let her solve it and the suitor would be hanged by the neck until dead.

Since the princess was beautiful and the kingdom enormous, princes, marquises, sages, and professors from all over came courting, and all were strung up at the gallows as the princess guessed their riddles, one after another.

There was a widow living in this kingdom who had a son that had not been spoiled by the ways of the world. People were unkind and called him Juan Bobo. Juan, having heard tell of the king's proclamation, decided that he, too, would go to the palace with a riddle for the princess. His cautious mother tried to stop him. But Juan Bobo had made up his mind. At last, with a heavy heart, the mother gave her permission.

While he saddled his mare, his mother made cassava cakes for Juan to take with him. Thinking it would be better for her good-hearted son to die peaceably on the road than on the gallows in the great city, she put a dose of poison into the cakes.

Juan Bobo set out. After traveling awhile he got off his mare and lay down to nap under a mango tree. While he slept, the mare found the cassava cakes and ate them all in one gulp. The cakes killed the mare instantly. Then four crows arrived to peck at the corpse, and the crows, too, were killed.

Juan woke up, saw what had happened, and continued his journey on foot after plucking the crows and stringing them around his neck. As he passed through some woods, seven thieves waylaid him and stole the plucked crows. When the thieves ate the crows, they fell over dead.

Juan took one of the thieves' rifles and continued on, keeping an eye out for something to eat. He saw a squirrel, took aim, but missed. Instead, his shot found a rabbit that happened to be pregnant. He skinned the rabbit, then built a fire to roast it, using some newspapers that were lying nearby.

He went on. He came to a river, and as he crossed the river he looked down from the bridge and saw a dead horse with three crows on it, floating in the water.

At last he reached the palace gates and asked permission to present a riddle to the princess. When they saw him at court, they laughed, and some were stricken with pain, knowing the poor man was about to die. But Juan Bobo, unconcerned, went up to the princess and said to her with great seriousness:

> I started out on Slowpoke, and
>   Slowpoke slaughtered four; when
>   these had murdered seven more, I
>   shot at what I thought I saw and
>   killed what I couldn't see;
> The flesh I ate was not yet born,
>   though fully cooked with words;
>   and when I crossed from there to
>   here, a corpse was carrying
>   three.

The princess began to think. She had three days to solve the riddle. The first two nights she tried to get the answer by having one of her maids, and then another, go to the room where Juan was staying. The third night the princess herself slipped into Juan's bedroom. "Let me have your nightgown," he said, "and also your ring. When morning comes I'll tell you what you need to know."

The princess did as she was asked, and when morning came, Juan whispered the answer in her ear.

So the princess explained the riddle before the court and the king sentenced Juan to the gallows. The poor man asked permission to speak. "She didn't know the answer," he cried, "until I told her what to say." The king asked for proof. Juan held up the nightgown and the ring. "Enough!" cried the king, and he gave orders for the wedding to proceed immediately.

The two were married and lived happily from that time on, for Juan Bobo turned out to be cleverer than all the great princes who had passed through the king's court.

Puerto Rico

⤜ 75. The Price of Heaven and the Rain of Caramels ⤛

I.

This was a man who hated to work and spent all his time going to wakes. One day he traveled to a village some distance from the city and came to a house where a corpse was laid out. Not one to miss a wake, he went in and sat down.

The dead woman's relatives were people of simple faith. He heard them asking, "How much is it?" It was the husband who wanted know. He was saying, "How much would it be for my wife? What does it cost for her to get to heaven?" And one of the relatives, who was also a man of honest faith, was saying, "I think a hundred pesos would be about right." Then the husband put a hundred pesos in the coffin, and when morning came they carried it out for burial.

None of this was lost on the visitor. The next night he went to the burial ground, dug up the coffin and with it the hundred pesos. He took the coffin back to the house of the bereaved family and propped it against the door.

The next morning one of the sons opened the door. The body fell on top of him, and he called out, "Look at this! Mother's come back. That hundred pesos we gave her wasn't enough. We'd better give her another hundred."

The next night the man from the city went to the burial ground again, took the extra hundred for himself, and brought the body back to the house. So they buried it again, with still another hundred. The day after that, there was the body at the door again. The husband looked out and saw the man from the city who had been at the wake, and he called him over. He said, "You know about these things. Tell me how much my wife needs to get to heaven." The man said, "Five hundred pesos."

"Bless my soul!" The husband turned to his sons and said, "We need another two hundred."

Then he whispered to the man from the city, "I'm going to let you take care of this. Take the two hundred and bury my wife so she'll be in paradise." The man from the city buried the woman's body for the last time and went away with five hundred pesos.

II.

Now, the man from the city went to another village, where he lived for many years. When he finally married he was getting old, and as luck would have it he took a wife who did nothing but scold him.

And one day he was out working in the woods when a team of mules passed by, loaded with packs of money. He ducked out of sight and heard the mule drivers say, "We'd better get rid of this stuff fast." "Nobody's looking. Let's hide it here." "We'll come back later when the coast is clear."

They buried the money, and the old man waited a little. Then he went home to his wife and said, "You know, some mule drivers left a load of money in the woods. We ought to go dig it up."

"Oh, stop it!" said the wife. "You expect me to believe there's buried treasure?" Then the minute she was by herself she went to the woods and dug it up. She came back and hid the money in the house, and the old man saw what she was doing but didn't open his mouth.

Then she said to him, "Hah! The dog needs to go out. Here, take this and tie her up in the yard," and she handed him a string of sausages. He tied up the dog with the string of sausages.

After that she said, "It's time to go to school now." And something I must tell you: this old man had gotten so slow-witted his wife was sending him to school every day. So off he went. He never disobeyed.

As soon as he'd gone, the wife went out and bought bagfuls of caramels, sour balls, and bonbons. That night she got up and sprinkled the patio with the caramels, the sour balls, and the bonbons.

In the morning she said, "Out of bed, you old duffer! Time to sweep the patio." He picked up the broom, and when he opened the door he called out, "Wife, look what happened last night! It rained caramels, sour balls, and bonbons!"

"Sweep them up!" she ordered.

A few days passed, and the mule drivers returned to the woods for their money. It was gone. They went into the village to investigate, and the first person they came to was the little old man. "Any idea who dug up our money?" "Oh, yes, in fact I saw you bury it and came home and told my wife, and she went back and dug it up."

The wife came out of the house. "So you dug up our money!" they said. "Your husband just told us."

"You tell *me* when I could have dug up money!" she said. The old man answered, "I remember! It was just before you sent me off to school." And the mule drivers looked at each other.

"Oh! And before that you had me tie up the dog with sausage links."

"When did anybody tie up a dog with sausage links?" they wanted to know.

"I'll tell you! It was the day it rained caramels, sour balls, and bonbons!"

The mule drivers shrugged their shoulders and went on their way, leaving the old man and his wife as rich as you please.

Mexico

꧁ 76. Pine Cone the Astrologer ꧂

Here's a story from the days when there were kings and queens.

It seems that the king of a certain city lost a precious ring. He issued a notice that a large sum of money would be paid to any astrologer who could read the stars and tell him where to look. There was a man who heard about this out in the countryside and came to town to offer his services.

The man from the country went by the name of Pine Cone. But he didn't mention that. He just came up to the king and said, "You lost a ring? You're looking for an astrologer? I'm the one who can help you." The king wasn't sure. In those days astrologers weren't hired without passing a test.

Now, in the city where all this was happening people rarely saw pineapples. So the king sent an order to the kitchen to have a plate of fruit brought in with a pineapple on it. "Give this to the man over there," said the king, "and ask him what it is."

The man lost his nerve for a moment. He slapped his hand on his head and said under his breath, "Pine Cone, Pine Cone! What have you gotten yourself into?"

The king picked up only the first word. He thought he heard "pineapple" and said, "You're hired. Go on up to the tower room and read the stars." Pine Cone climbed the stairs to the observatory and started living in style. He had a comfortable bed, and at every meal they brought him savory meats and all he could drink.

Now, Pine Cone had become the king's astrologer, but his head was not in the clouds. He noticed that the servants who brought him his food were always whispering back and forth. After he had been in the tower a few days his wife came for a visit. She was just what he had been waiting for. The moment he laid eyes on her he said, "Crawl under the bed, and when the servants bring me my lunch, cry, 'Thief!' as soon as the first one comes in."

The first servant entered the room. "Thief!" came an eerie voice from who knows where. The servant looked around. The other servant came in. Again, "Thief!" The two left the room exchanging whispers. Pine Cone said to his wife, "They're guilty."

Outside the door the servants were saying, "He's figured us out. Let's give him the ring now, before he tells the king." They came back in, and when they'd confessed, the astrologer said to them, "I'll keep your secret, but only if you take the ring out to the garden and put it in the peacock's food dish." And that's what they did.

Pine Cone went to the king and said, "Kill the peacock. You'll find the ring." And there it was. They brought it in to the king immediately, and the astrologer, naturally, collected the reward. My tale goes only to here; it ends, and the wind carries it off.

Panama

⇒ 77. The Dragon Slayer ⇐

There was a father who had three daughters. And the youngest, you know, was the one who attracted all the men. The other two were tired of being passed over and thought of a way to get rid of her.

"We'll take some of Father's money," said one of them, "and put it in her bed. Then we'll tell him she's been stealing." The other said, "Good, the proof will be right there in the bed, won't it?"

The next morning when the father went to count his money, it wasn't all there. He began to cry out loud. His eldest daughter heard him wailing and came running. She said, "Father, your money was stolen by your own daughter. Go look. You'll find it where she sleeps."

The father couldn't believe what he was hearing, but he looked anyway. When he saw the money in his daughter's bed, he ordered her to meet him at the door. He took hold of her with one hand, and with his machete in the other hand he dragged her toward the woods. She said, "Father, don't kill me. I'll go far away and never come back." She said it over and over until he loosened his grip. At last he said, "Very well. But you must keep your promise." Then he gave her a few tortillas and sent her on her way.

She wandered for miles, not knowing what she would do. Worn out and hungry, she sat down under a tree and began to eat the tortillas, you see, when an old woman dressed in rags came up to her and said, "Greetings, dear girl. Could you let me have just one of your tortillas? I haven't eaten in two days."

The girl said, "Dear mother, please help yourself. It hurts me that I don't have more to give you. My father ran me out of the house and made me promise never to come back. Here I am, the poorest of the poor. I don't know what I will do."

Now, you must know that this old woman was the Blessed Virgin Mary. When she had listened to the girl's story, she said, "My dear, don't you need work?" The girl said, "I need to find work right away, or I'll die of hunger."

"Here's what you must do. Farther on down the road you'll come to the kingdom of Quiquiriquí. The king there is very powerful, and I'm sure you'll find work in his palace. Take along this little wand, and whenever you need to know anything, just speak to it and say, 'O mighty little wand, by the might that Heaven gave you, tell me such-and-such.' Before you know it you'll have the answer."

The girl thanked the old woman and went on her way, and when she came to a place where the road branched into three roads she took out the wand and said, "O mighty little wand, by all the might that Heaven gave you, tell me, what lies down the road to the right?" It answered, "The road to the right is not for you. It leads to the dragon with seven heads, and each of the heads loves human flesh."

She asked again, "O mighty little wand, by the might that Heaven gave you, tell me, what lies down the road to the left?" And it answered, "The road to the left is not for you. It leads to the castle of the giant Bolumbí, who loves human flesh."

She asked once more, "O mighty little wand, by the might that Heaven gave you, tell me, what lies down the middle road?" The wand said, "The middle road is the road for you. It will take you to the kingdom of Quiquiriquí, where the king has the power to help you."

She took the middle road and walked on until she came to the king's palace. She went up to the door and asked the captain of the guard, "Is there any work here?" The captain said, "I don't know," but he led her into the palace, and when she got to the king, he said, "There's work in the kitchen. Go there. You'll find it."

Now, this king had become gloomy. Day after day he grew quieter, you see, until he was almost saying nothing. Then the girl in the kitchen remembered her wand, and she picked it up and said, "O mighty little wand, by the might that Heaven gave you, tell me, why is the king so gloomy?"

The wand answered, "As you know, not far from this kingdom is a dragon with seven heads. The dragon has told the king that he must send his son, the prince, to be eaten. Otherwise the dragon will come to the kingdom and start eating everybody. The prince must be sent off tomorrow at the latest."

"How could the dragon be killed?" asked the girl. "Very easily," answered the wand. "It takes a nap every day at twelve. Go there tomorrow and bring me with you. Use me to strike the dragon on its tail while it sleeps. It will never wake up."

The king, you know, had issued a proclamation that whoever could kill the dragon would be granted any wish. So the girl went off to the dragon's den and gave it a strong slap on the tail with the little wand. When it was dead, she cut out the tongues from its seven heads and went back to the palace.

As soon as she had left the dragon's den, a vassal of the king came along, saw the dead dragon, and said, "My luck is with me. I'll prove to the king that I killed the dragon and ask to marry his daughter, the princess."

The vassal rode back to the palace and went straight to the king. He said, "Majesty, I have killed the dragon. As proof, here are its seven heads. My wish is to marry the princess."

But at that moment the girl who had killed the dragon was arriving with the seven tongues. "This man is a liar," she said, and when she produced the tongues, the king believed her and sent the vassal to be shot by a firing squad.

Then the girl said, "Majesty, my wish is to marry your son, the prince." But now the king had second thoughts. He said, "I can't marry my son to a kitchen maid." She answered quickly, "Kings don't go back on their word."

He said, "You're right. The wedding will be held tomorrow evening." Nevertheless the girl was worried: she had nothing to wear. Then again she remembered the little wand, and when she took it out and spoke to it, it answered her, "Tonight before you sleep ask the Blessed Virgin to help you."

The miracle happened, and in the morning when she woke up, there was a dress of gold next to her bed. She wore it that evening, the prince fell in love with her, and the king could hardly believe that this was his kitchen maid.

The prince and his new princess lived happily. But you must know that the king had fallen in love with his son's bride. His only thought now was to get rid of the prince, so that he himself could enjoy the princess, and again he became gloomy. The princess consulted her wand: "O mighty little wand, by the might that Heaven gave you, tell me, why is the king so gloomy?"

The wand answered, "The king desires you and wants you for himself. He will declare a war, and as soon as his son, the prince, has gone off to battle, the king and his henchmen will follow and secretly kill him."

The princess asked, "How can this be prevented?" And the wand replied, "You must go to the giant Bolumbí and get the little ring that he wears on his tooth. When you have the ring, you can say, 'Little ring, change this into that.' Now, go to the giant exactly at twelve, when he takes his nap."

The princess set off for the giant's castle and arrived at twelve. She went in quietly. When she saw the snoring giant, with his mouth open, she slipped the ring off his tooth and ran back to her own palace.

The next morning the prince set off for war. Then the princess took out her wand and said, "O mighty little wand, by the might that Heaven gave you, tell me, where is the king now?" The wand replied, "The king is right behind the prince and about to kill him."

Quickly the princess reached for the ring and said, "Little ring, change the king into a wild pig." As it was ordered, so it was done. The prince saw the pig and shot it. And a fat one it was. When he and his companions had roasted it, they found it quite tasty. Then they went on and won the war and returned to the palace as safe as safe could be.

The prince and the princess lived happily for many years. They were always inviting me, and

Ruddy ruddy red,
My story is said.

Mexico

⮞ 78. Johnny-boy ⮜

A parish priest was making his rounds of the neighborhood when he noticed a little boy running along with his dog, calling out to it, "Come on, Johnny-boy! Come on, Johnny-boy!"

The priest thought, "A dog John? And to call it Johnny? Johnny-boy? Oh, the blessed name of the Evangelist and the Baptist, not to mention twenty-two Roman popes!" But then he thought, "Why blame the child for this sacrilege? It's the mother and father who are at fault." He stopped the boy and said, "Do you have parents at home?"

"No, father, I'm an orphan. But there's Pepa, my big sister. And Mama Señora, my grandmother."

"Where do they live?"

"Keep on down this street past the slaughterhouse, then take a left and it's not too far from there. Want me to go with you?"

"Please. I have to talk to your grandmother."

As they walked side by side, the child kept calling to the dog, "Come on! Come on, Johnny-boy!"

Johnny-boy. Each repetition drove another nail into the heart of the pious father in Christ.

When they finally reached the little doorway, the sister and the grandmother came out to greet the visitor. "Father, what an honor. You've blessed us. Who could have thought that we, poor as we are and so far out of the way, would ever see your face at our door or even so much as your picture."

"Dear daughters," said the priest, "I love nothing more than to visit my parishioners. And the poor are my favorites. Were they not the favorites of Our Lord? It's only that my duties keep calling me elsewhere."

"Thank you, father. Our humble house is yours. To see you fills us with joy."

"I wish I could say the same," said the priest, getting down to business. "I've come to talk to you about your little boy. I keep hearing him call his dog 'Johnny.' You must realize how disrespectful . . ."

The grandmother interrupted him, "Oh, that grandchild of mine! If I've told him once I've told him a hundred times, the dog's name isn't Johnny, it's John of God."

Nicaragua

⊰ 79. The Rarest Thing ⊱

There was a king who had three sons and a niece, and as fate would have it—don't you see?—the three fell in love with the king's niece, their cousin. "My niece can't marry all three," said the king, "and if I give her to one, there'll be no peace in the family."

To decide the matter he called his sons and said, "Listen, all three of you! Bring me a rarity I've never seen. Whoever can do it will marry my niece."

"I'll do it myself," said each of the sons.

"Be back in three months," said the king.

They took to the road and were gone in a wink. Well, the first of the three found a pair of spectacles for sale and snapped them up. Anyone who wore these marvelous glasses could see what was happening in distant cities. "In all the land there's nothing like this," said the first son to himself.

Then the second of the three found a carpet that flew from one town to the next in only ten minutes. "In all the land there's nothing like it," he exclaimed.

Finally, the youngest discovered a powerful apple; whoever waved it in front of the dead could make them wake up. "Hah," he said, "there's nothing like this in all the land. I can bring the dead back to life and make money."

The three got together at the place where they'd agreed to meet and said, "Here we are. Now what do we have?"

"A pair of glasses! Wait till I put them on, and we'll see what's happening at the palace. Uh-oh, what's this? There's a wake just getting started, and it's the king's niece who's laid out!"

"Good heavens, our cousin dead?"

"If only I were there," said the one with the apple, "I'd bring her back to life."

"Quick, jump on my rug," said his brother.

And in ten minutes they were there. The one with the apple rushed up to the coffin. Apple in hand, he made the sign of the cross over the dead niece's body. She sat up. Then he turned to the king and said, "Papa, she's mine. I've brought her back to life."

But his brother said, "What good would the apple have been without the carpet that got us here?"

And the eldest said, "What good is the apple or the carpet, without the glasses that told us we had to come? I should be the one who marries our cousin."

"Ah, no, no, no!" said the king [*laughter in the audience*]. "The three of you are equal. I can't give my niece to any of you. Now go! Find brides somewhere else!"

Don't you see? In their travels in some of those cities they'd noticed women. So the king said, "Go get your brides, and then you'll be married."

Guatemala / Antonio Ramírez

➣ 80. Prince Simpleheart ⬰

A king had three sons. The two older boys were as bright as a father could wish and had gotten through all their schooling. But the youngest was one of God's innocent creatures and everyone called him Prince Simpleheart.

The bright ones said to the king, "Give us our inheritance, so we can go out into the world." Simpleheart wondered if he might not go with them. But his brothers teased him, and the queen said, "What could you possibly do, numskull?" The king echoed her, "What could you possibly do? Better stay home."

The two bright ones set off down the road, each with his inheritance in a moneybag swinging from his belt. The youngest, although he hadn't been given a nickel, took it into his head to tag along. The two brothers waited for him to catch up, then gave him a licking with a green switch. But it was no use. He wouldn't turn back. The minute they hit the road again he was right behind them. They stopped and gave him a few more licks and twice again did the same. But he kept on.

When it got dark he could follow along without being noticed. He saw his brothers step into a thicket and thought, "They're making camp." He got as close as he dared and lay down under a tree that had three branches.

At midnight he was awakened by voices overhead. Three birds had arrived, one on each branch of the tree. The first said, "I've got to start singing! And when I do, I'll drop my knapsack."

The second bird inquired, "What's with the knapsack?"

"It's the one that fills up with money again whenever you empty it," replied the first. Then it opened its beak and the knapsack fell to the ground. Simpleheart turned his head to see where it landed.

The second bird said, "Now *I've* got to sing! When I do, I'll drop my little violin."

"Which violin is that?"

"The one that makes people dance and they can't stop." It opened its beak and down came the violin.

The third said, "Listen, girls, I've got to sing, too. When I do, this little cloak is going to fall."

"Cloak?" asked the other two.

"You know! The one that makes you invisible." It opened its beak and the cloak came fluttering down.

At the crack of dawn Simpleheart jumped up and collected the three objects. When his brothers saw him coming, they threatened to switch him again. But he showed them the marvelous things he had found and they calmed down. One took the knapsack. The other seized the violin, leaving Simpleheart with the cloak. So they traveled on for another day, making camp in the woods that night. As soon as Simpleheart was asleep, the two brothers sneaked off.

In the morning, seeing that his brothers had gone on, Simpleheart thought, "Why stick to the road? With the cloak to make me invisible, I'll be safe from the wild beasts and can take a shortcut through the forest." He struck off down a narrow path.

In a while he came to a tree loaded with sweet-smelling fruits. He filled his hat and his pockets, sat down on a log, and ate a few. Suddenly his head was heavy. He felt with his hand, and what was this? He'd grown horns like a stag.

"If my father could see me now, he'd never let me back in the palace. Oh well, the better to ward off those wild beasts." He threw away the rest of the fruits and went on. At a little brook he slipped and fell into a pool. Fortunately it wasn't deep. When he pulled himself out, behold! The horns were gone.

"Now I know what the cure is," he thought. He ran back and gathered up the fruits he'd left behind and continued on till he came to a city. Simple as he was, he nevertheless knew he had reached the capital of a great kingdom. He headed for the palace, thinking the king might buy some fruit. The princess was out on her balcony. "Your Highness," he called. "Fresh fruit for sale."

"Papa, there's a salesman here." The king came out, took a whiff of the sweet-smelling fruit, and bought the lot.

The next day word spread through the city that Their Majesties and all their servants had grown horns. People ran to the palace to get a look, but no one was allowed to come near. Simpleheart threw on his cloak and, being invisible, stole into the royal chambers. He got as far as the queen and the princess, and there they were with antlers on their heads, weeping bitter tears.

Knowing that his brothers must have come into the city by now, he left the palace to look them up. When he found them in their lodgings, they said to him, "Why don't you stay with us?" So he took advantage of their sudden generosity and asked to borrow the violin. Wrapped in the cloak and with the violin in hand, he stood at the palace gate and started scraping the bow on the strings. It made such a lively tune Their Majesties forgot they were wearing antlers and began tapping their feet.

They strutted out onto the balconies. People rushed to catch a glimpse and crowded so tightly into the plaza they had no room to dance themselves. The music picked up speed. At the sight of the royal family and all the servants with their antlers, whirling and prancing, the crowd let out with a roar.

The king shouted, "Stop, for a purse full of money!" But Simpleheart shouted back, "I want to marry the princess!" Desperate, the king said, "Very well." And Simpleheart put away the violin.

The next day he marched into the palace and announced he was the future husband of the princess. The king remembered his promise and allowed him to be brought forward. The king, the queen, and the princess stood behind a curtain to conceal their embarrassing antlers. But the king peeked out and recognized the fruit vendor from two days before. In a fury he ran around the end of the curtain, took Simpleheart by the ears, and threw him into a courtyard. "Lock him up and hang him at dawn!"

"At last," thought Simpleheart, "God has given up on me." But he thought again as he stared at the iron bars on the windows of his prison cell. They were in the form of crosses! "Why lose hope? I swear by these crosses that the princess will be my bride."

And it was lucky he still had the cloak folded up in his pocket. He called to the warden, "Think of it, my good man. Today it's me, tomorrow it could be you. Have pity and give me a breath of air. I'm suffocating. Open the door a crack." The jailer obliged, and Simpleheart, invisible in his cloak, slipped away.

He ran to his brothers' lodgings and said, "Let me have that knapsack a minute." He emptied it a few times and scooped up the money.

Then he was off to the shops, where he bought himself a doctor's outfit. He rented a furnished room and hung out a sign:

MEDICAL DOCTOR
SPECIALIZING IN ANTLERITIS
AND OTHER INFIRMITIES OF THE HEAD

Word of a new doctor in town reached the king, and Simpleheart was rushed to the palace. The king stated his terms, "My daughter's hand in marriage if you can remove these horns." The doctor replied, "I can. But I must warn you, the medicine hurts."

"No matter," said the king.

"Then get to work," ordered the doctor. "Have a tank built, five meters on each side and four meters deep, and fill it with water. I'll be back in three days." The doctor withdrew, bowing low and sweeping his arms.

When he returned, he inspected the tank and dribbled oils and perfumes. At each corner he set up a ram's-horn incense burner. "Now tell the king to come out in a bath towel."

The king appeared. "Down on your knees! I hate to do it, but this tapir-hair switch is the only thing that gets the blood moving. Ten years of research have proved it." The king kneeled, and the lashes came raining down on his back. Then the doctor threw him into the water and held him under until he nearly drowned. When he let him up, the horns were gone.

It was the queen's turn, but she only needed a half dozen lashes. And the princess needed no more than a touch with a silk handkerchief. Finally the servants were doctored, with or without the tapir switch, according to each case.

When the cures were complete, they honored the doctor at a banquet and a ball. A few days later he was married to the princess, and the king even gave him the crown of the realm. So that's how Prince Simpleheart became king of a powerful nation. And because his heart was good he called his two brothers to the palace and made them high-ranking ministers.

Costa Rica

⤜ 81. The Flower of Lily-Lo ⤛

A man and his wife had three sons. Their favorite was the youngest, and the whole town was in love with him, too. His older brothers, however, were jealous.

One day the mother fell sick, and doctors couldn't help her. No one knew what to do until a witch told them to look in the forest for a certain herb called the Flower of Lily-Lo. Nothing else would cure the mother's illness.

The father sent all three sons to find the flower. But when they got to the woods, the two older boys hid behind trees, and the youngest, thinking he was lost, began to cry, running this way and that way. Wandering in no particular direction, he came upon the flowers, picked a few, and started for home.

On the way he ran into his two brothers. When they saw that he had found the flowers, they fell into a fury and beat him. They dragged him to a hole, threw him in, and covered him up with rocks.

The two boys then brought the flowers to their father, and the father took them and made a potion. When he gave it to the mother, she was cured instantly. Noticing that the smallest boy had not returned, the father began wondering what had happened. The brothers said he must have lost his way.

The parents sent a search party to look for their son. But when two or three weeks had gone by and still he had not been found, they gave him up for dead. He must have been eaten by wild animals, they thought.

Now, in the meantime there was a boy who went out walking in the woods, and on his way back to town he came upon a curious tree covered with flowers. He picked one and blew on it, and the flower made a little song that said,

> Oh, little boy, don't blow on me;
> Don't blow again, no, no.
> My brothers they have killed me
> For the Flower of Lily-Lo.

The boy was startled, but when he blew again, and the flower repeated its little song, he began to think. He decided to fill his pockets with flowers and sell them in town.

Fate willed it that the boy should come stand outside the house where the parents of the lost child lived. The boy began to blow on the flowers, offering them for sale. Out of curiosity, people crowded around. The parents of the lost child recognized the voice of their son and came out into the street to see what was happening. They called the boy over and asked him for a flower. As the father blew on it, it sang,

> *Oh, father dear, don't blow on me;*
> *Don't blow again, no, no.*
> *My brothers they have killed me*
> *For the Flower of Lily-Lo.*

The father hardly knew what to think. He handed the flower to his wife, and she blew on it. Then she heard the flower say,

> *Oh, mother dear, don't blow on me;*
> *Don't blow again, no, no.*
> *My brothers they have killed me*
> *For the Flower of Lily-Lo.*

The parents called the brothers and made them blow on the flower. It said,

> *Oh, brothers mine, don't blow on me;*
> *Don't blow again, no, no.*
> *My brothers, you have killed me*
> *For the Flower of Lily-Lo.*

Hearing this, the mother and father threw chili peppers into the fireplace and locked the two brothers in the house, where they choked to death. Then they asked the little boy to take them to the flower tree. People from town followed behind. When they got to the place where the tree grew, they started pulling away the rocks. There was their little son asleep under the tree trunk. They took him into their arms, he woke up at once, and everyone cheered.

Ruddy ruddy red, my story is said, and yours is still to tell.

Mexico / Jorge Carlos González Avila

᠉ 82. My Garden Is Better Than Ever ᠊

There was a poor woman who never saw money. Yet, one day while sweeping she found six centavos. "What shall I do?" she wondered. "If I buy sugar, it won't last, and if I buy salt, it'll be gone before I know it."

At last she decided to get lettuce seed, and after she had sown it in a small plot and waited awhile, she harvested enough to sell. With the money she earned she was able to buy more seed, enough to make a large garden.

But there was a rabbit who tore things up just for the fun of it, and the rabbit began to ruin her garden. One day the poor woman came into the dooryard from her garden work, and a neighbor asked, "How are you doing? What's happening with your garden?"

"A rabbit is tearing it up," said the poor woman.

"Take my advice," said the neighbor. "There's an easy way to catch the rabbit. All you have to do is make a doll out of beeswax and put it in the path where the rabbit comes into the garden."

The poor woman listened, but she did not hear all the neighbor's words. Instead of using beeswax she made a doll out of rags. She put it in the garden. Later her neighbor asked, "How are you doing? What's happening with the rabbit?"

"Nothing, neighbor. The rabbit tore up the doll."

"What did you make it with?"

"Rags."

"No-o-o-o, neighbor, I told you *wax*."

The following day the poor woman tried again. This time she made the doll out of beeswax. That night when the rabbit arrived, he found the doll at the entrance to the garden. He said, "Good evening, little friend. May I have permission for lettuce?"

The doll said nothing. "Permission for lettuce?" said the rabbit again. No answer. The rabbit slapped it. "I'll make you answer," but his hand stuck fast. "Let me go. If you don't, I'll hit you again." He slapped the doll with his other hand. Now both hands were stuck and the rabbit was angry. "Let my hands go," he cried, "or I'll kick you." He did, and his feet stuck. Then he bit the doll, and his head stuck, too.

The next morning the owner went out to her garden. And what should she find but that she'd caught a rabbit. She made a cage out of sticks, put the rabbit inside, and after picking some vegetables, carried everything back to the house. Again the neighbor asked, "How are you doing, neighbor?"

"Very well," she answered, both hands full. "My garden is better than ever."

Mexico (Popoluca) / Anastasio García

⇒ 83. Juan Bobo and the Pig ⇐

Before she left for Mass, Juan Bobo's mama told him to watch the pig and the little chicks. When she'd gone, the pig started to squeal and the chicks tried to get out of the chicken yard. Juan Bobo saw that the pig wouldn't be quiet, and he said to it, "Ah, you want to go to Mass with Mama, right? But don't think I'm going to go with you."

He took out his mama's clothes and started to dress up the pig. He used the best things he could find, his mama's new black mantilla, her lace collar, and everything else. Then he brought the pig to the road, and when it refused to move, he gave it a crack of the whip and off it ran.

Meanwhile the chicks were refusing to be still. So he caught them and hung them upside down from a stick. When Mama came home from Mass, she asked, "Juan Bobo, where's the pig?"

He answered her a little worried, "You mean you didn't see it at Mass? I dressed it up and sent it. It was crying to go with you. And the chicks were about to get out of the yard, so I hung them upside down from a stick. Look. They're all perfectly quiet now." And when he said, "Just wait, the pig will be back before you know it," she whacked him until he was quiet himself.

Puerto Rico

⇒ 84. The Parrot Prince ⇐

If I tell it to know it you'll know how to tell it and put it in ships for John, Rock, and Rick with dust and sawdust, ginger paste, and marzipan, triki-triki triki-tran.

It's about a rich widower and his daughter, Mariquita, who was the apple of his eye. He doted on her without even thinking and gave in to her every whim. But she was all by herself when her father went out on business, and she began wishing she had sisters to keep her company.

Well then, in the house next door was a widow who had three daughters. Every time the widow saw Mariquita she gave her a little gift or something special to eat, while the daughters showered her with attention. They would say, "Tell your papa to marry our mama, then we'll be together all day long."

They kept at it until Mariquita imagined the world would be perfect if only this marriage could be brought about. She pestered her father to take the neighbor woman as his wife, pleading with him morning, noon, and night. Finally the father, for no other reason than to satisfy his daughter, said yes, and they had a wedding.

After that, things changed. Instead of gifts and tidbits, Mariquita's stepmother and stepsisters gave her dark looks and scoldings and whacked her with the backs of their hands.

Knowing she had brought it all on herself, she couldn't say a word to her father and had to suffer in silence. She would have gone on like this until who knows when, except that one day the whole thing boiled over. The sisters yanked her hair, and when she complained, the stepmother picked up a piece of stove wood and pummeled her with it. "Complain, will you? You had it coming! My daughters know you better than you know yourself!"

What they did know was that Mariquita was set to inherit her father's fortune, and because of it they couldn't stand the sight of her.

When the father came home that night, Mariquita told him the truth for a change. She refused to blame him, though. All she wanted was to live by herself in a certain little cottage her mother had left her, and the father at last agreed, since he could think of no other way to keep peace in the family.

Then one evening when Mariquita was sweeping her little dooryard, she heard a voice: "Mariquita, I'll help you sweep." Startled, she looked around but saw no one. The voice came again: "Look up in the *peumo* tree!" She looked, and there was a parrot. "Shall I come down?"

"Please! And be my friend, I'm so lonely. What can I get you? Nuts? Chocolate? Wine sops?"

"Not until after dark," he said. "Put a basin of water on your windowsill, a comb, a mirror, and a hand towel, and you'll see me later."

At midnight there was a whirring of wings. The parrot dipped himself in the basin, dried off, combed his feathers, and looked in the mirror. Then, as he bounded into the room, he became the most handsome prince you ever dreamed of.

I'll tell nothing at all of what they said to each other, except that when morning came the prince promised to be back that night and every night, and before he flew off he left a heavy bag. It was full of money. From then on Mariquita knew only happiness, and she began to wear silk and put on earrings and bracelets.

One of the stepsisters passed by the cottage one day and caught a glimpse of Mariquita through the open window. She ran back to her mother and sisters and told them she'd seen silk and jewels.

"Somebody's giving her money," said the mother. Then she instructed her eldest daughter, "Go pay a visit to little Mariquita. Spend the night and keep your ears open. Come back in the morning and tell us everything."

The next day the girl showed up at Mariquita's door with a hundred lies: "We can hardly stand it that you went away," "All the little gifts we gave you!" "What thanks did we get?" "How it hurts!" "We're dying to see you again."

Then she added, "I've come to spend the day with you. And the night!"

Nothing if not good-hearted, Mariquita said, "Thanks." But not wanting her stepsister to hear the prince arrive, she served her wine at dinner and kept refilling the glass until, when the stepsister stood up to go to bed, her head was spinning. By the time she lay down, a carriage could have rolled over her and she wouldn't have felt a thing.

She went home the next day with tales of fine furnishings, perfect housekeeping, and rare foods and wines, which made the mother and the sisters more jealous than they'd been before. Worse, she had seen nothing of what she had been told to watch for. The mother took hold of her middle daughter. "Go now, and see if you can do better. I'm warning you, don't sleep a wink!"

The girl set off, but she drank her dinner, just as her sister had done, and when she got back the following morning she couldn't say any more than she could have said before she went.

The youngest daughter, who was the most jealous of all, said, "Mother, I'm going right now! Trust me, I'll find out what we need to know!"

Off she ran. And when dinner was served, she only pretended to drink. She slept not a wink, her eye at the keyhole all night long. At midnight the parrot arrived at the windowsill, dipped in the basin, and became a prince. He sat close to Mariquita, caressing her, murmuring tenderly. By morning the stepsister's jealousy had nearly eaten her alive, yet there she was, still hunched over the keyhole. She saw the prince jump to the windowsill, bathe himself, and fly away. And not without leaving a sackful of money.

Moments later she was out the door. As soon as she could no longer be seen from the cottage she started to run. She couldn't wait to tell her mother. "Mama!" she announced. "Those ninnies fell asleep, but I stayed awake and saw it all, all, all!"

"We've got them now!" cried the mother. "That sow and her famous prince won't be whispering tonight!"

Then shortly before midnight she slipped up to the cottage window and without the slightest noise laid three sharpened knives on the windowsill. When the parrot landed, the knives cut into his flesh and he let out with a shriek. "Mariquita, my love, you've betrayed me! Today was the last day of my enchantment. I would have been free, and now I am lost. May you repent! When you do, come after me. You must put on a pair of iron shoes, and not until the soles are worn through will you find me." With that, he vanished.

Mariquita fell to weeping, then caught herself. "Why weep," she thought, "when I could be looking for my husband?" She ran to the cobbler and ordered iron shoes. The moment they were ready she pulled them on. She bundled up a change of clothes, a pair of scissors, and a little flask, and off she went.

She climbed mountains and crossed prairies, never stopping to rest. Aches and pains couldn't hold her back, not even exhaustion, though she felt it sorely. One day, when her strength had nearly ebbed away, she lay down in a thicket at the edge of a lake. She stretched out her legs and, oh bliss! the tips of her toes popped out. When she turned her shoes over she saw that the soles were completely worn through. "I've almost arrived," she thought. "I'll be with him soon."

Night was coming, but there was a rustling nearby and she couldn't sleep. Three duck women had landed at the edge of the lake:

"What kept you, comadre? And you, my goddaughter, what took so long?"

"Well, finally, comadre! That stupid husband of mine and my two older daughters, the good-for-nothings! I thought they'd never get to sleep. But here I am with my youngest, your goddaughter, comadre. She's a witch after our own hearts. But tell us the latest. What's happening with the parrot prince? Is he dead yet?"

"They say it'll be only three more days. His wounds won't heal. Those knives you laid on the windowsill were just the thing, comadre. His doctors will never guess the cure."

"And what's the cure?"

"Hush! Don't you know the walls have ears and the bushes have eyes?"

"Go on, tell us. There's nobody here but us three."

"Well, who'd ever guess that the prince would be cured if they just took a feather from the right wing of each of us and waved it over the prince's wounds after dipping it in our blood? Of course they'd have to kill us first."

"But how would they ever guess? The Devil wouldn't allow it."

When their meeting was over, the three waddled into the reeds at the waterside and settled down for the night.

Mariquita waited until she was certain the ducks had fallen asleep. Then she went up to the closest of the three, which was none other than her own stepmother, and sliced off its head with one clip of her scissors. She took a feather from its right wing and poured a few drops of its blood into her flask. The next duck she came to was her stepsister, and she did the same; and the same again with the stepsister's godmother. After that she changed into men's clothing and hurried toward the city.

Running into the palace she yelled out to the king, "I'm a doctor!" She gave her orders: "I must be left alone with the prince." When she reached his room, his eyes were already closed. She dipped one of the feathers into the flask and waved it gently over his wounds.

The next morning the king came in and asked, "How is my son?"

"See for yourself, sire. The worms have left, and the wounds are starting to close." When the king had gone, Mariquita took the second feather, dipped it into the witches' blood, and as she waved it in the air the prince opened his eyes.

The day after that she soaked up the rest of the blood with the third feather, passed it back and forth over the prince's body, and he sat up and was well. Then she told him everything that had happened.

When the king came in, his joy was so great I haven't the words to describe it. He gave his consent to the marriage, and they celebrated with much rejoicing throughout the kingdom.

And I can tell you it's true, since they had me to the wedding banquet and fed me until I nearly burst.

With that my tale is done, and the wind blows it into the sea.

Chile

➦ Chain Riddles ⇐

I.

"Where's the corn?"
"Under a metate."
"Where's the metate?"
"In a gopher hole."
"Where the hole?"
"Covered by a crab."
"Where's the crab."
"Eaten by a heron."
"Where's the heron?"
"Perched in a tree."
"Where's the tree?"
"Fell in the water."
"Where's the water?"
"A deer drank it up."
"Where's the deer?"
"Scared off by a fire."
"Where's the fire?"
"Put out by the rain."
"Where's the rain?"
"Carried off by the wind."
"Where's the wind?"
"It blew away behind the mountain."

Mexico (Mixe)

II.

Comadre frog, where's your husband?
"Coming, madam."
"What's he wearing?"
"His little suit."

"And what's its color?"
"Green-and-yellow."
"Are we off to Mass?"
"I have no blouse."
"Shall we hear the sermon?"
"I have no shawl."
No bread to eat and nothing at all.

Puerto Rico

III.

The moon, the moon, Santa Rosa,
Where did Rosa go?
"She went for two red-hot coals."
"Why the fire?"
"To cook the corn."
"Why the corn?"
"To make pancakes."
"Why the pancakes?"
"For Grandfather to take to the orchard."
"What's Grandfather want in the orchard?"
"He went for a vine."
"Why the vine?"
"To beat Grandmother, so she'll get up
    from the kitchen and bring a jug
    of water."
"Why the water?"
"For the chickens to drink."
"Why the chickens?"
"To lay the eggs."
"Why the eggs?"
"For food for the priest."
"Why the priest?"
"To say a little Mass."

Ting-a-ling, the milk palm nut,
Ting-a-ling, the *coyol* palm nut.

Mexico (Zapotec)

IV.

"The king and queen have gone for water."
"Where's the water?"
"The chicks drank it up."
"Where are the chicks?"
"They're eating little bones."
"Where are the bones?"
"The king took them."
"Where's the king?"
"He went to say Mass."
"Where's the Mass?"
"He wrapped it in paper."
"Where's the paper?"
"It flew to heaven."

New Mexico

V.

"Where are you going, daddy-long-legs?"
"Over there."
"Why over there?"
"To get a white flower."
"Why the flower?"
"To put at the feet of a girl."
"What happened to the girl?"
"Bitten by a white snake."

"Where's the snake?"

"We killed it."

"Where did you throw it?"

"Into the fire."

"Where are the ashes?"

"The old church was patched up with them."

"And the old church?"

"Collapsed."

"Who knocked it down?"

"A crippled sheep gave it a kick."

"And where's the sheep?"

"A coyote ate it."

"Where's the coyote?"

"A vulture ate it."

"Where's the vulture."

"Flew away."

Mexico (Otomi)

VI.

"Let's hunt."

"My rifle's broken."

"Where are the parts?"

"I burned them."

"Where are the ashes?"

"Eaten by a falcon."

"Where's the falcon?"

"Went to the sky."

"Where in the sky?"

"Fell."

"Then where did it fall?"

"Went in a well."

"Where's the well?"

"Disappeared."
"Where'd it disappear?"
"Into your belly button."
"True."

Mexico (Yucatec Maya)

PART EIGHT

➣ 85. A Dead Man Speaks ➢

My cousins Andrés, Francisco, and Santiago had wanted to come to the United States for a long time. They were coming to see us, but they got on the wrong train, and instead of coming to Austin they went to Oklahoma. While there, they worked as cowboys.

Once while the three were out on the range, one of their fellow cowboys became ill. They took the cowboy to the nearest house, which was a two-room abandoned shack. The cowboy died, and the others put his body on some planks in one of the rooms and placed a candle at the head of the body and another at the foot.

Then one of the cowboys suggested a game of cards to while away the time. My cousin Francisco objected. He said, "There's a dead man in the next room. We can't be disrespectful."

The others refused to hear. They began to play cards and drink whiskey. One of the candles began to burn very low, and they had no other, so Andrés told Francisco, "Go into the other room and get one of the candles."

Francisco went into the room where the dead man lay. As he clutched the candle, the dead man raised himself up slightly. Francisco tripped, threw down the candle, and fell against the planks. The candle at the head of the body blew out and the planks flew up into the air. As they did so the dead man was thrown forward on Francisco. His elbows pricked Francisco and he heard a shrill voice say, "You must respect dead men."

At this, Francisco screamed, "Help, the dead man is killing me!"

When the cowboys heard this, they ran out of the shack. Andrés was the first to recover, and he went back to see what had happened to Francisco. Francisco had fainted. The cowboys revived him, but they didn't go back to the cards and whiskey. They never again played or drank when they were around a dead man.

Texas / Mrs. Charles G. Balagia

⇒ 86. The Bear's Son ⇐

A man and his wife were very poor. The man would go looking for wild honey.

One day when he'd had some success, he told his wife he was going off to make a sale. But then he said, "No, I'd better not. There's a bear that comes out of the forest along the road I'd have to take."

"Never mind," said his wife. "I'll go myself."

"And if the bear comes out?"

"God prevent it!"

"Very well, if you wish." He gave her six bottles of honey packed in a basket. She went out the door saying, "May the hand of God protect me!"

When she got to the forest, the animal was there. She could hear him coming. He seized her roughly, and the honey bottles fell out on the road. But the bear didn't want the honey. He picked up the woman and carried her to his cave. It was a huge cave, big as a church. When she looked it over, she saw that it was quite nice, like a house.

The bear said to her, "I'm going out now. Stay here or I'll kill you. Is that clear?" When he returned, he brought tidbits of meat, neatly wrapped in *guaruma* leaves. "I can't eat this," she said. "It's not cooked."

He understood. He made a little fire in a corner of the cave and grilled the meat. Every night he would go out, and before it was light he would return. During the day he stayed with the woman. They lived on. After a year she had a little boy.

"Dear God!" she thought. "What have I gotten into?" But she did her duty and brought up the child. His diet was raw meat, which he ate eagerly. Before she knew it, she had a fifteen-year-old boy on her hands, his lower body covered in fur, the rest of him human, except that his eyes were round like a bear's.

"Look at me! Fur down to my feet! Is that animal my father?"

"He loves you. He loves your animal half, and he loves your human half, too," said the mother.

But the boy knew the bear's ways, and he had been told many times that the bear would kill his mother if she tried to leave. He said, "Mother, watch me!" He picked up a log and broke it in half. "Don't kill him for my sake," she said. "Do it for yourself!"

That night the boy waited until the bear settled down to sleep, then he beat him with half a log. He didn't stop until the bear was dead. "Now let's get out of here!" said the mother. "We've got to get you baptized."

"What's 'baptized,' mother?"

"It's something that happens in a church."

"It sounds good."

They walked until nightfall and stopped at a deserted cabin. In the morning the boy said, "Before you take me to be baptized, you must let me see what a real man looks like."

"My son, a man would kill you."

"I'm strong."

"But men have ideas that are greater than your strength. Even if they don't kill you, with their ideas they make you do things you don't want to do. Go, but I warn you."

He made her promise to wait for him in the little cabin. She wept and said, "God protect you."

He walked for a while, came to a clearing, and saw an ox. From his mother's description he knew that men were smaller than this, but he decided to take no chances. "Are you a man?" The ox shook its head. Its master had just unyoked it after a day's work.

"Look at the back of my neck," said the ox. "All the hair's worn off! It's the man's doing. You never know what to expect!"

"But you're bigger than he is."

"It doesn't matter. He has the ideas. When he takes the yoke off, he puts me on a rope and ties it to that stake over there. Always another idea!"

"When I find him, I'll kill him and set you free."

The ox just shook its head, and the boy walked on.

He came to a pasture where a horse was grazing. This could be it. This could be the man. The ears were fairly small, as the boy had been told to expect. "Are you a man?" The horse spoke up, "The man is the one who just took off my saddlebags. Look where my hair is rubbed off. When he rides me, I can throw him, and I can kick him with my hooves. But it doesn't help me. He has a whip and makes me carry heavy loads."

The boy walked on. He came to a house with some outbuildings. There was a burro chained in the yard. The boy thought, "This is it. Look at that white belly! That worried face!" He said, "Are you a man?"

"The man is the one who puts me on this chain. Just look at it! It's made of iron. He knows if he uses a rope I'll chew it."

"I'm going to set you free," said the boy. "Not possible," said the burro. And the boy walked on. A dog was barking. Could it be a man?

"Who are you barking at?"

"You, in case you're a thief. Master's orders!"

"And who's your master."

"The man."

Already a man was running out of the house. He came and greeted the bear's son, and they shook hands. He asked the boy, "What can I do for you?"

"I'm here to fight. One of us will kill the other."

"Kill?" said the man. He was carrying an ax on his shoulder. "But aren't you looking for work? I need help. Work first. We'll fight later." He lifted the ax and drove the blade into a pine log. "Here, put your hands next to the blade, so you can pick up this log. We'll see how strong you are."

"Both hands?" asked the boy.

"Yes, with your arms crossed." Then the man removed the blade, and the log snapped shut on the boy's hands. He shouted for help as the man put the ax on his shoulder again and slowly walked back to the house, ate his lunch, took his nap; got up, had his dinner, and went to bed. In the morning he freed the boy, sending him off to his mother with crushed hands. As he passed by the burro, it said, "Didn't I tell you?" And the horse and the ox said the same, "Didn't I tell you?"

When he reached the cabin, his mother greeted him: "Didn't I tell you?" Then she rubbed his hands with grease and healed him. "Now enough of this!" she said. "I'm taking you to be baptized."

When they got to the church, the priest eyed the strapping young man and said, "I'll not only baptize him, I'll be his godfather. Just leave him with me." The priest found him a bed in a little room in the parish house and gave him food. That day the bear's son became acquainted with tortillas. Whatever he was given he ate. And he worked without pay.

"Son, I have workers making a cornfield. Go give them a hand."

"Yes, father." And when breakfast was finished, he went off to the forest without any tools, not even a machete. He got to the little clearing, where the priest had twenty-five men. The overseer greeted him, "We've been at it for five days." Yet practically nothing had been cleared.

The bear's son stared at the enormous trees all around him. They reminded him of the forest where he had lived with his mother and his father the bear. He told the men, "I was born in a place like this." He felt comfortable there, and he walked around, sizing up the trees.

When he got back to the priest, he said, "You have twenty-five men, and they've done almost nothing. Give me a fifty-pound machete and I'll do the work myself."

The priest went to the blacksmith and ordered the machete. "But who could lift such a thing?" asked the smith. "My beautiful godson!" said the priest. "He's half a bear and half a man."

The next morning the workers saw the godson coming with a fifty-pound machete and fled in terror. In just one day he cleared the entire two-acre plot, leaving only the largest trees. "For these I'll need a hundred-pound ax," he said. So the priest went back to the blacksmith and ordered the ax. The day after that, the trees were felled. The following day he did the burning. The day after that, the planting. And then the weeding. Finally the harvesting.

"My son, you've done all this work without any payment," said the priest.

"What do you mean by 'payment,' father?"

"Here!" He took two pesos out of the drawer. "Go get yourself a drink of rum."

"What's 'rum,' father?"

"Go over to the *cantina*. The *cantinero* will sell it to you."

He went into the *cantina* and ordered rum. When he returned, he asked his godfather for two more pesos. Then two more, and two more after that. When he'd finished his last glass, he reached for a jug and drained it. "Enough of that!" said the *cantinero*. "I'm calling the authorities."

"What are 'authorities'?"

The *cantinero* sent his little boy to bring the police. But the police couldn't capture the bear's son. He pulled all the rum off the shelf, five kegs, and finished it up. When he got back to the priest, the *cantinero* and the police were running up behind him. "Don't worry," said the priest. "I'll pay for it. You'll get your money." To himself he said, "Money? You won't get any from me." Then he thought, "I've got to get rid of this godson. What a worker! He's good. But he's an animal. I can't keep him here."

Out in the bush there were tigers, the worst of them a tigress that had given birth to three cubs. She dragged people to her den to feed the little ones. The priest said to his godson, "Tomorrow morning I want you out in the bush to bring back a cow I've got and three calves. Be careful of the cow. She has a hot temper."

"Father, how do you get a cow to come to you?"

"Call to her, *ton-ton-ton.*"

He got his ropes ready, a long, heavy one and three lighter ones, and went out to the bush. *Ton-ton-ton.* Before he knew it, he'd almost stepped on the tigress. He lassoed her, but she wouldn't lie still. "She's just as mean as my godfather said she was." He punched her, reminding himself, "Easy! I mustn't kill her. She's my godfather's cow." Punching her gently, he tied her up until she couldn't move. He jumped! One of the little cubs was behind him, then another and then another. He tied up all three and dragged the four of them back to town. People were gasping. They couldn't believe what they saw.

"Father, here's your cow. What a temper! And these calves!" But when he turned his back, the priest called the police. Four shots, and the mother and her cubs lay dead. "Father, what have you done? Poor creatures! I brought them to you so they could live!" He held the animals in his arms. "The little calves, how I loved them! Father, it would have been better to leave them in the bush." He went to his room and lay down on his bed, angry.

The next day he was still miserable. But the priest wasn't finished. He said, "Tomorrow I have another job for you. There's an old farmhouse I own, out in the country. Spend the night there and rid the place of ghosts!" Then to himself he said, "He'll die of fright. No one who goes there comes back alive."

The following day the boy set out with a blanket and a machete and reached the old farmhouse shortly after dark. He went in and lay down, and in less than a minute he was snoring. Suddenly he woke up. There was a light in the next room. "Well, it's about time. My godfather said there were ghosts."

He put on his shoes and went to investigate. A steer was being hoisted onto a huge dining table. "Whoever you are, out!" said the boy. "This is my godfather's house."

"Come eat," said a voice.

"Not hungry," said the boy. "I came with a full stomach. And you! Clear out! I'm warning you!" But he could see that the table was nicely set. There were knives all in a row, and already the steer was being carved. The voice kept urging him, "Eat!" He pulled up a chair and in spite of himself ate everything that dropped on his plate. When he'd finished the last mouthful, he felt sleepy again and went back to his blanket. This time he locked the door, but again he was awakened. The voice was calling down to him from the ceiling:

"I'm about to fall!"

"How did you get in here?"

"I'm falling!"

"All right, fall! And get out, so I can sleep."

An arm dropped to the floor, then another arm.

"What's this? Piece by piece? Get it over with and clear out, so I can get back to sleep."

A thigh came down and hit the floor with a thud. Then a shank, then the other thigh and the other shank. Then the head, *pum!* And at once the pieces rejoined and made a man.

"All right, so you pulled yourself apart and now you're together again. I'm trying to sleep!"

"Don't you know I'm a ghost?"

"Ghost? I can't be bothered."

"Not even if there's buried treasure? Go cut a pine stick and make me a torch. I'll show you."

"Make it yourself."

The ghost cut a stick and made the torch as best it could. Then it led the boy to where the treasure was hidden. "Here it is, all my silver. It's for the priest to say a Mass for my sake on the feast of St. Anthony. Whatever is left over is for you."

"You mean you played those tricks on me just because of this?"

"Yes, because I am a soul in torment."

"Then go. I'll take care of the rest." The ghost disappeared, and the boy went back to his blanket. The next morning, when he saw the priest again, he told the whole story, not forgetting the treasure, and together they went back to the farmhouse with iron tools. The boy showed the priest where he had eaten the steer and where he had slept on the blanket. The priest blessed both rooms, then got out the tools and started digging. The chest was so heavy the boy had to lift it for him. Then he carried it home to the parish house on his back.

When the feast of St. Anthony arrived, the priest said a Mass for the soul in torment, who years before had been owner of the farmhouse. Now the poor soul could rest in the hands of God; and the money, in the hands of the priest, for what was left from the Mass he kept for himself.

And this priest, mind you, did not pay wages. He said, "Dear godson! How hard I've made you work! You've done everything I've asked. It hurts me to think how you could have been killed."

"It's all right, father. I'm leaving now."

"My dear son! If you must! Here, take a few tortillas." But the boy refused. He was annoyed. He had gotten up angry that morning. And still he said, "Look, you are my godfather. You baptized me. My mother brought me to you for baptism, and you took me in. God protect you."

"Go, my son. God protect you."

The boy disappeared, and nobody knows where he went. That's the story, just to here and no further.

Honduras (Lenca) | Hipólito Lara

⇒ 87. Charity ⇐

A certain king was devoted to the poor. On Friday of each week he fed the needy people in his town. He ordered his servants to prepare the meals, then he himself handed them out.

All the poor came regularly except one man, who had not been informed. When at last the news reached him, he presented himself, and the king, seeing him for the first time, said, "Tell me, are you one of the poor?"

"Poorer than the mice themselves," answered the man. "I have a wife to provide for and my parents, too. And so many children! And so little to give them!"

Hearing all this, the king commanded his servants to make meat pies for the following Friday. He wanted to help the man who had waited so long to come forward, but he didn't want to cause a stir among the rest of the poor. When the pies were done, the king opened one of them and slipped a gold doubloon inside. Then he put the crust back and set the pie aside.

When the time came to hand out the food, the king gave the desperately poor man two pies instead of one, without saying a word. The man was glad to get them and started for home. On the way he met another poor man headed for the palace and, realizing that this man would get there too late to receive a pie, gave him one of his own, keeping the other for himself.

The following Friday the king was astounded to see the man he had treated so generously returning for more. Thinking the man had frittered away the doubloon, he said to him angrily, "What did you do with the gold doubloon I put in your pie last week?"

"Doubloon? I didn't find it," said the man. "But I gave one of the pies to another man who was poor and in need."

"Then I've helped someone without intending to!" cried the king. He was pleased and asked the man to follow him. He led him to his treasure room, thinking to save him from his poverty once and for all. But when he tried his keys, none would turn in the lock. Suddenly a voice spoke to him from the crucifix attached to the wall. It was Our Lord, saying, "He whom I have made poor you may not make rich."

The king heard the words and was taken aback. Then he understood that it was not proper to favor this man, and from that time on he helped him no more or less than he helped all the others.

Argentina / Manuel de Jesús Aráoz

➣ 88. Riches Without Working ⇐

A little old woman had a son who never worked, but the son had a girlfriend whose father was a rich *hacendado*. The boy was eighteen, and it was time for him to have a wife. He told his mother to go to the *hacendado* with a marriage proposal.

The mother refused. She said, "Why would they listen to a proposal from you? They'd run me off the property." But the boy said, "Give it a try! When you get to the door, just ask if they wouldn't mind talking to that boy's mother." The old woman kept refusing.

But at last she went. When she got to the door of the *hacendado*'s house, the servants paid no attention to her. Then after a while they asked her what she wanted. She answered, "Oh, a little something."

At that point the *hacendado* and his daughter came out, and the father said politely, "You've gone to a lot of trouble to come here. You've been kind enough to bring us a message." But then he said, "You people are dirt poor. You want riches without working. Work! If you're not too lazy to try it. See if you can earn something for a change."

The little old woman trembled so hard she could scarcely hear the words. She hurried off to tell her son how she had been treated. The boy said, "That's enough. Don't go back. Tomorrow morning kill me a chicken to take to the woods. I'll bring back a load of firewood so they won't be able to say I'm lazy."

When the sun came up, the mother packed the chicken and a basket of tortillas, and the boy set off in high spirits. He walked for a while, not far enough to reach the edge of the forest, then he thought, "What's the point? I'd better stop and eat. It's getting late." He broke the chicken into pieces, ate some, then laid the rest aside. When he reached for another piece, he saw that it had been nibbled.

Cautiously he stood back and watched. He saw a mouse come out. He said to himself, "The mouse takes my food and runs off. Where does it go?" He searched until he found the nest. Then he said to the mouse, "You thief! You've stolen my chicken. You and all your children are going to pay for this."

The mouse folded its hands together and prayed to him, "You won't kill my children, will you?" The boy said, "Friend! You finished off my food!" But the mouse said, "Don't kill us. Instead, take all of us home with you. Give us a bed and plenty to eat, and I'll see to it that you marry the daughter of the *hacendado* who has rejected you."

"Can you mean it?" said the boy. Then he picked up the mouse and its family and tucked them into his serape. When he got back to the house, his mother asked, "Where's the firewood? Did you bring it?" But the boy just said, "Hey! Get me some cotton."

"Why cotton?"

"For the mouse's bedclothes."

The mother said, "If you've got a mouse, put it here. I'll kill it." "No," said the boy, "the mice are going to give us everything we need." So the mother went out and bought a pound of cotton and hurried home. With the cotton the boy made a nest and put the mice to bed.

That night, advised by the mouse, the boy went to his girlfriend's.

He knew that the *hacendado* kept all his money in a chest. He found the chest and made a small hole in it. Then he fished out a piece of silver, brought it home, and showed it to the mouse. From that night on, the mouse began carrying the silver, piece by piece, until not a single cent remained in the *hacendado*'s money chest.

Soon the old woman was buying meat for the mouse family, and the boy was riding a fine horse. The horse pranced, and the boy would ride to his girlfriend's like a prince.

Before long the girlfriend's mother took sick. The *hacendado* had to sell off part of his land to pay for a cure. The cure failed and the mother died. After that the *hacendado* himself became sick, and all the rest of his land was sold off to pay the expenses. They knew, at least, that there was money in the chest. But when they went to get it, the chest was empty.

At last the girlfriend's father died, and she became an orphan. She went to her boyfriend's and asked if he had any money. The boy thought for a while, then said to himself, "If I don't tell her the truth, I'll never have what I want." Finally he said yes, the two were married, and of course they were rich.

As for the mice, they were spared no comforts, hidden away where no one could harm them. They were given everything that mice could want until at last the happy couple died of old age.

Mexico (Nahua)

⇒ 89. Let Somebody Buy You Who Doesn't Know You ⇐

Don Jesús Nutmeg was a good Catholic and the soul of simplicity. His beliefs were pure. He was not a man who questioned the faith.

Now, they had a farmer's market in Chiantla, and Don Jesús was there to buy a mule. With his money piled in his pack basket he attracted the notice of thieves, never lacking at farmer's markets, and two of the thieves started to follow him.

Don Chús walked around and around until he saw a mule that pleased him, and after calling attention to its defects, with the owner pointing out its merits, he settled the bill and took his purchase to where he had lodgings for the night. He tied the mule to a stake and threw it some hay.

He knew better than to fall asleep and kept coming out of his room to make sure the mule was still there. Meanwhile the two thieves had been keeping an eye on him. The moment he let up his guard, they untied the mule, and one of them led it away while the other tied himself to the rope and got down on his hands and knees.

A little later, when Nutmeg came out with his torch light, instead of the mule he found a man on all fours chewing hay. He couldn't think what to say. But without coming too close, he crossed himself and finally said, "In the name of the Almighty, what are you doing here?"

The thief answered, "Oh, sir! My benefactor! You see before you a man who fell out of favor with his mother and father, and because of it a witch enchanted me and changed me into a mule. She said, 'Astray in your life, you will now be astray in the world. You will not return to your former shape until you are owned by a believer who is sincere in his faith.' And from then on I endured nothing but hardship. I was sold at auction, and that man, Scholar Corncob, bought me. But he's such a heretic, I couldn't become my old self until my luck willed it that you, who are a saint, should buy me. I just became me again a half hour ago. All I need is to be untied. But how can I do it? My hands still feel like hooves."

"Well!" said Don Chús. "If I let you go, how do I get my money back? Do I get it from you?"

The thief said, "You know I have nothing. Let me be free, give me your blessing . . . and give me five pesos. God will pay you back. Mind you, have you ever known God to renege on a debt?" Moved by compassion, Don Chús sent the man on his way.

The following day Don Chús went back to market to get a replacement for the lost mule. His act of charity had made him lighthearted.

As he looked around, his glance fell on an animal that seemed quite similar to the one he had lost. He noted its size, its coloring, its brand. Then he took out the bill of sale from the previous day and compared all the identifying marks. When he was satisfied that the animal was the one he had bought two days before, he looked it in the eye and said, "You rogue, let somebody buy you who doesn't know you."

Guatemala

⤳ 90. The Mouse King ⤆

All right, they say that in those olden days there was a hut where a peasant couple lived at the edge of a forest, and they had a pretty daughter. The daughter went out for a walk in the forest and found a white mouse asleep at the base of a tree. She picked it up and said, "I'm going to take this home."

It was a beautiful little thing she'd found. Well, wasn't it? But the mouse spoke to her and said, "Don't take me, I beg you. Don't make me a prisoner. I'm the king of the mice, and if you let me go free I'll give you anything you ask for." The girl said, "Ah, that I would like!"

The mouse said, "Whenever you need anything, just come to the base of this oak tree and say, 'My little mouse, my little white mouse, come, I need you.' And there I'll be. I'll give you whatever you ask."

The girl's mind worked quickly. She said, "I'll ask you right now. Change my family's hut into a nice farmhouse."

"It's done," said the mouse. "Go, and you'll see."

She ran off. When she got home, what a surprise! Where the hut had been, there was a magnificent villa. Her parents were overjoyed, and so was she. She thought, "I'll have to go thank the mouse." At that moment her lover appeared. He was only a small farmer, and it was necessary to tell him the truth, "You don't appeal to me anymore. I've come up in the world. Look at this beautiful house!"

Then she began to think, "I was stupid. Why did I ask for a house? I should have mentioned a castle."

She returned to the oak tree and called out, "My little mouse, my little white mouse, please give me a castle." When she got back home, there was the castle. Before she could reach the door, a handsome young nobleman came up to her and asked if he could be her husband.

At the very idea her face lit up. But then she thought, "No, I can do better than this." She brushed the nobleman aside and went back to the oak tree. She announced, "I want to be queen. I want you to give me a queen's palace."

She was asking for something fantastic, wasn't she? She said to the mouse, "I want to marry a king."

"Very well," said the mouse. She went back. There was the castle, fit for a king. She got to the door, and who should come out to greet her but the king's son. These were the wonderful days, long ago, so it was probably the king of England. Or wherever.

Anyway, he asked her to marry him, and of course she said yes. But then she went back to the mouse, who was starting to be annoyed. It said, "Look, you're too ambitious. Nothing satisfies you. You want one thing and then you want another, always something better, and then something still better. Be careful."

"Don't worry," she said. "Everything's perfect. I'm about to marry the son of the king. All I need now is for him to do everything I tell him to do, so I'll be the one who rules the kingdom."

The mouse, finally, had had enough, and it looked her in the eye and said, "I already told you, don't be so ambitious. Now go home."

She left for home, thinking when she got there she'd find the prince as meek as a lamb, ready to do whatever he was told. Imagine her surprise when she found the same miserable little house she had had before, the same little hut, and there were her poor parents in their same old clothes. She looked down, and her beautiful dress was gone. All the fine clothes, the great house, the carriages, everything had become nothing. You know what I mean?

Do you realize? Every time she asked for something, the mouse deceived her, so she only thought she saw it, no? The mouse was testing her. And what did she do but ask for more and still more. The mouse had great powers of mind that caused her to see what she wanted to see.

But at last she stepped over the line and the mouse made her see what was real.

Bolivia / Amalia de Ordóñez

≥ 91. Mariquita Grim and Mariquita Fair ≤

Long ago there lived a woman with a daughter and a stepdaughter, both called Mariquita. But people called the daughter Mariquita Grim and the stepdaughter Mariquita Fair. The one was a fright to look at with a temper to match, while the other was a kind-hearted soul and as pretty as a picture.

Mother and daughter lost no opportunity to torment Mariquita Fair. They made her do all the work and gave her beatings on top of that. Yet she never complained.

One day she was handed a pig and told to raise it. She thought, "Now I have a little friend to play with." But as soon as the stepmother saw that the pig had brought her some happiness, she said, "Tomorrow we'll kill it and put it in the larder."

And that's what happened. The next day, over Mariquita's protests, they butchered the pig. Mariquita was handed the innards. "Take these to the river and wash them off," shouted the stepmother. "Don't lose any, or you won't even live to regret it!"

The stepdaughter went to the river and began cleaning the innards. She had just finished when a fish swam by and carried off the liver. Mariquita began to cry, fearing that if she came back with anything missing she'd be butchered herself.

A dog came along, and the girl said, "Dog, please help me find my pig's liver. If I go home without it, my stepmother will kill me."

"Bandage my sore paw," said the dog, "and I'll bring you the liver." But when she had bandaged the paw, the dog said, "A little old man will be coming soon. He's the one who can help you."

When the little old man came by, the girl said, "Father, please help me. I lost a pig's liver in the river. If I don't find it, my stepmother will do me in."

"Trim my beard," he said, "and I'll get it for you."

Mariquita, good as she was, trimmed the old man's beard, and as soon as she'd finished he ran off, saying, "A little old woman will be here soon. She's the one who can help you."

The little old woman appeared, and Mariquita said, "Mother, help me! I've lost a pig's liver, and they'll kill me if I go home without it."

The old woman, who was the Virgin herself, said, "See that little house, over there? Go mess it up! Kill the dog, cut off the parakeet's head, wring the rooster's neck, and give the baby a sound whipping! Can you do all that?"

"Yes, ma'am," answered the girl.

"Then leave me the basket with the innards, and when you see it again you'll find that nothing is missing."

The girl ran to the house and went in. Angel that she was, instead of doing what she had been told to do, she swept the floor, put everything in order, gave the dog its dish, fed the parakeet and the rooster, put soup on the fire, bathed the baby and tucked it into bed, then hid behind the door.

When the old woman arrived and looked around, she was well pleased. "Who's my housekeeper?"

The dog woofed:

> *Behind the door! She's the one!*
> *Catch her quick, before she can run!*

The rooster crowed:

> *Behind the door! She's the one!*
> *Catch her quick, before she can run!*

The old woman pulled back the door, and when she saw Mariquita she placed her hand on the girl's forehead and said, "Here's my handprint; a star it will seem. The more you scrape it, the more it will gleam."

She was handed a mirror, and in the reflection she saw a star as beautiful as anything you could imagine. She asked, "Would you let me have a cloth to cover my head? If my stepmother sees me with a star she'll be so jealous she'll give me a beating." The old woman handed her a kerchief, also the basket with the pig's innards complete, and Mariquita set off for home.

As she came through the door her stepmother said, "What's that on your forehead?" and she tore off the kerchief. When she saw the beauty mark, she took a knife and scraped at it. But the more she scraped the more it glowed. She began to scream, "Explain yourself or I'll cut your throat. Where did you get that star?"

The girl told everything. Then the stepmother called to her daughter and said, "Tomorrow you'll go to the river and wash pig's innards. When you come back you'll have one of these stars on your forehead."

Said and done. Early the next morning they killed another pig and put the innards in a basket. When the daughter got to the river, she began scrubbing and rinsing. She waited for a fish to swim by, and when none appeared she dropped the liver in the water and started to wail. A dog came along. "Hey, dog!" she said. "Get me that liver!"

"If you'll bandage my paw," said the dog.

"Bandage? I don't put bandages on dogs."

The dog made no reply and ran on. A little old man came by. "Hey, old man! Jump in the water and fetch me that liver!"

"Would you trim my beard?"

"Ask me to trim your beard? How dare you!"

Without another word the old man walked on. Then the little old woman came along. "Old woman, would you get me that liver I dropped?"

"I'll try to find it for you," said the old woman, "if you'll help me with my housework. Could you straighten things up? And then could you start the soup, bathe the baby, fill the water jar, and put out food for the dog and the parakeet and the rooster?"

The girl dropped her basket at the old woman's feet and headed for the little house. When she got there, she said to herself, "What could the old woman have been thinking of?" Ill-tempered as she was, she picked up the trash basket and emptied it all over the floor. She broke

the dishes, whipped the baby, smashed the water jar, beat the dog until
it was nearly dead, and twisted the necks of the parakeet and the rooster until they were both gasping. Then she hid behind the door. When
the little old woman came in, she exclaimed, "Who could have done
this to me?"

The dog gave a barely audible woof:

> *Behind . . . the door! She's the . . . one!*
> *Catch her quick, before she can run!*

and fell over dead. The rooster cackled from the depths of its throat:

> *Behind . . . the door! She's the . . . one!*
> *Catch her quick, before she can run!*

and breathed its last. The little old woman pulled back the door, and
when she saw Mariquita she put her hand on the girl's forehead, saying,
"Where I place my hand a cockscomb will show; try to slice it off and
you'll make it grow."

The girl picked up her basket and went off cheerfully, imagining she
had a star on her forehead. When her mother saw her coming, she said,
"Daughter, what's on your forehead?"

"A star, what else?"

"Goodness no! Look for yourself!" And she shoved a mirror in front
of her.

One look at the horrible cockscomb and the girl burst into tears.
"Mama," she cried, "cut it off!" The mother began slicing away with a
knife. But the more she sliced, the more it grew.

Time passed, and as the two girls became women they remained
true to form, the one as lovely as could be, the other as frightful as ever.
The king's son was about to take a wife. He issued an invitation for all
the young women to come to the palace so he could choose among
them. The stepmother, naturally, would have hidden Mariquita Fair,
but she had no choice in the matter. Those who failed to present their
daughters were to be punished.

When the day of the ball arrived, the prince himself stood at the door to receive the guests. Mariquita Fair was announced. The prince took one look at the beautiful star on her forehead and fell helplessly in love. "Will you be my bride?" he asked. "Yes," she said, and in no time there was a wedding.

When the prince discovered how Mariquita Fair had suffered at the hands of her stepmother and her stepsister, he threw them out of the kingdom. There was nothing for them to do but wander from place to place, everyone fleeing at the sight of the cruel-looking mother and the horrid daughter with the cockscomb sprouting from her head.

Cuba

➣ 92. The Compadre's Dinner ⭠

A man and his wife were so stingy that if somebody came to the door while they were eating they'd hide their food under a towel. The husband had a compadre, and one day the compadre said to a neighbor, "I'm going to my friends' for dinner."

"No!" said the neighbor. "How is it possible?"

"I'll make you a bet," said the man, and he went off to his compadre's. They saw him coming and quickly put their dinner under a towel. The man came in, went over to the towel, and sat on it. The wife said, "You're not comfortable. Sit somewhere else."

"I'm fine," said the man.

Hours went by. Still the compadre was seated on the towel. The husband and wife were dying of hunger. Finally the woman said, "Compadre, stretch out on this bed."

"I'm not particular," he said. "I'll just spend the night where I am."

The compadre lay down on the towel and pretended to snore. The husband whispered to his wife, "I'm so hungry. Go out to the kitchenshed and make us a *majarete*. If he sees you, tell him you're making a pot of starch."

The compadre saw the woman headed for the kitchen and followed her. "Señora, you and I are exactly the same," he said. "We can't sleep, and we both have to starch clothes! Look, I have a handkerchief here that was supposed to have been starched for me, and it never got done. I'm going to have to do it myself." He put the handkerchief over his hand and scooped all the pudding out of the pot. Then he went back to the towel and settled down again.

The woman followed him into the house and whispered to her husband, "He put his handkerchief into the pot and scooped up the *majarete.*"

"All right!" said the husband finally. "Go and make *three* tiny little bread rolls." The compadre pretended to be sleeping soundly. The wife went back to the kitchen, made the three little rolls, and put them on the hearth to bake. The compadre suddenly appeared and said, "What won't happen next! Here you are sleepless again, and I can't sleep either." He began to ramble on. As he talked, he stood in front of the hearth and played with the poker.

"I'm thinking how we three are compadres," he said, "and someday I'll be coming into a nice little inheritance. But why would I want it? I'd give it to you." Tapping the poker in the embers, he broke the three little rolls into tiny bits.

The woman went back to the house and reported to her husband, "He completely ruined the rolls." The compadre lay down again and pretended to snore, this time so loudly the woman had go outside.

Before she left, she whispered to her husband, "Here's what you do. Slip out through the window with a bite to eat, and if he hears you chomping he'll think there's a burro on the patio eating our lettuce."

Hearing the sounds from the patio the compadre jumped up and pounded on the wall to frighten off the burro. He ran outside with a stick and delivered so many blows that he killed his compadre.

"What have you done to my husband?" cried the woman.

"Husband?" said the compadre. "I thought it was a burro."

Dominican Republic / Carmen Sánchez

≫ 93. The Hog ≪

A man who had a hog ready for butchering began to think how he might keep it for himself. When his neighbors killed hogs they always shared meat with him. Now it was his turn.

The day before the hog was to be killed, the owner's compadre suggested a plan. "We'll butcher it tonight," he said. "I'll help you. Then tomorrow you'll say, 'A thief came during the night and took my hog.'"

The owner agreed. After dark, when everyone else was in bed, they got together and did the butchering. The next morning the man went out to slice some bacon for breakfast and couldn't find the hog anywhere. His compadre, it seems, had gotten up early and taken the whole thing.

The man went knocking on doors to ask if anyone had seen his hog. The first house he came to was his compadre's.

"Compadre!" he said. "The hog's been stolen!"

"Yes, of course," said the compadre. "Now you're supposed to tell the other people."

"But it really is stolen. Somebody came and took it."

"Shame on you," said the compadre. "You won't even share it with me after all my help. May God spare you!"

Colorado / Presciliano López

≫ 94. Two Sisters ≪

A poor woman had three children. Every day she went to her rich sister's house to bake the bread. It's how she made a living for her three little ones. In the evening, when her work was done, she was careful not to wash the dough from her hands until she returned home, so she could give the wash water to her children for their supper.

One day her sister asked her what she was feeding her young ones that made them so fat. How could she do it, poor as she was, when her sister, who was rich, had children who were skinny? Her sister told her the truth: "I wash up at home every night and my little children make their supper out of it."

The rich sister said, "You'll have to stay later than usual tonight. Wash your hands right here and feed the water to your skinny little nieces and nephews." So the poor woman washed up at the rich woman's house. When she finally got home to her children, she washed her hands again in order to make do, as best she could, for her own family.

The day after that, as she was hurrying home from her work, she met an old man on the road. He said, "When you get back to your children, you'll find things changed, and whatever is there will be yours for the taking."

By the time the poor woman got to her house, the place had become a beautiful finca with a herd of cattle in the pasture, and on top of that, there were three chests of silver money. The poor thing was delighted. Immediately she sent her son to her sister's for a grain measure to total up the silver.

When the little boy came for the measure, the aunt asked, "What's it for?" He told her, "My mother's measuring grain," and she said, "Where did your mother get grain?"

"A neighbor sent it over to us."

The boy ran back to his mother, and the mother measured the money. But the measure had a crack in it, and a piece of silver got stuck in the crack. When the boy returned the measure, his aunt noticed the coin. She said, "Tell your mother to come here at once. I have to talk to her."

The child brought the message to his mother, and she ran to see what her rich sister wanted. When she got there, the sister asked, "Where did this money from?" The poor thing answered, "Oh dear, it must have come from God."

"The next time God comes to see you," said the sister, "send him over to my place." Then one day God arrived at the rich woman's house unannounced, and since she had always supposed that God traveled in style, and here was a beggar at her door, she ordered her servants to turn the dogs on him.

The poor old man ran away. And less than half an hour after he disappeared, the woman's house and everything she owned crumbled to dust. She was forced to beg for charity at the door of her sister who had formerly been poor. The rest of her life she went from door to door crying for alms, scraping together what little she could to keep her children alive.

Puerto Rico

⇒ 95. The Ghosts' Reales ⇐

There was a man who owed money to everybody. He tried first one thing and then another, but he could never find a way to get out of debt. If he didn't owe a real, he owed a céntimo, and there were always three or four bill collectors at the door.

Finally, worn out by so many creditors, he told his wife he had thought of a way to get rid of them. He would pretend to die, and she would pretend to wail. But she must tell all the neighbors, and especially the creditors, that it was her husband's wish that she alone should sit with the corpse until the following morning.

The wife did exactly as she had been told. The creditors came, and each said, "I forgive him." But there was one who would not forgive. He said, "Your husband owes me a real." The man kept waiting to be paid. He refused to go away. If there was nothing left but the burnt stub of a candle, the wife would have to give it to him.

When evening came, the coffin was carried to the church. The wife began to sit watch by herself, according to her husband's request, while the man who was owed the real stood inside the church door waiting for his candle stub.

At midnight seven thieves came down the street looking for a place to divide the money they had stolen that night. Seeing a light in the church, they went in. Without paying attention, they sat down next to the casket where the corpse was laid out. Hearing the commotion, the man who was supposed to be dead sat up in the casket, and one of the thieves screamed. The rest turned around to look, and when they saw the dead man rising up they rushed out of the church, leaving their money on the floor.

The husband and wife wasted no time. They picked up all the money and got away.

The creditor who hadn't been paid was still behind the door. He started to cry out, "My real, my real, my real!" The thieves, just coming back to the church to get their money, heard the cries. Thinking that ghosts were dividing the loot, with only a real for each one, they reckoned the church was filled with the dead and ran away terrified, this time with no thought of ever returning.

Dominican Republic / Julio Antonio Medina

PART NINE

➤ 96. The Bad Compadre ⬅

A merchant named Mariano went to sell a little bread and a little sugar and a little meat. He went to make a journey, and when he returned, he brought much money.

His compadre, Juan, heard about it. Then Juan said to his wife, "Do me favor, do me an errand. Go see our compadre, maybe talk to his wife." The woman went, she talked to the man. "Do me a favor, compadre. Sometime when you go on a trip, tell your compadre. Do him that favor. 'I'll follow along, I want to make that trip' is what your compadre is saying."

"All right," said Mariano, "I'll be gone for a week, and I'll earn a little money. I'll buy a little bread and a little meat and a little sugar and a little sausage. That's what I'll take with me."

"Thank you, I'll tell your compadre," and she returned to her husband and told him what Mariano had said.

"Well, all right," said Juan. "I'll be gone for a week, but I won't take much with me, only a little bread and a little meat and a little sugar and a little sausage. That's what I'll take, I'll take it and sell it." So Juan got a little money and bought the bread and bought the meat and bought the sugar and bought the sausage. A week later he went on the business trip with his compadre. They went together.

Now Mariano knew magic, and when Juan lagged behind, Mariano went on ahead and made a spell. A swarm of leaf-cutter ants appeared, and he left them there in the road. When Juan came along, he could not get by them. Quickly he put down his bag and took out four pounds of sugar, pouring it in front of the leaf-cutter ants, together with half the bread. And with that they went running off the road.

When Juan caught up with his compadre, he found him in the shade.

"Well," said Mariano, "why don't you walk faster? I've been here a long time. I've been waiting for you."

"Well, yes, compadre," replied Juan. "I walk slowly." And again his compadre set off at full speed and Juan lagged behind.

Juan came to a bend in the road, and right there in front of him were two snakes. Frightened, he quickly took out two pounds of meat, one pound for one snake, one pound for the other. After eating the meat, they gave him permission to pass.

When at last he caught up, his compadre said, "Well, why can't you walk faster?" and "What have you been doing?"

"Nothing, compadre."

"Come on, let's go. Time is passing."

"All right," said Juan.

Then Mariano went off at full speed, and Juan lagged behind again. He was not a good traveler. When he got to a turn in the road, he saw two coyotes. Quickly he took out all the bread that was left and half the meat. He gave it to them, and they ate it up. Then they ran off into the woods, and Juan went on and caught up with his compadre.

"Well, compadre, what happened to you?"

"Nothing, compadre."

"Why were you so far behind?"

"Well, compadre, I got a little tired."

"Come on, let's go. Already the sun is going down."

"All right, compadre," said Juan. Then Mariano ran on ahead and made more magic. He made two hawks appear and left them there in the road. Poor Juan was unable to pass, because the hawks were ready to eat him. Quickly he took out all the sausage and threw it in front of them. They carried it right off, giving him permission to pass. Continuing on, he caught up with his compadre.

"Well, compadre," said Mariano, "can't you go a little faster?"

"Well, yes, compadre, but I got a little tired. I had to slow down."

"Compadre, I'm going to tell you something. Don't fall behind anymore, because we're just about to reach the plantation that I'm headed for."

"All right," said Juan. Then Mariano ran ahead and made more magic against his compadre. He called up two jaguars, and when Juan came along, there they were, right in the middle of the road, waiting to eat him. Juan was frightened. But he took out his last piece of meat and threw it in front of the jaguars, and they ran off. That was all the meat he had, and Mariano had hoped he would be killed. But God did not give the jaguars permission to eat poor Juan.

When he caught up with his compadre, Mariano said, "Oh, why can't you walk faster?"

"Well, yes, compadre, I do walk slowly."

"Did you meet any animals on the road?"

"No, I didn't see any."

"Well, don't lag so far behind, because we're almost to the plantation."

"All right, compadre."

By the time they arrived at the plantation, the sun had gone down, and they had to look for a place to sleep. But first Mariano went to the owner of the plantation and talked to him. "I've brought along a servant who works wonderfully. And you will see for yourself how he does everything I say. And well, tomorrow I will show you this servant. But such a servant! He works wonderfully! Wonderfully!"

"All right, all right," said the owner. "Let's leave it at that."

Next morning Mariano brought his compadre to work, and when evening came, the poor man returned very tired. Then the bad Mariano went to the owner again and said, "Now, patrón, I am going to tell you something. You give me a little money because I found our servant. And let me tell you what this servant told me. He said, 'I don't want this work, it's too easy.' That's what he told me. And then he said, 'I'll mix a quintal of sugar and a quintal of salt, the two quintals mixed, and when morning comes I'll give you the sugar in one bag and the salt in another.' This is how our servant talks, patrón!"

"Well, all right," said the owner, "and if he doesn't do it, I'll have him punished."

Then the owner called poor Juan. "Look here, son, is it true that you say you can sort out a quintal of sugar and a quintal of salt from two quintals mixed?"

"No, sir," replied Juan, "I never said that."

"Oh yes you did," said Mariano. "My servant speaks only the truth."

"Well now, we'll give you a quintal of each," said the owner. And at that moment, right in front of poor Juan, they mixed the salt with all the sugar. Now it was done.

At eight o'clock that night Juan went to sleep, and the poor man quickly dreamed. He dreamed that the ants were saying to him, "Son, do not worry. We will take care of it, and at six in the morning you will find a bag of sugar and a bag of salt. Yes, it is true, and the bags will be well filled."

Morning came. Mariano said, "Did you do what we talked about?"

"Compadre, I did not do anything."

Mariano went to look at the bags, and there they were, the salt and the sugar, completely separated. He went running to the owner of the plantation. "Patrón, patrón," he called at the door.

The patrón got out of bed. "What do you want?"

"Sir, come quickly. Our servant has done it. What I told you was not a lie. Our servant works wonderfully. And let me tell you what he told me. He say he wants to do something big. So I said to him, 'Make a cornfield of five hundred mecates. Make it on the side of the mountain and have it ready by six tomorrow morning.' And he says, 'So what! I can do it.' That's what he says, patrón."

"All right," said the patrón, "I will call the man.

"Now, is it true that you say you can have a cornfield of five hundred mecates ready by six o'clock tomorrow morning?"

"No, sir, I didn't say that."

"Oh yes he did," said Mariano. "Our servant tells the truth. Five hundred mecates by tomorrow morning. Have your foreman there at half past five."

Juan was silent.

That night the animals came. They cleared the forest and planted the cornfield. At three o'clock the foreman was sent for. He went with the other men. They went to see the cornfield, and it was true. There it was. The foreman measured it. Five hundred mecates, all done. Then he came back and delivered the record of it to the owner of the plantation.

Then the bad compadre went by another road to see the patrón. He said to him, "You see, I told you how well our servant works. But now, patrón, he says, 'I wish they would tell me to make a four-story house with a clock at the top, and the clock with four bells in it, and the house all plastered and whitewashed inside, with a garden and a water tank in front, and the lady of the house, the daughter of the patrón, with a beautiful new baby at her breast, by five o'clock tomorrow morning. All these things I would do.' That's what our servant says, patrón, and our servant speaks only the truth."

"Well, thanks to my servant if he will do me that favor," said the patrón. "And let us see if he can bring a child to the breast of my daughter! If he does not, I will turn him over for punishment. And all the work must be finished tomorrow morning at six. Now let me call him. Juan, come here!"

"Sir?" answered Juan.

"Can you really do what you say, my servant? Is it true you can do all this work?"

"No, sir."

"And it must be done by six tomorrow morning."

"As you wish, sir," said Juan. And Juan went to sleep. He dreamed. He did not dream thoughts. Rather, all the animals spoke to him in his sleep.

"Juan, we are telling you not to worry. We will do the work," said the animals in his dream. And it was true. They did the work in one night. The coyotes made the bricks. The snakes did the plastering. The hawks laid the bricks, and the leaf-cutter ants brought the beams.

The hawks went to get the clock. They both went. One brought the clock, and one brought the child from another country. All these things they brought, and they finished the whole house and painted it. And when the daughter of the patrón went inside, she felt nothing. But once inside, she felt a child at her breast.

When morning came, there was the garden, and there was the water tank, all well made. At six o'clock the owner of the plantation arrived. He looked, and there was the garden and all the rest, done in one night.

Then Mariano went to the owner and said, "Patrón, now you see what I told you. The servant is very good, this servant of ours. All he promised, all of it he has done. And you will pay me well, because I am the one who told you he would do it."

"All right, Mariano, I will pay you well, because now I have a big house with a clock. Yes, I will pay you well. Come get your money this afternoon."

"All right, patrón. But Juan will be coming to ask you for money too. Don't give him much. No, give it to me, because I found the man."

"All right," said the patrón.

That afternoon at five o'clock, Mariano and his compadre both went to get their pay. The patrón gave poor Juan only a little, while Mariano got much.

That night Juan slept at the plantation, as he had done before. And in his dream the animals said to him, "Poor Juan, it is a shame what Mariano has done to you, what has happened to you because of your compadre, how he has mistreated you, and all because we did you a favor and did the work for you ourselves. Now the place has been pointed out where we will be waiting for Mariano. Do not be afraid. We will catch hold of him, and we will take his life, because we feel badly about what happened, and it is better that his bones remain in that place.

"You are free, because the sin is Mariano's. You bought the meat, you made the expense, and now, in that place, we will put in your hand all the money he has. When we take the money, we will give it to you, Juan." This is what they told him in his dream.

In the morning he arose, and it was true. When he arrived at that place, there were the animals in the road with his compadre, Mariano, who had gone on ahead. The animals caught hold of him, but they did nothing to Juan. The punishment of God was on his compadre, and all his bones remained in that place.

Then when Juan reached his town, Mariano's wife went to see him.

"Hello, compadre."

"Come in, comadre."

"Please, compadre, in what place did your compadre stay?"

Juan said to her, "Comadre, he took too many drinks, and because he feels a little sick, he will be delayed. He stays in the tavern."

"All right, compadre. Well, thank you. Then he will come in a little while."

Guatemala (Cakchiquel) / Francisco Sanchez

⇒ 97. Black Chickens ⇐

This was a husband whose wife had her eye on another man. The husband kept watching, but the more he watched the less there was to see. One day he began thinking what to do and announced he was going off to work in his fields. The minute he was out of sight, the wife called, "Come, honey. At last he's gone." Little by little the lover eased himself toward the house. The woman kept making signals, waving him on. She stepped out the door, motioning with her hand. "It's all right, he's not here! Finally!"

Meanwhile the husband, instead of going to the fields, headed for church, because he knew his wife went there often to pray, asking the statues to make miracles. He went inside and stood behind the Christ with his arms outstretched behind the arms of the cross.

After a while the wife came into the church and bowed down and said,

> *Father, listen!*
> *Make me a miracle.*
> *Make my husband blind.*
> *Take away my husband's*
> *   eyesight,*
> *So my lover can be with me*
> *   in the house.*

Then she bent over and prayed again,

> *Father, listen!*
> *Make me a miracle.*
> *I'll give you a candle*
> *   worth two reales,*
> *Tomorrow a candle*
> *   worth one real,*
> *Day after tomorrow,*
> *   half a real,*

Day after that,
a quarter real.

When her prayer was finished, she cried out, "Father! Talk to me now! What would be good to give my husband, to make him blind?"

Then she heard a miracle. It was the voice of her husband coming from behind the crucifix. The voice said, "What would be good is black chickens."

The woman went home from church happy. Now she knew what to feed her husband to make him lose his eyesight.

Already the sun was high. The man thought, "I'll go home and have a few words with my wife about not bringing my lunch to the field," though he hadn't been to the field at all. When he got to the house, he threw the door open and said, "Where were you? What happened to my lunch?"

"I couldn't get finished with the sweeping. Then I killed a chicken and it took me forever to pluck it."

"Come on," he said. "I'm hungry."

She put the chicken in a pot and cooked it up nice with a chili sauce. "Here it is," she said. "Eat!" While her husband was eating, she set aside a pan of special stew. "What's that for?" he wanted to know. "It's for me," she answered. But she wasn't telling the truth. The stew was for her lover.

When evening came, the husband said, "Listen, do you think I'm not seeing very well?" The wife answered, "Oh, God!" But immediately her mood became happier.

In the morning the husband went off again, and again he came back before noon, complaining. "Why didn't you bring me anything to eat?"

"I was too busy plucking this chicken. Besides, there's nothing to bring you. We don't have anything in the house but these chickens."

The next day she killed another chicken and cooked it up. In the evening her husband said, "Listen! More and more I keep seeing less!" Then the woman was convinced that the black chickens were the good ones.

The day after that she killed another chicken, and in the evening her husband said, "Now I see nothing at all!"

Then the lover showed up behind the house, not far away. The wife motioned him with her hand, whispering, "Come on! He can't see a thing!"

The husband shouted, "Where are you? Are you here?"

"Yes. Hush! I'm right here."

"Heaven help me!" said the husband. "What a terrible thing it is to be blind! I'll never be able to work again. How can I go deer hunting?" While he rambled on, the wife slipped outside. Her lover was there. They embraced. "Come in," she whispered. "What can he do to us now? He's completely blind." Little by little the lover edged his way into the house.

The wife sat down to grind corn with her lover in front of her, caressing her. From his chair in the far corner the husband looked away and kept talking, "What a thing it is not to see anyone! What will become of me? I'll end up dying an early death." Then he said to his little son, "Come here, son. Come get advice from your father. Let me tell you how you must work, what you must do to support yourself."

And all the while the wife and the lover were tickling each other in front of the husband. He went on, "If it is God's will, so be it. I've become blind. My life's work reaches to here and no farther. My son, bring me my Remington, so I can give you lessons on how to handle a weapon."

The boy brought the rifle. "Let's see now, son. Come closer, so I can teach you to shoot." Then the two of them took hold of the Remington, pointing it away. "This is what you do when you have to kill a deer. Aim under the foreleg, straight for the heart." The wife was laughing.

"So, my son, if it's a bird, you have to shoot the wing. If it's a deer, you shoot under the foreleg." And then, "If it's a goat, you do it this way." Bang! He blew the lover backwards with a single shot. Then he took the strap off the rifle and whipped his wife until she fell to the floor. "What trouble!" she said. "And don't get the idea it'll happen again!"

"Why not?" he said. "Go ahead and try it!"

The next day two neighbor women stopped by the house. They said to the wife, "Aren't you coming with us?" "Where to?" "To the altar." "No thanks! Not for me!" said the wife.

"Why not?" said the husband. "Go ahead, try it!" Then the wife helped him pick up the dead man, and they dragged him outside like a dog. The police came and questioned the husband, "What's this?" "I caught him with my wife." "But you shot him three times?" "No, never, I shot him once." Then the captain picked up the dead man, and they carried him off.

A few days passed. The two neighbors came by again, and the wife was out in the yard gazing at the hills. The neighbors said, "What makes you so superior?" "What do you mean?" "We don't see you at church or at the dances anymore." "No thanks, that's not for me."

"Why not?" said the husband. "Go ahead, try it!"

"How can I go to church when the statues don't tell me the truth? Why promise them candles?"

"You mean you don't like their miracles? Why not?"

"How stupid do you think I am? How crazy? My lover was to blame; it was all his fault. I shouldn't have done it. Perhaps I won't do it again."

Mexico (Tepecano)

➢ 98. Doublehead ➢

There was a married man whose wife disappeared every night. He wasn't aware of it, because in the morning when he got up, there she was, fixing his lunch bag.

A neighbor advised him, "Your wife goes out after dark. She spends the night with somebody else. See for yourself. She puts a stick of wood under the covers so you think she's next to you."

The man took a look. It was true. When morning came he stopped at the neighbor's house. "You were right. Her head went out, her arms went out, her legs went out. Only her body stayed behind."

The next night he watched again, and again she came apart. The neighbor said, "Let her know what you've seen. Keep a bowl of ashes next to the bed, and put salt in it. Rub it on the place where she comes apart. Then wait for her to return."

That night when the head came back, it tried to clamp on. Not good! It tried again. Not good! It fell off, came back, and tried again. Not good!

The arms came. Not good! The legs. Not good! Then the head said, "Get up."

"What do you want?"

"Get up. I want to know why you did such a miserable thing. And to keep you from doing it again, I'm going to clamp onto you!"

She fastened herself to her husband. From then on he had two heads. When he went to work, his wife's head went with him. When he ate, she ate too; and when she answered a call of nature, it was through her husband's body.

When it was time to sleep, she detached herself from her husband and lay beside him, chatting amiably.

But at his slightest move, she was on the alert. He could not get away from her.

One day they were walking in the woods and came to a sapodilla tree. One of the fruits had fallen to the ground. The man picked it up and split it open. He gave half to his wife's head and ate the other half himself. "This is delicious," he said.

"Climb up and see if you can find another one."

"All right," said the husband. "You stay here." He took off his coat and laid it on the ground, so the head would have a nice place to sit while he climbed the tree. He found another fruit and threw it down on the coat. He broke off another, but it turned out to be green. "I got a green one," he said. He threw it away, and it hit a deer that was passing by. The deer began to run.

The wife's head heard the deer and thought it was her husband trying to escape. She rushed off in pursuit, and when she caught up with the deer she fastened herself to its rump. The deer ran on, trying to shake off the head. What with all the brambles the deer passed through, the head finally died and fell off.

The husband climbed out of the tree. He cried, "My wife is gone! She must have thought I was running away. I'll never find her now. What can I do?"

He went to confession.

Then in later years when he was asked for the story, this is what he told: "The priest said I had to keep looking for my wife's head. I looked in the woods; I looked everywhere. When I found it I went back to the priest, and he said, 'Bury it!' And after that I had to sweep the grave. He told me to go every day and report what I saw. Once, while I was watching, a little calabash tree grew out of the ground. I told the priest. He said, 'Keep watching. See what happens.'

"The tree grew larger. Here and there a little blood oozed out. I described it to the priest. He said, 'Keep watching.' Then a calabash fruit began to form, and as soon as it was ripe I could hear a commotion inside. I kept watching. When the fruit burst, I saw that it was filled with little children. I told the priest, and he said I should go into town to get pieces of cloth.

"As more fruits ripened, little children started falling from all parts of the tree. I dressed them with the cloth to cover their nakedness, just as the priest had told me. And when the last of them had fallen from the tree, I gathered them up in my arms and brought them home."

El Salvador (Pipil)

⇒ 99. Littlebit ⇐

Learn to tell it and tell it to teach it.

There was a needy old couple, miserable in every way. The husband was a water carrier, and the wife took in laundry. But as hard as they worked, the money they earned barely kept them from starving to death.

One night when they were talking, "How poor we are!" "So all-alone!" the old wife said. "If at least we had a child, even if it was just a little bit of a thing, it could help us over the rough spots. There'd be someone to talk to in the evenings and take care of us in case we got sick."

"How true," said the old water carrier. "But what's the use of wishing?"

At that a voice came booming down from the roof, "You shall have the child you wish!"

The two old people looked at each other, stupefied. "Goodness, it's getting late." "We'd better be off to bed."

Next day as usual they got up at dawn. The old man left to haul water for his customers, and his wife started scrubbing the clothes. No sooner had she begun her work than she felt something wriggling in the sleeve of her blouse. She thought, "It must be a lizard or whatever," and she shook her right arm and the something fell into the washtub. She couldn't see what it was, but she heard a squeaky little voice, "Mama, pick me out of the water before I drown."

The poor old soul strained her eyes and saw a baby boy so tiny he was nearly invisible, bobbing up and down in the soapy water. She caught him at once.

Then she and her old husband brought him up, showering him with all kinds of love and attention. They called him Littlebit, and the name fit, because he was no bigger than your little finger.

He grew, but not in size, only in strength. And when he shouted, his voice was louder than any man's.

No one suspected the old people were raising a child. He was so pretty, they kept him well hidden for fear someone would steal him. He was all their comfort and entertainment, their consolation in life.

Seven years went by, and the old parents became so feeble they couldn't work anymore, and their meager savings came to an end. When there was nothing left but thirty cents, the old laundress said to Littlebit, "My son, take ten cents. Go to the butcher and bring back some meat."

Littlebit arrived at the butcher shop and rapped on the counter. The butcher looked around and saw no one. "Who's rapping?"

"It is I, Littlebit," said a big voice that startled the butcher. "Give me ten cents' of meat scraps."

The butcher heaped the scraps on the counter and with effort managed to see a tiny man holding a coin scarcely six inches off the floor.

"And how will you carry ten cents' of meat scraps? What you're ordering is bigger than you are."

"Sir, be serious. If you sold me a whole steer I'd be able to carry it."

"Very well," said the butcher. "Give me the ten, and you can have that steer hanging up in the window."

Littlebit took the butcher at his word, threw the steer over his shoulder, and ran off. The butcher just stood there with his mouth open. At the sight of a steer traveling down the street upside down, people crossed themselves. No one could see Littlebit. He was under the carcass.

Delighted with their son's purchase, the old parents sent him off to buy five cents' of bread.

Littlebit walked into the bakery and rapped on the counter. "Who's rapping?"

"It is I, Littlebit." The voice was like thunder. "Give me five cents' of bread."

The baker leaned over the counter and could hardly believe what he saw. "And how will you carry five cents' of bread?"

"How? The same as any other customer. You could sell me that breadbasket on the counter there, and you'd see me carrying it off."

"Then give me the five cents."

"Here, take it. And please put the basket on my shoulder."

The baker lowered the basket slowly, worrying that he might crush his tiny customer. But the moment Littlebit felt the load touch his shoulder he was out the door. The baker watched in amazement as the basket went gliding down the street.

The parents greeted it joyfully, and immediately they sat down to a full meal. Then the old woman said, "Let's slice enough of this steer for a couple more days. Tomorrow I'll make jerky out of the rest. It'll keep us in beef forever!" They chatted on contentedly. That night the old woman said, "Who'd mind a sip of tea?"

The little man said, "Mama, give me ten cents. I'll get you five cents' of sugar and five cents' of tea herb."

"Take it, my child."

Littlebit arrived at the corner grocery. "Who's rapping?"

"Littlebit! I'd like five cents' of sugar and five of the tea herb." The grocer leaned over the counter. "But child! How could you carry it?"

"It's not your problem, sir. If you like, give me a case of sugar and a barrel of herb and watch me carry the whole thing without any help."

"Well then, pass me the ten cents and take the case and the barrel."

"Here's the ten. Could you tie the case to the barrel?"

The storekeeper rolled his eyes but filled the order just the same, then stood speechless as the case and the barrel sped through the door and down the street.

You can imagine how happy the old people were when they saw this precious cargo coming in. No more dying of hunger. What else could they wish for? They all took a deep draught of tea and went to bed.

The next day the old woman jerked the steer meat. When she was finished, she said to no one in particular, "If only we had a few onions, and with all this jerky, we could make a *valdiviano.*"

"Mama, isn't there five cents left? Let me have it. I'll get the onions." She gave him the five and he was out the door. As he headed for the street he noticed one of those miniature penknives people wear as trinkets. He picked it up and dropped it in his moneybag.

He hadn't gone but a few more steps when he came to a farmer with a load of onions in two heavy saddlebags, one on each side of his horse.

"Hear me, friend! Sell me five cents' of those onions." The farmer looked around but couldn't see the customer. He was hidden in the tall grass at the edge of the pavement.

"Five cents' worth of those onions!" he repeated. And as soon as the words had left his mouth a cow came by, eating the grass, and Littlebit found himself inside the cow's stomach. But he kept on hollering from inside the cow, "Five cents for some onions! Listen here, my mother's waiting!"

The farmer scratched his head and kept looking around. Who would know that a voice like that could come from a cow?

Now, it wasn't until he had been completely swallowed that Littlebit realized what had happened to him. But he wasn't afraid. He took his penknife out of his moneybag and carved his way to freedom, hardly clean but safe and sound. The cow, meanwhile, fell over dead. Littlebit took hold of it by the tail and dragged it home. "Now this will make more jerky." His parents bathed him and gave him a change of clothes, and he ran back to the farmer, shouting, "How about it, friend? Can I get five cents' of onions or what?"

"But, child, that would be half a dozen! Just one of these onions alone would crush you."

"You're dreaming, friend. Take five cents for both your saddlebags and watch me."

An easy five cents, thought the farmer, and he took the money, then dropped his jaw as he watched his saddlebags and all his onions disappearing down the street.

It wasn't long before Littlebit's fame had spread through the whole country and the king was asking to see him. Since the capital was not close by, Littlebit needed a horse. So he caught a mouse and trained it. He made the bridle and the stirrups from a hairpin; he cut his saddle from an old kidskin glove, the reins and the rest of the harness from a shoestring. For his sword he hung the little penknife from his belt with the blade open. Then he jumped on his mount and was off to the city.

When he arrived, he was suddenly the toast of the town. The king, the queen, the princes, the princesses, and all the grandees and dames of the court ran after him. He was certified as the chief wonder of the realm, and the king found a spot for him next to the throne. But Littlebit explained that he couldn't stay. His parents were old and in misery. He would have to return to them, for without his support they would die.

Such a good son! The king loved to hear it. "Bring your old parents to us," he cried. "We'll give them everything they need." And in short order they were all together in the palace.

When the king's enemies declared war, Littlebit pushed the artillery to the field of battle, and with his roaring voice he shouted all the orders from the general to the front lines. For his services he was decorated with medals and ribbons and given the rank of field commander. He lived out the rest of his days loved and honored throughout the kingdom.

Chile / Manuel Oporto

⇒ 100. Rosalie ⇐

A young man who had started out from home to earn some money came to a hut where a giant lived with three daughters, and falling in love with the youngest, he made up his mind to stay. "You may stay and be my son-in-law," said the giant, "but only if you can perform the four tasks that I will give you." The young man agreed.

"First," said the giant, "I have a great desire to take my bath the moment I get out of bed instead of having to go all the way down to the lake. Tonight you will bring the lake up to the hut, so that when I wake in the morning I can sit on my bed and put my feet in water. Use this basket to carry it."

The young man hardly knew what to think. But the giant's youngest daughter, whose name was Rosalie, told him not to worry. That night, while everyone else was sleeping, Rosalie went down to the lake, and with her skirt she swept the water up to her father's bedside. When the giant awoke, he was astonished to find the water lapping the leg posts of his bed.

Next the giant took a large pot, threw it into the deepest river he could find, and told his future son-in-law to bring it back home. After diving many times, the young man was about to give up, for the river was so deep he could not reach the bottom. Then Rosalie told him to go with her to the riverbank that night, and she would dive. But he must call her name when she reached the bottom, otherwise she would be unable to rise to the surface again. This they did, and the following morning the giant found the pot once more in the house.

The next task was to make a cornfield of a hundred mecates. The young man must clear and burn the forest, do the planting, and at midnight of the same day bring back a load of fresh young ears. He set to work at daybreak but by sunset had accomplished practically nothing.

Then Rosalie stretched out her skirt, and all the forest was immediately felled. Using the same magic, she dried the brush, burned it, sowed the corn, raised the plants, and harvested the young ears, so that the young man was able to take them to her father at midnight.

Furious, the giant went to his wife to ask her how they could get rid of this would-be son-in-law. "We'll have him thrown from a horse," said his wife, and they arranged that she herself would turn into a mare, the giant would become the saddle and stirrups, and Rosalie would be the bridle. Rosalie, however, overheard their conversation and warned the one who loved her to treat the bridle carefully and not to spare the horse and the saddle.

Next morning the giant told the young man to go out into the savanna, where he would find a mare already saddled. He was to mount her and bring her back to the house. Meanwhile the giant and his wife and Rosalie took a shortcut through the forest, and by the time the young man arrived, they had changed themselves into the fully saddled mare.

The young man, who had brought along a stout club, jumped onto the mare's back, and before she had a chance to buck, he began beating her as hard as he could. All but paralyzed by the blows, the mare was unable to throw her rider, and after a few moments she sank exhausted to the ground.

The young man returned to the hut, where a little later he was joined by the giant and his wife, bruised all over and worn out.

The son-in-law had now completed his four tasks, but the giant, going back on his word, told him there were yet more. That night Rosalie decided they must run away, while the giant and his wife would still be sore from the beating. When the two were asleep, Rosalie took a needle, a grain of white earth, and a grain of salt, and spitting on the floor, slipped quietly out of the house to meet the young man.

At daybreak the giant called to Rosalie to get up. "It's all right, Papa, I'm getting up, I'm combing my hair," replied the spittle. It spoke with the voice of the giant's daughter, so he suspected nothing.

A little later the giant again called to Rosalie, asking her if she was dressed yet. Again the spittle replied, "I'm combing my hair." By this time, however, the spittle was almost dry and could only answer in a whisper. Suspicious, the old lady went into Rosalie's room and discovered the trick that had been played on them.

Then the giant set out in pursuit of the fleeing couple, rapidly gaining on them. When he had nearly overtaken them, Rosalie turned herself into an orange tree, and the young man disguised himself as an old grandfather. Stopping next to the tree, the giant asked if a young couple had gone by.

"No," replied the old grandfather, "but stay a moment and rest, and eat some of these oranges." The giant tasted the oranges and immediately lost his desire to run after his daughter and the young man. Returning to his hut, he explained to his wife that he had been unable to overtake them.

"You fool!" cried the old lady. "That orange tree was Rosalie."

Again the giant set out in pursuit. When he was once more at the point of overtaking them, Rosalie turned the horse they were riding into a church, her young man into the sacristan, and herself into an image of the Virgin. When the giant reached the church, he asked the sacristan if he had seen any sign of the missing pair.

"Hush!" replied the sacristan. "You must not talk here, the priest is just about to sing Mass. Come inside and see our beautiful Virgin."

The giant entered the church, and the moment he laid eyes on the statue he lost all thought of pursuing the young couple. Returning once again to his hut, he told his wife how he had seen the Virgin and had decided to come home.

"You fool, you fool!" cried the old lady. "The Virgin was Rosalie. You are too dim-witted to be of any use. I'll catch them myself."

The giant's wife set out at full speed. Rosalie and the young man traveled as fast they could, but the old lady ran faster, and gradually she caught up with them. When she was almost within reach, Rosalie cried out, "We can't fool her, we'll have to used the needle."

Stooping down, she planted the needle in the ground, and immediately a dense thicket grew up. For the moment they were out of danger. As the old lady cut her way through the thicket, the young couple fled on. At last she got clear of the thicket and began gaining on them once more.

When her mother had nearly caught up with them, Rosalie threw down the grain of white earth, and immediately a mountain rose up. Again the couple fled away, as the old lady, half out of breath, scrambled to the top of the steep slope, then slid down the other side.

Clear of the mountain at last, she continued on, rapidly gaining on her daughter and the young man. When she had almost overtaken them, Rosalie threw down the grain of salt, and it became an enormous sea. Rosalie herself became a sardine, the young man a shark, and their horse a crocodile. The old lady waded into the water, trying to catch the sardine, but the shark drove her off. "Very well," said the old lady. "But you must remain in the water seven years."

When the seven years were up and they were free at last, they came out on dry land and made their way to the town where the young man's grandparents lived. Rosalie, however, could not enter the town, because she had not been baptized. She sent the young man ahead, telling him to return with half a bottle of holy water, and on no account was he to embrace his grandparents, for then he would instantly forget his Rosalie.

The young man arrived at his old home and greeted his grandparents, but he would not permit them to embrace him. Feeling tired, he decided to rest awhile before returning to Rosalie with the holy water. Soon he was fast asleep, whereupon his grandmother, bending over him, softly kissed him. When he awoke, he no longer had any recollection of Rosalie.

For days Rosalie waited for him to come back. At last, one morning, seeing a little boy playing at the edge of the town, she called to him and asked him to get her some holy water. The boy brought it to her, and she bathed herself with it and entered the town. There she learned that the one she loved, at the urging of his grandparents, was about to marry another young woman.

Rosalie went straight to the grandparents' house, but the young man did not know who she was. Nevertheless, she succeeded in having the marriage postponed three days. Then she prepared a great feast and invited all the elders of the town as well as the young man she loved. In the center of the table she placed two dolls she had made: one that resembled herself; the other, the young man.

The guests arrived and sat down to the feast. Then Rosalie pulled out a whip and began thrashing the doll that represented the man.

"Don't you remember how you were told to carry water in a basket?" she cried, and "Whang!" the whip cut through the air. As it struck the doll, the man himself cried out in pain.

Again she spoke to the doll, "Don't you remember the pot at the bottom of the river and how I brought it up for you?" "Whang!" and again the young man cried out in pain.

"Don't you remember the cornfield you had to make and the fresh young ears I grew for you?"

"Whang!"

"And the seven years we spent in the sea?"

"Whang!"

Again the young man shrieked in pain. Then his memories returned to him, and forgetting his bride-to-be, and with a cry of joy, he threw himself into Rosalie's arms.

Mexico (Yucatec Maya)

⤜ 101. A Day Laborer Goes to Work ⤛

There was a little man, a little laborer. Every day he went off to his work. He and his wife lived near their comadre and her husband. During the day, while the man was at work, the comadre would watch to see what the wife was doing.

In the morning after the man had left, the wife would follow her husband to bring him his meal. Later she would come back to feed her animals. This was all that the neighbor could see.

In the evening the man would pass his comadre's house on his way home. They lived in friendship, these two compadres, but the man's wife and the comadre were not friendly.

Well, this woman, that's the comadre, told the man a lie. She said she kept seeing a stranger at his house. "He comes and sits in your place. Sometimes your meal arrives early, doesn't it? And sometimes late? Well, first the stranger has to eat. Then he lies in your bed." Of course this wasn't true, but here's how she told it: When she saw the compadre on his way home, she stopped him and said, "So, you're back from work, compadre?"

"Yes, dear comadre, I've returned."

"Ah, you poor thing. How tired you are every day."

"I'm tired, but I have to look for work to meet my expenses. I have to earn money to take care of my family."

"You poor thing. Here you are dying of hunger and thirst, and a stranger comes to eat in your house."

"Who is it?"

"A man. He comes and talks with your wife. First they eat, then they make love. Finally she brings you your tortilla. You can't believe how it hurts me to tell you this. He comes in the morning at eight, nine, ten o'clock. He keeps your wife from bringing you your little meal. He keeps her busy."

"Comadre, it can't be true. Are you sure?"

"Yes, very sure."

The man was angry now, and he went on his way. "I'm going, comadre. We'll see each other tomorrow." She answered him, "Good, compadre."

He was nearly home now. It was their custom for the wife to come out on the patio as soon as she saw her husband arriving from work. She went out to greet him. He was enraged, he didn't greet her, he just seethed with anger. He punched her and slapped her in the face and kicked her. Unable to control his anger, he took out his knife and stabbed her. The wife fell down and died.

Now it dawned on him what he had done, and as he saw his wife fall, the realization came over him and he repented and asked God to forgive him. Then he got his blanket out of the house and left. He was afraid because of what he had done. He went out on the road, and as night fell he kept going.

About three in the morning he came to a house at the roadside. A light was burning. An old woman lived there with a little boy. The man asked permission to come in. He said, "Good evening, lady. Good evening, lady." He said it three times. He wasn't sure what he was saying. He was in a daze.

"Good evening?" she said. "Rather, good morning. Dawn is almost here."

"Ave Maria! I thought it was night."

"No, it's nearly dawn already, it's three in the morning. You must have been walking all night."

"Lady, permit me to rest awhile."

"Where are you going?"

"I'm going to a city, to ask for one or two days' work. I need to earn a little money."

"Come in and rest," said the lady.

He rested. He just napped without sleeping, because he kept remembering his wife. He thought about God and said to himself, "Who knows if what my comadre told me is true? I killed my wife." He was almost in tears, and all his thoughts were of God. The old woman let him rest about two hours, then said, "Are you ready to get up, dear man? It's time for work. You'll need to be there at sunrise." The man was incredulous. "Where? Are you sure?"

"Yes, there are some big men who are looking for help, because none of their workers ever return."

"How will I find this place?"

"Get up," said the lady. "I'm going to give you some coffee and dry tortillas. You'll need them, the work is very hard. The little boy will show you where the rich men live, who give out the work."

The man drank his coffee and ate his tortillas. He barely got them down, he was so upset over what he had done to his wife. They gave him another mug of coffee and a plate of beans. He said thanks but had to refuse. "Wait," said the woman, "the little boy will walk with you awhile to show you the way, and then he'll return here."

The man went off with the boy to where the big men lived. He called to the men and greeted them as they came out. One of them said, "You're looking for work? Good." Immediately the big man saddled his horse, threw on the reins, and mounted. Then he drove the little man like an animal out to the forest. "This is the place," he said. "Clean out these trees, make me a decent piece of land for planting." He handed him a big ax to work with, but it was dull and useless. "You'd better work," he said. "Or else!"

The little man started to chop at the trees, but they wouldn't fall. All he could do was bang on them and make noise.

About ten o'clock the little boy came again to bring the man tacos and water. "How is the work going?"

"Good," said the man. "I'm getting there, a little at a time."

"You've cut down some trees? Where are they?"

"These blessed trees! They only make noise, they don't want to fall."

"I know. That's the kind of work these men have. What were you thinking? Why did you come here?"

"I had to have work."

"Well," said the boy, "here's food. While you're eating, I'll help you with some of them." He picked up the ax, and with one or two chops the trees thundered and fell.

The man kept eating his lunch. "Ave Maria," he said to himself, "how does this boy do it?" In less than an hour the boy had piled up ten trees. "Well, with these you ought to get by," he said. "When the big man comes back to see what you've done, he won't be able to touch you."

At eleven o'clock the big man appeared. "How much have you done? Ah, good, good. I think you are better than I am. But don't let up." The big man was carrying a whip, and his horse was bucking. "Hurry! Work!" And he went off to check on his other fields, while the little man kept on working, making no progress.

The next day they gave him more work. When he went back at night, the old woman asked him, "How is it going?"

"Slowly."

"I know," said the woman. "They want you to hurry. If you don't, they beat you. That's their custom, you have to be fast. Each day I'll send the boy to help with the work, so they won't harm you. As long as you're with me, nothing will happen to you."

The next day the big man gave him a sickle to harvest wheat. The sickle wasn't sharp, it kept sliding off, and the blessed wheat refused to be cut. At ten o'clock the little boy arrived with the lunch. "How much have you done?"

"I'm working as fast as I can, but the sickle is useless."

"Here," said the boy, "eat, and I'll help you." He picked up the sickle and began swinging it back and forth. In no time there was a mound of wheat. "Now you'll be safe when the big man comes." And the little man trembled at the thought. "Hurry," said the boy, "finish eating and get back to work. I have to leave now, so he won't find me here."

The big man arrived. He said, "What have you been up to? Blast! You're better than I am!" He wanted to be angry at the little man, but he couldn't. "Do you want to eat? Here, I've brought you some food." But the man said no. The old woman had told him, "Don't eat anything they give you."

"All right, don't! But if you're hungry, let me know. I'll give you food. On top of that, you're earning your pay." But it wasn't true. They were cheating him. There was no pay except beatings for not working fast enough.

The next morning the old woman told him, "You'll be getting another kind of work today." She knew all about it. "It won't be the same as before," she said. "They've been testing you."

"Whatever they give me, God will help me."

"Yes, the boy will come bring you a taco," she said, "but you must work."

So once again he arrived at the house of the big man. "Now you are going to plow furrows where you cut down the wheat," he was told. "Go hitch up a team and get the plow." But they gave him two bad mules that didn't want to be hitched. They bit him and kicked him. The little boy had advised him, "Don't be afraid when you try to hitch the big man's mules. Just punch them and you'll subdue them. These animals they give you are like wild beasts."

And they gave him the mules and he roped them together. It was work. They bit his hands. "Ave Maria!" cried the laborer, and he kept his thoughts on God. He put on the reins and the mules bit his hands again. He slapped them around. They were so wild that fire came from their mouths and eyes. They didn't want to be driven or pull the furrows.

The little boy came again and asked, "How much work have they done?"

"They don't want to go."

"Ah, they'll go," said the boy. "You eat, and I'll help you with a furrow or two."

Well, he took hold of the animals and spoke to them slowly. Immediately they began to pull furrows. They cut every row in the field. But when the man finished eating and tried to take charge of his team, they bit him again, and they kicked him until fire poured from their hooves and their eyes and their noses. "Hit them, punch them if they do that to you," said the boy. "Beat them, don't be afraid of them. That's why they gave you a whip." The man listened and beat the mules. And the mules cried out, "Compadre, stop! You're killing us!"

At last it was evening, and the man untied the mules. He put them in the corral, gave them food, and went home to the house of the little old woman.

"How much have you worked?" she asked. "How tired you look."

"Yes, tired. Those animals they gave me wouldn't move."

"Ah, that's the way they are. Well now, you've done your penance. Now you can go back to your own house. Rest. Tomorrow you go home." The man rested, he lay down, they gave him food. Tortillas and beans. And water, no pulque.

About three in the morning the old woman said, "Are you up?"

"Yes, lady, I'm awake."

"Now you may go to your house. Your wife is there, crying. She lights a candle for you and remembers you. She is all right. You beat her. But what you did to her was not your fault. It was the fault of your comadre—the one you drove like an animal yesterday, the one you tied up. You were punished for what you did to your wife, and your comadre was punished also. You drove her, and she pulled the plow. Now go to your wife. She is crying, thinking she has lost you. She doesn't know where you went. Go see her."

"Yes, lady. Thank you." He got up.

"Go on, go see her now. Forget what was done to her, forget what we've talked about." And the old woman showed him her bleeding heart, and it was the dear Virgin, with the mark of the wound on her breast.

"Don't always believe what people tell you," she said. "Believe what you see. Now, when you pass your comadre's house, you will talk with her. Her eyes are blackened from what you did to her yesterday."

He went home and greeted his comadre, whose house was on the road near his own. She was black and blue and cut up from the beating. "Ah, dear compadre," she said, "you punished me yesterday."

"So, it was you?"

"Yes, it was me."

"But I only did what the boss told me to do. I was carrying out orders. I didn't know it was you."

"Ah, so that's how it was, compadre. I told you a lie. And for this, I believe, we went to the place where the Devil lives."

Mexico (Otomí) / Jesús Salinas Pedraza

➤ 102. The Moth ⬅

A man and a woman lived happily together with their only child, a little boy.

But the man went off on a journey, leaving his wife in tears, and while he was away she spent the nights sleeplessly spinning.

One night, as the little boy lay awake, he asked his mother, "What is it that flutters there beside you, that I hear you talking to?" The mother answered, "Oh, just someone who loves me, a little friend who comes and keeps me company."

When the man returned from his journey, his wife was out of the house. He began talking with his son, asking him how his mother had spent the nights while he was gone. "Someone who loves her came every night," said the little boy, "and she stayed up late, spinning and talking to him."

Hearing this, the man went out to look for his wife. When he found her, he threw her over a cliff and killed her.

Then one night, as he sat before the fire, thinking of what had happened, his little boy cried out, "There he is, Mama's lover! The one who kept her company!" and he pointed to the moth that had come to his mother's side during the long nights of her husband's absence. Realizing his mistake, the man became strangely quiet. His grief overwhelmed him, he no longer moved, and at last he stopped breathing and his body grew cold.

Peru (Quechua)

➣ 103. The Earth Ate Them ⥸

An old man had three daughters who were constantly in want. He was so tight he refused to buy food, and it was all they could do to keep body and soul together.

One day, as the old man lay dying, he called his daughters to his bedside and whispered his last request: they must bury him with all his money, in gold and silver coins, which they would find in a bag hidden behind a panel in the wall. He had to instruct the girls how to find this moneybag, since they had no idea it existed. Naturally the daughters said they would do as their father wanted.

The old man died, and the girls laid the bag in his coffin.

Many days went by, and finding themselves desperately poor the three sisters got together and decided to steal the purse from their father's grave. They were sure he would never miss it. Besides, it would save them from starvation. The eldest, they agreed, should be the one to go after it.

The next day, late, just at vespers, the eldest sister went to the cemetery and fetched the moneybag. She brought it home and set it aside, thinking they would be able to start using it the following morning.

But that very night, before they had finished their dinner, there came a knock at the door, and when they looked through the keyhole, there was their father, returned from the other world.

Frightened half to death, they crouched in a corner and refused to open up. The next morning they brought the money to the cemetery and put it back in the coffin.

A few days later, in dire need, they stiffened their resolve and decided to try again. This time the second oldest was elected to go. And off she went. But that night again the father came knocking, and the next day they returned the money as they had done the time before.

After a few more days the youngest sister announced that she was going to bring home the moneybag and keep it no matter what. If the father came for it again, she'd open the door and face him down.

She went to the cemetery just as she'd said she'd do, brought home the bag, and hid it where the father would not be able to see it if and when he arrived.

That night at his customary hour he knocked on the door. The youngest sister called, "Who's there?"

"Your father!" came a hollow voice as if from the earth.

She opened the door and there stood a skeleton. The two older sisters shrank back in horror. But the youngest motioned him to his old chair, and he settled himself noiselessly the way ghosts do. While the older sisters held their breath, the youngest spoke up:

"And your legs, Father?"

"The earth ate them," answered the ghost.

"And your hands and your arms, Father?"

"The earth ate them."

"And your ears, Father?"

"The earth ate them."

"And your hair and your beard, Father?"

"The earth ate them."

"And the bag full of money, Father?"

"You mean you didn't take it?" came the hollow voice, picking up strength. In a fury the ghost jumped out of the chair and disappeared, much to the dismay of the sisters, who were consoled nevertheless by the bag of money hidden safely away. In fact—

They were happy as the dickens
And ate chickens.

Argentina

EPILOGUE

TWENTiETH-CENTURY MYTHS

One should always fear spirits, gods, and ancestors, but never the living.

proverb / Aymara (Bolivia)

Resisting Hispanic influence, oral literature of strictly Amerindian origin flourished throughout the twentieth century, hardly as an afterthought but vigorously in many areas from New Mexico to Argentina. While folklorists turned their attention to transplanted Old World lore, anthropologists continued to document native cultures that had been little known, transcribing oral tales in quantities far surpassing the Hispanic collections. Even in Indian Mexico, which had been written off by early-twentieth-century authorities as hispanicized, purely native lore was found to have survived, notably among the Lacandon Maya of Chiapas and the Huichol of Jalisco. And to an impressive degree among other Mexican groups as well, not to mention more remotely situated cultures in Costa Rica, Colombia, Venezuela, Ecuador, Peru, Bolivia, Paraguay, and Argentina.

Indian lore, wherever it is unmixed with Iberian tradition, cannot be called Latino; and, as noted elsewhere in this book, the mixing, when it does take place, occurs in one direction only. Indian storytelling techniques and subject matter are not absorbed by Ibero-American communities; that is, not at the level of folklore. They have had a pronounced effect, however, on Latin American literature, as can be seen in the fiction and poetry of Rosario Castellanos, Miguel Asturias, Mario Vargas

Llosa, Ernesto Cardenal, and many others, who have looked upon Indian narrative art as a cultural resource. This is not the same as bringing the symbolic Indian into literature as a tragic or noble figure. What is meant is that Indian oral art has become a literary influence, as with the Peruvian Vargas Llosa, who retells twentieth-century Machiguenga tales in his novel of 1987, *El hablador* (The storyteller), creating a bridge, if a troubling one, between Hispanic and Indian traditions—troubling for the Hispanic side because the fictional *hablador* actually crosses that bridge in a renunciation of Western culture.

We may speak of Indian folklore, yet Indian narratives cannot comfortably be called folktales; they have both the immensity and the inwardness that Europeans associate with an earlier stratum in their own culture, when myth was freely produced. Indian storytellers do distinguish between serious tales and those told for entertainment only. But exact terminology would be hard to adjust to the very brief sampling that can be offered here, to which the term "myth" in the original Greek sense, "story," may be broadly applied. This follows the custom of some, if not all, anthropologists.

The twelve myths given below have been chosen to reflect the main anthology, opening with a tale that suggests the power of stories themselves and closing—in both cases, though to different effect—with a final question: Can death be permanent? In between are some of the other familiar themes—marriage, world creation, and romantic courtship. Observe that money and nonsense, those durable staples of European folklore, are not represented. And there are some reversals. Instead of "The Witch Wife," we have "The Buzzard Husband"; in place of the male Creator, at least three instances in which the Creator is female.

It can be noticed that Indian tellers have a way of pulling the story out of the social sphere and into the wider world of nature. A countertendency, often revealed in the same stories, draws the listener into the depths of personality, safely beneath the necessary world of social ills. The result, we may say, is medicinal, a kind of healing. The similar claim that European folktales are a form of folk psychotherapy is well known, if controversial. With myth, the proposition is less easy to ignore, though the line of inquiry, since the target is elusive, must again be controversial. "The Condor Seeks a Wife," with its heroine who retreats to the safety of her mother's lap, and "The Priest's Son Becomes an Eagle," with its sudden escape into nature, may be considered in this light.

Just as Old World folklore has its standard fairy tales and Aesopic fables, Indian lore has tale types that jump from language to language, spreading out over large geographical areas. Three of these are included here. The first, "The Buzzard Husband," belongs to Mexico and Central America. The second, "The Dead Wife," is a pan-Indian type, more common in North America than in Latin America and with a history of documentation that goes back to at least the early 1600s. The third, "The Revolt of the Utensils," also a pan-Indian myth, has an even older pedigree.

In much the same way that European tales can be traced to such sources as the medieval *Gesta Romanorum* and the fifth-century *Panchatantra* of India, native American myths have early colonial and pre-Columbian prototypes. A case in point is "The Revolt of the Utensils," which appears in the sixteenth-century *Popol Vuh*, the sacred book of the Quiché Maya of Guatemala. Written in alphabetic script in the 1550s by one or more Maya scribes, the *Popol Vuh* incorporates stories that recall pictorial versions on Maya vases of a thousand years earlier. The myth of the rebellious utensils, in which the earth is rid of an early, imperfect race of humans, tells a story of cultural destruction. The people's cooking pots, griddles, grinding stones, weapons, and other artifacts rise up against their masters and put them to death, returning the world to a state of nature. Although this particular story has so far not been found on an ancient Maya vase, a version of it is illustrated on a pre-Inca pot from Peru, showing the combative utensils with arms, legs, and angry little faces. The modern version given below, from the Tacana of Bolivia, has the utensils in a playful mood, holding their power in reserve—perhaps as a gentle reminder that the war between nature and culture, if seemingly resolved in favor of culture, is not finished yet.

⇒ 104. Why Tobacco Grows Close to Houses ⇐

In former times tobacco plants were people. They loved stories, and for this reason they always lived close to the walls of houses. That way they could lean forward and listen whenever stories were about to be told.

Even if they just heard talking they would get as close to the walls as possible and listen. Therefore the Mother arranged her creation so that tobacco plants would never grow anywhere except around houses, up close to the walls. There they can listen easily. In addition the Mother commanded that tobacco be chewed with coca leaves, because that way tobacco can hear the stories directly from the mouths of the tellers.

Kogi (Colombia)

⇒ 105. The Buzzard Husband ⇐

Once there was a man long ago. He was very lazy. A loafer. He didn't want to do anything. He didn't want to work. When he went to clear trees, he asked for tortillas to take along. But he only went to eat.

Lying on his back in the woods, watching the buzzards gliding in the sky, he said, "Come on down, buzzard, come here, let's talk! Give me your suit!" The buzzard never came down.

Every day the man returned home. "How is your work?" his wife would ask.

"There is work to do, there is still work to do. There is quite a bit because it can't be done easily. There are so many large logs," the man would say. And he left and he came back. And he left and he came back. And that's how the year passed.

The poor woman's heart! "My corn is about to be harvested," she said. But how could her corn be harvested? Sleeping is what the man did. He spreads out his woolen tunic. He goes to sleep. He makes a pillow out of his tortillas.

"God, My Lord, holy buzzard, how is it that you don't do anything at all?" he would say. "You fly, gliding easily along. You don't work. But me, it's hard with me. I'm suffering terribly. What agony I suffer! Look at my hands! They have lots of sores already. My hands hurt, so now I can't work. My hands are worn out. I don't want to work at all."

Maybe Our Lord grew tired of it. The buzzard finally came down.

"Well, what is it you want with me, talking that way?"

"It's just that you seem so well off," said the man. "Without a care you fly in the sky. Now me, I suffer so much. I suffer a lot, working in my cornfield, and I haven't any corn. I'm poor. My wife is scolding me. That's why, if you just wanted to, you could take my clothes, and I'll go buzzarding."

"Ah!" said the buzzard. "Well, I'll go first to ask permission. I'll come back, depending on what I'm told."

"Go, then!"

"Wait for me."

The man waited. He sat down, waiting for the buzzard. "Why don't you come to change places with me? I can't stand it anymore, I'm tired of working," he said. He had taken his ax and his little billhook with him to clear the land. He cleared a tiny bit. He felled two trees, then he returned home again.

"How about it, have you finished clearing your land?" asked his wife.

"Oh, it seems to be nearly ready."

"Ah," she said. And another day passed.

"So, I'm going again today," he said. "Get up, please, and make me a couple of tortillas."

"All right," said the wife, and the man went off to talk to the buzzard. He sat down immediately. "God, I'm hungry already. I have too much work."

"Oh?" said someone. It was the buzzard, coming down. It landed.

"What? What do you say?"

"Our Lord has given permission. He says we can change places. He says for you to go, and me to stay."

"But won't my wife realize that it isn't me anymore?" asked the man.

"No, she won't know. It's by Our Lord's command," said the buzzard, and he took off his feathers. He shook off all his feathers. The man took off his pants, his shirt, his wool tunic, everything. The other one put them on, and when he finished putting on the wool tunic, the clothes began to stick on. And you see, the buzzard's feathers and everything, they too began to stick on.

"See here," said the one who had been a buzzard, "don't do anything wrong. Let me tell you how we eat. We see fumes coming up when there is a dead horse, or sheep, or whatever. You'll see that if it's a small meal there are only a few fumes. If the meal is bigger, then the fumes go high. If you see lots of fumes coming up, go, because it's a very big meal. Go now! Go on! Go have fun! But come back in a few days."

"All right, I'll come back, I'll come talk to you then."

After the man who had been a buzzard worked at clearing his land for three days, the buzzard who had been a man returned. "God, it's true, I'm no good for anything," he said. "Already you've done a good job clearing the land. Look how much work you've done! My wife prefers you. Did she tell you I was good for nothing?"

"She didn't tell me much of anything. 'Why do you stink so? You reek!' is what she said."

"And what did you tell her?"

"'Oh yes,' I said, 'I certainly do stink. It's because I'm working. In the past I used to lie to you. I never used to work. I just slept all the time. But now go see for yourself, if you want. When I burn our land, go look! Go and help me watch the fire.'"

"And will you take her along?"

"Yes," he said. And the wife went along when the burning of the trees began. He took her along. "Sit here. First, I'll clear the fire lane. I'll make a fire lane around our land," he said.

"All right," she replied. The wife sat down and prepared her husband's meal. Then they ate.

The smoke from the burning trees was coming up. It was curling up. The buzzard who had been a man thought it was his meal. He remembered. When they had exchanged clothes, the other one had said, "You'll see fumes rising in the sky."

When the smoke came up from the trees that were burning, that's when the buzzard came whooshing down. He landed right in the fire and burned up.

"Is the buzzard so stupid?" said the wife. "That's what the disgusting thing deserved, dying like that."

"It was the command of Our Lord," said the husband. "But never mind. Our corn will be harvested now. In a week we'll come to plant it."

"All right!" said the wife. They left. They went home. "See here," said the husband, "I'm just covered with soot. I'll change. It's because I sweat so. That's why you say I stink."

How would she know he was a buzzard?

Do you know how it was discovered? A neighbor said to her, "Oh, why don't you want to admit it? Your husband turned into a buzzard."

She told her husband, "I was right that you stink so! You see, you're a buzzard."

"Oh, what concern is that of ours?" he said. "What people won't come and tell you! Who knows if it's so?"

"Ha, how come it isn't true? I was right, it's a buzzard's stink. I was right that you're a buzzard."

"Who knows?" he said. "I never felt that I was a buzzard. Just because I sweat, it seems I have a bad odor."

"Oh, forget it," she said, "so long as you provide for me."

They had things now. They ate now. The woman's husband wasn't a loafer anymore. He worked well.

Those are the ancient words.

Tzotzil Maya (Mexico)

➣ 106. The Dead Wife ⇐

A Mískito named Nakili had lost his wife, whom he loved very much. He went to her grave, and there, suddenly, he found himself in the presence of her *isiñni* [disembodied soul]. The soul, which was only about two feet high, announced that she was now starting on her journey to Mother Scorpion [the spirit of the hereafter].

The man wanted to go with her, but she told him that such a thing was out of the question, because he was still alive. But he insisted and would not be persuaded to stay behind. So they started out together, and as she led the way, she turned off onto a very narrow trail that he had never seen before.

They arrived at a place where there were many moths flying about. She was afraid of them and did not dare to proceed. But he chased them off, and they continued on their way.

After a while the trail led between two low pine trees, so close together that the wife could barely pass. The husband, being his normal size, was unable to squeeze through. Instead, he walked around the two pine trees.

Continuing on, they came to a gorge spanned by a bridge the width of a human hair. Below was a huge pot of boiling water attended by *sikla* birds. The wife, small and light as she was, was able to walk over this narrow bridge. But Nakili did not find the distance across very great, and so he jumped it.

Then they arrived at a very large river, where there was a canoe paddled by a dog. This river was swarming with *bilim* [a tiny fish], which the soul thought were sharks. On the opposite shore they could see the country of Mother Scorpion, and everyone there appeared to be happy.

When the souls of those who had not led a righteous life tried to cross the river, the canoe would overturn, and the souls would be eaten by the *bilim*. The wife was ferried across safely by the dog, while the husband managed to swim alongside.

On the far shore they were received by Mother Scorpion, a very tall, stout woman with many breasts, to whom the inhabitants of the place came occasionally to suck like babies. She appeared to be angry at

Nakili for having come, and she ordered him to go back to earth. He begged her to let him stay, because he loved his wife very much and did not wish to be separated from her. She agreed finally that he could remain.

In this country no one had to work. There was plenty of excellent food and drink and no lack of amusements. But after staying for some time, Nakili longed to go back to earth in order to see his children again. Mother Scorpion allowed him to leave on condition that he would not return to the hereafter until he died. Then she put him in a huge bamboo rod, which she placed on the river. After a while he noticed high waves and realized that he was on the ocean, and finally a gigantic breaker threw him ashore, just in front of his own hut.

Mískito (Nicaragua)

⮞ 107. Romi Kumu Makes the World ⮜

In the beginning the world was made entirely of rock and there was no life. Romi Kumu [Woman Shaman] took some clay and made a cassava griddle. She made three pot-supports and rested the griddle upon them. The supports were mountains holding up the griddle, the sky. She lived on top of the griddle.

She lit a fire under the griddle. The heat from the fire was so intense that the supports cracked and the griddle fell down on the earth below, displacing it downward so that it became the underworld; the griddle became this earth. She then made another griddle which is the layer above this earth, the sky.

She made a door in the edge of the earth, the Water Door, in the east. There was lots of water outside, and when she opened the door the waters came in and flooded the earth.

The waters rose inside the house. All the possessions in the house became alive. The manioc-beer trough and the long tube for sieving coca became anacondas; the post on which resin is put to light the house became a cayman and the potsherds and other flat objects became piranha fish. These animals began to eat the people.

The people made canoes to escape the flood but only those in a canoe made from the *kahu* tree survived. Everyone else and all the animals were drowned.

The survivors landed on top of the mountain called Ruriho near the Pirá-paraná. There they began to eat each other as there was no food, and the animals that survived ate each other too.

Then the rains and floods stopped and it was summer. The sun stayed high in the sky, and it became hotter and hotter and drier and drier. This went on till the earth itself caught fire. The earth burned furiously and everything was consumed. The fire was so hot that the supports of the layer above cracked, and it came crashing down.

Barasana (Colombia)

108. She Was Thought and Memory

The sea existed first. Everything was dark. There was no sun, no moon. There were no people, no animals, no plants, only the sea, everywhere. The sea was the Mother. She was water, water everywhere. She was river, lake, stream, and sea, existing in all places. And so, in the beginning there was only the Mother. She was called Gaulchováng.

The Mother was not a person, not anything, nothing at all. She was *alúna* [soul, life, or desire]. She was the spirit of what would come, and she was thought and memory. The Mother existed only as *alúna* in the lowest world, the lowest depth, alone.

When the Mother existed in this manner, the earths, the worlds, were formed above her, up to where our world exists today.

Kogi (Colombia)

➢ 109. Was It Not an Illusion? ➤

Was it not an illusion?

The Father touched an illusory image. He touched a mystery. Nothing was there. The Father, Who-Has-an-Illusion, seized it and, dreaming, began to think.

Had he no staff? Then with a dream-thread he held the illusion. Breathing, he held it, the void, the illusion, and felt for its earth. There was nothing to feel: "I shall gather the void." He felt, but there was nothing.

Now the Father thought the word. "Earth." He felt of the void, the illusion, and took it into his hands. The Father then gathered the void with dream-thread and pressed it together with gum. With the dream-gum *iseike* he held it fast.

He seized the illusion, the illusory earth, and he trampled and trampled it, seizing it, flattening it. Then as he seized it and held it, he stood himself on it, on this that he'd dreamed, on this that he'd flattened.

As he held the illusion, he salivated, salivated, and salivated, and the water flowed from his mouth. Upon this, the illusion, this, as he held it, he settled the sky roof. This, the illusion, he seized, entirely, and peeled off the blue sky, the white sky.

Now in the underworld, thinking and thinking, the maker of myths permitted this story to come into being. This is the story we brought with us when we emerged.

Witoto (Colombia) / Rosendo (no surname)

⟫ 110. The Beginning Life of the Hummingbird ⟪

Our First Father, the absolute, grew from within the original darkness.

The sacred soles of his feet and his small round standing-place, these he created as he grew from within the original darkness.

The reflection of his sacred thoughts, his all-hearing, the sacred palm of his hand with its staff of authority, the sacred palms of his branched hands tipped with flowers, these were created by Ñamanduí as he grew from within the original darkness.

Upon his sacred high head with its headdress of feathers were flowers like drops of dew. Among the flowers of the sacred headdress hovered the first bird, the Hummingbird.

As he grew, creating his sacred body, our First Father lived in the primal winds. Before he had thought of his future earth-dwelling, before he had thought of his future sky—his future world as it came to be in the beginning—Hummingbird came and refreshed his mouth. It was Hummingbird who nourished Ñamanduí with the fruits of paradise.

As he was growing, before he had created his future paradise, he himself, Our Ñamandu Father, the First Being, did not see darkness, though the sun did not yet exist. He was lit by the reflection of his own inner self. The thoughts within his sacred being, these were his sun.

The true Ñamandu Father, the First Being, lived in the primal winds. He brought the screech owl to rest and made darkness. He made the cradle of darkness.

As he grew, the true Ñamandu Father, the First Being, created his future paradise. He created the earth. But at first he lived in the primal winds. The primal wind in which our Father lived returns with the yearly return of the primal time-space, with the yearly recurrence of the time-space that was. As soon as the season that was has ended, the trumpet-vine tree bears flowers. The winds move on to the following time-space. New winds and a new space in time come into being. Comes the resurrection of space and time.

Mbyá Guaraní (Paraguay)

⇒ iii. Ibis Story ⇐

Once in the old days, as spring was drawing near, a man looked out of his lodge and saw an ibis flying overhead. Joyously he cried out to the other lodges, "An ibis has just flown over my lodge. Come see!" The people heard him and came rushing out, crying, "Spring has returned! The ibises are flying!" They leaped for joy and talked loudly.

But the ibis is a delicate and sensitive woman. She must be treated with respect. When she heard the commotion made by those men, women, and children, shouting on and on so raucously, she became angry. Deeply offended, she called forth a thick snowstorm with bitter frost and much ice. Snow fell and kept falling for whole months. Snow fell incessantly, the entire earth was covered with ice, and it was agonizingly cold. The water froze in all the waterways. Many, many people died. They couldn't board their canoes or travel to get food. They couldn't even leave their dwelling places to gather firewood. Heavy snow lay everywhere. More and more people died.

After a long time the snow stopped falling. Soon the sun came out and shone so brightly that all the ice and snow melted. The earth had been covered with it, even up over the mountaintops. But now there was much water flowing into the channels and into the open sea. The sun grew so hot that the mountaintops were scorched—and remain bare to this day. The ice in both the broad and the narrow waterways melted. Then at last the people could get down to the beach and board their canoes and go find food. But on the high mountain slopes and in the deep valleys the ice held fast—and still does. The sun was not hot enough to melt it. It can yet be seen, extending even out into the sea, so thick was the ice sheet that once lay over the earth. The bitterest of frosts and a dreadful snowfall: all of it was brought about by the ibis. Indeed, she is a delicate and sensitive woman.

Since then the Yamana have treated the ibis with great reverence. When she approaches their lodges, the people keep still. They make no noise. They hush up the little children to keep them from shouting.

Yamana (Chile)

≥ 112. The Condor Seeks a Wife ≤

A condor fell in love with a young woman tending her flock of sheep. He changed himself into a young man and came and stood beside her where her flock was grazing.

"What do you do here?" he asked.

"I graze my flock," she answered, "and with my slingshot I chase away the fox who comes to eat my lambs and the condor who tries to catch me in his talons."

"Would you like me to stay with you and help you chase the fox and scare away the condor?"

"Oh no," she replied, "for then I would lose my freedom. I love my sheep and I love to be free. I do not wish to marry."

"Then I will go. But you have not seen the last of me."

The next day the condor returned, again disguised as a young man. "We can talk, can't we?" he asked.

"Yes, we can talk," she said. "Tell me, where do you come from?"

"I come from the high mountaintops, close to the thunder. I see the first light of dawn and the last light of evening. Won't you go there with me?"

"No, I do not care for your mountaintops. I prefer my pasture and my sheep. And I love my mother. She would cry for me if I were gone."

"I will say no more," he said. "But do me a favor. I have a burning itch behind my shoulder. Lend me the long pin from your shawl so I can scratch it." She lent him the pin, and when he had finished using it he went away.

The next day he returned. "You have bewitched me," he said. "I cannot live without you. Come away with me now."

"No, I must not. My sheep would miss me. My mother would cry."

"Ah," he said suddenly, "I have the same burning itch behind my shoulder. If only you would rub it for me with your smooth fingers, you would cure me forever."

As he bent over, she climbed onto his back, and the moment he felt her resting on his shoulders he became a condor and flew into the sky.

After a long voyage they reached a cave near the summit of a mountain. In the cave lived the condor's mother, an ancient lady with faded plumage. And in other caves on the same peak were other condors. A great multitude.

The condors greeted the young woman's arrival with shouts of joy and noisy flappings of their wings. The old mother was delighted to see her son's bride and anxiously cradled her in her huge wings, for she was shivering in the cold air.

At first the girl was happy with her young condor. He was affectionate. But he brought her nothing to eat.

Finally she said to him, "Your tender caresses make my heart happy. But I am growing weak with hunger. Don't forget that I must eat and drink. I need fire. I need meat. I need the good things that grow in the earth."

The condor took flight. Discovering an untended kitchen, he stole some hot coals from the hearth and carried them home. With his beak he opened a spring in the mountainside and brought back water. From the fields and pathways far below he collected bits of flesh from dead animals. He dug up gardens and brought home potatoes.

The meat was foul-smelling. The potatoes had gone soft. Nevertheless, the young woman was overcome with hunger and devoured this unpleasant food. She wished for bread, but the condor was unable to provide it.

After a while she began to feel homesick. She wearied of the bad food and the constant embraces of the amorous condor. She began to be thin and her body grew feathers. She laid eggs. She hatched her chicks.

Meanwhile the young woman's mother was weeping in her empty house. Pitying her, a parrot who lived in the neighborhood came and spoke to her, "Do not weep, dear woman. Your daughter is alive in the high mountains. She is the wife of the great condor. But if you will give me the corn in your garden and enough room in your trees to perch and nest, I will bring her back to you."

The mother accepted this offer. She gave the parrot her corn patch and room to nest in her trees.

The parrot flew to the mountaintop. He chose a moment when the condors were off guard and picked up the young woman and carried her back to her mother's side. She was thin and ill-smelling from the poor food she had eaten. The glossy feathers that hung about her gave her the appearance of an outcast human dressed up like a bird. But her mother received her gladly. She washed her body with the tears from her eyes. She dressed her in the finest clothes she had. Then she held her in her lap and gazed at her with complete satisfaction.

Angry over the loss he had suffered, the condor set out in search of the parrot. He found him in the garden, stuffed with corn, flitting from tree to tree.

He swooped down on the parrot and devoured him whole. But the parrot went straight through the condor's body and came out the other end. The condor swallowed him again, and again he came out. Furious, the condor seized the parrot, tore him to pieces with his talons, and swallowed him piece by piece. But for each piece he swallowed, a little parrot came out the other end. And this, they say, is the origin of the parrots we know today.

Quechua (Bolivia)

⋟ 113. The Priest's Son Becomes an Eagle ⋞

They were living in Hawiku. The village priest had one son and four daughters. All the girls in the village wished to marry this son of the priest. Every night a girl came with a basket of flour on her head and climbed up the ladder. The boy and his father were eating their supper. The father said, "You ought to be a married man, the girls are all anxious to marry you. Choose one to be your wife." The girl came down the ladder. She was dressed in white moccasins, and she had a fine red-and-black-bordered white blanket over her shoulders. His mother said, "You're coming, aren't you?" The girl said, "Yes." The boy's mother asked her to eat with them. She ate, and after eating she said, "Thank you." They said to her, "What is it that you have come to ask?" She said, "I was thinking of your son." The father and mother said to her, "Go with him into the inner room."

In this room the boy stayed every day weaving a white blanket. It was in the loom. He said to the girl, "We must not sleep together tonight. In the morning come to this room and weave this blanket, and if you are able to do this, you shall be my wife. If you are not, we shall not marry." That night they slept apart.

Next morning she got up to grind before the father and mother of the boy had waked. When the mother had made ready the morning meal and they had eaten, the girl went back into the inner room and tried to weave the blanket, but she could not. When she found that she could not, she went back to her home weeping. She was ashamed.

The next-eldest sister came to ask for the boy, but she, too, had to return to her home when he saw that she could not weave; the third sister came and was turned away. Everybody was watching the house of the priest's son. Every morning they saw a girl go home weeping.

That night the youngest sister went to the well to get water. She was wishing that someone would teach her to weave. She heard someone speak to her. She looked all about but she could not find where the voice came from. At last the voice said, "Here I am in the top of this flower stalk." She looked, and saw that it was Spider Woman. Spider Woman said to her, "On the morning of the day you are to go to the house of the youth, come back to the spring, and I shall climb into your ear. I will go with you to his house and teach you how to weave."

The next morning she went back to the spring, and Spider Woman climbed into her ear. She put on her white moccasins and white puttees and her white blanket, and they went to the house of the youth. His mother said, "You're coming, aren't you?" She put out a seat for her and brought food. The girl ate, and when she finished, she said, "Thank you." The mother took away the food, and they said, "What is it that you have come to ask?" She answered, "I was thinking of your son." They said, "Go with him into the inner room."

When they had gone into the other room, he said to her, "We shall not sleep together tonight. In the morning if you are able to weave this blanket, you shall be my wife." They slept apart.

In the morning they ate their morning meal. When they had finished, she went into the inner room, and went directly to the loom and sat down. Spider Woman said to her, "First pull out that short stick. Pull the lower bar out toward you. Now put the ball of cotton thread in between the warp." Everything that she had to do Spider Woman told her. The youth sat close beside her and he saw that she understood how to weave the blanket on his loom. He said, "My dear, now we shall be married and we shall have a long life."

That morning everyone was watching for the girl to come weeping out of the youth's house. But no one came, and they knew that she had married the youth. Her sisters were very angry. After that she always stayed in the house and did the weaving, and her husband helped his father hoeing the fields.

Whenever he came home, his wife asked him, "My dear, do you love me?" Every time he came in she asked him again, "My dear, do you love me?" The youth did not like this. He thought, "I must find out whether you really love me."

The next day when he and his father were hoeing in the fields he said to him, "My father, is there any way I can find out if my wife loves me?" His father answered, "My son, you can call the Apaches."

There were crows flying about the cornfield, and he told the crow, "Go to the Apaches and tell them the priest's son has called them to come against the people of Hawiku." The crow flew off to the Apaches. He sought out the Apache priest and said, "The priest's son at Hawiku has sent for you to come and fight him and his wife." The Apache said, "Very well. Tomorrow we will come." They made ready to go to Hawiku on the following day.

In the morning the priest's son told his wife to dress in her white moccasins and puttees, and to put on her blanket dress and a red-and-black-bordered white blanket and over that an embroidered white blanket. He said, "I and my father are going out to our field to hoe. Bring us a lunch of parched-corn meal." She went out to the field and took the parched-corn meal. They built a shelter for her to sit in while they were working. At noon they soaked the meal and had lunch. The youth told his father to go home, and the old man went back to the village. He could see the dust in the distance where the Apaches were coming.

The Apaches crept up in ambush. They hid from cedar to cedar. At last they were near. The youth took out his arrows. He had twenty arrows and he shot them all and killed many of the enemy. When the arrows were gone the Apaches killed him and he fell. His wife ran away.

The boy's father went to the bow priests and told them to make proclamation that in eight days they would dance the yaya dance. When the eighth day came everyone was ready for the dance. All the women had dyed red wool to embroider their blanket dresses fresh, and they wore their white deer-skin moccasins and puttees. The priest's son's wife dressed also and went with her sisters to the dance. She did not give a thought to her dead husband. In the middle of the morning the dance began. The yaya leader went up to the wife and her sisters and said, "Shall I tie your blanket?" He took out his deer-bone needle and sewed together their blankets and put them into the dance circle.

The priest's son came in from the west and climbed up to the tops of the houses around the plaza. He saw his wife and her sisters going into the dance, and he saw that his wife never gave a thought to him. Soon the yaya leaders came up to the priest's son and put him also into the dance. They pushed him into the circle next to his wife. She looked up at him and recognized him. Tears ran down her cheeks. Immediately he turned into an eagle and flew up to the houses where he had been standing. Then he flew away giving his eagle cries. That is why we value eagle feathers so much, because the eagle is the priest's son.

Zuni (New Mexico)

➤ 114. The Revolt of the Utensils ⬅

In the old days clay pots and other objects were like people. They could talk, visit, dance, and make chicha.

One day a man left his house, and the pots decided they would go to the garden and the stream to get the maize and the water to make maize chicha. Off they went to the garden, the stream. They got the maize and the water. Then they made the chicha.

They felt happy. "Now we will make music and have dancing," they said, and when they had prepared the chicha, they made the music and had the dancing. They were in good spirits, they were enjoying each other's company. When they had played for a long while, they realized that the man of the house would soon return. They began to put everything back. They cleaned up, and the place was just as it had been.

The man came back. He looked around. "Everything is in order," he said—and all the pots doubled up with laughter.

Tacana (Bolivia)

➤ 115. The Origin of Permanent Death ⇐

After the first death, the hummingbird was sent to get clay in order to make a more durable human. Then the cricket was sent to get lightweight balsa wood. Finally, the beetle was sent to get stones to mix in with the new creature to give it firmness.

And so they started to make a human who could withstand death. The cricket returned right away with the lightweight wood. And the hummingbird came with the clay. But the beetle never showed up. Its job was to bring the stone, but it never came back.

After a long wait, and it still had not returned, they decided to make the human being out of clay. Having no stones, they just used clay, and those balsa sticks. Then they blew the breath of life into it, and the human being was finished.

And then Etsa [the sun] said, "Did I not ordain that humans be made also of stone? Was it not my wish that humans be immortal? Had I not determined that even old people would become children again? I had indeed determined that humans would be immortal. But now I say they must die." He pronounced this solemn judgment: "Now let full-grown men and newborn children die. Let young men die who have not yet had children, and young women who have not yet married."

Whatever is made of earth and fragile clay must it not break? The earthen bowl, though it is made well, does it not break? We ourselves are made the same.

Shuar (Ecuador) / Píkiur (no surname)

NOTES

All translations are from the Spanish and by the editor unless otherwise noted. Tale type numbers, if preceded by "AT," are from Aarne and Thompson. Types from Boggs 1930, from Hansen, and from Robe 1973 are so indicated. Motif numbers are from Stith Thompson's *Motif-Index*. Folktale distributions have been derived mostly from these same indexes, keeping in mind that Spanish-American tales are generally supposed to have been channeled through Spain from remoter origins in Europe, the Middle East, and India. Thus distributions outside the presumed Asian-European-Hispano-American pathway are not taken into account here.

Introduction:

Ramón Pané and Taino lore (Stevens-Arroyo, pp. 74, 78, 88, 103, 137, 168–9). Colombian female deity (Anglería, p. 645). Sahagún as "physician" (Sahagún 1982, pp. 45, 67). Toledo and Sarmiento (Urton, p. 29; Bendezú, p. 393). Montezuma and Inkarrí (Bierhorst 1990, pp. 204–5; 1988, pp. 235–7). Tzotzil view of European kings (Laughlin 1977, p. 78). Aesop in Nahuatl (Kutscher et al.). Cuban tale of eleven thousand virgins (Feijóo, vol. 2, p. 178). Female divinity in the Sierra Nevada de Santa Marta (Reichel-Dolmatoff 1951; 1978, pp. 23–5; Reichel-Dolmatoff and Reichel-Dolmatoff 1961, p. 347; Tayler 1997, pp. 35, 147). Pedro de Urdemalas "alive in the hearts of the Guatemalan people" (Lara Figueroa 1981, pp. vii, 20). Antonio Ramírez (Lara Figueroa 1981, pp. 112–13). Tía Panchita (Lyra, pp. 3–8). José Rivera Bravo (Anibarro de Halushka, pp. 448–9). Mazatec folk-Bible recitation (Laughlin 1971, p. 37). Martin Gusinde on women narrators (quoted in Wilbert, p. 3). Stanley Robe east of Guadalajara (Robe 1970, p. 36).

Prologue: Early Colonial Legends

[Epigraph]: Lumholtz, vol. 1, p. 516.

[Introductory Note]: "Told in the book of Amadis" (Díaz del Castillo, ch.

87). Alexander Pope, "Windsor Forest," ll. 411–12. Incas emerged through cave openings (Sarmiento, pp. 213–16; Cobo, ch. 3).

1/I. The Talking Stone, tr. and adapted from Tezozomoc, ch. 102; and Durán, ch. 66 (the two sources derive from a presumed Nahuatl manuscript provisionally called Crónica X).

The legend recalls the great round-stone that had been carved during the reign of Tizoc (1481–86), a generation before Montezuma's time. This was a cylindrical piece of basalt eight and a half feet in diameter and three feet high. The prisoner, drugged, was stretched over the upper flat surface and held down by attendants, while a priest cut open the breast and removed the still-beating heart. The stone of Tizoc, as it is now called, is displayed at the National Museum of Anthropology in Mexico City.

Huitzilopochtli: principal god of the Aztecs, a god of war.

1/II. Montezuma's Wound, tr. and adapted from Durán, ch. 67; and Tezozomoc, ch. 103.

Two other, similar tales were current in sixteenth-century and early-seventeenth-century Mexico. In one, a noblewoman dies and is buried. Four days later she breaks out of her grave and goes to tell Montezuma that Mexico will be conquered by strangers (Sahagún 1979, libro 8, cap. 1). In the other, the king's own sister, Papantzin, dies and is laid to rest in a cave, where, returning to life, she hears an angel predict the coming of the Spaniards and the conversion of the Indians to Christianity. She reports this to Montezuma, who is so distraught that he refuses to see her ever again (Torquemada, bk. 2, ch. 91).

1/III. Eight Omens, tr. from the Nahuatl in Sahagún 1979, libro 12, cap. 1.

The disconsolate mother of the sixth omen prefigures the famous "weeping woman," *la llorona,* of modern Mexican folk belief. People say they hear her at night, especially in abandoned places and along streams, crying for her lost children.

12 House: the year 1517.

1/IV. The Return of Quetzalcoatl, tr. and adapted from Tezozomoc, chs. 106–8, and Durán, ch. 69.

The account confuses the reception given Juan de Grijalva, who arrived on the coast in 1518, with the similar reception for Cortés in 1519. It was Cortés who arrived with Malintzin, the Nahua woman who had joined his party farther down the coast and was serving as his interpreter—and mistress—by the time he reached Aztec territory. Loyal to Cortés, Malintzin proved invaluable in the Conquest. Her name is dubiously enshrined in the modern term *malinchismo,* meaning attachment to foreign influences with disregard for Mexican values. The emblems of Quetzalcoatl, presented to Cortés as gifts from Montezuma, were among the treasures sent back immediately to Europe, where they were put on display. Albrecht Dürer saw them in Brussels in the summer of 1520 and wrote in his journal, "All the days of my life I have seen nothing that rejoiced my heart so much as these things, for I have seen among them wonderful works of art" (quoted in Keen, p. 69).

Mexico Tenochtitlan: the more important of the two boroughs, or twin cities, that formed the Aztec capital, Mexico; the other borough was Tlatelolco.

1/V. Is It You?, tr. from the Nahuatl in Sahagún 1979, libro 12, cap. 16.

Here the story definitely passes from legend into stylized history-telling, no more or less reliable than the mutually conflicting accounts preserved in the letters of Cortés and in Bernal Díaz's *Historia verdadera* (True history).

Itzcoatl, Montezuma the elder, Axayacatl, Tizoc, Ahuitzotl: Montezuma (more fully Montezuma the younger) is naming his predecessors in chronological order, stating that all of them had been simply waiting for Quetzalcoatl to return and claim the throne.

2/I. Mayta Capac, tr. from Sarmiento, chs. 16–17.

The events on which the legend is based occurred more than two hundred years before the Conquest of 1533. But in this mid-sixteenth-century version we hear that already in Mayta Capac's time the Incas "lived by thievery," thus sowing the seeds of culpability that will justify their future destruction. At so early a date the empire, if it may be called that, did not extend beyond the Valley of Cuzco. The town of Oma, which produced Mayta Capac's mother, was only two leagues from Cuzco itself; and the Alcahuiza, alternately called Culunchima, were original Cuzco natives whose ancestors had been subdued three generations earlier by the first Incas. The story, therefore, tells of a rebellion, said to have been the first major test of Inca rule (Cobo, ch. 7).

2/II. The Storm, tr. from the Quechua-German text in Trimborn and Kelm, ch. 23. The translations of this tale and the next have been compared with the Spanish versions in Urioste and the English in Salomon and Urioste.

Topa Inca Yupanqui added more territory to the empire than any other Inca, acquiring the gods of the various tribes he had subdued. Yet, according to the story, he was bedeviled by a rebellion and survived only because the god Macahuisa sent a storm against his enemies. This tale of the Inca's weakness, significantly, comes not from the official records of Cuzco but from the conquered province of Huarochirí, where Macahuisa and his "father," Pariacaca, were among the homegrown deities.

Coral (*mullu*): translation follows Trimborn and Kelm. Lara 1971, p. 177, has "red-colored marine shell that used to be offered to the gods in Inca times."

2/III. The Vanishing Bride, tr. from the Quechua-German text in Trimborn and Kelm, ch. 14.

With the reign of Topa Inca Yupanqui's son, Huayna Capac, the legends become more pointed and more ominous. This one, among the most mysterious, incorporates a version of the American Indian Orpheus myth, so called by folklorists who note its resemblance to the Greek myth of Orpheus and Eurydice. The basic plot is of a hero who attempts to fetch a bride or wife from the underworld and fails. The story in this case is told twice. The first time around, the Indian people themselves lose the bride; the second time, they lose both the bride and the Inca. The Inca's subjects are here divided into three fictional classes, condor (the proverbial sky dweller of Peruvian lore), hawk (a bird of earthly elevations), and swallow (nesting inside the earth)—implying that the three tiers of the universe (sky, earth surface, and underworld), or, better, the entirety of human society, became bereft. On account of its underworld associations the swallow is the principal actor. (But Salomon and Urioste, offering a different interpretation, suggest that the people are being described as shamans, whose bird familiars simply give them power to fly to the other world.) For another, modern version of the Orpheus myth see "The Dead Wife," from the Mískito of Nicaragua, no. 106, below.

Cajamarca: the definitive incident of the Peruvian conquest, the execution of the Inca Atahualpa, occurred in this Andean town about halfway between Quito and Cuzco.

2/IV. A Messenger in Black, tr. and adapted from Pachacuti (the text is to be found four-fifths of the way through this relatively brief chronicle).

As mentioned above in the introductory note, the epidemic that spread south from Panama is thought to have been typhus (or plague). But "faces covered with scabs" implies smallpox. The final detail is not fantastic; Inca mummies were brought out in litters on ceremonial occasions.

2/V. The Oracle at Huamachuco, tr. from Sarmiento, ch. 64.

The idol destroyed by Atahualpa was the statue of the god Catequilla. Its broken pieces were scattered, according to the *Relación de la religión y ritos del Perú* (written about 1561), which adds further details: "After the arrival of the Christians in this land, there was an Indian woman who had thoughts of Catequilla. A small stone appeared before her; she picked it up and brought it to the grand sorcerer [native priest] and said, 'I found this stone.' Then the sorcerer asked the stone, 'Who are you?' and the stone, or rather the Devil speaking through the stone, replied, 'I am Tantaguayani, son of Catequilla.'" Thereafter another "son" of Catequilla came to light, and the two were "multiplied" until there were some three hundred throughout the district, promptly established as objects of worship. In a deed recalling the fury of Atahualpa, the Augustinian fathers collected all of these objects and "burned them and smashed them and did away with the sorcerers" (*Relación,* pp. 25–7).

3. Bringing Out the Holy Word, translated from the Nahuatl, Bierhorst 1985a, pp. 269–73.

This catechistic version of holy scripture was prepared by Don Francisco Plácido, Indian *gobernador* of the town of Xiquipilco (the title "don" here indicates a member of the old Indian nobility). Chanted for the benefit of the town of Azcapotzalco, whose patron saint was the apostle Philip, the piece has a prelude and an envoy (neither of which is included here), greeting the people of Azcapotzalco and, at the end, summoning the ghost of St. Philip. Evidently the catechistic portion is intended to explain how the apostles, including Philip, fit into the history of the world. As an account of the doctrine on which the Latin American folk-Bible cycle is based, it is complete in itself. Compare the folk-Bible stories, nos. 55–73.

Lords and princes: the Aztec nobility.

Folktales: A Sixteenth-Century Wake

[Epigraph]: *Los muertos al pozo y los vivos al negocio* (Pérez, p. 123).

[Introductory Note]: Information on wakes (Reichel-Dolmatoff and Reichel-Dolmatoff 1961, pp. 378–82; Vázquez de Acuña, pp. 45–8; Chapman, pp. 186–95; Lara Figueroa 1981, pp. 112–25; Campa, p. 196; Laughlin 1971; Portal, p. 38; Carvalho-Neto 1961, p. 319). "Ah serene, ah Sir Ron . . ." (Cadilla de Martínez, p. 240).

4. In the City of Benjamin, tr. from Carvalho-Neto 1994, no. 39. Motif J1185.1 Sheherezade.

"Benjamin" translates *Benjuí,* an old Spanish name for the aromatic gum benjamin or benzoin, evidently intended here as a means of transporting the listener to the Orient. The story, clearly, is a variant of the framing tale of the *Thousand and One Nights,* where it is written that a king named Shahriar was betrayed by his wife while visiting with his brother, whose wife had betrayed *him.* Concluding that women could not be trusted, Shahriar from then on took a new wife every night, killing her in the morning. After three years people fled with their daughters. Needing a wife, Shahriar ordered his vizier to get him a virgin. The vizier's elder daughter, Sheherezade, who had read a thousand stories, offered to be the bride, provided she could bring along her younger sister. On the wedding night the sister asked for a story, the king assented, and Sheherezade began her recitation. On the thousand-and-first night, after she had borne three sons, she begged the king to spare her for the children's sake; he wept and relented.

The tale that follows also stems from a Near East lineage but moves more decisively into Latin American territory.

5. Antuco's Luck, tr. from Saunière, pp. 286–97. Motifs N531 Treasure discovered through dream; H1226.4 Pursuit of rolling ball of yarn leads to quest; N512 Treasure in underground chamber; N813 Helpful genie.

The blood-red talisman beneath the cross implies the Sacred Heart (mentioned finally by name in story no. 101); here it subdues the genie of Middle Eastern lore in a characteristically Hispanic touch. The realistic locales, including the Alameda in Santiago, as well as the name Antuco, borne by both a town and a volcano in Bío-Bío province, mark this novella-like tale as a Chilean creation. Though the novella may be regarded as a literary form, such tales "are also widely told by the unlettered, especially by the peoples of the Near East; the action occurs in a real world with a definite time and place, and though marvels do appear, they are such as apparently call for the hearer's belief" (Thompson 1946, p. 8). The story is discussed in the introduction, p. 8. See also the comments to nos. 13 and 51, below.

6. Don Dinero and Doña Fortuna, tr. from Andrade 1930, no. 269.

Assignable to AT type 945 Luck and Intelligence, but deserving of a special Hispanic subtype, Money and Luck, reported also from New Mexico (Rael, no. 93). In one of the New Mexican variants the characters are even styled Don Dinero and Doña Fortuna, as here (Brown et al., pp. 140–3).

7. Mistress Lucía, tr. from Corona, pp. 43–50. AT type 403 The Black and White Bride (California, Chile, Costa Rica, Dominican Republic, Mexico, New Mexico, Puerto Rico, Europe, India, Middle East).

Alacrán: lime prickly ash (*Zanthoxylum fagara*), an old-fashioned remedy for migraine.

8. St. Peter's Wishes, tr. from Feijóo 1960, pp. 48–9. AT type 759.

See comment to no. 27.

9. The Coyote Teodora, tr. from Izaguirre, pp. 168–70. Motifs G211 Witch in animal form; G266 Witches steal; G271.2.2 Witch exorcised by holy water; G271.4.5 Breaking spell by beating the person or object bewitched.

One of the most unusual of the Latin American Witch Wife tales. The more familiar types are represented by nos. 30 and 98.

10. Buried Alive, tr. from Miller, pp. 266–8. AT type 612 The Three Snake-Leaves (California, Mexico, New Mexico, Panama, Europe, India, Middle East).

The helpful mouse, who drops the flower that revives the wife, is typical of the American versions. In Grimm's (no. 16) the helper is a snake, who uses three green leaves.

11. The Three Gowns, tr. from Mason 1925, pp. 572–4. AT type 510B

The Dress of Gold, of Silver, and of Stars (Cuba, Dominican Republic, Mexico, New Mexico, Puerto Rico, Europe, India, Middle East).

The not-so-hidden subtext of this provocative Cinderella tale concerns the parents of the young couple. The girl's marriage-minded father gets left behind for making his intentions too plain. His more subtle counterpart, the boy's mother, is less easily separated from her son and, together with her disarming touch of insanity, is incorporated in the new *ménage.*

The lion skin, perhaps, is a development from old Spanish versions in which the orphaned heroine has no proper clothes to wear. A modern variant from the Spanish province of Cáceres begins, "Once there was an orphan girl and she went about the world dressed in an animal hide" (Taggart 1990, p. 101).

12. The Horse of Seven Colors, tr. from Sojo, pp. 183–8. AT type 530 The Princess on the Glass Mountain (Cuba, Mexico, New Mexico, Venezuela, Europe, India, Middle East). With the addition of motifs D1234 Magic guitar; B401 Helpful horse; Q2 Kind and unkind; L13 Compassionate youngest son; S165 Mutilation: putting out eyes; N452 Secret remedy overheard in conversation of animals (witches). The helpful horse appears in Old World variants, but that it must be "of seven colors" is a Latin American requirement.

A parody of the Cinderella stories, with the sexes reversed, this richly developed tale might have been called "The Three Fancy Suits." The vanity of the hero as he changes from one dazzling outfit to the next matches Cinderella herself, while the exaggerated cruelty of the two older brothers far outstrips the stepsisters of the classic versions. To be compared with nos. 11 and 28.

13. The Cow, tr. from Rael, no. 55. AT type 1415 Lucky Hans (New Mexico, Puerto Rico, Europe, India, Middle East).

Compadrazgo, the institution that binds the community, at least in theory, spells trouble in folktales. It is one of the signature themes of Latin American folklore, in which the mere mention of the endearing term of address, compadre, is a signal that someone is about to be victimized or betrayed. In practice, the compadre is the godfather of one's child; the godfather's wife is called comadre. Reciprocally, the godparents use the same terms in addressing the child's parents, establishing a social kinship that implies trust and mutual aid. The story "Antuco's Luck," no. 5, is most unusual for treating the relationship without a hint of derision. Typical tales, in addition to no. 13, are nos. 22, 23, 92, 93, 96, and 101. In no. 84 the witches comfortably address each other as comadre.

14. Death and the Doctor, tr. from Andrade 1930, no. 230. AT type 332 Godfather Death (Dominican Republic, Ecuador, Guatemala, Mexico, New Mexico, Panama, Europe, India, Middle East).

Once again, as in no. 4, sheer storytelling saves a human life.

15. What the Owls Said, tr. from Portal, pp. 89–90. Hansen type 613

[Hero Overhears Secrets and Cures Illness] (Costa Rica, Dominican Republic, Guatemala, Mexico, Peru, Puerto Rico).

In spite of its American Indian flavor, the tale is an Old World type found throughout Europe, where it is usually embedded in a somewhat longer narrative classified as The Two Travelers (AT 613). The remedy overheard in a conversation of animals or witches (motif N452), traceable to the *Pentamerone* and the *Panchatantra,* appears also in nos. 12, 80, and 84 of the present collection. But the details of the remedy at hand, as well as the satire on Western-style doctoring, are particular to this Mazatec version from Oaxaca State. The casting of corn kernels, the identification of an animal as the cause of disease, the liquid medicine (rum, or *aguardiente,* in this case), and the egg (which must be passed over the patient's body) are standard features of Oaxaca folk medicine—probably indigenous except for the egg treatment, which is most likely of Spanish origin (Parsons 1936, pp. 120–2, 376, 493–8). Note that the offending animal is a toad, as also in the old Peruvian variant (see comment to no. 84).

16. Aunt Misery, tr. from Ramírez de Arellano, no. 95. AT type 330D Bonhomme Misère. Closely related to AT type 330 The Smith Outwits the Devil (Argentina, Chile, Colombia, Costa Rica, Dominican Republic, Guatemala, Mexico, New Mexico, Puerto Rico, Europe).

The hero of the story is always male, except here.

17. Palm-tree Story, tr. from Reichel-Dolmatoff and Reichel-Dolmatoff 1956, no. 70. Type AT 327 The Children and the Ogre (Chile, Colombia, Cuba, Dominican Republic, Guatemala, Mexico, New Mexico, Peru, Puerto Rico, Europe, India).

The strange opening, in which the hero is expelled from his mother's womb and immediately tries to help people, makes little sense until the last line of the story. No other version has either the surprise ending or the initial episode that sets it up.

18/I. The Letter Carrier from the Other World, tr. from Laval 1968, no. 67. AT type 1540 The Student from Paradise (Argentina, Chile, Mexico, Europe, India, Middle East).

In Old World versions a student tells a woman he comes from Paris. She understands him to say paradise and gives him money and goods to take to her deceased husband. In a Mexican variant he tells her that her husband is in Hell. She asks what her husband needs for his journey home and gives the trickster a horse, clothing, and money.

18/II. The King's Pigs, tr. from Lara Figueroa 1981, no. 4. AT type 1004 Hogs in the Mud (Argentina, Arizona, California, Chile, Guatemala, Mexico, New Mexico, Puerto Rico, Texas, Europe, India, Middle East).

One of the most commonly recorded stories about Pedro de Urdemalas.

Often told in series with other, similar tales. Outside the Spanish- and Portuguese-speaking world the trickster is given different names. The version in Grimm's (no. 192) is told of the "master thief."

18/III. The Sack, tr. from Laval 1968, no. 68. AT type 1737 The Parson in the Sack to Heaven (Argentina, Chile, Dominican Republic, Guatemala, Mexico, New Mexico, Puerto Rico, Europe, India, Middle East).

Once again the old contrast between town and country, as in no. 75, where the man from the city goes out to the country to fleece the mourners at a wake. Here, Pedro de Urdemalas dresses up as a friar and heads for the countryside to beg for alms. The implication is that country people are easily duped. But in no. 14, "Death and the Doctor," the man from the country goes to the city with a trick for working cures; and in no. 18/I Pedro himself is the country boy who rides into town with a money-making scheme.

18/IV. Pedro Goes to Heaven, tr. from Chertudi 1964, pp. 97–9. AT type 330 The Smith Outwits the Devil (Argentina, Chile, Colombia, Costa Rica, Dominican Republic, Mexico, New Mexico, Puerto Rico, Europe).

The middle part of the story, with the Devil stuck in the tree, is a variation on no. 16.

Old namesake: St. Peter, i.e., San Pedro, who shares his name with Pedro de Urdemalas.

19. A Voyage to Eternity, tr. from Anibarro Halushka, no. 25. AT type 470 Friends in Life and Death (Bolivia, Colombia, Europe).

Though rare in Latin America, the story is an established folktale type heavily reported from Iceland to Russia and from Spain to Turkey. The storyteller, who says, "I'm not sure, but I think this was in Spain," shows that he considers the tale to be legendary rather than strictly fictional. For more on this narrator see introduction, pp. 13–4.

20. Mother and Daughter, tr. from Reichel-Dolmatoff and Reichel-Dolmatoff 1956, no. 84.

The little tale, barely more than a motif, may be regarded as a pious variant of AT type 310 The Maiden in the Tower, widespread in Europe, with variants in Cuba, the Dominican Republic, and Puerto Rico. In that story a virgin kept in a tower is visited by a witch who climbs up on the girl's hair. Here the witch has become the heroine's own mother, caught in Purgatory. She does her time there, however, since apparently the narrator does not wish us to think she has cheated by climbing up too soon.

21. The Bird Sweet Magic, tr. from Lyra, pp. 112–20. AT type 551 The Sons on a Quest for a Wonderful Remedy for Their Father (Argentina, Costa Rica, Dominican Republic, Mexico, New Mexico, Panama, Puerto Rico, Europe, India, Middle East) + AT type 505 The Grateful Dead (essentially the same distribution).

The Grateful Dead is the story of a hero who pays for the burial of a penniless stranger; the dead man's grateful spirit then follows the hero and helps him. In combination with the tale of the young son who seeks a cure for his father's blindness and in the process wins a princess, as here, the story has an antecedent in the Book of Tobit in the Hebrew Apocrypha. Tobit, who buried the penniless dead, was himself stricken by blindness; and the spirit who followed his questing son was the angel Raphael. With the angel's help the son finds a miraculous cure for his father's blindness and wins the hand of Sarah, daughter of Raguel.

This Costa Rican version comes from the woman we know only as Panchita, who nonetheless emerges as an imposing figure in Latin American folklore. Her stories have been indexed and repeatedly cited by folklorists. She had a wide-ranging repertoire of tales, and it is said that she possessed the "charm and wit" (*el gracejo y la agudeza*) that were required of storytellers who performed at wakes (Noguera, p. xv). For more on tía Panchita see introduction, pp. 12–3.

22. Death Comes as a Rooster, tr. from Feijóo 1960, p. 80. AT type 1354 Death for the Old Couple (Cuba, New Mexico, Europe, India).

23. The Twelve Truths of the World, tr. from J. M. Espinosa, no. 50. Motifs S224 Child promised to devil for acting as godfather; H602.1.1 Symbolic meaning of numbers one to [. . .] twelve.

The prayer, sometimes called "The Twelve Words Turned Back," is thought to have originated in India and to have traveled to Europe by way of the Middle East. Aurelio Espinosa says the earliest known version is in a Persian tale from the *Book of Arda Viraf,* in which the questions and answers begin as follows: What is the one? The good sun that lights the world. What are the two? Drawing breath and exhaling. What are the three? Good thoughts, good words, and good deeds. What are the four? Water, earth, plants, and animals. What are the five? The five Persian kings, Kai-Kabad, Kai-Khusrov, Kai-Lorasp, etc. In a Jewish version the twelve words are God, the two tablets of Moses, the three patriarchs, the four mothers of Israel, and so forth (A. M. Espinosa 1946–47, vol. 3, pp. 119–20, 133). A non-Jewish Venezuelan version likewise includes the two tablets of Moses (Olivares Figueroa, pp. 86–9). Other Latin American versions—of the prayer only—have been recorded from Argentina, Chile, and Puerto Rico. Versions of the story without the prayer come from Ecuador (Carvalho-Neto 1994, nos. 48–50).

An old Spanish belief is that it is necessary to know the twelve "words" because the soul on its journey to the hereafter must cross a bridge where the Devil is waiting to ask the twelve questions (Espinosa).

Folk Prayers. I and VI, tr. from Vázquez de Acuña, pp. 38 and 35. II, tr.

from Laval 1916, p. 25. III, IV, and V, tr. from Olivares Figueroa, pp. 85, 86, and 84–5.

These are not canonical prayers, and no. III is actually a curse. The Reichel-Dolmatoffs have written that death is almost always taken to be the result of black magic; and during the wake "suspicions are voiced concerning the dead person's enemies, but a name is never mentioned" (Reichel-Dolmatoff and Reichel-Dolmatoff 1961, p. 381).

The brief *ensalmo* (incantation) to St. Anthony, patron saint of courtship, has been included as a bridge to the story that follows.

24. The Mouse and the Dung Beetle, tr. from Rael, no. 32. Robe type 559 Dung Beetle (Colorado, Mexico). The similar tale from which this one has evidently been derived, AT type 559 Dung Beetle, is widespread in Europe and known also from Mexico and New Mexico.

St. Anthony, who finds lost objects and helps lovers, is probably the most frequently mentioned saint in Latino folktales. It is said that in New Mexico, if the saint refused to grant a petition, his image used to be hung upside down in a well with the head submerged until he changed his mind (A. M. Espinosa 1985, p. 74).

25. The Canon and the King's False Friend, tr. from J. M. Espinosa, no. 3. AT type 883A The Innocent Slandered Maiden (New Mexico, Europe, India, Middle East).

Well known in medieval literary sources, including the *Gesta Romanorum*, but evidently rare in Latin America.

26. The Story that Became a Dream, tr. from Laval 1920, no. 19. AT type 1364 The Blood-brother's Wife (Argentina, Chile, Europe, Middle East).

The Chilean storyteller brings the old tale down to contemporary reality. The two knights who swear blood brotherhood in the old European versions are now a pair of idlers making their daily rounds through the city streets.

27. St. Theresa and the Lord, tr. from Wheeler, no. 40. AT type 759 God's Justice Vindicated (Argentina, Cuba, Guatemala, Mexico, New Mexico, Panama, Puerto Rico, Europe, India, Middle East).

The incidents vary, but the situation is always the same. An incredulous companion travels with an inscrutable master, who perpetrates injustices, finally explaining their hidden meaning. The old version given in Islamic scripture is a parable on the virtue of unquestioning faith (Koran 18:65–82). A flippant Cuban version turns the story into a joke about the battle of the sexes (no. 8).

Gorda: a bulky tortilla, about the thickness of a finger, carried as food for the road by rural people in Mexico.

28. Rice from Ashes, tr. from Chertudi 1960, pp. 138–42. AT type 510A

Cinderella (Argentina, California, Chile, Colombia, Costa Rica, Cuba, Dominican Republic, Ecuador, Mexico, New Mexico, Puerto Rico, Europe, India, Middle East).

The familiar story, but with some unusual details. Here it is the prince, not Cinderella, who has the fairy godmother; and instead of the glass slipper, a gold cup from the belly of a lamb (motif H121 Identification by cup). The tasks required by the stepmother at the beginning of the story are common folkloric elements, though not usually attached to Cinderella (motifs H1091.1 Task: sorting grains: performed by helpful ants, and H1091.2 Task: sorting grains: performed by helpful birds).

29. Juan María and Juana María, tr. from Recinos 1918a, no. 8.

Strictly speaking not a folktale, but the kind of story folklorists today would call an urban legend. Despite the label, the setting does not have to be urban, but it must be contemporary. The tale should have a suspenseful story line and sensational, even grisly details. There may be an element of the supernatural. Nevertheless the account is passed along as a true recent happening. An example that has long been popular in North America is "The Vanishing Hitchhiker," in which the spirit of a young woman tries to hitchhike home every year on the anniversary of her death (Brunvand, pp. 165–70).

30. The Witch Wife, tr. from Reichel-Dolmatoff and Reichel-Dolmatoff 1956, no. 83. Hansen type 748H [Witch Wife Who Visits Cemetery Changes Spying Husband into Dog] (Colombia, New Mexico, Puerto Rico).

The story of the wife slipping out of the house and spied on by her husband, who discovers she's a witch, is one of the most characteristic of Latin American folktales (see also nos. 9 and 98). However, this version, which has the wife's alarming rice diet, the graveyard scene, the husband changed into a dog, the dog-loving baker, and, finally, the wife's comeuppance, can be traced to the *Thousand and One Nights,* as noted by Laughlin, who found the same story among the Tzotzil Maya of Chiapas State, Mexico (1977, pp. 75–6).

31. O Wicked World, tr. from Chertudi, vol. 1, no. 92. Boggs type 1940E [The Widow's Dog Named World] (Argentina, Cuba, Spain). The Cuban version is in Feijóo, vol. 2, p. 142.

Buñuelos: doughnuts, fritters.

32. The Three Sisters, tr. from Reichel-Dolmatoff and Reichel-Dolmatoff 1956, no. 79. AT type 707 The Three Golden Sons (California, Chile, Colombia, Dominican Republic, Mexico, New Mexico, Panama, Puerto Rico, Europe, India, Middle East).

One of the best-known international folktales. As is often the case with Latin American folklore, the Colombian version is remarkably close to the version in the *Thousand and One Nights.*

33. The Count and the Queen, tr. from Rael no. 487. AT type 1418 The Equivocal Oath (Colorado, Europe, India).

34. Crystal the Wise, tr. from Saunière, pp. 260–8. AT type 891 The Man Who Deserts His Wife and Sets Her the Task of Bearing Him a Child (Chile, Europe, India, Middle East).

Versions in which the heroine starts out as a schoolteacher, as here, are especially popular in southern Europe. The Chilean variant has the teacher serving the national beverage, *mate,* here translated "tea." But the geographical hints (train to Paris, betrothal to a Spanish princess) suggest an Italian origin for this story. In fact it is very close to a variant in the great Sicilian collection of Giuseppe Pitrè, summarized by Saunière in her comparative notes and translated into English in Calvino (no. 151, "Catherine the Wise").

35. Love Like Salt, tr. from Wheeler, no. 54. Subtype of AT 510 Cinderella, indexed separately as AT 923 Love Like Salt (Arizona, California, Cuba, Guatemala, Mexico, New Mexico, Puerto Rico, Europe, India, Middle East).

The heroine of the tale is one of the pluckier Cinderellas, like the heroine of no. 11, in contrast to the long-suffering stepdaughters of nos. 28 and 91. The King Lear motif (M21), which has the father rejecting the youngest and most honest of his three daughters, is a regular feature of Love Like Salt in both the Old World and the New. If the emphasis placed on salt seems odd to the modern reader, it may help to remember an old saying recorded for Latin America: The Devil will come to a table without salt (Redfield, p. 131).

36. The Pongo's Dream, tr. from Arguedas and Carrillo, pp. 127–32.

The story of the dream in which a great man is covered in honey and a poor man in excrement, whereupon the two lick each other, has been recorded for India (Shulman, pp. 199–200) and presumably made its way to Peru via the Middle East and Spain. It is not indexed for either Europe or Latin America, however. Arguedas obtained this version in Lima from a Quechua-speaking *comunero,* who had come from the region of Cuzco. Subsequently Arguedas learned that two Peruvian colleagues had heard versions of the same tale (Arguedas, p. 9).

Pongo: An Indian menial of the lowest order, charged with kitchen and stable work, traditionally a kind of doorman whose more or less permanent station was the vestibule. Hence the name "pongo," from Quechua *punku,* "door" (Luna).

37. The Fox and the Monkey, adapted from the Aymara-English text in La Barre, pp. 42–5.

Animal tales depend for their effect almost totally on body language and vocal manipulation and thus defy translation. But because of their wide popularity the anthologist cannot in good conscience ignore them. In Latin America, as elsewhere, the little stories are often told in sequences of two or more. The trickster and his companion dupe are generally Rabbit and Coyote in Mexico and Central America, Fox and Tiger in parts of South America. Armadillo, Lion, Monkey, Squirrel, and other creatures may be substituted. The sequence at hand joins these elements:

Motif W151.9 Greedy person (animal) gets hand (head) stuck in food jar (Bolivia, Brazil, India).

Motif K841 Substitute for execution obtained by trickery (Americas, Europe, India).

AT type 1530 Holding Up the Rock (Argentina, Chile, Dominican Republic, Guatemala, Mexico, New Mexico, Puerto Rico, Europe).

AT type 34 The Wolf Dives into the Water for Reflected Cheese (Costa Rica, Dominican Republic, Guatemala, Mexico, New Mexico, Puerto Rico, Europe).

38. The Miser's Jar, adapted from Gordon, pp. 134–6. AT type 1536B The Three Hunchback Brothers Drowned (Argentina, Belize, Bolivia, Chile, Guatemala, Mexico, New Mexico, Puerto Rico, Europe, India, Middle East).

The story is also told of Pedro de Urdemalas, with Pedro as the fool who keeps burying the cadavers (Lara Figueroa 1982, no. 31).

39. Tup and the Ants, adapted from J. E. S. Thompson, pp. 163–5.

Stories about slash-and-burn agriculture, often minutely descriptive, belong to the Indian side of Mexican and Central American storytelling. But the various narrative elements in this particular tale—the three brothers, the unpromising hero, the helpful ants, the literal fools (who in this case cut trees instead of cutting them *down*)—suggest Hispanic models. Motif J2461.1 Literal following of instructions about actions.

40. A Master and His Pupil, tr. from Recinos 1918a, no. 6. Robe 1712 (Guatemala).

Not indexed for Europe or Latin America except Guatemala. But a Triestine version is in Pinguentini (no. 30); English translation in Calvino (no. 44, "The Science of Laziness").

"Drydregs" translates *Pososeco,* "Idler" is *Jaragán.* Recinos's anonymous informant evidently had a weakness for Dickensian surnames. Compare the "Don Jesús Nutmeg" and "Scholar Corncob" of no. 89.

41. The Louse-Drum, tr. from Riera-Pinilla, no. 57. AT type 621 The Louse Skin (Argentina, Colombia, Mexico, New Mexico, Panama, Puerto Rico, Europe, India, Middle East).

42. The Three Dreams, tr. from Lara Figueroa 1982, no. 39. AT type 1626 Dream Bread (Argentina, Cuba, Guatemala, Mexico, New Mexico, Puerto Rico, Europe, India, Middle East).

The Guatemalan narrator allows himself to describe the Indian as "this something or other that might be human." And in the somewhat similar tale from Peru, "The Pongo's Dream" (no. 36), the Indian is asked, "Are you human or something else?" In both cases the Indian triumphs, discreetly, by means of a dream. But who might tell such story? An Indian? Or, to use the Guatemalan term, would it be a *ladino?* The answer is the former, in the Peruvian case; the latter, in the Guatemalan. Our narrator, here, is an agricultural worker with two years of schooling, born in the tiny hamlet of La Juez in the community of La Montaña, *municipio* of Sansare, *departamento* of El Progreso, northeast of Guatemala City.

43. The Clump of Basil, tr. from Ramírez de Arellano, no. 29. AT type 879 The Basil Maiden (Argentina, Bolivia, Chile, Dominican Republic, New Mexico, Mexico, Puerto Rico, Europe).

The opening, "Well, sir," is a formula that may be used by either a man or a woman and has nothing to do with who happens to be listening.

Riddles. I, tr. from Mason 1916, no. 322. II, VI, VII, VIII, X, XXV, tr. from Ramírez de Arellano, nos. 452a, 512, 391, 529b, 430, 396. III, IV, V, XIV, XV, XXII, XXIII, XXVI, XXVII, XXVIII, tr. from Lehmann-Nitsche, nos. 551, 186, 196, 66, 60a, 656d, 284, 608a, 57a, 677b. IX, XI, XII, tr. from Recinos 1918b, nos. 12, 10, 38. XIII, tr. from the Nahuatl-Spanish text in Rámirez et al., p. 62. XVI, tr. from the Spanish in A. Espinosa 1985, p. 166. XVII, XIX, XXIV, tr. from the Quechua-Spanish text in Kleymeyer, pp. 21, 17-8, 23. XVIII, XX, tr. from Andrade 1930, nos. 276, 172. XXI, tr. from Dary Fuentes and Esquivel, p. 117. XXIX, tr. from the Cashinahua in Abreu, no. 5908. XXX, tr. from the Yucatec Maya and Spanish text in Andrade 1977, folio 1648.

Hispanic riddles vary little or not at all from nation to nation; and many have been taken into Indian languages without change, including even so venerable an item as the riddle of the Sphinx (no. XXIV). Others deserve to be called native American (nos. XVII, XXIX). Whether riddles were originally native to the Western Hemisphere is a question folklorists have debated. An eighteenth-century Maya manuscript contains riddles of unquestionable Indian content, for example:

> Son, go bring me the girl with the watery teeth. Her hair is twisted into a tuft. Fragrant shall be her odor when I remove her garments. [Answer:] It is an ear of green corn cooked in a pit (Roys, p. 130).

A sizable collection of Nahua riddles is preserved in Sahagún's sixteenth-century *Historia,* including:

What is it that says to itself, "You go this way, I'll go that way, and we'll meet on the other side"? [Answer:] loincloth (Sahagún 1979, libro 6, cap. 42, fol. 198v).

Even so, it could be argued that such riddles, while they may be called native—and as old as they are—were inspired by Spanish models.

44. The Charcoal Peddler's Chicken, tr. from Mason 1924, no. 36. AT type 332B Death and Luck (California, Chile, Mexico, New Mexico, Puerto Rico, Spain).

45. The Three Counsels, tr. from A. M. Espinosa 1911, no. 4. AT type 910B The Servant's Good Counsels (Chile, Cuba, Dominican Republic, Guatemala, Mexico, New Mexico, Puerto Rico, Europe, India, Middle East).

The earliest recorded European version of the House of Death episode is in the *Gesta Romanorum:* A certain prince, who lived in an isolated country house, met a merchant while out hunting one day and invited him home. When they arrived, the merchant marveled at the richness of the place and congratulated his host on his good fortune. The prince's wife joined them at supper and ate from a human skull. That night in his sleeping alcove the merchant saw two cadavers hanging by their hands from the top of the partition. In the morning the prince explained that his wife had been unfaithful to him and was being punished by having to eat from the skull of her lover, whom the prince himself had put to death. The two corpses were the prince's brothers-in-law, murdered by the lover's son. Finally, as the merchant took his leave, the prince advised him not to judge good fortune on appearances (A. M. Espinosa 1946–47, vol. 2, p. 279).

46. Seven Blind Queens, tr. from Laval 1968, pp. 180–7. AT type 462 The Outcast Queens and the Ogress Queen (Chile, India).

Widespread in India but not indexed for Europe or elsewhere in Latin America. In another Chilean version the outcast women, blinded, are the king's nieces; the jealous queen sends their brother for lion's milk, drinks it, and dies, whereupon the king lives happily with his nieces and nephew (Hansen, p. 58).

47. The Mad King, tr. from Boggs 1938, no. 5. AT type 981 Wisdom of Hidden Old Man Saves Kingdom (Florida, Mexico, Europe, India, Middle East).

The story was collected in the Tampa area in the 1930s, at which time Tampa had by far the largest Hispanic community in Florida, centered around a cigar industry that had been moved south from New York to avoid organized labor. Most of the workers were from Cuba, some from Mexico.

In Old World versions of the same tale the king's reason for executing the old people is to save food in time of famine. In a Mexican variant the king is overthrown and the boy who has hidden his old father becomes ruler and governs wisely (Wheeler, no. 3).

48. A Mother's Curse, tr. from Ramírez de Arellano, no. 89. Motif C12 Devil invoked appears unexpectedly.

49. The Hermit and the Drunkard, tr. from Carvalho-Neto 1994, no. 25. AT type 756 The Three Green Twigs (Argentina, Chile, Ecuador, New Mexico, Puerto Rico, Europe). The Ecuadorean variant is closest to the subtype 756B The Devil's Contract.

In European versions the sinner must do penance by wandering aimlessly or carrying a sack of stones until his staff sprouts or three green twigs grow on a dry branch. Here, quite simply, he gets to Heaven by pounding his chest with a stone.

50. The Noblewoman's Daughter and the Charcoal Woman's Son, tr. from Hernández Suárez, pp. 260–4. Hansen type 930B [Noble Daughter and Coal Seller's Son] (Cuba)—a subtype of AT 930 The Prophecy (Puerto Rico, Europe, India, Middle East).

51. The Enchanted Cow, tr. from Saunière, pp. 308–17. Motifs B411 Helpful cow, F841 Extraordinary boat, N512 Treasure in underground chamber, E30 Resuscitation by arrangement of members.

The naming of each character and the realistically defined locales (a small village near Constitución, a fair in Chillán) give this story the quality of a novella, as with no. 5, "Antuco's Luck."

52. Judas's Ear, tr. from J. M. Espinosa, no. 21. AT type 301A Quest for a Vanished Princess (Chile, Costa Rica, Guatemala, Mexico, New Mexico, Puerto Rico, Europe, India, Middle East).

53. Good Is Repaid with Evil, tr. from Olivares Figueroa, pp. 48–9. AT type 155 The Ungrateful Serpent Returned to Captivity (Argentina, California, Chile, Cuba, Costa Rica, Guatemala, Dominican Republic, Mexico, New Mexico, Nicaragua, Peru, Puerto Rico, Venezuela, Europe, India, Middle East).

Versions of this ancient fable are found in the *Panchatantra,* the *Gesta Romanorum,* La Fontaine, and other literary sources. Perhaps the oldest is the Aesopic variant recorded in Greek by the second-century author Babrius. According to Babrius, "A farmer picked up a viper that was almost dead from the cold, and warmed it. But the viper, after stretching himself out, clung to the man's hand and bit him incurably, thus killing the very one who wanted to save him. Dying, the man uttered these words, worthy to be remembered: 'I suffer what I deserve, for showing pity to the wicked'" (Perry, p. 187).

The title by which the fable is most commonly known in Latin America, "Good Is Repaid with Evil," is itself a proverb: *Un buen con un mal se paga.*

54. The Fisherman's Daughter, tr. from Reichel-Dolmatoff and Reichel-

Dolmatoff 1956, no. 71. Motif S241 Child unwittingly promised: "first thing you meet" + AT type 425A Cupid and Psyche (California, Chile, Colombia, Costa Rica, Dominican Republic, Mexico, New Mexico, Panama, Puerto Rico, Europe, India, Middle East).

A wild ride through European motifs and American Indian symbolism. The unintended sacrifice to the water spirit is purely Old World (motif S241), and the sequence of bedroom scenes, culminating in the broken prohibition, follows the story of Cupid and Psyche (AT 425A). But the suggestion of paradise lost ("your easy days in this house are finished"), despite the biblical parallel, has an Indian flavor (with hat, sandals, and machete); and the means of redemption—the magical hair from the "mother" who dwells high in the mountains—rests on the old Indian mythology of northern Colombia. The story is discussed in the introduction, p. 11.

55. In the Beginning, Laughlin 1971, pp. 37–8. Genesis 1:1–2:3.

Depending on context, the stories that make up the folk-Bible cycle may be called legends or folktales; legends if regarded as true, folktales if treated as fictional (as in a Tepecano version of the Nativity story that ends with the folktale formula, "I pulled my tale from a basket, tell me another if I ask it" [*Y entro por un chiquihuite roto, y cuéntame otro*]—Mason 1914, p. 166). Some, like no. 55, are folk versions of Scripture. Others, like 67, are entirely noncanonical. At least two, 61 and 68, are pre-Columbian myths adapted to a new religious climate.

56. How the First People Were Made, Parsons 1932, pp. 287–8. Genesis 2:5–25 + motif E751.1 Souls weighed at Judgment Day.

Revising the doctrine of original sin, the teller has Adam cultivating his field from the first day, even digging a ditch in the Garden.

57. Adam's Rib, adapted from Foster, pp. 236–7. Genesis 2:21–24.

Here again, as in the preceding tale, Adam is at work in the Garden, unmoved by the scriptural distinction between paradise and the world east of Eden. Cf. Genesis 3:23–24, "Therefore the Lord God sent him forth from the garden of Eden, to till the ground from whence he was taken. So he drove out the man; and he placed at the east of the garden of Eden Cherubims, and a flaming sword which turned every way, to keep the way of the tree of life."

58. Adam and Eve and Their Children, A. M. Espinosa 1936, p. 119. Genesis 3:1–24 + motifs A1650.1 The various children of Eve and F251.4 Underworld people from children which Eve hid from God.

Unlike the tellers of the two preceding stories this narrator accepts the theory of work as punishment for original disobedience—yet promptly turns the tale into an American Indian emergence myth. First, however, a detour through strictly noncanonical European folklore. The digression, which serves as a bridge, comes from a story well known in the Grimm's version (no. 180), where Eve has seven pretty children and twelve who are ugly; out of shame, when the Lord comes to visit, she hides the ugly ones. The Lord blesses the seven, giving each an enviable destiny (king, prince, etc.). Thinking to secure comparable blessings for her remaining twelve, she brings them out of hiding, only to have the Lord anoint them as servants, laborers, and tradesmen. In Isleta hands, the tale accounts for the unequal destinies of whites and Indians as well as the origin of Indian nations, believed to have emerged from within the earth.

59. God's Letter to Noéh, adapted from Parsons 1936, p. 350. Genesis 6:5–13.

60. God Chooses Noah, tr. from Lehmann 1928, pp. 754–6. AT type 752C* The Discourteous Sower (Chile, Colombia, Ecuador, Guatemala, Mexico, New Mexico, Europe).

The tale is usually told of Christ, who meets the discourteous sower while fleeing his persecutors; or it is told of Mary and Joseph on their way to Bethlehem. It is the only story in the folk-Bible cycle that can still be found in Hispanic communities, though it is much more popular in Indian settings, especially in Mexico and Guatemala.

Phalluses: explicitly phallic stones are found at archeological sites in the Maya area; in Oaxaca, naturally occurring stones regarded as phallic have ritual significance, though in the present story the reference evidently signals little more than the farmer's contempt.

61. The Flood, tr. from Lehmann 1928, pp. 753–4.

This twentieth-century Mixe version from Oaxaca is very close to a sixteenth-century Aztec account that derives from pre-Columbian pictographic sources (Bierhorst 1992, pp. 143–4). The resemblance to the biblical version, slight in any case, would appear to be coincidental. But God, angels, the ark, and pairs of animals are introduced in other versions of the same story collected from Indian narrators in central and southern Mexico (Horcasitas, pp. 194–203). A recurring theme in these basically native flood stories is the prohibition against work. The saved man is ordered not to work as the flood approaches; and, similarly, he must not make fire after the waters have subsided. For his disobedience he is punished, suggesting a comparison not with the ordeal of Noah but with the predicament of Adam, who disobeys, then finds he has no choice but to work. To explicate this cause and its effect, whether relating to Adam or to Noah, has been the uncertain work of theologians and mythologists.

62. A Prophetic Dream, Laughlin 1971, pp. 38–9. John 19:41–20:31.

The story of Christ's appearance following the Resurrection is here changed into a prophecy of his coming. In the biblical account Mary Magdalene enters the garden where Christ was entombed and finds him standing beside the sepulcher. He warns her, "Touch me not; for I am not yet ascended to my Father: but go to my brethren, and say unto them, I ascend unto my Father." The disciples are informed, but the one named Thomas doubts.

63. The White Lily, tr. from Howard-Malverde, p. 211.

The conception is not always immaculate. According to a Nahua account, Mary met Joseph while washing her father's dirty clothes; the couple eloped, Mary riding a donkey (Taggart 1983, p. 103). In a Mazatec version, Joseph impregnates Mary. But since she has other suitors as well, a test is required; Mary hands each a dry reed, and only Joseph's sends forth roots (Laughlin 1971, pp. 39–41). According to a Tepecano story, Mary was Joseph's helper in the woodworking business; at the same time there were devils who wanted to marry her on account of her beauty. When she became pregnant, though she was a virgin, Mary's father decreed that the man whose staff sprouted flowers would be her husband. The devils competed against Joseph, and Joseph was the winner (Mason 1914, p. 164).

64. The Night in the Stable, adapted from Tax, pp. 125–6. Luke 2:1–20 and Matthew 2:2, with motif H71.1 Star on forehead as a sign of royalty.

Though it does not appear in modern indexes, the Nativity tale of the rewarded cow and the punished mule has a long history in European folklore (Dähnhardt, pp. 12–16), with Indian variants from Ecuador, Guatemala, Mexico, and New Mexico (Howard-Malverde, p. 199; Incháustegui, pp. 212–13; Laughlin 1977, pp. 331–2; Parsons 1918, p. 256; Siegel, p. 121; Williams García, p. 73).

65/I. Why Did It Dawn?, Taggart 1983, p. 103.

As early as the mid-sixteenth century Jesus was identified with the sun in Christianized Nahuatl writings (Bierhorst 1985b, p. 367). By the late twentieth century the idea was widespread in Mexico and Guatemala. "To the Nahuas it is absolutely self-evident that [. . .] Jesus Christ is a manifestation of the sun" (Sandstrom, p. 236).

65/II. That Was the Principal Day, Laughlin 1977, p. 332.

66. Three Kings, A. M. Espinosa 1936, pp. 118–19. Matthew 2:1–12. Stories explaining how Indians became poor are widely distributed in Latin America, though the events are usually linked to the Creation rather than the Nativity. Among the Seri of northern Mexico it is said that Indians and other groups were originally in a giant bamboo, each at a node, peering out. At the top were the Seris, next the Gringos, then the Chinese, the Apaches, the Yaquis, and, lowest, the Mexicans. Each in turn came out to meet God and received presents. The Mexicans, who were made the richest, got money, guns,

houses, clothing, and food. Too proud to take gifts, the Seris ended up with nothing but seaweed to cover their nakedness and had to pull it out of the ocean themselves (Coolidge and Coolidge, pp. 107–8; Kroeber, p. 12).

67. The Christ Child as Trickster, tr. from Howard-Malverde, pp. 199–201.

This is rare lore indeed. Remotely similar stories are to be found in the Infancy Gospels, influential in the late Middle Ages, especially the Gospel of Pseudo-Matthew, where we may read, "A bed of six cubits was ordered of Joseph, and he told his lad to cut a beam of the right length, but he made it too short. Joseph was troubled. Jesus pulled it out the right length" (James, p. 78). But neither in Pseudo-Matthew nor elsewhere in the apocryphal scriptures is there clear evidence of the child as trickster.

68. Christ Saved by the Firefly, Redfield, p. 65.

The same is told in the *Popol Vuh*, regarding the twin heroes Hunahpu and Xbalanque. Imprisoned by the lords of death, the two boys are given cigars and ordered to keep them lit through the night. Cleverer than their guards, the heroes escape after attaching fireflies to the ends of the unlit cigars (Tedlock, p. 119). Evidently the story has deep pre-Columbian roots, judging by a scene painted on a Maya vase from northern Guatemala, dated A.D. 600–900, in which the firefly is shown holding the lighted cigar (Coe, p. 99). In a modern variant, also from Guatemala, the prison guards see the firefly and think Jesus is "sitting there smoking a cigarette" (Tax, p. 126).

69. Christ Betrayed by Snails, J. E. S. Thompson, p. 161.

One of the most unusual incidents in the story of Christ's persecution and flight. We are not told what punishment the snails received.

70. Christ Betrayed by the Magpie-jay, Laughlin 1977, p. 26.

Laughlin points out that the magpie-jay is an extremely noisy bird; and in a Guatemalan version that has a rooster noisily betraying Christ, the rooster is punished by being made the bird of sacrifice.

71. The Blind Man at the Cross, Laughlin 1971, pp. 47–8. Matthew 27:1–56 + motif D1505.8.1 Blood from Christ's wounds restores sight.

Thompson's *Motif-Index* mentions only a medieval French source. According to a modern Nahua version, the blind man regained his sight and immediately wailed, "God save me! I have stabbed my compadre" (Ziehm, p. 159). In a Laguna account from New Mexico the spurting blood not only heals the blind man but becomes the agent of a new Creation: "From the spattered blood all living beings came, horses and mules and all creatures" (Parsons 1918, p. 257).

72. The Cricket, the Mole, and the Mouse, Laughlin 1971, pp. 48–50. Matthew 27:57–66, Luke 24:1–3.

The unusual tale of how the sepulcher was opened is evidently known in Ecuador as well as in Mexico. Among the Quichua of Imbabura in the Ecuadorean highlands it is told that once in the month of harvests, when all the grains were gathered, Jesucristo came to give each creature its proper grain. A mouse presented himself and said, "I will open the sepulcher so you may get out when the enemies kill you and bury you." Jesucristo replied, "If you do me this favor, you shall live forever as the master of every grain and hidden almost always in the house of man" (Parsons 1945, p. 147).

73. As If with Wings, Laughlin 1971, p. 52. Mark 16:19, Acts 1:9.

74. Slowpoke Slaughtered Four, tr. from Ramírez de Arellano, no. 22. AT type 851 The Princess Who Cannot Solve the Riddle (Argentina, Chile, Costa Rica, Dominican Republic, Ecuador, Mexico, New Mexico, Puerto Rico, Venezuela, Europe, India, Middle East).

Also known as The Shepherd's Riddle, the tale has an easily recognizable variant in the *Thousand and One Nights*: A young man down on his luck sells his parents for a suit of fine clothes and a horse. While on the road, thirsty, he drinks the horse's sweat. Arriving at the palace of a king who has promised his daughter to anyone who proposes a riddle she cannot solve, he offers, "The water I drank was neither of earth nor of Heaven." The princess is stumped. That night she comes to his bed and sleeps with him in exchange for the answer. She leaves her nightclothes, and the next day he catches her once and for all with the riddle, "A dove came to visit me and left its feathers in my hands."

75. The Price of Heaven and the Rain of Caramels, tr. from Wheeler, no. 158. Robe type 1341E [The Money in the Coffin] (Mexico) + AT type 1381B The Sausage Rain (Mexico, New Mexico, Panama, Europe, India).

The two tales are dissimilar, though in each case the trickster ends up with the money. The technique of doubling, or telling complementary tales in tandem, is a feature associated more with Indian than with Hispanic storytelling. Coincidentally, the money placed in the coffin recalls the actual custom of putting money on the chest of the corpse during a wake to help pay for food and drink (Carvalho-Neto 1961, p. 313).

76. Pine Cone the Astrologer, tr. from Riera-Pinilla, no. 58. AT type 1641 Doctor Know-All (Argentina, Chile, Dominican Republic, Guatemala, Mexico, New Mexico, Puerto Rico, Venezuela, Europe, India, Middle East).

77. The Dragon Slayer, tr. from Wheeler, no. 57. AT type 300 The Dragon Slayer (Argentina, California, Chile, Colombia, Dominican Republic, Guatemala, Mexico, New Mexico, Puerto Rico, Europe, India) + AT type 510A Cinderella (see no. 28).

Heroines in trouser roles, though not unheard of in Old World lore, are a frequent and striking feature of Latin American folk narrative. Among these, the female dragon slayer who rescues a prince in distress is surely the most unexpected. The widow who liberates three princesses and becomes general of the king's armies (no. 52) ranks as a close second. Others are to be found in nos. 11, 25, 33, 34, 84, and 97.

Quiquiriquí: literally, cock-a-doodle-doo, the never-never land of Hispanic folktales.

Ruddy ruddy red, / My story is said (*colorín colorado, este cuento se ha acabado*): a formulaic closing of Spanish origin. *Colorín* means "ruddy" and by extension denotes the linnet (in Spain) or the bright red seeds of the coralbean, *Erythrina coralloides* (in the Americas). A Spanish variant is *punto colorado, cuento terminado* (red dot, the story is over—Taggart 1990, p. 180).

78. Johnny-boy, tr. from Peña Hernández, pp. 222–3.

Twenty-two Roman popes: The story was collected before the reign of Pope John XXIII.

John of God (Juan de Dios), 1495–1550, founder of the Brothers Hospitalers of St. John of God, canonized 1690.

79. The Rarest Thing, tr. from Lara Figueroa 1982, pp. 20–21. AT type 653A The Rarest Thing in the World (Dominican Republic, Guatemala, Mexico, New Mexico, Puerto Rico, Europe).

In a version from New Mexico the princess is to wed the man who offers her the best gift, but when three suitors arrive, each claiming his gift is the best, she tells them to shoot arrows and bring them back to her. They're still looking (Rael, no. 223).

80. Prince Simpleheart, tr. from Noguera, pp. 105–14. AT type 566 The Three Magic Objects and the Wonderful Fruits (Argentina, Chile, Costa Rica, Mexico, New Mexico, Puerto Rico, Europe, India, Middle East).

The tapir switch adds a tropical American touch to this essentially Old World tale.

81. The Flower of Lily-Lo, adapted from A. Paredes, no. 41. AT type 780 The Singing Bone (Argentina, Bolivia, Chile, Costa Rica, Cuba, Dominican Republic, Ecuador, Mexico, New Mexico, Panama, Puerto Rico, Europe, India, Middle East).

One of the world's most popular folktales. Typical Old World versions have the murder revealed by a flute, harp, or other instrument made from the victim's bones. In Spain and Latin America the crime is usually signaled by a flower, often called the Flower of Lily-Lo or Lililón.

82. My Garden Is Better Than Ever, adapted from Foster, p. 218. AT type 175 The Tarbaby and the Rabbit (Argentina, Chile, Colombia, Costa Rica, Dominican Republic, El Salvador, Guatemala, Mexico, New Mexico,

Nicaragua, Puerto Rico, Venezuela, Africa, Europe, India). The Salvadoran variant is in Schultze Jena, p. 133.

The most familiar of the Brer Rabbit stories. Widely diffused in Indo- and Hispano-America, it is generally believed to have been brought to the New World from Africa. The more elaborate (and controversial) theory of Aurelio Espinosa postulates an Indic origin, and from India two parallel routes of diffusion to the Americas, one through Africa to the Antilles and Brazil, the other through the Middle East and Spain to Mexico and Spanish South America (A. M. Espinosa 1946–47, vol. 2, pp. 163–227).

83. Juan Bobo and the Pig, tr. from Ramírez de Arellano, no. 114. Hansen type 1704** [The Fool as Babysitter] (Cuba, Puerto Rico).

A great many Puerto Rican versions have been recorded. In most, the chicks are replaced by a baby that won't stop crying. The fool quiets it by sticking a pin in its head.

84. The Parrot Prince, tr. from Laval 1920, no. 9. AT type 432 The Prince as Bird (California, Chile, Dominican Republic, Guatemala, Mexico, New Mexico, Puerto Rico, Europe, India, Middle East) with the addition of motif H1125 Task: traveling until iron shoes are worn out (Chile, Mexico, New Mexico, Panama, Puerto Rico, Europe).

The remedy overheard in a conversation of animals (motif N452) is a narrative trick deeply entrenched in Old World lore and evidently known in the New World since at least the turn of the sixteenth century. It makes its American debut in a Quechua manuscript of 1608 from the province of Huarochirí in the central highlands of Peru. A rich man, according to the story, had been stricken with an incurable illness. "Wise men and sages were called in, just as the Spaniards consult learned sages and doctors, but not a single one could recognize the disease." At that moment a poor beggar was coming over the mountain and took it into his head to lie down and rest. As he was falling asleep, two foxes arrived, one from the valley, the other from the high plains. The one from the valley said, "Brother, how are things up above?" "Just fine, just fine. But there's a gentleman in Anchicocha [. . .] who is very sick, and he's called in all the sages to tell him what the illness is and not a one can diagnose it. But I tell you, the trouble is that . . ." And having overheard the cause of the disease, the beggar comes into town, asks if anyone is ill, and proceeds to work the cure. The remedy includes removing a snake from the roof of the house and a two-headed toad from beneath the grinding stone (Trimborn and Kelm, pp. 33–7). See comment to the Mexican variant, "What the Owls Said," no. 15, above.

And put it in ships for John, Rock, and Rick . . . : discussed above in the introductory note, p. 47.

Peumo: a small evergreen tree (*Cryptocarya alba*) native to Chile.

The walls have ears and the bushes have eyes: a formulaic expression widely used in European folk narrative whether or not there are walls or bushes in the story.

Chain Riddles. I, adapted from Scott, p. 239. II, tr. from Cadilla de Martínez, p. 252. III, tr. from the Zapotec by Langston Hughes in Covarrubias, pp. 346–7. IV, tr. from A. M. Espinosa 1916, p. 516. V, adapted from Bernard and Salinas 1989, p. 103. VI, Burns, p. 18.

The first of these six patter-chants is said to be a riddle. The second, third, and fourth are nonsense rhymes used in children's games. The fifth is recited as a story; the sixth, at the end of a story to break the spell of enchantment.

85. A Dead Man Speaks, tr. from Pérez, pp. 94–5. Motif E235 Return from dead to punish indignities to corpse.

Latin American folklorists would call this little story a *caso,* or happening. The term used in English is "memorate," meaning a reminiscence, especially one that includes a brush with the supernatural. A memorate is told as a factual occurrence by someone who claims to have witnessed it or, second hand, by a person who *knows* the person who witnessed it. Distanced from the original narrator, it might eventually become an "urban legend" (see no. 29).

86. The Bear's Son, adapted and tr. from Chapman, pp. 215–33.

One of the most popular and most variable Hispanic folktales, also known as Juan Oso (John the Bear). This gritty Honduran version is unusual for its labor-oriented reworking of narrative elements, avoiding the usual swashbuckler-wins-princess motifs, and for its poignant sociological undercurrent—a native American bildungsroman created almost entirely from Old World folkloric materials. The main elements may be summarized:

Motif B635.1 The Bear's Son (Bolivia, California, Chile, Guatemala, Honduras, Mexico, New Mexico, Puerto Rico, Europe).

Motif B600.2 Animal husband provides characteristic animal food (see note to no. 112, below).

AT type 157 Learning to Fear Men (Argentina, Chile, Guatemala, Honduras, Mexico, New Mexico, Puerto Rico, Europe, India, Middle East).

AT type 38 Claw in Split Tree (Guatemala, Honduras, Mexico, New Mexico, Puerto Rico, Europe, India, Middle East).

Motif J1758 Tiger mistaken for domestic animal.

AT type 326 The Youth Who Wanted to Learn What Fear Is (Bolivia, Chile, Dominican Republic, Guatemala, Honduras, Mexico, New Mexico, Puerto Rico, Europe, India, Middle East).

Guaruma: a large tree of Mexico and Central America, *Cecropia peltata,* with leaves like fig leaves.

87. Charity, tr. from Chertudi, vol. 1, no. 54. AT type 841 One Beggar Trusts God, the Other the King (Argentina, Mexico, Europe, India, Middle East).

88. Riches Without Working, tr. from Boas and Arreola, pp. 1–5. Robe type 545G [The Mouse as Helper] (Mexico).

Perhaps a remote variant of the familiar Puss-in-Boots tale (AT type 545 The Cat as Helper), which has been collected repeatedly in Mexico. The creativity of American Indian storytelling is at work here.

Hacendado: the owner of a hacienda.

89. Let Somebody Buy You Who Doesn't Know You, tr. from Recinos 1918a, no. 5. AT type 1529 Thief Claims to Have Been Transformed into a Horse (Chile, Guatemala, Honduras, Mexico, Panama, Europe, Middle East). The Honduran variant is in Ortega.

Chiantla: a town just north of Huehuetenango, in Indian country.

Chús: short for Jesús.

Scholar Corncob: *Pascasio Taltusa,* literally, "a vacationing student, a man called corncob," in other words, a rustic intellectual. Compare the students who try to outwit the Indian in another tale from Guatemala, no. 42, and the similarly Dickensian surnames in yet another Guatemalan story, no. 40.

90. The Mouse King, tr. from Anibarro de Halushka, no. 39. AT type 555 The Fisher and His Wife (Bolivia, Cuba, New Mexico, Europe, Middle East).

In the usual story a grateful fish, in exchange for being thrown back, grants all the wishes of the fisherman's wife until she wishes to be God. Only in the Bolivian and Cuban versions are the wishes granted by a mouse. With an unusually fine-pointed moral the Bolivian narrator turns an ordinary parable into a miniature psychological drama.

91. Mariquita Grim and Mariquita Fair, tr. from Hernández Suárez, pp. 264–9. AT type 480 The Spinning-Women by the Spring (Cuba, Mexico, New Mexico, Europe, India, Middle East).

The contrast between the kind and the unkind, who treat a stranger courteously or with disrespect, is one of the commanding themes in these folktales. Here it forms the basis for one of the lesser known Cinderella stories.

92. The Compadre's Dinner, tr. from Andrade 1930, no. 294. Hansen type 1545** [The Reluctant Hosts] (Cuba, Dominican Republic, Puerto Rico, Spain). The Cuban variant is in Feijóo, vol. 1, pp. 76–7.

Majarete: a native dish of Cuba and the Dominican Republic (a sort of a custard made from cornmeal, honey, and other ingredients, served as a dessert).

93. The Hog, tr. from Rael, no. 54. AT type 1792 The Stingy Parson and the Slaughtered Pig (New Mexico, Europe).

94. Two Sisters, tr. from Mason 1924, no. 10. AT type AT750F The Old Man's Blessing (Argentina, Puerto Rico).

95. The Ghosts' Reales, tr. from Andrade 1930, no. 270. AT type 1654 The Robbers in the Death Chamber (Cuba, Dominican Republic, Ecuador, Mexico, New Mexico, Panama, Europe, India, Middle East).

Wakes are normally held at home. But in a note to the Ecuadorean variant of this tale Carvalho-Neto writes, "It was formerly the custom to hold wakes in church in front of the high altar" (1994, pp. 11–12).

96. The Bad Compadre, tr. from the Cakchiquel Maya by Robert Redfield, in Redfield, pp. 243–51. AT type 531 Ferdinand the True and Ferdinand the False (Costa Rica, Guatemala, Mexico, New Mexico, Europe, India, Middle East) + AT type 554 The Grateful Animals (Argentina, Cuba, Guatemala, Mexico, New Mexico, Puerto Rico, Europe, India, Middle East).

Rarely do we learn the provenance of a particular version or the story-teller's own evaluation of the tale. But the anthropologist Robert Redfield supplies some information: "Story told by Francisco Sanchez, Nov. 18, 1940. He said that his friend Antonio Perez told it to him and that it had been told to Antonio by his mother-in-law. Francisco said it was a true story, and he interrupted himself several times to make sure I was understanding its significance. He dwelt on the bad conduct of Mariano, who tried to prevent his own compadre from making money. 'Business is free to everyone. It was a sin to do this to his compadre.' He also spoke of the evil nature of Mariano's magic. 'This power was not of God but of the Devil.' Before he had told all the story in Cakchiquel, he told me the conclusion in Spanish; he wanted me to know that Mariano was going to get his just deserts."

97. Black Chickens, tr. from Mason 1914, no. 17. AT type 1380 The Faithless Wife (Mexico, Europe, India, Middle East).

Widely known in the Old World but apparently recorded for Spanish America only in this Tepecano variant from Mexico. It is remarkably close to peninsular Spanish versions, in which the faithless wife, seeking to make her husband blind, consults the statue either of St. Anthony or of Christ. Her husband, speaking from behind the statue, advises her to feed him ham, chops, and wine; or, in another version, black chickens and red wine. Somewhat different but still recognizable is an ancient Indic version recorded in the *Panchatantra*: A woman spends all her time making biscuits, which she secretly feeds to her lover with butter and sugar. Her husband asks why she makes biscuits, and she says she offers them to the local goddess. When she goes off to bathe, her husband follows and hides behind the statue of the goddess. Hearing his wife ask the statue, "What can I give my husband to make him blind?" he answers, "Biscuits with butter and sugar!" She returns home and feeds him accordingly. He pretends to be blind, using the opportunity to catch the wife with the lover, whom he thrashes soundly (A. M. Espinosa, vol. 1, nos. 33 and 34; vol. 2, pp. 160–2).

98. Doublehead, tr. from the Pipil-German text in Schultze Jena, pp. 23–6.

The witch wife who leaves the house at night, having removed her head or her skin, is the subject of tales reported from El Salvador, Mexico, and Puerto Rico. The husband uses ashes, or more often salt, to prevent her from getting back into her skin or to keep her head from rejoining her body; and in some versions the head is carried off by an animal. This much is perhaps of Hispanic origin, though the folklorist Elsie Parsons suspected African influence. The El Salvador versions, in a decidedly Indian touch, have the widowed husband becoming the father of innumerable children; and from this flow further tales, forming a mythological cycle in which the children's adventures lead to the origin of corn.

Similar Witch Wife stories of possible Hispanic origin are in Hartman pp. 144–6; Laughlin 1977, pp. 65–6, 72–3, 179–82; Mason 1926 (summarized in Hansen, pp. 82–5); Parsons 1936, p. 364; Preuss 2000; Redfield and Villa Rojas, p. 334; and J. E. S. Thompson, p. 158. Further variants are cited in Laughlin 1977, p. 66. For African-American versions see Dorson, p. 246. Two other subtypes of the Witch Wife tale are represented by nos. 9 and 30 in the present collection.

Observe that the widower's myriad children are not average-sized humans. Like the Aztec rain dwarfs and the diminutive war gods of Zuni mythology, they are little people. And in fact, the whole mythology (of which the tale at hand is merely a portion) reveals that the widower's children are none other than the mischievous "rain boys," who will eventually bring corn into the world (Schultze Jena).

99. Littlebit, tr. from Laval 1968, pp. 187–93. AT type 700 Tom Thumb (Chile, Dominican Republic, New Mexico, Panama, Puerto Rico, Europe, India, Middle East).

Known everywhere in Europe, including Spain, the tale of the thumbling first appears in European literature in R. Johnson's *The History of Tom Thumbe* (1621) and in a subsequent treatment in verse, also published in England, the anonymous *Tom Thumbe, His Life and Death* (1631). In the latter version a married couple wishes for a child, and with the aid of Merlin a boy, the size of a thumb, is born. His adventures begin when he falls into a food dish and is eaten by a beggar. Passed as waste, he is recovered by his mother, who ties him to a leaf. Eaten by a cow, he is again passed as waste. His mother cleans him up, and he goes off to plow a field. He is swallowed by a giant. Passed into the sea, he is swallowed by a fish. The fish is caught, Tom is rescued, and he lives out the rest of his days at King Arthur's court.

Valdiviano: stew made from jerked meat (a Chilean dish).

100. Rosalie, adapted from J. E. S. Thompson, pp. 167–71. AT type 313 The Girl as Helper in the Hero's Flight (Argentina, Chile, Cuba, Dominican Republic, Mexico, New Mexico, Panama, Puerto Rico, Venezuela, Europe, India, Middle East).

The name Rosalie is an unusual feature of this Yucatec Maya version. In Spain as in Latin America the heroine is usually Blancaflor. She is Rosella in the variant given by Basile in the *Pentamerone* (ninth story of the third day).

101. A Day Laborer Goes to Work, adapted from Bernard and Salinas 1976, pp. 1–17.

Life portrayed as a descent into hell. Though the story echoes folkloric motifs, it cannot be reduced to a handful of formulas. The plantation owner, encountered in so many of these Hispano-Indian tales, has become the Devil. The Virgin, now in the role of a dutiful wife, sends food to the fields, enabling the laborer to carry out his penance. The stereotypical witch wife, identified by her transformation into a mule, has become simply the woman next door, as the homely, folkloric moral articulated by the Virgin—"Don't always believe what people tell you"—is buried beneath the larger reality of hardship and crisis.

Though it has not been indexed, the tale evidently has variants. In a similar story from the Ixil Maya of Guatemala, a poor man leaves his wife in search of money and is led into hell. There the patrón, identified as a *ladino,* instructs him to perform labor with the aid of a stubborn mule. The poor man beats the mule, who turns out to be his own comadre, sentenced to hell for a sin she had committed. When the man returns home, he learns from his wife that the comadre is in her own house, all black and blue from the wounds the man had given her in the afterworld (Colby and Colby 1981, pp. 188–94).

102. The Moth, tr. from Arguedas and Carrillo, pp. 78–9.

The redemption earned by the distraught husband in the preceding tale is not in store for his counterpart in this typically harsh Peruvian story. Again, there are no type or motif numbers by which the tale can be pigeonholed.

103. The Earth Ate Them, tr. from Jijena Sánchez, no. 30.

Finally, in a less serious vein, another original tale, original at least so far as European lore is concerned. A variant of this Argentine story has been recorded from neighboring Paraguay: A rich widow tells her niece to put all her jewels in her coffin when she dies. After the burial, following an entertaining and well-attended wake, a rogue sneaks into the cemetery to steal the jewels. While he is yanking at one of the combs, he unintentionally pulls the dead woman's hair, and the corpse opens its eyes. Terrified, the thief tries to get away, snags his poncho on the coffin, and thinks the corpse is reaching for him. When he finally runs off, he has lost his mind, and his hair has turned white (Carvalho-Neto 1961, p. 195).

Epilogue: Twentieth-Century Myths

[Epigraph]: *Hay que temer a los espíritus, a los dioses, a los antepasados, pero no a los hombres vivos* (Otero, p. 233; the English translation is in Fox, p. 289).

104. Why Tobacco Grows Close to Houses, tr. from Reichel-Dolmatoff 1951, p. 60.

The Mother: The creative spirit in Kogi religious belief, said to be "mother of the world." See also no. 108.

105. The Buzzard Husband, a composite drawn from three versions translated from the Tzotzil Maya by Robert Laughlin, in Laughlin 1977, pp. 50–1, 246–51, 342–3.

The story is widely told in Mexico and Guatemala, especially among Maya groups but also among the Nahua and as far north as the Yaqui of Sonora and Arizona (Laughlin 1977, p. 51; Bierhorst 1990, pp. 119, 217; Peñalosa 1996, pp. 87–8).

106. The Dead Wife, adapted from Conzemius, 159–60. Motif F81.1 Orpheus.

Here in a variant from the Mískito of Nicaragua is the so-called Orpheus myth of native America, widely told throughout the hemisphere (Hultkranz; Bierhorst 1990, pp. 119, 217; Wilbert and Simoneau, p. 565). The four-hundred-year-old version from Peru, no. 2/III, "The Vanishing Bride," is more in keeping with the general type in that it has the hero breaking a prohibition and thus losing the wife or bride he is attempting to bring back from the afterworld—as in the Greek myth of Orpheus and Eurydice. In the opinion of folklorists the parallel between Old and New World versions is coincidental.

A motif index fully attuned to native America might include the following additional items characteristic of Mexican and Central American Indian lore: Souls of the dead as moths or butterflies; Dog as ferryman to the afterworld; Tree of breasts suckles infants in the afterworld (Bierhorst 1991, pp. 155–6). The first two are similar to Stith Thompson's motifs E734.1 Soul in form of butterfly (Europe, Asia); and A673 Hound of hell (Europe, India, Middle East). Yet the various American tales in which these motifs appear, including the Mískito "Dead Wife," suggest an independent origin.

107. Romi Kumu Makes the World, Hugh-Jones, p. 263. Motifs A1010 Deluge and A1030 World-fire.

Though freely distributed in both hemispheres, the idea of a world fire belongs particularly to South American Indian mythology. The Revolt of the Utensils, discussed in the introductory note, p. 303, is an American Indian specialty, cropping up here in the fourth paragraph of the story.

Pirá-paraná: river in southeastern Colombia, part of the Amazon basin.

108. She Was Thought and Memory, tr. from Reichel-Dolmatoff 1951, p. 9.

There are nine preliminary worlds, one above the other; the Mother resides in the first and lowest, with human life gradually taking shape in the second through ninth worlds (Reichel-Dolmatoff 1951, pp. 9–18, 60).

109. Was It Not an Illusion?, tr. from the Witoto-German text in K. T. Preuss 1921, pp. 166–7.

Had he no staff?: Note that in the myth that follows, no. 110, the Creator has a "staff of authority."

Iseike (EE-say-ee-kay): a mysterious adhesive described by one of Preuss's native informants as something "like tobacco smoke, like cotton flocking."

110. The Beginning Life of the Hummingbird, tr. from the Mbyá Guaraní and Spanish text in Cadogan, pp. 13–15.

The first in a cycle of creation myths known by the general name ayvu rapyta (origin of human speech). The manner in which Cadogan came to record these stories is of interest, since for a number of years he had been able to obtain only the non-esoteric lore of the Mbyá and had no inkling of any further, secret lore. His relationship to the tribe changed, however, after he secured the release of an important tribal member who had been incarcerated by Paraguayan authorities on a murder charge. When the tribal cacique came to the city of Villarrica to receive the prisoner, the freed man turned to the cacique and asked if he had ever discussed with Cadogan the ayvu rapyta. The chief said no. Then the freed man proposed that Cadogan be regarded as "a true member of the seat of our hearthfires," and following that pronouncement interviews were set up with knowledgeable elders, including the freed man and the cacique himself, who dictated the myths (Cadogan, pp. 9–11).

Ñamanduí: another name for the First Father.

Hummingbird: synonymous with the First Father.

The primal time-space: winter.

A new space in time: spring.

111. Ibis Story, tr. from the German in Gusinde, pp. 1232–3 (with help from the English version in Wilbert, pp. 25–6).

An unusual myth, told among the Yamana of Tierra del Fuego and apparently nowhere else. The underlying thought, typically Indian, is that the cataclysms of the formative era might yet be revisited. Reason enough to "hush up the little children" when the ibis woman appears.

112. The Condor Seeks a Wife, tr. from M. R. Paredes, pp. 65–7. Motif B600.2 Animal husband provides characteristic animal food.

The unpleasantly realistic setting of the condor colony with its daily fare of carrion identifies the tale as a typical native American myth, concerned with the fine distinctions between nature and culture. The sentimentalizing tone and the mention of sheep may be regarded as modern growths. The key motif, B600.2, is registered by Thompson only for Greenland and Canada; and for Argentina, Colombia, and Paraguay by Wilbert and Simoneau. Many other New World locations could be added—including Honduras (see "The Bear's Son," no. 85). Compare the similar treatment of food in "The Buzzard Husband," no. 105.

113. The Priest's Son Becomes an Eagle, tr. from the Zuni by Ruth Benedict, in Benedict, vol. 1, pp. 179–82. The first sentence of the fourth paragraph carries out Benedict's instruction, "Repeat for two more of four sisters."

The compulsive use of the number 4, typical of Indian storytelling north of Mexico, contrasts with the obligatory number 3 of European lore. Thus four girls come courting. Notice that the girl climbs up a ladder, then climbs down; this would have been necessary since old-style Pueblo dwellings were entered from the roof. The guest is greeted with the customary expression "So you've come?" here translated "You're coming, aren't you?" The rough equivalent is "Welcome." Benedict comments that the Zuni distrust of demonstrativeness is given extreme expression in this tale. At the time the story was recorded Benedict was compiling an index of Southwest Indian mythology (never completed), which would have included the motif "Death sought by summoning the Apaches." Note that the "priest" is an officiant of the native religion, not a Catholic priest.

And all this takes place in Hawiku, a long-abandoned village twelve miles southwest of a present-day Zuni pueblo. It was in Hawiku that the explorer Coronado first encountered Zuni warriors in the year 1540.

114. The Revolt of the Utensils, tr. from the German in Hissink and Hahn, no. 230.

A recurring theme in American Indian mythology. Usually the story is set in the time of Creation, especially as part of the world flood, as in no. 107. Here the Tacana storyteller is merely playing with the old familiar tale. In another, somewhat more alarming Tacana version it is said that the utensils all began to knock about when the moon was eclipsed; when it reappeared, they fell lifeless. Harking back to the ancient days, a third Tacana story recalls that utensils rebelled against the people during an eclipse of the sun. More typically, still another of the Tacana myths states, "Before the great Flood inundated the earth and destroyed it, the pots, grating boards, weapons, and other utensils rebelled against the people and devoured them" (Hissink and Hahn, nos. 4, 39, and 40). See the discussion in the introductory note, p. 303.

115. The Origin of Permanent Death, tr. from the Shuar-Spanish text in Pellizzaro, pp. 86–92.

The narrator, Píkiur, is a fifty-seven-year-old man, married, monolingual in the language of the Shuar.

REGISTER OF TALE TYPES
AND SELECTED MOTIFS

The register, or list, of tale types offers the folklorist a quick summary of contents more meaningful than the table of contents itself. But even the nonfolklorist, who has a nodding acquaintance with folktales, will recognize a few of the types by their catchwords: Cinderella, The Grateful Dead, The Tarbaby and the Rabbit, Tom Thumb, and others. The sequence of type numbers, established in 1910 by the Finnish folklorist Antti Aarne, has achieved canonical status over the years. No one has attempted to change it, though many have added to it, including Thompson, Boggs, Hansen, Robe, and Peñalosa (whose works will be found entered in the bibliography), simply by attaching letters or asterisks to the basic numbers. Thus the series is both immutable and, to some extent, flexible. For the Latin Americanist its chief limitation, the Euro-Indic straitjacket, is its greatest virtue, offering a ready means of distinguishing the imported from the native, since stories of purely American Indian origin do not have generally acknowledged type numbers.

The "type" is a more or less complex arrangement of "motifs." Thus the recurrence of a "type" strongly indicates borrowing rather than independent invention.

Some stories, even within the Old World tradition, are sufficiently original to elude the type list. Most of these, however, have one or more motifs that can be usefully noted, though the identification of a motif is no guarantee of Old World origin. Stith Thompson's standard *Motif-Index,* unlike the tale-type sequence, incorporates a sprinkling of American Indian references.

In the lists that follow, the corresponding story numbers are appended in square brackets. All types are accounted for, insofar as possible. But motifs are here recognized only for stories or parts of stories that cannot be typed (though if a listed motif recurs in typed stories, the numbers of those are here given in addition to the number of the untyped story). The abbreviation AT stands for Aarne and Thompson.

TYPES

Animal Tales

AT 34 The Wolf Dives into the Water for Reflected Cheese [37]

AT 38 Claw in Split Tree [86]

AT 155 The Ungrateful Serpent Returned to Captivity [53]

AT 157 Learning to Fear Men [86]

AT 175 The Tarbaby and the Rabbit [82]

Ordinary Folktales

AT 300 The Dragon Slayer [77]

AT 301A Quest for a Vanished Princess [52]

AT 310 The Maiden in the Tower [20]

AT 313 The Girl as Helper in the Hero's Flight [Blancaflor] [100]

AT 326 The Youth Who Wanted to Learn What Fear Is [86]

AT 327 The Children and the Ogre [17]

AT 330 The Smith Outwits the Devil [16, 18/IV]

AT 330D Bonhomme Misère [16]

AT 332 Godfather Death [14]

AT 332B Death and Luck [44]

AT 403 The Black and White Bride [7]

AT 425A Cupid and Psyche [54]

AT 432 The Prince as Bird [84]

AT 462 The Outcast Queens and the Ogress Queen [46]

AT 470 Friends in Life and Death [19]

AT 480 The Spinning-Women by the Spring [91]

AT 505 The Grateful Dead [21]

AT 510 Cinderella [35]

AT 510A Cinderella [28, 77]

AT 510B The Dress of Gold, of Silver, and of Stars [11]

AT 530 The Princess on the Glass Mountain [12]

AT 531 Ferdinand the True and Ferdinand the False [96]

Robe 545G [The Mouse as Helper] [88]

AT 551 The Sons on a Quest for a Wonderful Remedy for Their Father [21]

AT 554 The Grateful Animals [96]

AT 555 The Fisher and His Wife [90]

Robe 559 Dung Beetle [24]

AT 566 The Three Magic Objects and the Wonderful Fruits [80]

AT 612 The Three Snake-Leaves [10]

AT 613 The Two Travelers [15]

Hansen 613 [Hero Overhears Secrets and Cures Illness] {15}

AT 621 The Louse Skin [41]

AT 653A The Rarest Thing in the World {79}

AT 700 Tom Thumb [99]

AT 707 The Three Golden Sons [32]

Hansen 748H [Witch Wife Who Visits Cemetery Changes Spying Husband into Dog] {30}

AT 750F The Old Man's Blessing [94]

AT 752C* The Discourteous Sower [60]

AT 756 The Three Green Twigs [49]

AT 756B The Devil's Contract [49]

AT 759 God's Justice Vindicated [8, 27]

AT 780 The Flower of Lily-Lo [81]

AT 841 One Beggar Trusts God, the Other the King [87]

AT 851 The Princess Who Cannot Solve the Riddle [74]

AT 879 The Basil Maiden [43]

AT 883A The Innocent Slandered Maiden [25]

AT 891 The Man Who Deserts His Wife and Sets Her the Task of Bearing Him a Child [34]

AT 910B The Servant's Good Counsels [45]

AT 923 Love Like Salt [35]

Hansen 930B [Noble Daughter and Coal Seller's Son] {50}

AT 945 Luck and Intelligence [6]

AT 981 Wisdom of Hidden Old Man Saves Kingdom [47]

AT 1004 Hogs in the Mud [18/II]

Jokes and Anecdotes

Robe 1341E [The Money in the Coffin] [75]

AT 1354 Death for the Old Couple [22]

AT 1364 The Blood-Brother's Wife [26]

AT 1380 The Faithless Wife [97]

AT 1381B The Sausage Rain {75}

AT 1415 Lucky Hans [13]

AT 1418 The Equivocal Oath [33]

AT 1529 Thief Claims to Have Been Transformed into a Horse [89]

AT 1530 Holding Up the Rock {37}

AT 1536B The Three Hunchback Brothers Drowned [28]

AT 1540 The Student from Paradise [18/I]

Hansen 1545** [The Reluctant Hosts] [92]

AT 1626 Dream Bread [42]

AT 1641 Doctor Know-All [76]

AT 1654 The Robbers in the Death Chamber [95]

Hansen 1704** [The Fool as Babysitter] [83]

AT 1737 The Parson in the Sack to Heaven [18/III]

AT 1792 The Stingy Parson and the Slaughtered Pig [93]

Boggs 1940E [The Widow's Dog Named World] [31]

SELECTED MOTIFS

Mythological Motifs

A673 Hound of hell [106]

A1010 Deluge [3, 61, 107, 111]

A1030 World-fire [107]

A1650.1 The various children of Eve [58]

Animals

B401 Helpful horse [12]

B411 Helpful cow [51]

B600.2 Animal husband provides characteristic animal food [86, 112]

B635.1 The Bear's Son [86]

Tabu

C12 Devil invoked appears unexpectedly [48]

Magic

D1234 Magic guitar [12]

D1505.8.1 Blood from Christ's wounds restores sight [71]

The Dead

E30 Resuscitation by arrangement of members [51]

E235 Return from dead to punish indignities to corpse [85]

E734.1 Soul in form of butterfly [106]

E751.1 Souls weighed at Judgment Day [56]

Marvels

F81.1 Orpheus [106]

F251.4 Underworld people from children which Eve hid from God [58]

F841 Extraordinary boat [51]

Ogres

G211 Witch in animal form [9, 80, 84]

G211.1.2 Witch in form of horse [30, cf. 101]

G266 Witches steal [9]

G271.2.2 Witch exorcised by holy water [9]

G271.4.5 Breaking spell by beating the person or object bewitched [9]

Tests

H71.1 Star on forehead as a sign of royalty [64]

H121 Identification by cup [28]

H602.1.1 Symbolic meaning of numbers one to [. . .] twelve [23]

H1091.1 Task: sorting grains: performed by helpful ants [28, 96]

H1091.2 Task: sorting grains: performed by helpful birds [28]

H1125 Task: traveling until iron shoes are worn out [84]

H1226.4 Pursuit of rolling ball of yarn leads to quest [5]

The Wise and the Foolish

J1185.1 Sheherezade [4]

J1758 Tiger mistaken for domestic animal [86]

J2461.1 Literal following of instructions about actions [39]

Deceptions

K841 Substitute for execution obtained by trickery [37]

Reversal of fortune

L13 Compassionate youngest son [12, 21]

Ordaining the Future

M21 King Lear judgment [35]

Chance and Fate

N452 Secret remedy overheard in conversation of animals {12, 15, 84, cf. 80}

N512 Treasure in underground chamber {5, 51}

N531 Treasure discovered through dream {5}

N813 Helpful genie {5}

Rewards and Punishments

Q2 Kind and unkind {12, 21, 28, 60, 91, 94}

Unnatural Cruelty

S165 Mutilation: putting out eyes {12}

S224 Child promised to Devil for acting as godfather {23}

S241 Child unwittingly promised: "first thing you meet" {54}

Traits of Character

W151.9 Greedy animal gets head stuck in food jar {37}

GLOSSARY OF NATIVE CULTURES

The population figures, which are very rough approximations, have been gathered from different sources, principally the Summer Institute of Linguistics.

Aymara. A major ethnic group of the central Andes, numbering more than three million in northwestern Bolivia, southern Peru, and northern Chile.

Aztec. *See* **Nahua.**

Barasana. A small Amazonian tribe of southeastern Colombia with fewer than 500 members.

Cakchiquel Maya. One of the Mayan groups of the Guatemalan highlands west of Guatemala City, numbering more than 300,000.

Cashinawa. Also **Cashinahua.** A forest tribe of about 2,000 on the Peru-Brazil border, mostly in Peru.

Cora. A Uto-Aztecan tribe of about 15,000 in the Western Sierra Madre of Nayarit State, Mexico.

Guaraní. One of the two national languages of Paraguay, with Spanish; spoken by nearly five million Paraguayans (95 percent of the population) and by hundreds of thousands of native people in neighboring areas of Argentina.

Inca. A small tribe that conquered the Valley of Cuzco in the southern Peruvian highlands and became the ruling elite of a vast empire; the king, or emperor, was called *the* Inca. *See* **Quechua.**

Isleta. One of the Rio Grande pueblos of northern New Mexico, with a population of about 2,500.

Kekchi Maya. A Mayan group of more than 300,000 in eastern Guatemala with about 9,000 in Belize.

Kogi. Also **Kogui** or **Cagaba.** A Chibchan people of the Sierra Nevada de Santa Marta, northeastern Colombia, with an estimated population of 4,000 to 6,000.

Lenca. An ethnic group of 50,000 in Honduras, now Spanish-speaking with a only a few speakers of the Lenca language now remaining.

Maya. *See* **Yucatec Maya.**

Mayan. A language family of southern Mexico and Guatemala, including Cakchiquel, Kekchi, Quiché, Tzotzil, Yucatec, and many others.

Mazatec. A people of Oaxaca State, Mexico, with a population of about 35,000 native speakers.

Mbyá Guaraní. A people of eastern Paraguay with 7,000 native speakers and an additional 5,000 in adjacent areas of Brazil.

Mískito. The principal native group in Nicaragua, with a population of about 150,000.

Mixe. A people of northeastern Oaxaca State, Mexico, numbering over 30,000.

Nahua. A term now used by scholars to designate the Nahuatl-speaking peoples of Mexico, past and present, including the pre-Columbian Aztecs. There are over a million Nahuatl speakers today, mostly in central Mexico.

Otomi. Called **Ñähñu** by the Otomi themselves. A central Mexican group numbering more than 200,000.

Pipil. An ethnic group of 200,000 in El Salvador, now mostly Spanish-speaking, related to the Nahua of Mexico.

Popoluca. A people of southeastern Veracruz State, Mexico, numbering over 50,000.

Quechua. The language of the Incas of Cuzco, imposed upon most of the native tribes of the central Andes, now spoken throughout the Peruvian highlands. Additional Quechua peoples are in Bolivia and Argentina. *See also* **Quichua.**

Quiché Maya. A Mayan group of the Guatemalan highlands with a population of 600,000.

Quichua. The Ecuadorean variety of Quechua, spoken by more than four million people.

Shuar. Formerly called **Jívaro.** A native group of over 30,000 in eastern Ecuador.

Tacana. A forest tribe of the eastern slopes of the Andes in Bolivia, numbering 3,500.

Tepecano. An ethnic group of the Western Sierra Madre of Jalisco State, Mexico, formerly speaking a Uto-Aztecan language, now Spanish-speaking.

Tzotzil Maya. A Mayan group of Chiapas State, southern Mexico, population 300,000.

Witoto. Also **Huitoto.** An Amazonian tribe of 2,000 in southeastern Colombia with an additional 1,000 in neighboring Peru.

Yamana. Also **Yahgan.** A small native group of Tierra del Fuego, southern Argentina, now culturally extinct.

Yucatec Maya. Also **Yucateco** or **Maya.** The Maya of the Yucatan Peninsula, numbering three-quarters of a million.

Zapotec. A group of closely related peoples of Oaxaca State, Mexico, with a total population of about 600,000.

Zuni. A Pueblo group of western New Mexico, numbering 10,000.

BiBLiOGRAPHY

Sources for the stories are preceded by an asterisk and followed by the story number(s) in square brackets.

Aarne, Antti, and Stith Thompson. 1973. *The Types of the Folktale: A Classification and Bibliography.* Folklore Fellows Communications, no. 184. Helsinki: Suomalainen Tiedeakatemia.

Abrahams, Roger D. 1999. *African American Folktales: Stories from Black Traditions in the New World.* New York: Pantheon Books.

Abreu, J. Capistrano de. 1914. *Rã-txa hu-ni-ku-ĩ: a lingua dos caxinauás.* Rio de Janeiro: Leuzinger.

*Andrade, Manuel J. 1930. *Folk-Lore from the Dominican Republic.* New York: American Folklore Society. [6, 14, 92, 95]

————. 1977. "Yucatec Maya Stories." Microfilm Collection of Manuscripts on Cultural Anthropology, no. 262. Joseph Regenstein Library, University of Chicago.

Anglería, Pedro Mártir de. 1964–65. *Decadas del Nuevo Mundo.* 2 vols. Mexico: José Porrúa e hijos.

*Anibarro de Halushka, Delina. 1976. *La tradición oral en Bolivia.* La Paz: Instituto Boliviano de Cultura. [19, 90]

Arguedas, José María. 1969. *El sueño del pongo: cuento quechua / Canciones quechuas tradicionales.* Santiago, Chile: Editorial Universitaria.

*Arguedas, José María, and Francisco Carrillo. 1967. *Poesía y prosa quechua.* Lima: Biblioteca Universitaria. [36, 102]

Bendezú Aybar, Edmundo. 1980. *Literatura quechua.* Caracas: Biblioteca Ayacucho.

*Benedict, Ruth. 1935. *Zuni Mythology.* 2 vols. New York: Columbia University Press. [113]

*Bernard, H. Russell, and Jesús Salinas Pedraza. 1976. *Otomi Parables, Folktales, and Jokes.* International Journal of American Linguistics, Native American Texts Series, vol. 1, no. 2. Chicago: University of Chicago Press. [101]

————. 1989. *Native Ethnography: A Mexican Indian Describes His Culture.* Newbury Park, Calif.: Sage.

*Bierhorst, John. 1985a. *Cantares Mexicanos: Songs of the Aztecs.* Stanford: Stanford University Press. [3]

————. 1985b. *A Nahuatl-English Dictionary and Concordance to the Cantares Mexicanos with an Analytic Transcription and Grammatical Notes.* Stanford: Stanford University Press.

————. 1988. *The Mythology of South America.* New York: William Morrow.

————. 1990. *The Mythology of Mexico and Central America.* New York: William Morrow.

————. 1992. *History and Mythology of the Aztecs: The Codex Chimalpopoca.* Tucson: University of Arizona Press.

*Boas, Franz, and José María Arreola. 1920. "Cuentos en mexicano de Milpa Alta, D. F." *Journal of American Folklore* 33: 1–24. [88]

Boggs, Ralph S[teele]. 1930. *Index of Spanish Folktales.* Folklore Fellows Communications, no. 90. Helsinki: Suomalainen Tiedeakatemia.

Boggs, Ralph Steele. 1937. "Spanish Folklore from Tampa, Florida" ("I. Background" and "II. Riddles"). *Southern Folklore Quarterly* 1, no. 3 (September): 1–12.

*————. 1938. "Spanish Folklore from Tampa, Florida: (no. V) Folktales." *Southern Folklore Quarterly* 2, no. 2 (June): 87–106. [47]

Briggs, Charles L. *See* Brown et al.

Brotherston, Gordon. *See* Kutscher et al.

Brown, Lorin W., Charles L. Briggs, and Marta Weigle. 1978. *Hispano Folklife of New Mexico.* Albuquerque: University of New Mexico Press.

Brunvand, Jan Harold. 1986. *The Study of American Folklore.* New York: Norton.

Burns, Allan F. 1983. *An Epoch of Miracles: Oral Literature of the Yucatec Maya.* Austin: University of Texas Press.

Cadilla de Martínez, María. 1933. *La poesía popular en Puerto Rico.* Madrid: Universidad de Madrid.

*Cadogan, León. 1959. *Ayvu rapyta.* Universidade de São Paulo, Faculdade de Filosofia, Ciencias e Letras. Boletim 227, Antropologia 5. São Paulo. [110]

Calvino, Italo. 1981. *Italian Folktales.* Trans. George Martin. New York: Pantheon Books.

Campa, Arthur L. 1979. *Hispanic Culture in the Southwest.* Norman: University of Oklahoma Press.

Carrasquilla, Tomás. *Cuentos de Tejas Arriba (Folklore Antioqueño).* Medellín: Editorial Atlantida, 1936.

Carvalho-Neto, Paulo. 1961. *Folklore del Paraguay.* Quito: Editorial Universitaria.

————. 1969. *History of Iberoamerican Folklore: Mestizo Cultures.* Oosterhout, The Netherlands: Anthropological Publications.

*————. 1994. *Cuentos folklóricos del Ecuador (sierra y costa).* Quito: Abya-Yala. [4, 49]

*Chapman, Anne. 1985. *Los hijos del copal y la candela: ritos agrarios y tradición oral de los lencas de Honduras.* Mexico: Universidad Nacional Autónoma de México. [86]

*Chertudi, Susana. 1960, 1964. *Cuentos folklóricos de la Argentina.* 2 vols ("primera serie" and "segunda serie"). Buenos Aires: Instituto Nacional de Antropología. [18/IV, 28, 31, 87]

Cobo, Bernabé. 1979. *History of the Inca Empire.* Trans. Roland Hamilton. Austin: University of Texas Press.

Coe, Michael D. 1978. *The Maya Scribe and His World.* New York: Grolier Club.

Colby, Benjamin N., and Lore M. Colby. 1981. *The Daykeeper: The Life and Discourse of an Ixil Diviner.* Cambridge: Harvard University Press.

*Conzemius, Eduard. 1932. *Ethnographical Survey of the Miskito and Sumu Indians of Honduras and Nicaragua.* Washington, D.C.: Bureau of American Ethnology, Bulletin 106. [106]

Coolidge, Dane, and Mary Roberts Coolidge. 1971. *The Last of the Seris.* Glorieta, N.M.: Rio Grande Press. Originally published 1939.

*Corona, Pascuala. 1945. *Cuentos mexicanos.* Mexico. [7]

Covarrubias, Miguel. 1967. *Mexico South: The Isthmus of Tehuantepec.* New York: Alfred A. Knopf.

Dähnhardt, Oskar. 1909. *Natursagen: Eine Sammlung naturdeutender Sagen, Märchen, Fabeln, und Legenden.* Vol. 2: Sagen zum Neuen Testament. Leipzig and Berlin: B. G. Teubner.

Dary Fuentes, Claudia, and Aracely Esquivel. 1985. "Una muestra de la tradición oral del caserio 'El Soyate,' municipio de Oratorio, Santa Rosa, Guatemala." *Tradiciones de Guatemala: Revista del Centro de Estudios Folklóricos,* no. 23–4: 83–124. Universidad de San Carlos de Guatemala.

Déleon Meléndez, Ofelia Columba. 1985. *Folklore aplicado a la educación guatemalteca.* Guatemala: Universidad de San Carlos, Centro de Estudios Folklóricos.

Díaz del Castillo, Bernal. 1976. *Historia verdadera de la conquista de la Nueva España.* Mexico: Editorial Porrúa.

Dorson, Richard M. 1967. *American Negro Folktales.* Greenwich, Conn.: Fawcett.

*Durán, Diego. 1967. *Historia de las Indias de Nueva España e islas de la tierra firme.* Edited by Angel M. Garibay K. Vol. 2: *Historia.* Mexico: Editorial Porrúa. [1/I, 1/II, 1/IV]

*Espinosa, Aurelio M. 1911. "New-Mexican Spanish Folk-Lore, III. Folk-Tales." *Journal of American Folklore* 24: 397–444. [45]

———. 1916. "New-Mexican Spanish Folk-Lore, X. Children's Games." *Journal of American Folklore* 29: 505–35.

*———. 1936. "Pueblo Indian Folk Tales." *Journal of American Folklore* 49: 69–133. [58, 66]

———. 1946–47. *Cuentos populares españoles.* 3 vols. Madrid: Consejo Superior de Investigaciones Científicas/Instituto Antonio de Nebrija de Filología.

———. 1985. *The Folklore of Spain in the American Southwest: Traditional Spanish Folk Literature in Northern New Mexico and Southern Colorado.* Edited by J. Manuel Espinosa. Norman: University of Oklahoma Press.

*Espinosa, José Manuel. 1937. *Spanish Folk-Tales from New Mexico.* New York: American Folklore Society. [23, 25, 52]

*Feijóo, Samuel. 1960, 1962. *Cuentos populares cubanos.* 2 vols. Havana: Universidad Central de las Villas/Ucar García (vol. 1) and Imprenta Nacional (vol. 2). [8, 22]

*Foster, George M. 1945. *Sierra Popoluca Folklore and Beliefs.* University of California Publications in American Archaeology and Ethnology, vol. 42, no. 2. Berkeley. [57, 82]

Fox, Hugh, ed. 1978. *First Fire: Central and South American Indian Poetry.* Garden City, N.Y.: Anchor Books/Doubleday.

García Sáiz, Valentin. 1957. *Leyendas y supersticiones del Uruguay.* Montevideo.

*Gordon, G. B. 1915. "Guatemala Myths." *Museum Journal* 6: 103–44. [38]

Grimm's Fairy Tales. 1944. New York: Pantheon Books.

*Gusinde, Martin. 1937. *Die Yamana (Die Feuerland-Indianer,* vol. 2). Mödling bei Wien, Austria. [111]

Hansen, Terrence Leslie. 1957. *The Types of the Folktale in Cuba, Puerto Rico, the Dominican Republic, and Spanish South America.* Berkeley: University of California Press.

Hartman, C. V. 1907. "Mythology of the Aztecs of Salvador." *Journal of American Folklore* 20: 143–7.

*Hernández Suárez, Dolores. 1929. "Cuentos recogidos en Camagüey." *Archivos del Folklore Cubano* 4: 251–69. Republished under the name Dolores Hernández Ruiz, same title, *Archivos del Folklore Cubano* 5 (1930): 61–70. [50, 91]

*Hissink, Karin, and Albert Hahn. 1961. *Die Tacana,* vol. 1: Erzählungsgut. Stuttgart: W. Kohlhammer. [114]

Horcasitas, Fernando. 1988. "An Analysis of the Deluge Myth in Mesoamerica." In *The Flood Myth,* edited by Alan Dundes, 183–219. Berkeley: University of California Press.

*Howard-Malverde, Rosaleen. 1981. *Dioses y diablos: tradición oral de Cañar Ecuador/Amerindia: Revue d'Ethnolinguistique Amérindienne, numéro spécial 1.* Paris: A. E. A./Université de Paris VIII, Centre de Recherche. [63, 67]

*Hugh-Jones, Stephen. 1979. *The Palm and the Pleiades: Initiation and Cosmology in Northwest Amazonia.* Cambridge, England: Cambridge University Press. [107]

Hultkranz, Åke. 1957. *The North American Indian Orpheus Tradition.* Statens Etnografiska Museum Monograph Series, 2. Stockholm.

Incháustegui, Carlos. 1977. *Relatos del mundo mágico mazateco.* Mexico: Instituto Nacional de Antropología e Historia.

*Izaguirre, Carlos. 1943. "Adivinanzas, leyendas y tradiciones, y bombas." *Boletín de la Biblioteca y Archivo Nacionales,* año 3, no. 6: 167–74. Tegucigalpa. [9]

James, Montague Rhodes. 1953. *The Apocryphal New Testament.* Oxford.

*Jijena Sánchez, Rafael. 1946. *Los cuentos de Mama Vieja.* Buenos Aires: Versol. [103]

Keen, Benjamin. 1971. *The Aztec Image in Western Thought.* New Brunswick, N.J.: Rutgers University Press.

Kleymeyer, Carlos David. 1990. *¡Imashi! ¡Imashi! adivinanzas poéticas de los campesinos indígenas de la sierra andina ecuatoriana/peruana.* Quito: Abya-Yala.

Kroeber, A. L. 1931. *The Seri.* Southwest Museum Papers, no. 6. Los Angeles.

Kutscher, Gerdt, Gordon Brotherston, and Günter Vollmer. 1987. *Aesop in Mexico.* Berlin: Gebr. Mann.

*La Barre, Weston. 1950. "Aymara Folktales." *International Journal of American Linguistics* 16: 40–5. [37]

Lara, Jesús. 1971. *Diccionario qhëshwa-castellano, castellano-qhëshwa.* La Paz: Amigos del Libro.

*Lara Figueroa, Celso A. 1981. *Las increíbles hazañas de Pedro Urdemales en Guatemala.* 2d ed. Guatemala: Universidad de San Carlos, Centro de Estudios Folklóricos. [18/II]

*———. 1982. *Cuentos populares de Guatemala,* primera serie. Guatemala: Universidad de San Carlos, Centro de Estudios Folklóricos. [42, 79]

*Laughlin, Robert M. 1971. "In the Beginning: A Tale from the Mazatec." *Alcheringa: Ethnopoetics,* no. 2 (summer): 37–52. New York. [55, 62, 71, 72, 73]

*———. 1977. *Of Cabbages and Kings: Tales from Zinacantán.* Smithsonian

Contributions to Anthropology, no. 23. Washington, D.C.: Smithsonian Institution Press. [65/II, 70, 105]

Laval, Ramón A. 1916. *Contribución al folklore de Carahue (Chile)*. Madrid: Victoriano Suárez.

*⸻. 1920. *Contribución al folklore de Carahue (Chile), segunda parte: leyendas y cuentos populares.* Santiago: Imprenta Universitaria. [26, 84]

*⸻. 1968. *Cuentos populares chilenos.* Santiago: Editorial Nascimento. Originally published 1910–25. [18/I, 18/III, 46, 99]

Lehmann, Walter. 1910. "Ergebnisse einer Forschungsreise in Mittelamerika und México 1907–1909." *Zeitschrift für Ethnologie* 42: 687–749.

*⸻. 1928. "Ergebnisse einer mit Unterstützung der Notgemeinschaft der Deutschen Wissenschaft in den Jahren 1925/1926 ausgeführten Forschungsreise nach Mexiko und Guatemala." *Anthropos* 23: 749–91. [60, 61]

Lehmann-Nitsche, Robert. 1911. *Adivinanzas rioplatenses.* Folklore Argentino, 1. Buenos Aires: Universidad de La Plata.

Lumholtz, Carl. 1987. *Unknown Mexico: Explorations in the Sierra Madre and Other Regions, 1890–1898.* 2 vols. New York: Dover. Originally published 1902.

Luna, Lizandro. 1957. "El pongo." *Tradición: Revista de Cultura,* no. 19–20: 19–24.

*Lyra, Carmen (i.e., María Isabel Carvajal). 1936. *Los cuentos de mi tía Panchita.* San José, Costa Rica: Imprenta Española. Originally published 1920. [21]

*Mason, J. Alden. 1914. "Folk-Tales of the Tepecanos." Edited by Aurelio M. Espinosa. *Journal of American Folklore* 27: 148–210. [97]

⸻. 1916. "Porto-Rican Folk-Lore: Riddles." Edited by Aurelio M. Espinosa. *Journal of American Folklore* 29: 423–504.

⸻. 1922. "Porto-Rican Folk-Lore: Folk-Tales." Edited by Aurelio M. Espinosa. *Journal of American Folklore* 35: 1–61.

*⸻. 1924. "Porto-Rican Folk-Lore: Folk-Tales." Edited by Aurelio M. Espinosa. *Journal of American Folklore* 37: 247–344. [44, 94]

*⸻. 1925. "Porto-Rican Folk-Lore: Folk-Tales." Edited by Aurelio M. Espinosa. *Journal of American Folklore* 38: 507–618. [11]

⸻. 1926. "Porto-Rican Folk-Lore: Folk-Tales." Edited by Aurelio M. Espinosa. *Journal of American Folklore* 39: 227–369.

⸻. 1927. "Porto-Rican Folk-Lore: Folk-Tales." Edited by Aurelio M. Espinosa. *Journal of American Folklore* 40: 313–414.

⸻. 1929. "Porto-Rican Folk-Lore: Folk-Tales." Edited by Aurelio M. Espinosa. *Journal of American Folklore* 42: 85–156.

*Miller, Elaine K. 1973. *Mexican Folk Narrative from the Los Angeles Area.* Austin: American Folklore Society/University of Texas Press. [10]

*Noguera, María de. 1952. *Cuentos viejos.* 3d ed. San José, Costa Rica: Lehmann. [80]

*Olivares Figueroa, R. 1954. *Folklore venezolano,* vol. 2: prosas. Caracas: Ministerio de Educación. [53]

Ortega, Pompilio. 1949. "Que te compre quien no te conoce." *Boletín del Comité Nacional del Café,* p. 697. Tegucigalpa.

Otero, Gustavo Adolfo. 1951. *La piedra mágica: vida y costumbres de los indios callahuayas de Bolivia.* Mexico: Instituto Indigenista Interamericano.

*Pachacuti Yamqui Salcamaygua, Juan de Santacruz. 1927. "Relación de antigüedades desde reyno del Perú." In *Historia de los incas y relación de su gobierno,* edited by Horacio H. Urteaga. Lima: Sanmartí. [2/IV]

*Paredes, Américo. 1970. *Folktales of Mexico.* Chicago: University of Chicago Press. [81]

*Paredes, M. Rigoberto. 1949. *El arte folklórico de Bolivia.* 2d ed. La Paz. [112]

*Parsons, Elsie Clews. 1918. "Nativity Myth at Laguna and Zuñi." *Journal of American Folklore* 31: 256–63.

————. 1932. "Zapoteca and Spanish Tales of Mitla, Oaxaca." *Journal of American Folklore* 45: 277–317. [56]

*————. 1936. *Mitla: Town of the Souls and Other Zapoteco-Speaking Pueblos of Oaxaca, Mexico.* Chicago: University of Chicago Press. [59]

————. 1945. *Peguche, Canton of Otavalo, Province of Imbabura, Ecuador: A Study of Andean Indians.* Chicago: University of Chicago Press.

*Pellizzaro, Siro. 1980. *Ayumpúm (Mitología shuar,* vol. 5). Sucua, Ecuador: Mundo Shuar. [115]

*Peña Hernández, Enrique. 1968. *Folklore de Nicaragua.* Masaya, Nicaragua: Editorial Unión (Cardoza). [78]

Peñalosa, Fernando. 1996. *The Mayan Folktale: An Introduction.* Rancho Palos Verdes, Calif.: Yax Te' Press.

*Pérez, Soledad. 1951. "Mexican Folklore from Austin, Texas." In *The Healer of Los Olmos and Other Mexican Lore,* edited by Wilson M. Hudson (Texas Folklore Society, publication 24), pp. 71–127. Austin and Dallas: Texas Folklore Society and Southern Methodist University Press. [85]

Perry, Ben Edwin. 1984. *Babrius and Phaedrus { . . . } Greek and Latin Fables in the Aesopic Tradition.* Cambridge: Harvard University Press.

Pinguentini, Gianni. 1955. *Fiabe, leggende, novelle, satire paesane, storielle, barzellette in dialetto triestino.* Trieste: E. Borsatti.

Pino Saavedra, Yolando. 1967. *Folktales of Chile.* Trans. by Rockwell Gray. Chicago: University of Chicago Press.

*Portal, María Ana. 1986. *Cuentos y mitos en una zona mazateca.* Colección Científica, Serie Antropología Social. Mexico: Instituto Nacional de Antropología e Historia. [15]

*Preuss, Konrad Theodor. 1921, 1923. *Religion und Mythologie der Uitoto.* 2 vols. Göttingen: Vandenhoeck & Ruprecht. [109]

Preuss, Mary H. 2000. "The Cat-Witch." *Latin American Indian Literatures Journal* 16, no. 2: 181–2.

Radin, Paul. 1917. *El folklore de Oaxaca.* Edited by Aurelio M. Espinosa. New York: Stechert.

*Rael, Juan B. 1977. *Cuentos españoles de Colorado y Nuevo México.* 2d ed. 2 vols. Santa Fe: Museum of New Mexico Press. [13, 24, 33, 93]

Ramírez, Arnulfo G., José Antonio Flores, and Leopoldo Valiñas. 1992. *Se tosaasaanil, se tosaasaanil: adivinanzas nahuas de ayer y hoy.* Tlalpan, Mexico: Instituto Nacional Indigenista/Centro de Investigaciones y Estudios Superiores en Antropología Social.

*Ramírez de Arellano, Rafael. 1926. *Folklore portorriqueño.* Madrid: Avila. [16, 43, 48, 74, 83]

*Recinos, Adrián. 1918a. "Cuentos populares de Guatemala." *Journal of American Folklore* 31: 472–87. [29, 40, 89]

———. 1918b. "Adivinanzas recogidas en Guatemala." *Journal of American Folklore* 31: 544–9.

*Redfield, Robert. 1945. "Notes on San Antonio Palopo." Microfilm Collection of Manuscripts on Cultural Anthropology, no. 4. Joseph Regenstein Library, University of Chicago. [68, 96]

Redfield, Robert, and Alfonso Villa R[ojas]. 1934. *Chan Kom: A Maya Village.* Washington, D.C.: Carnegie Institution of Washington.

*Reichel-Dolmatoff, Gerardo. 1951. *Los kogi.* Vol. 2. Bogotá: Iqueima. [108]

———. 1978. "The Loom of Life." *Journal of Latin American Lore* 4: 5–27.

*Reichel-Dolmatoff, Gerardo, and Reichel-Dolmatoff, Alicia. 1956. *La literatura oral de una aldea colombiana.* Divulgaciones etnológicas, vol. 5. Barranquilla, Colombia: Universidad del Atlantico, Instituto de Investigación Etnológica. [17, 20, 30, 32, 54]

———. 1961. *The People of Aritama: The Cultural Personality of a Colombian Mestizo Village.* Chicago: University of Chicago Press.

" Relación de la religión y ritos del Perú hecha por los primeros religiosos agustinos que allí pasaron para la conversión de los naturales." 1865. In *Colección de documentos inéditos, relativos al descubrimiento, conquista y colonización de las posesiones españolas en América y Oceania,* vol. 3, pp. 5–58. Madrid.

*Riera-Pinilla, Mario. 1956. *Cuentos folklóricos de Panamá.* Panama: Ministerio de Educación, Departamento de Bellas Artes. [41, 76]

Robe, Stanley L. 1970. *Mexican Tales and Legends from Los Altos.* Berkeley: University of California Press.

———. 1972. *Amapa Storytellers.* Berkeley: University of California Press.

———. 1973. *Index of Mexican Folktales.* Berkeley: University of California Press.

Roys, Ralph L. 1967. *The Book of Chilam Balam of Chumayel.* Norman: University of Oklahoma Press. Originally published 1933.

*Sahagún, Bernardino de. 1979. *Códice florentino.* 3 vols. Mexico: Secretaría de Gobernación. Facsimile of MS. 218-200, Palatine Collection, Laurentian Library, Florence, Italy. [1/III, 1/V]

———. 1982. *Florentine Codex: General History of the Things of New Spain.* Edited by Arthur J. O. Anderson and Charles E. Dibble. Part 1: Introductions and Indices. Santa Fe: School of American Research and University of Utah.

Salomon, Frank, and George L. Urioste. 1991. *The Huarochirí Manuscript: A Testament of Ancient and Colonial Andean Religion.* Austin: University of Texas Press.

Sandstrom, Alan R. 1991. *Corn Is Our Blood: Culture and Ethnic Identity in a Contemporary Aztec Indian Village.* Norman: University of Oklahoma Press.

*Sarmiento de Gamboa, Pedro. 1965. "Historia de los incas" [Historia indica]. In *Biblioteca de autores españoles,* edited by Carmelo Sáenz de Santa María. Vol. 4. Madrid: Atlas. [2/I, 2/V]

*Saunière, Sperata R. de. 1975. *Cuentos populares araucanos y chilenos.* Santiago: Editorial Nascimento. Originally published in *Revista de Historia y Geografía,* nos. 21–32 (1916–18). [5, 34, 51]

*Schultze Jena, Leonhard. 1935. *Indiana,* vol. 2: *Mythen in der Muttersprache der Pipil von Izalco in El Salvador.* Jena, Germany: Gustav Fischer. [98]

Scott, Charles T. 1963. "New Evidence of American Indian Riddles." *Journal of American Folklore* 76: 236–44.

Shulman, David Dean. 1985. *The King and the Clown in South Indian Myth and Poetry.* Princeton: Princeton University Press.

Siegel, Morris. 1943. "The Creation Myth and Acculturation in Acatán, Guatemala." *Journal of American Folklore* 56: 120–6.

*Sojo, Juan Pablo. 1953–54. "Cuentos folklóricos venezolanos." *Archivos Venezolanos de Folklore,* año 2–3, tomo 2, no. 3: 175–89. [12]

Stevens-Arroyo, Antonio M. 1988. *Cave of the Jaguar: The Mythological World of the Taínos.* Albuquerque: University of New Mexico Press.

*Taggart, James M. 1983. *Nahuat Myth and Social Structure.* Austin: University of Texas Press. [65/I]

———. 1990. *Enchanted Maidens: Gender Relations in Spanish Folktales of Courtship and Marriage.* Princeton: Princeton University Press.

————. 1997. *The Bear and His Sons: Masculinity in Spanish and Mexican Folktales.* Austin: University of Texas Press.

*Tax, Sol. 1949. "Folk Tales in Chichicastenango: An Unsolved Puzzle." *Journal of American Folklore* 62: 125–35. [64]

Tayler, Donald. 1997. *The Coming of the Sun: A Prologue to Ika Sacred Narrative.* Monograph no. 7. Oxford: Pitt Rivers Museum, University of Oxford.

Tedlock, Dennis. 1996. *Popol Vuh: The Mayan Book of the Dawn of Life.* Rev. ed. New York: Simon and Schuster/Touchstone.

*Tezozomoc, Hernando Alvarado. 1975. *Crónica mexicana.* Edited by Manuel Orozco y Berra. Mexico: Editorial Porrúa. Reprint of 1878 ed. [1/I, 1/II, 1/IV]

*Thompson, J. Eric S. 1930. *Ethnology of the Mayas of Southern and Central British Honduras.* Anthropological Series, vol. 17, no. 2. Chicago: Field Museum of Natural History. [39, 69, 100]

Thompson, Stith. 1946. *The Folktale.* New York: Holt, Rinehart and Winston.

————. 1955–58. *Motif-Index of Folk Literature.* 6 vols. Bloomington: University of Indiana Press.

Torquemada, Juan de. 1975. *Monarquía indiana.* 3 vols. Mexico: Editorial Porrúa.

*Trimborn, Hermann, and Antje Kelm, eds. 1967. *Francisco de Avila.* [Avila, Francisco de, "Tratado y relación de los errores, falsos dioses, y otras supersticiones . . . de Huarocheri . . ."] Berlin: Mann. [2/II, 2/III]

Urioste, George L. 1983. *Hijos de Pariya Qaqa: la tradición oral de Waru Chiri.* 2 vols. Syracuse: Syracuse University, Maxwell School of Citizenship and Public Affairs.

Urton, Gary. 1999. *Inca Myths.* Austin: University of Texas Press.

Vázquez de Acuña G., Isidoro. 1956. *Costumbres religiosas de Chiloé y su raigambre hispana.* Santiago, Chile: Universidad de Chile, Centro de Estudios Antropológicos.

Weigle, Marta. *See* Brown et al.

*Wheeler, Howard T. 1943. *Tales from Jalisco Mexico.* Philadelphia: American Folklore Society. [27, 35, 75, 77]

Wilbert, Johannes, ed. 1977. *Folk Literature of the Yamana Indians: Martin Gusinde's Collection of Yamana Narratives.* Berkeley: University of California Press.

Wilbert, Johannes, and Karin Simoneau. 1992. *Folk Literature of South American Indians: General Index.* Los Angeles: UCLA Latin American Center.

Williams García, Roberto. 1972. *Mitos tepehuas.* Mexico: SepSetentas/Secretaría de Educación Pública.

Ziehm, Elsa, ed. 1968. *Nahua-Texte aus San Pedro Jícora in Durango,* vol. 1: *Mythen und Sagen.* Berlin: Gebr. Mann.

Zingg, Robert M. 1977. *The Huichols: Primitive Artists.* Millwood, N.Y.: Kraus Reprint.

PERMISSIONS ACKNOWLEDGMENTS

Acknowledgment is made for permission to reprint, adapt, or translate the following. For additional information see bibliography and notes, above.

ALFRED A. KNOPF: "The moon, the moon, Santa Rosa . . ." (chain riddle) from *Mexico South: The Isthmus of Tehuantepec* by Miguel Covarrubias. Copyright © 1946 by Alfred A. Knopf, Inc. Reprinted by permission of Alfred A. Knopf, a division of Random House, Inc.

ASSOCIATION D'ETHNOLINGUISTIQUE AMERINDIENNE: "The Christ Child as Trickster" and "The White Lily" translated from *Dioses y diablos: tradicion oral de Canar Ecuador (Amerindia: Revue d'Ethnolinguistique Amerindienne, Paris numero special 1, 1981)* by Rosaleen Howard-Malverde. Reprinted by permission of the Association d'Ethnolinguistique Amerindienne.

JOHN BIERHORST: "The Condor Seeks a Wife," "Legends of the Inca Kings" (with revision), and "The Moth" as translated in *Black Rainbow: Legends of the Incas and Myths of Ancient Peru* (Farrar, Straus and Giroux, 1976), edited by John Bierhorst; "The Beginning Life of the Hummingbird," "The Pongo's Dream" (with revision), and "Was It Not an Illusion?" as translated in *The Red Swan: Myths and Tales of the American Indians* (Farrar, Straus and Giroux, 1976), edited by John Bierhorst; "Montezuma" from *The Hungry Woman: Myths and Legends of the Aztecs* (Morrow, 1984), edited by John Bierhorst; "The Miser's Jar," "Tup and the Ants," and "Rosalie" as adapted in *The Monkey's Haircut and Other Stories Told by the Maya* (Morrow, 1986), edited by John Bierhorst. Reprinted by permission of John Bierhorst.

CAMBRIDGE UNIVERSITY PRESS: "Romi Kumu Makes the World" from *The Palm and the Pleiades: Initiation and Cosmology in Northwest Amazonia* by Stephen Hughes-Jones. Reprinted by permission of the Cambridge University Press.

CENTRO DE ESTUDIOS FOLKLORICOS, UNIVERSIDAD DE SAN CARLOS DE GUATEMALA: "The King's Pigs" translated from *Las increibles hazanas de Pedro Urdemales en Guatemala* by Celso A. Lara Figueroa. Reprinted by